the Accursed Vampire

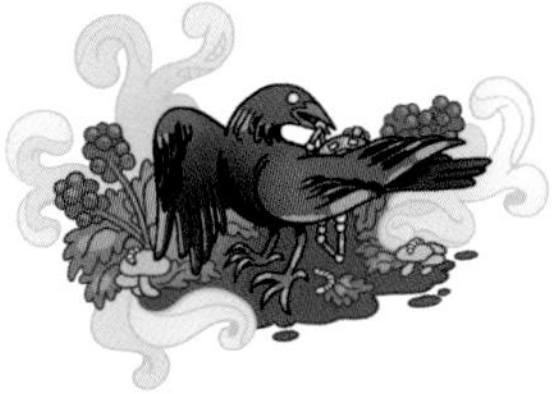

Quill Tree Books is an imprint of HarperCollins Publishers.
HarperAlley is an imprint of HarperCollins Publishers.

The Accursed Vampire

For information address HarperCollins Children's Books,
a division of HarperCollins Publishers,
195 Broadway, New York, NY 10007.
www.harperalley.com

ISBN 978-0-06-295434-3 (paperback)
ISBN 978-0-06-295435-0 (hardcover)

The art for this book was rendered digitally.
Typography by Catherine San Juan

21 22 23 24 25 GPS 10 9 8 7 6 5 4 3 2 1

❖

First Edition

Madeline McGrane

Quill Tree Books
Imprints of HarperCollinsPublishers

HARPER
alley

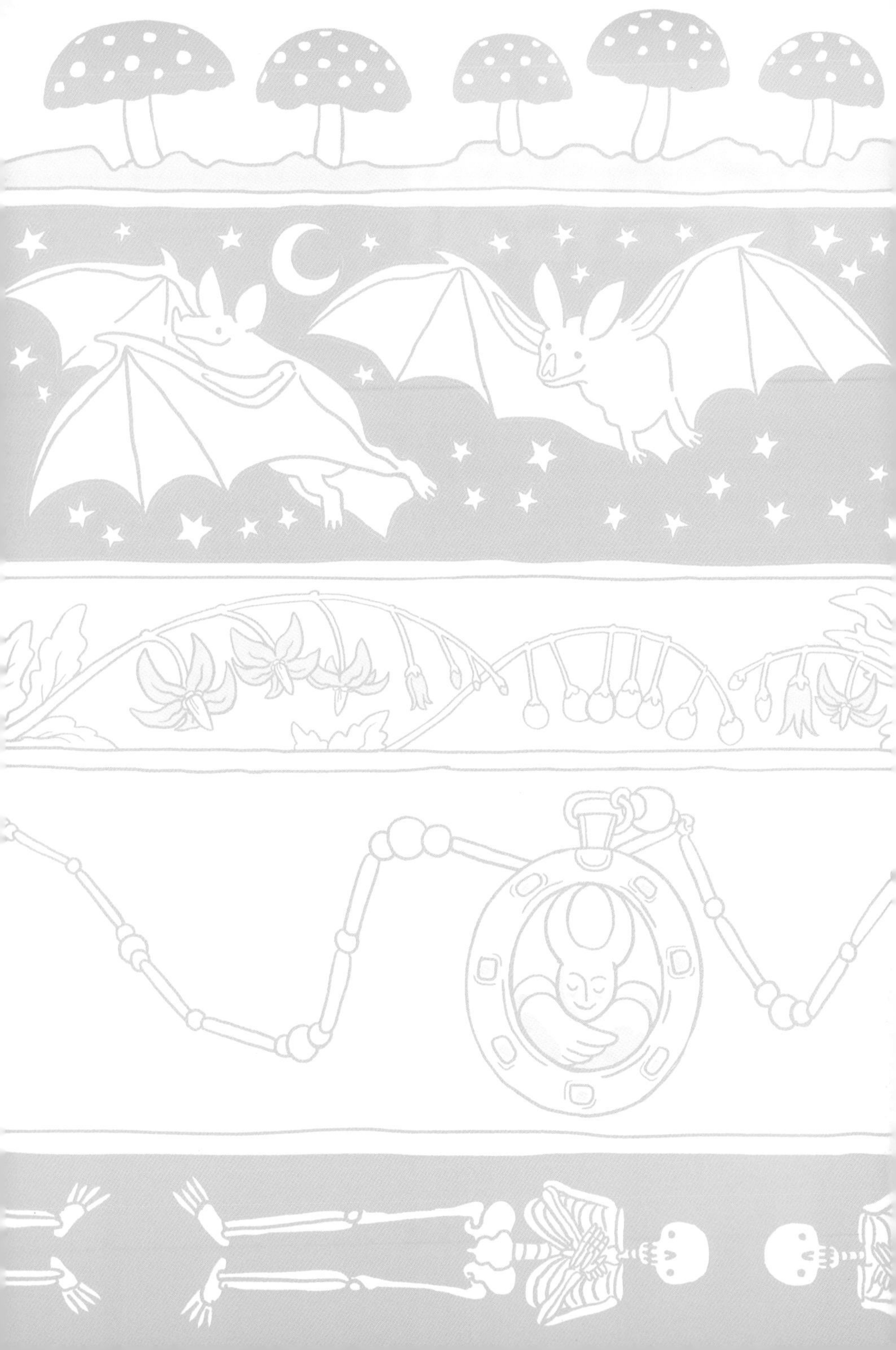

CHAPTER ONE

Dragoslava

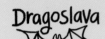

b. 1460
They're a vampire
and they wear a
really cool cape.

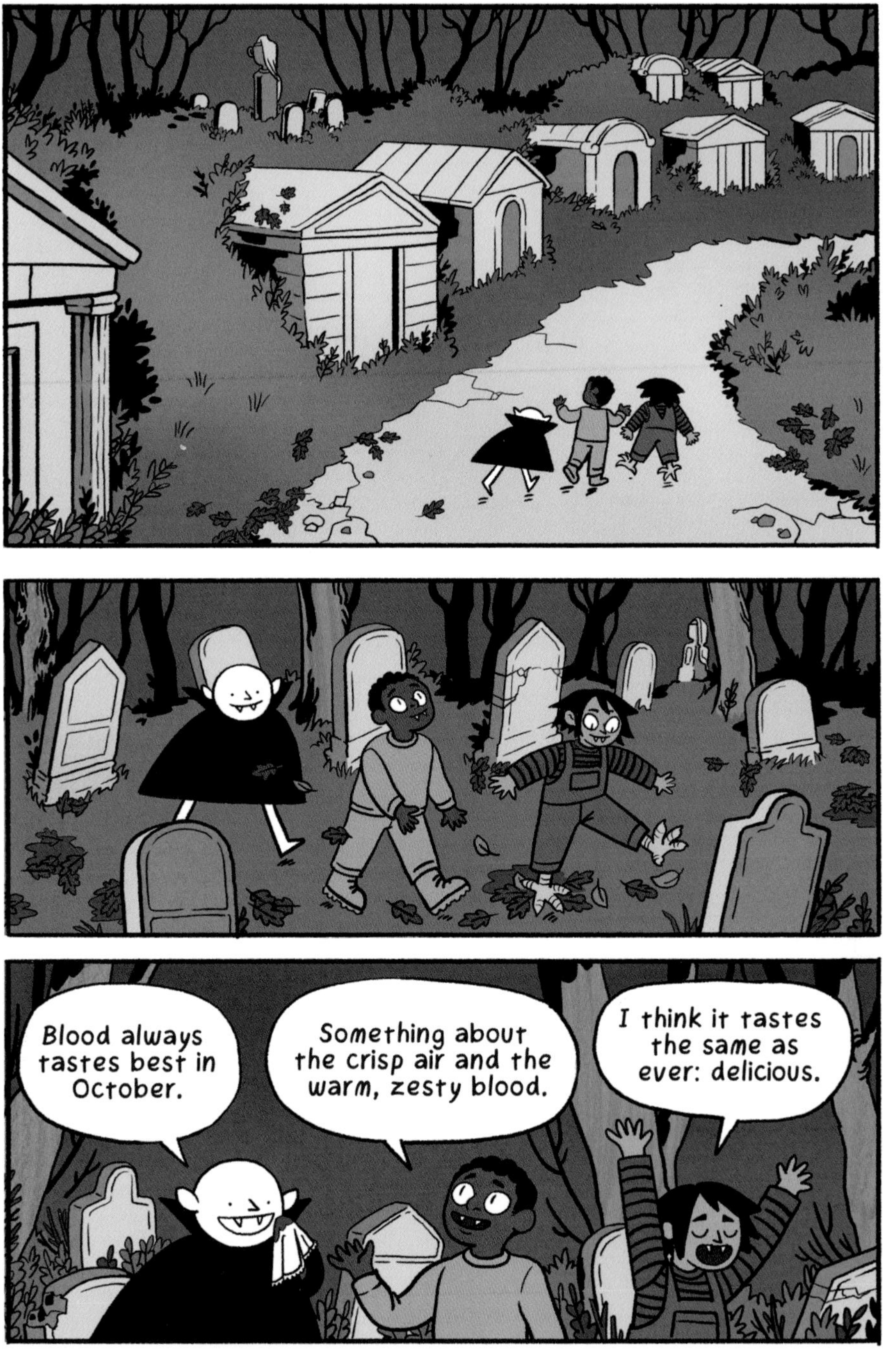
Blood always tastes best in October.
Something about the crisp air and the warm, zesty blood.
I think it tastes the same as ever: delicious.

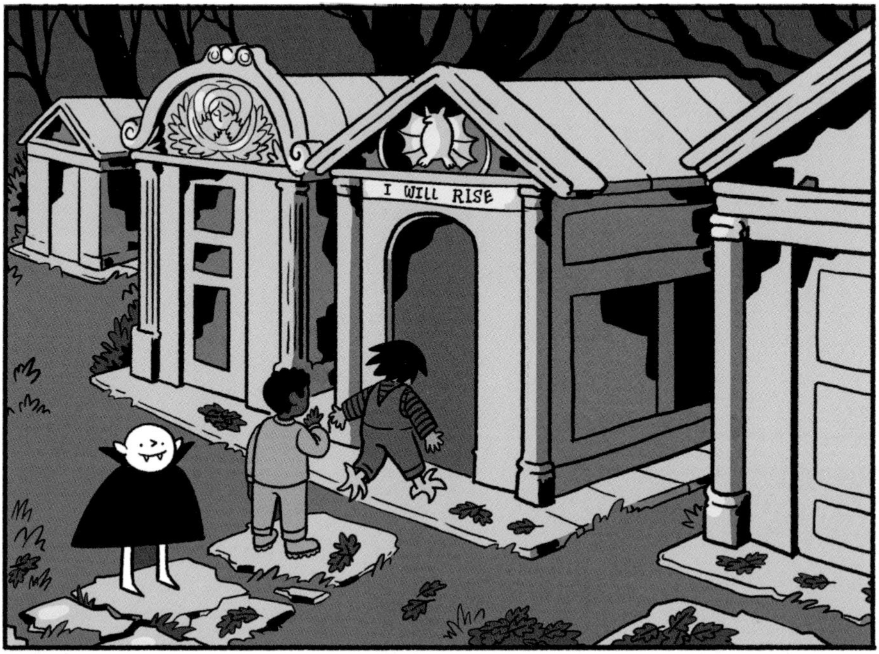
I WILL RISE

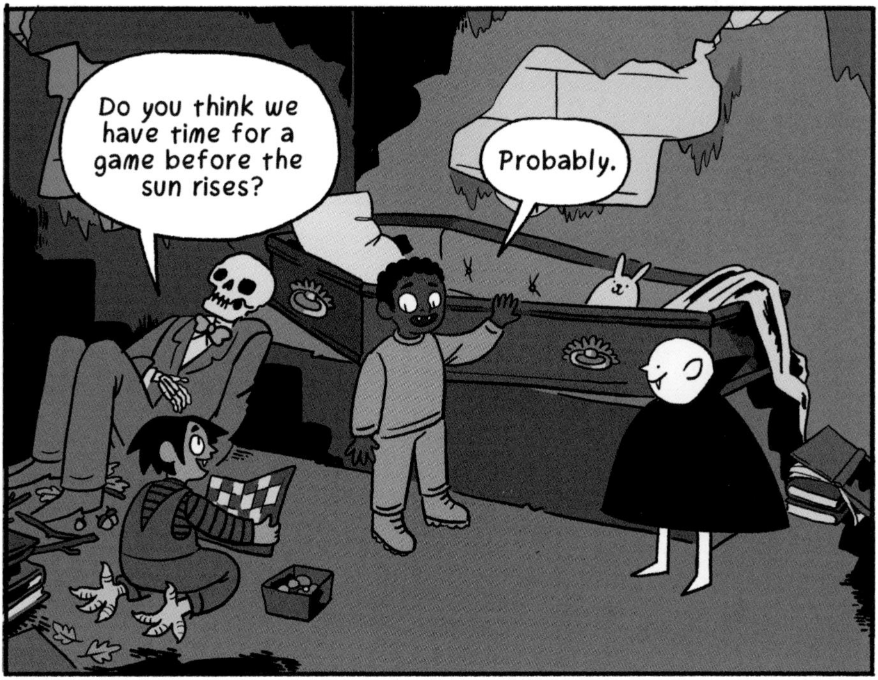
Do you think we have time for a game before the sun rises?
Probably.

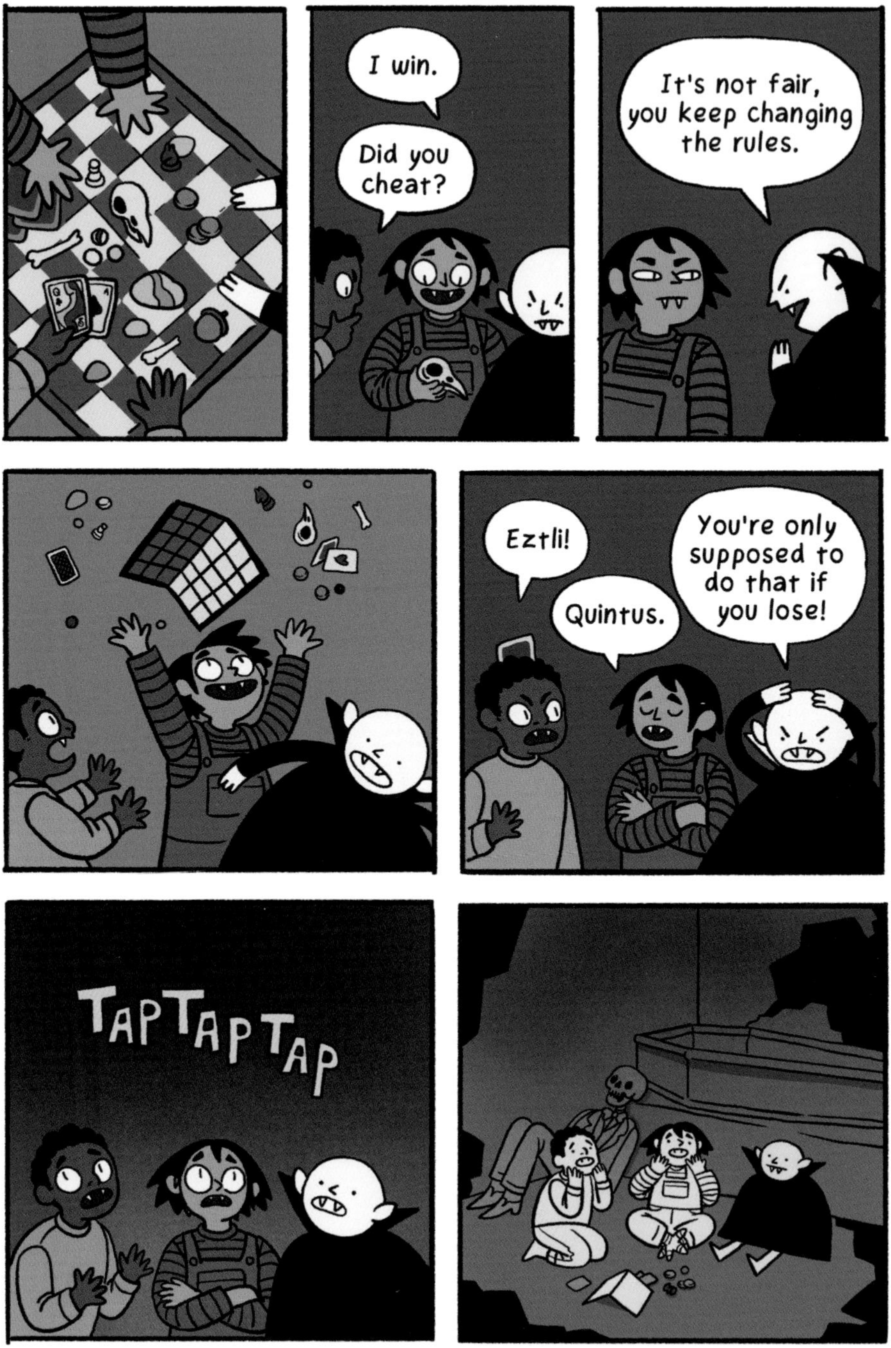
I win.
Did you cheat?
It's not fair, you keep changing the rules.
Eztli!
Quintus.
You're only supposed to do that if you lose!
TAP TAP TAP

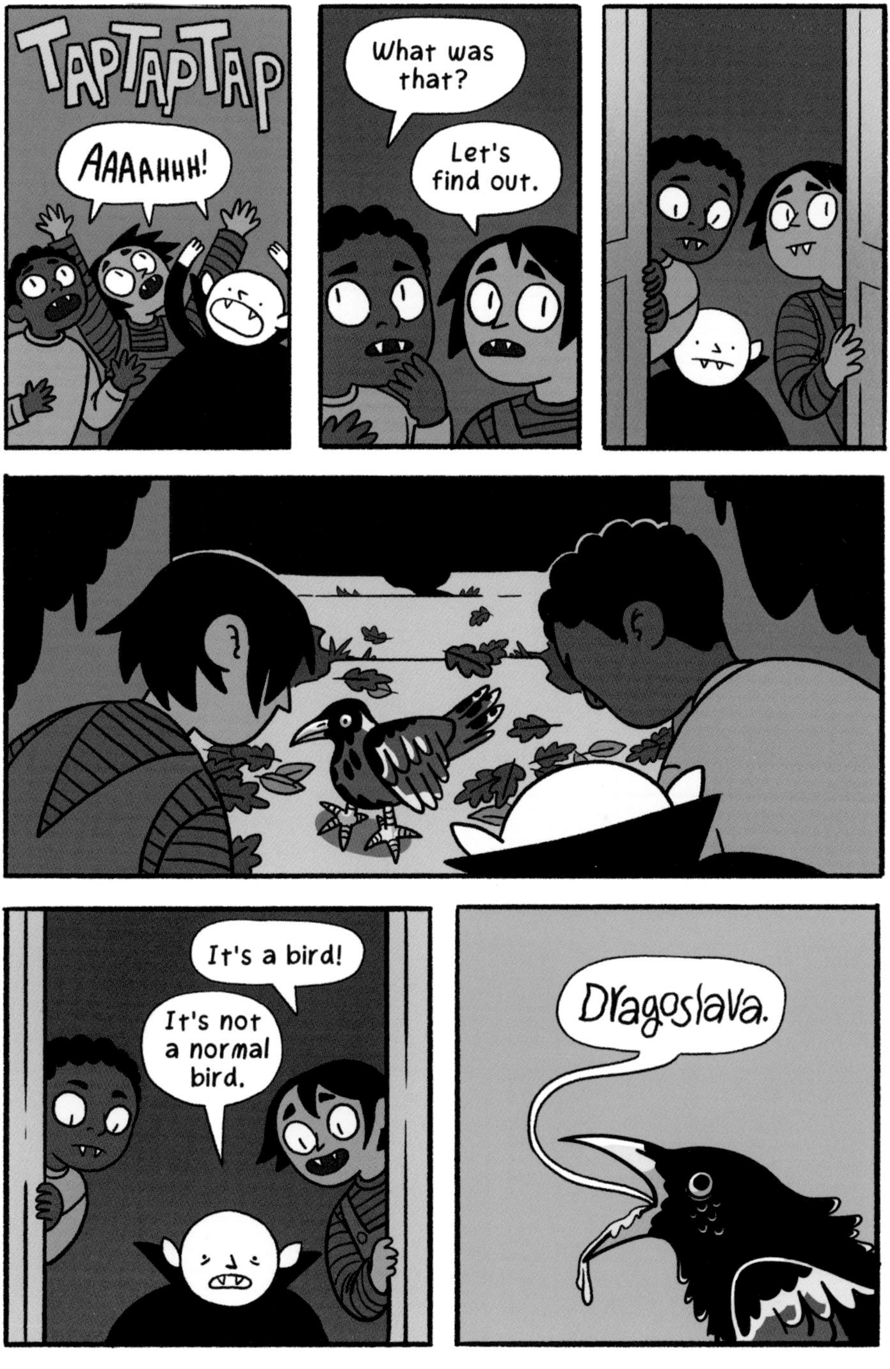
TAPTAPTAP
AAAAHHH!
What was that?
Let's find out.
It's a bird!
It's not a normal bird.
Dragoslava.

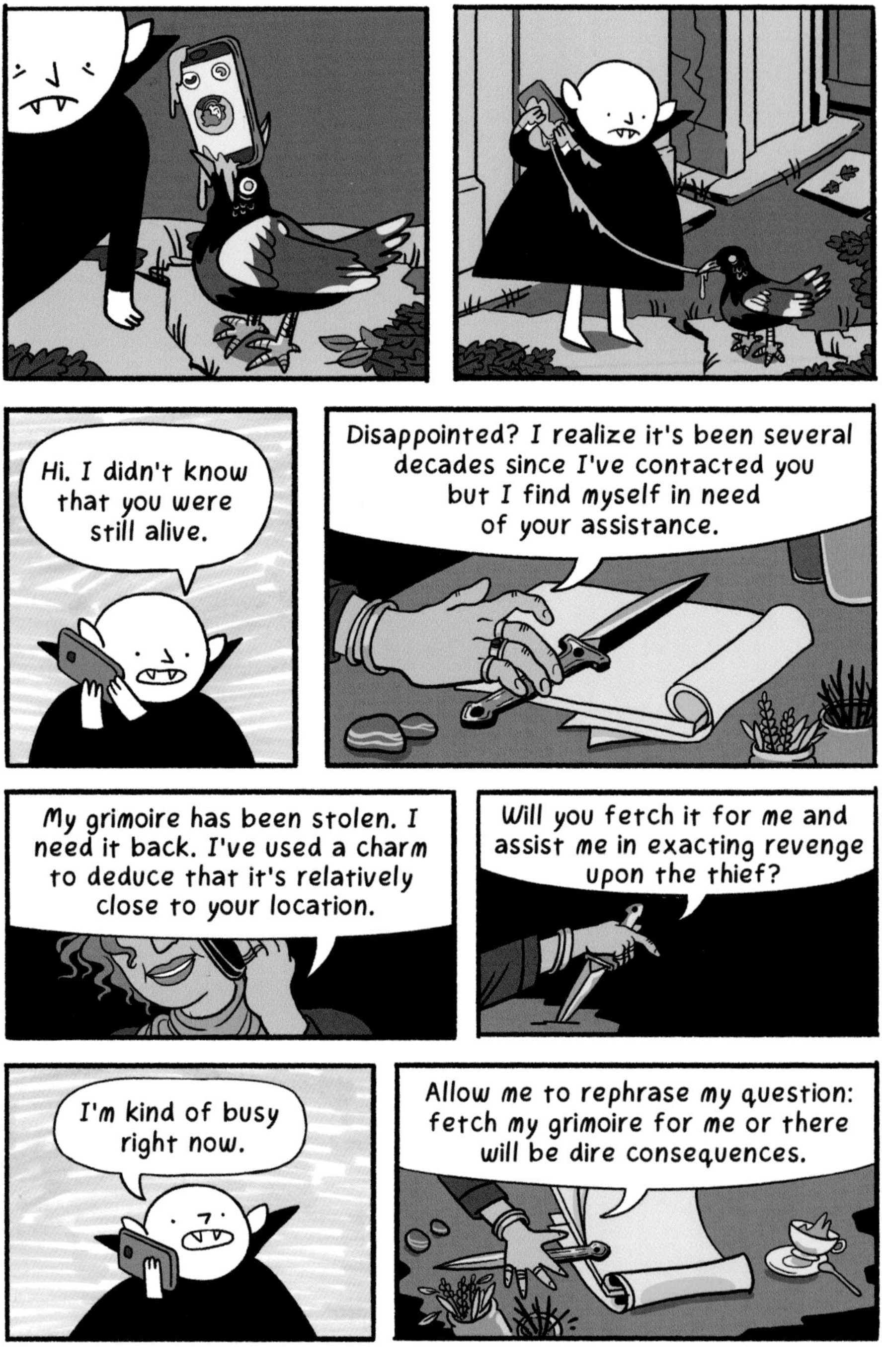
Hi. I didn't know that you were still alive.
Disappointed? I realize it's been several decades since I've contacted you but I find myself in need of your assistance.
My grimoire has been stolen. I need it back. I've used a charm to deduce that it's relatively close to your location.
Will you fetch it for me and assist me in exacting revenge upon the thief?
I'm kind of busy right now.
Allow me to rephrase my question: fetch my grimoire for me or there will be dire consequences.

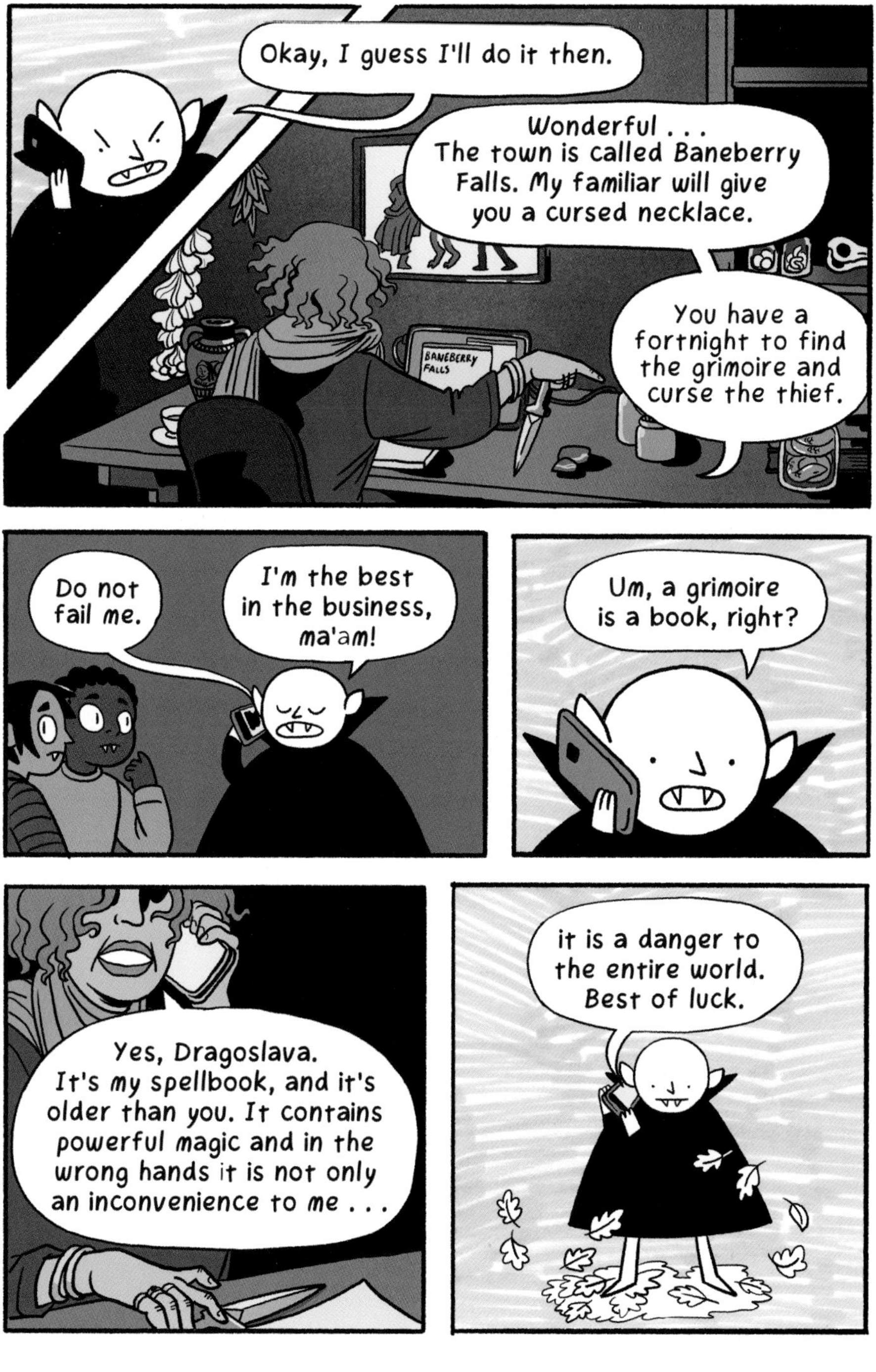
Okay, I guess I'll do it then.
Wonderful . . . The town is called Baneberry Falls. My familiar will give you a cursed necklace.
You have a fortnight to find the grimoire and curse the thief.
BANEBERRY FALLS
Do not fail me.
I'm the best in the business, ma'am!
Um, a grimoire is a book, right?
Yes, Dragoslava. It's my spellbook, and it's older than you. It contains powerful magic and in the wrong hands it is not only an inconvenience to me . . .
it is a danger to the entire world. Best of luck.

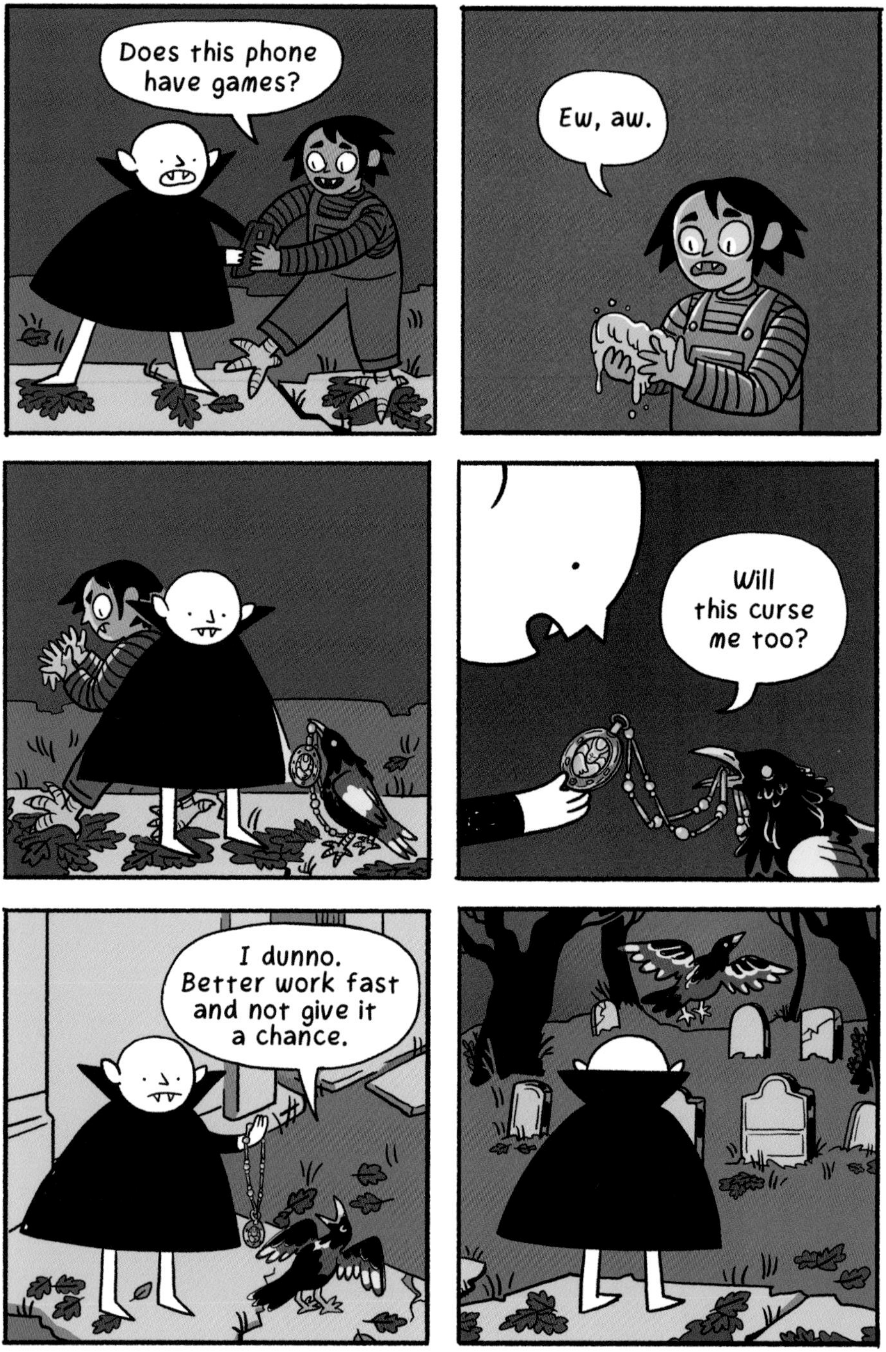
Does this phone have games?
Ew, aw.
Will this curse me too?
I dunno. Better work fast and not give it a chance.

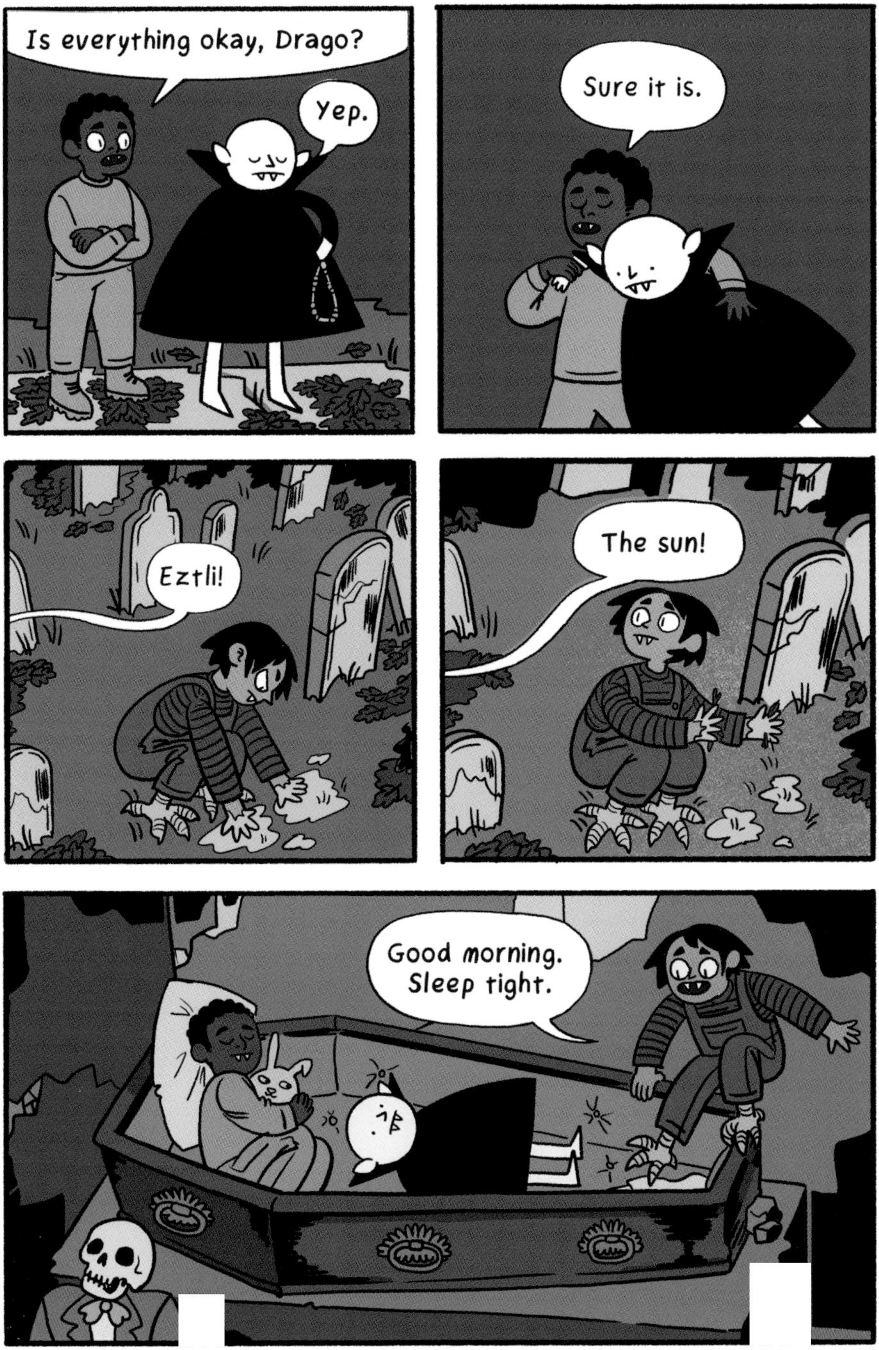
Is everything okay, Drago?
Yep.
Sure it is.
Eztli!
The sun!
Good morning. Sleep tight.

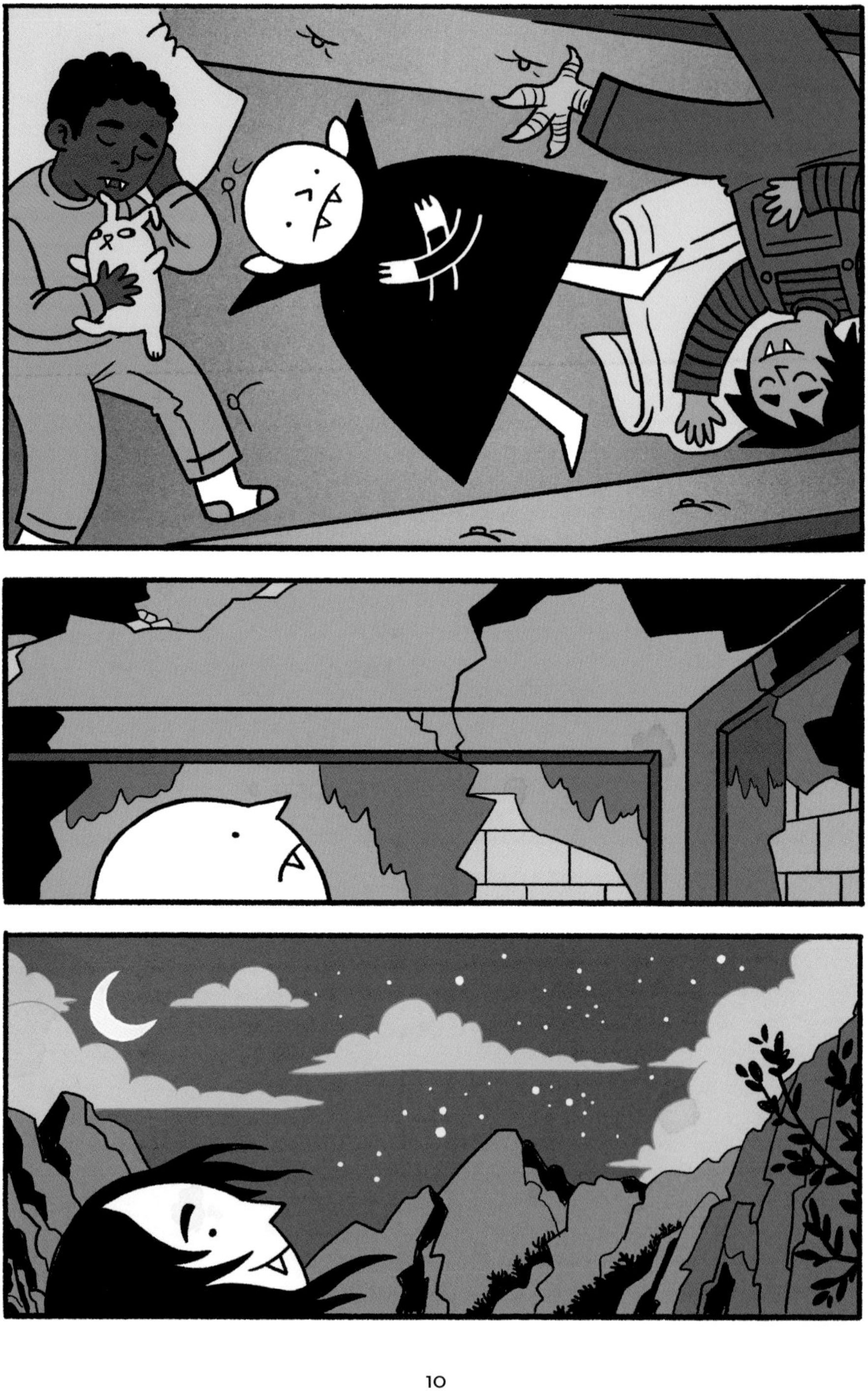

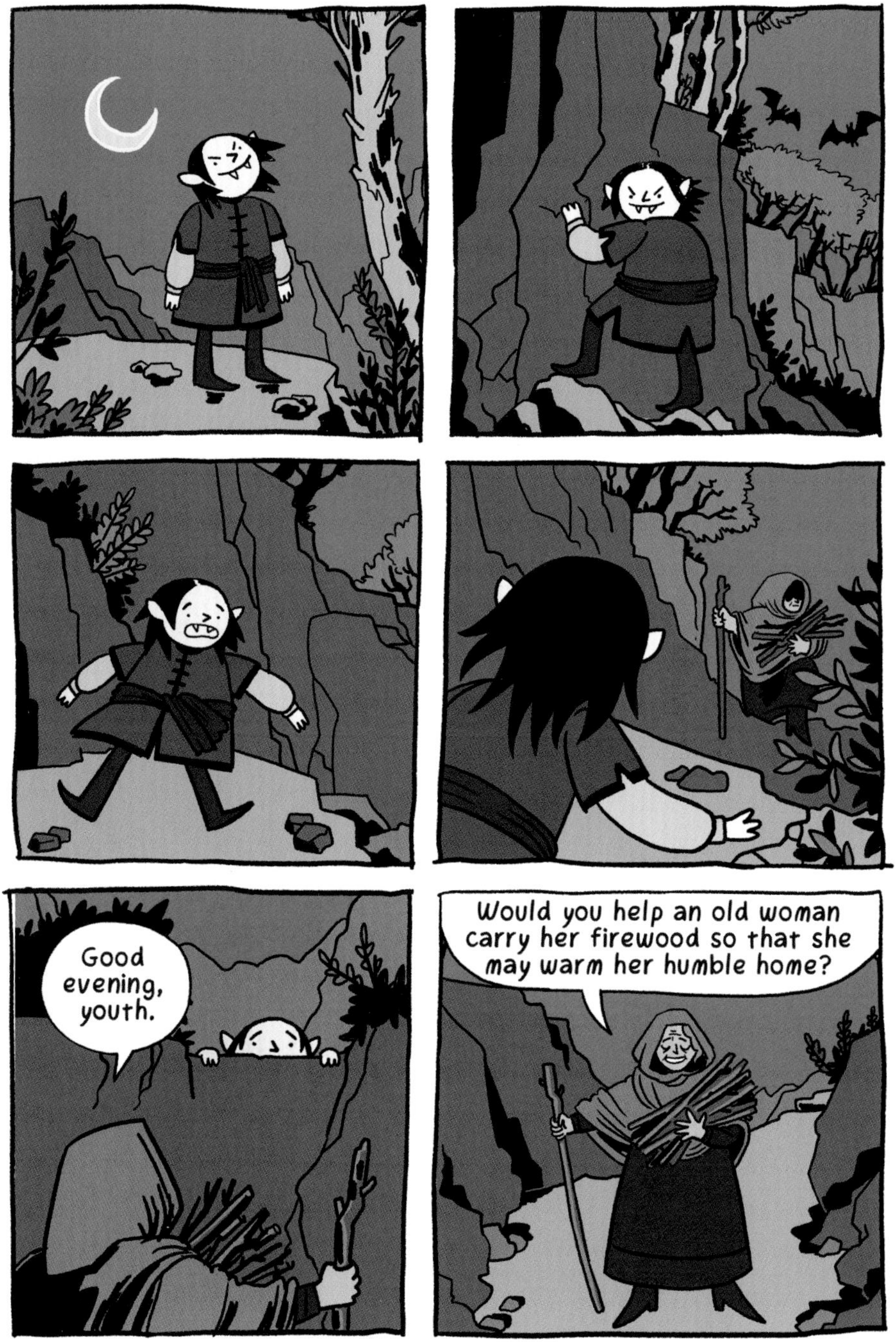
Good evening, youth.
Would you help an old woman carry her firewood so that she may warm her humble home?

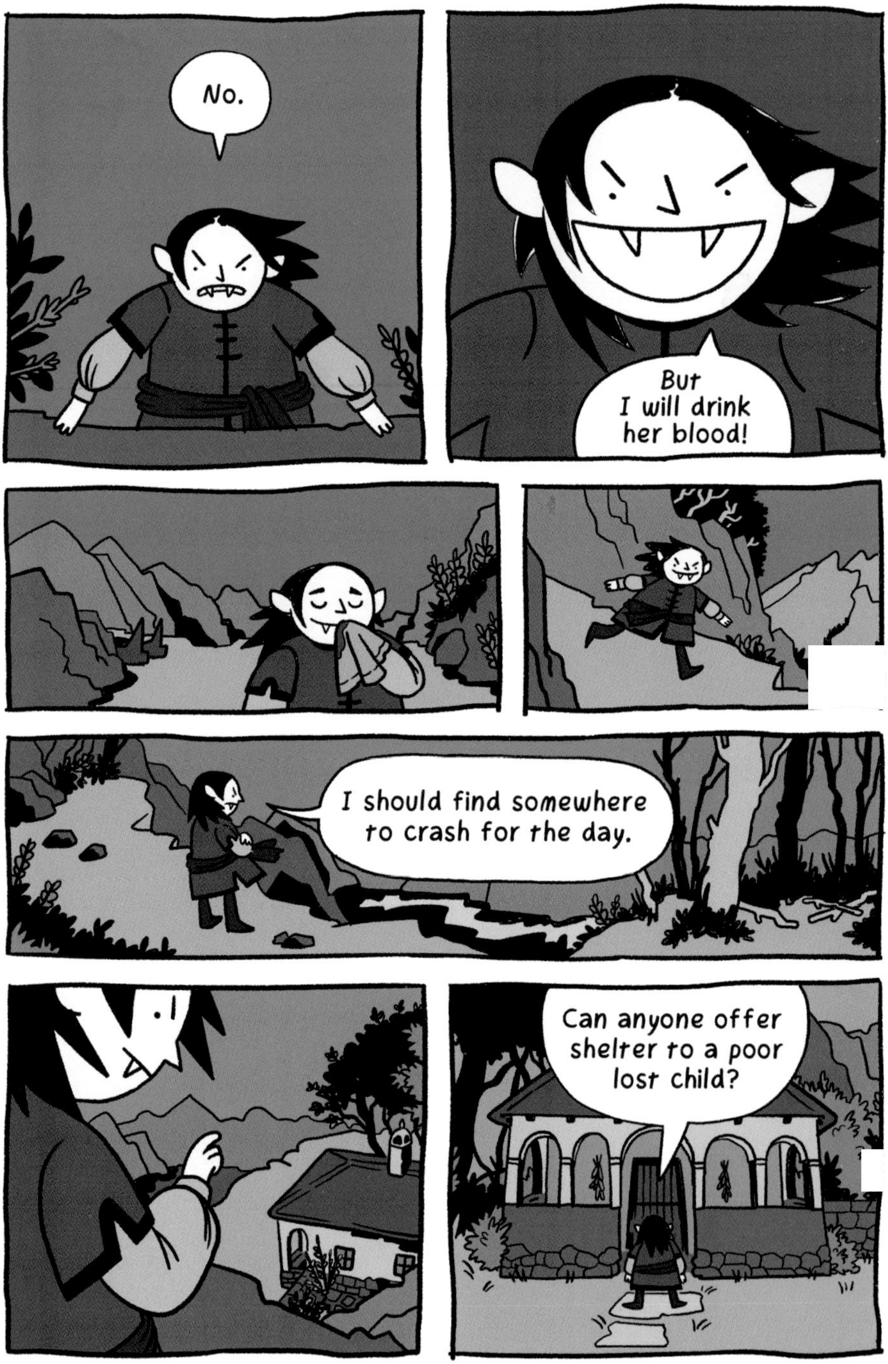
No.
But I will drink her blood!
I should find somewhere to crash for the day.
Can anyone offer shelter to a poor lost child?

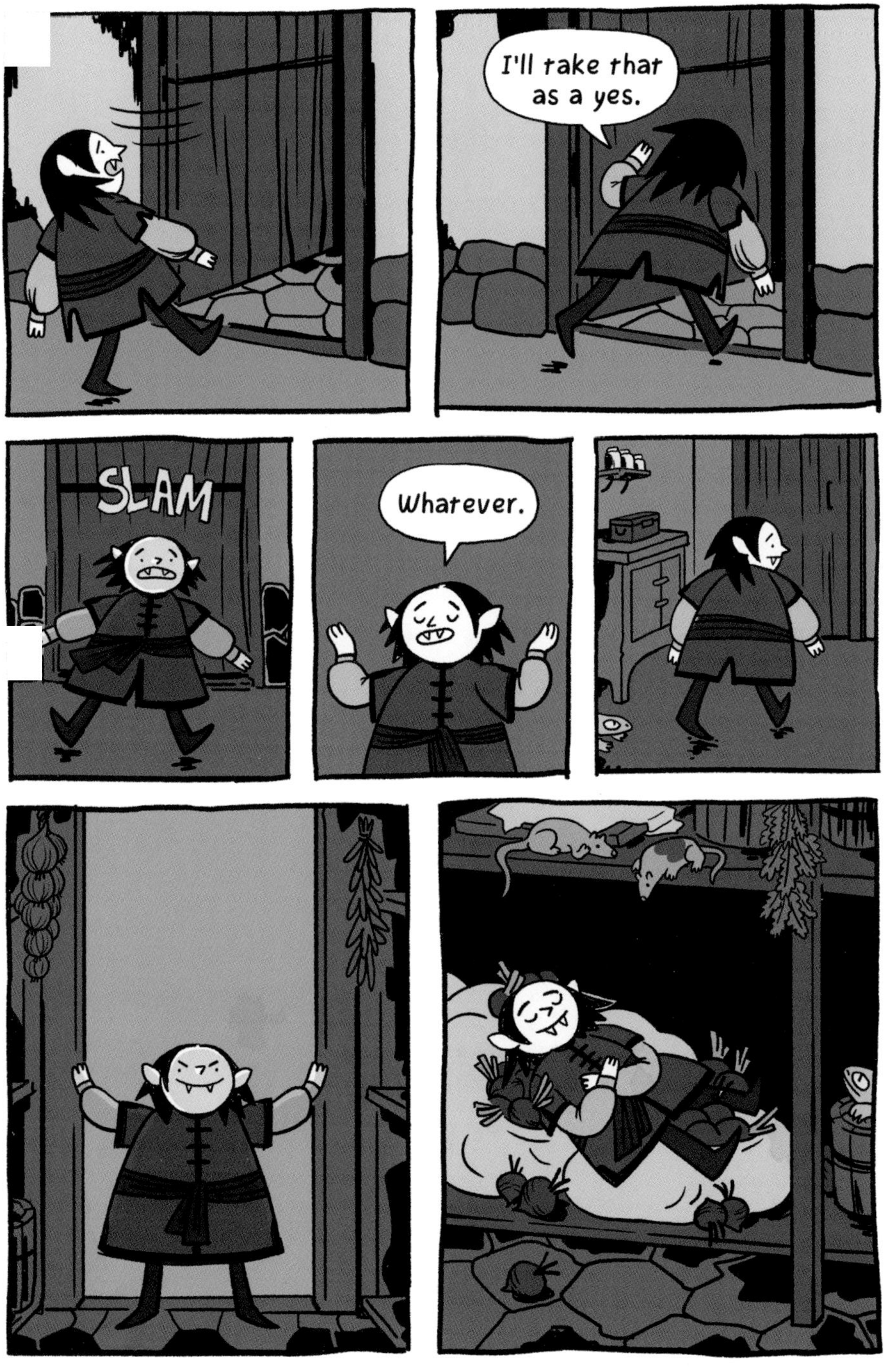
I'll take that as a yes.
SLAM
Whatever.

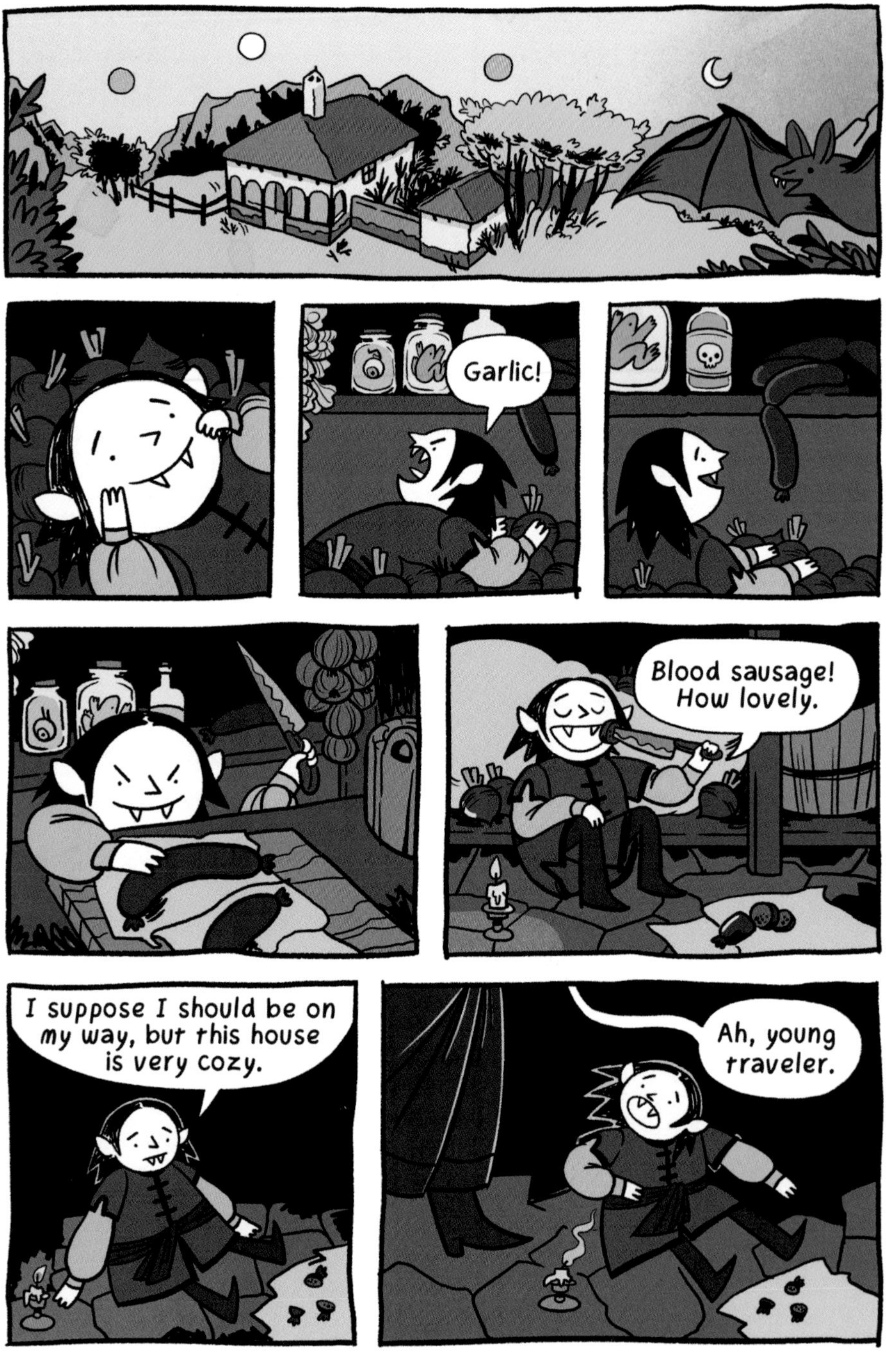
Garlic!
Blood sausage! How lovely.
I suppose I should be on my way, but this house is very cozy.
Ah, young traveler.

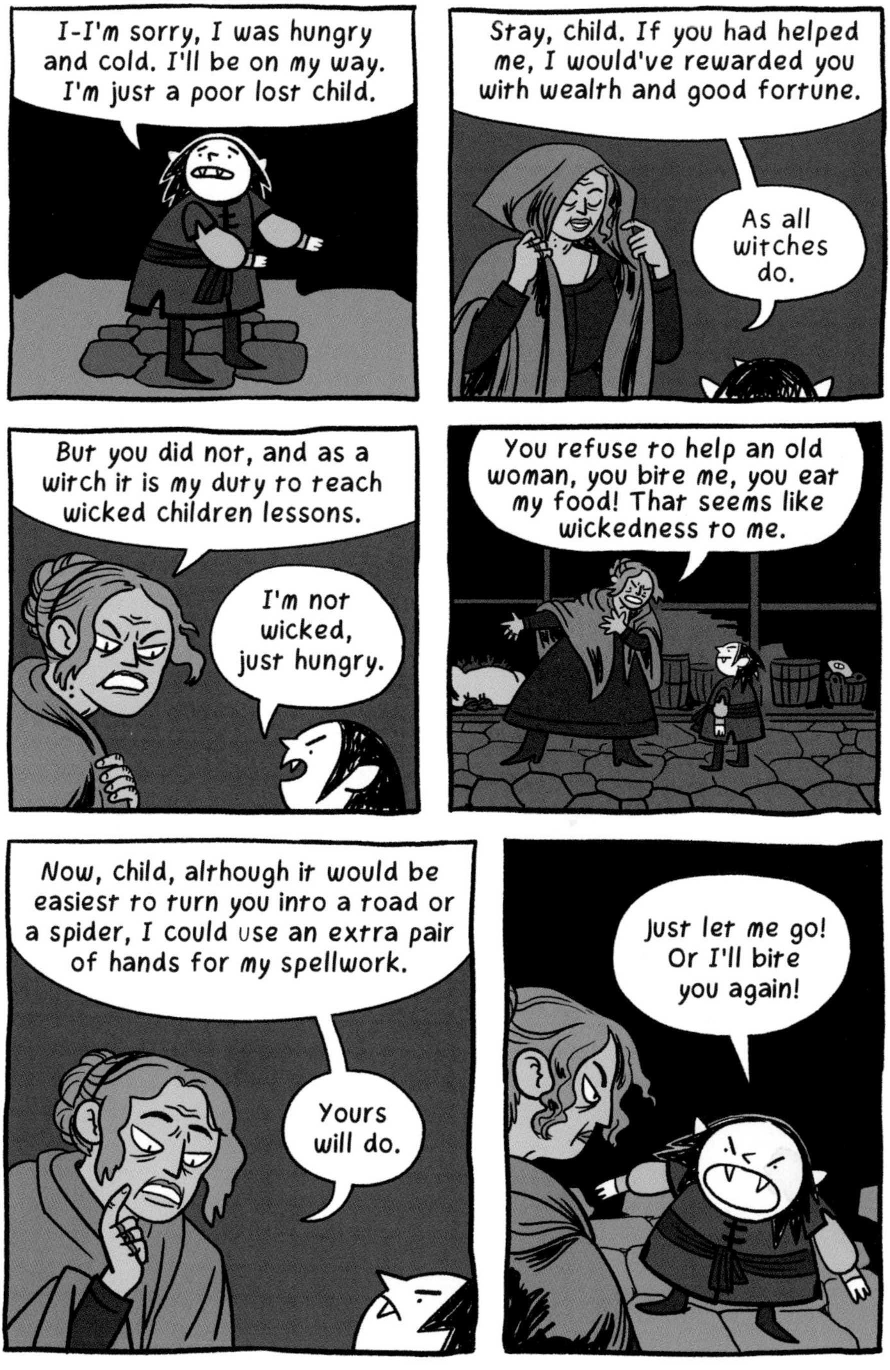
I-I'm sorry, I was hungry and cold. I'll be on my way. I'm just a poor lost child.
Stay, child. If you had helped me, I would've rewarded you with wealth and good fortune.
As all witches do.
But you did not, and as a witch it is my duty to teach wicked children lessons.
I'm not wicked, just hungry.
You refuse to help an old woman, you bite me, you eat my food! That seems like wickedness to me.
Now, child, although it would be easiest to turn you into a toad or a spider, I could use an extra pair of hands for my spellwork.
Yours will do.
Just let me go! Or I'll bite you again!

That was merely a test to see if you're hardworking, as all children should be. I am not a weak old woman, I am strong and powerful...
and you have incurred my wrath.

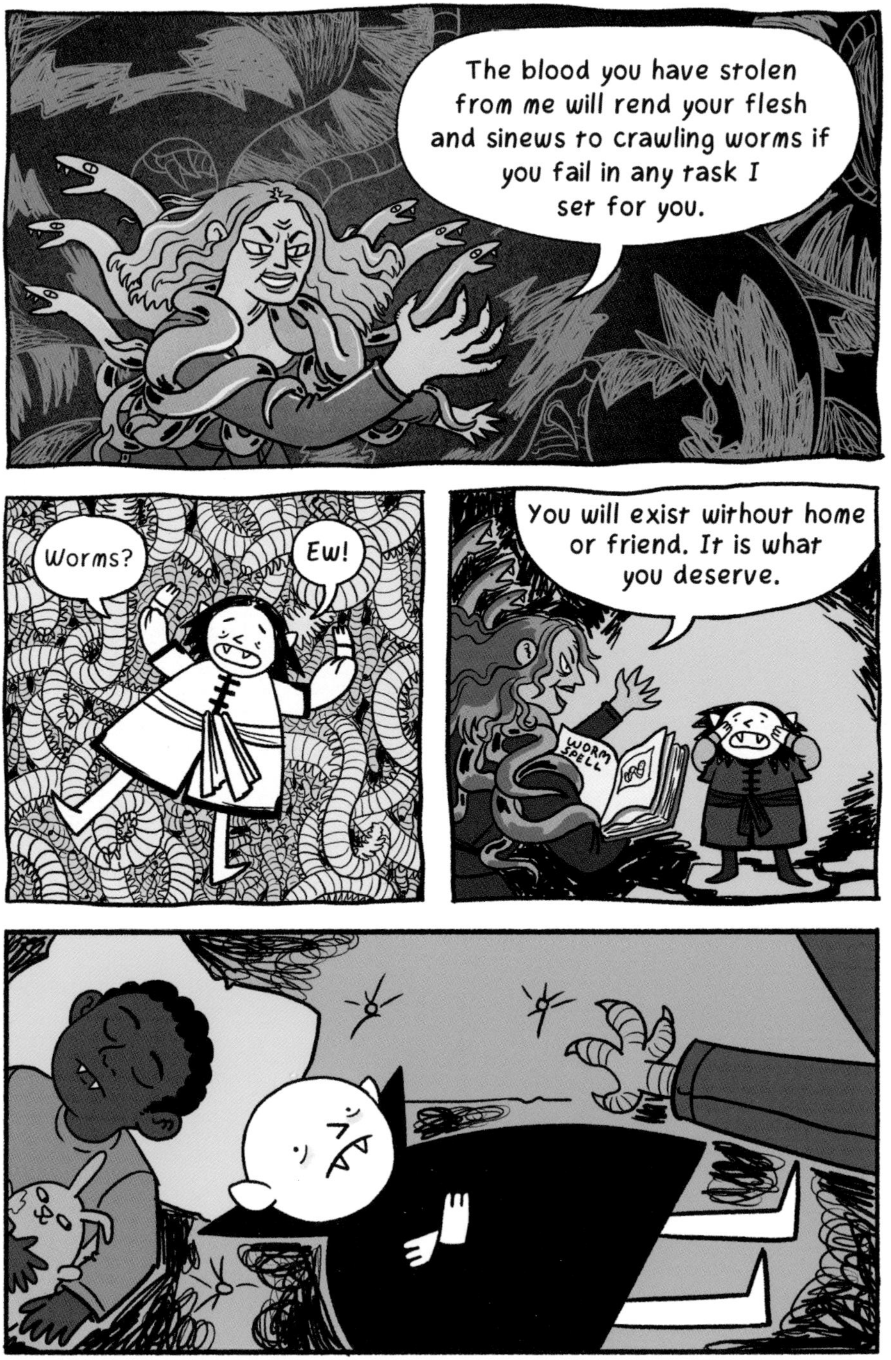
The blood you have stolen from me will rend your flesh and sinews to crawling worms if you fail in any task I set for you.
Worms?
Ew!
You will exist without home or friend. It is what you deserve.
WORM SPELL

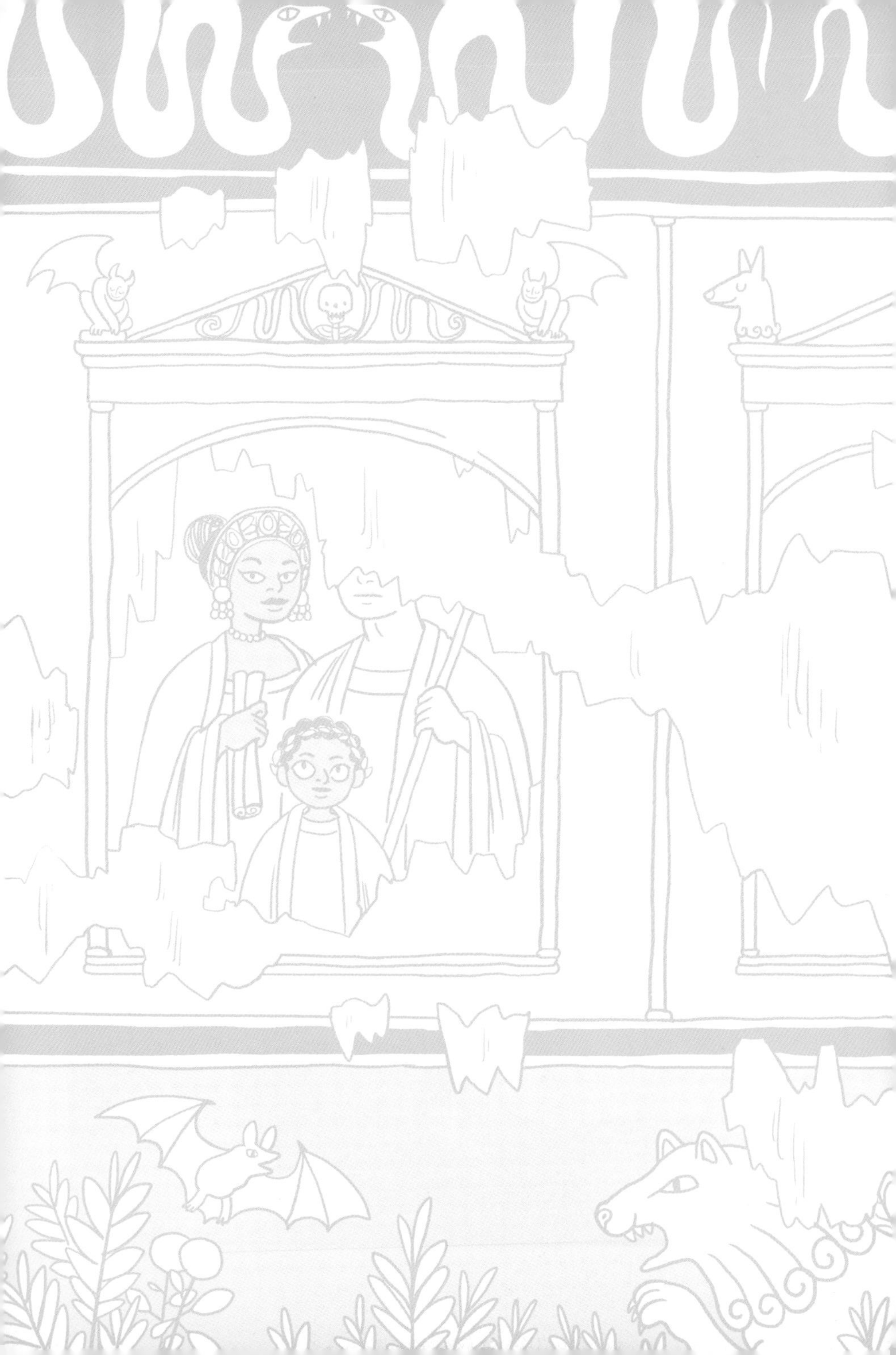

CHAPTER TWO

QuintUS

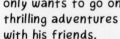

b. 129 BCE
His mom is the queen of a
subterranean vampire
society, but Quintus
only wants to go on
thrilling adventures
with his friends.

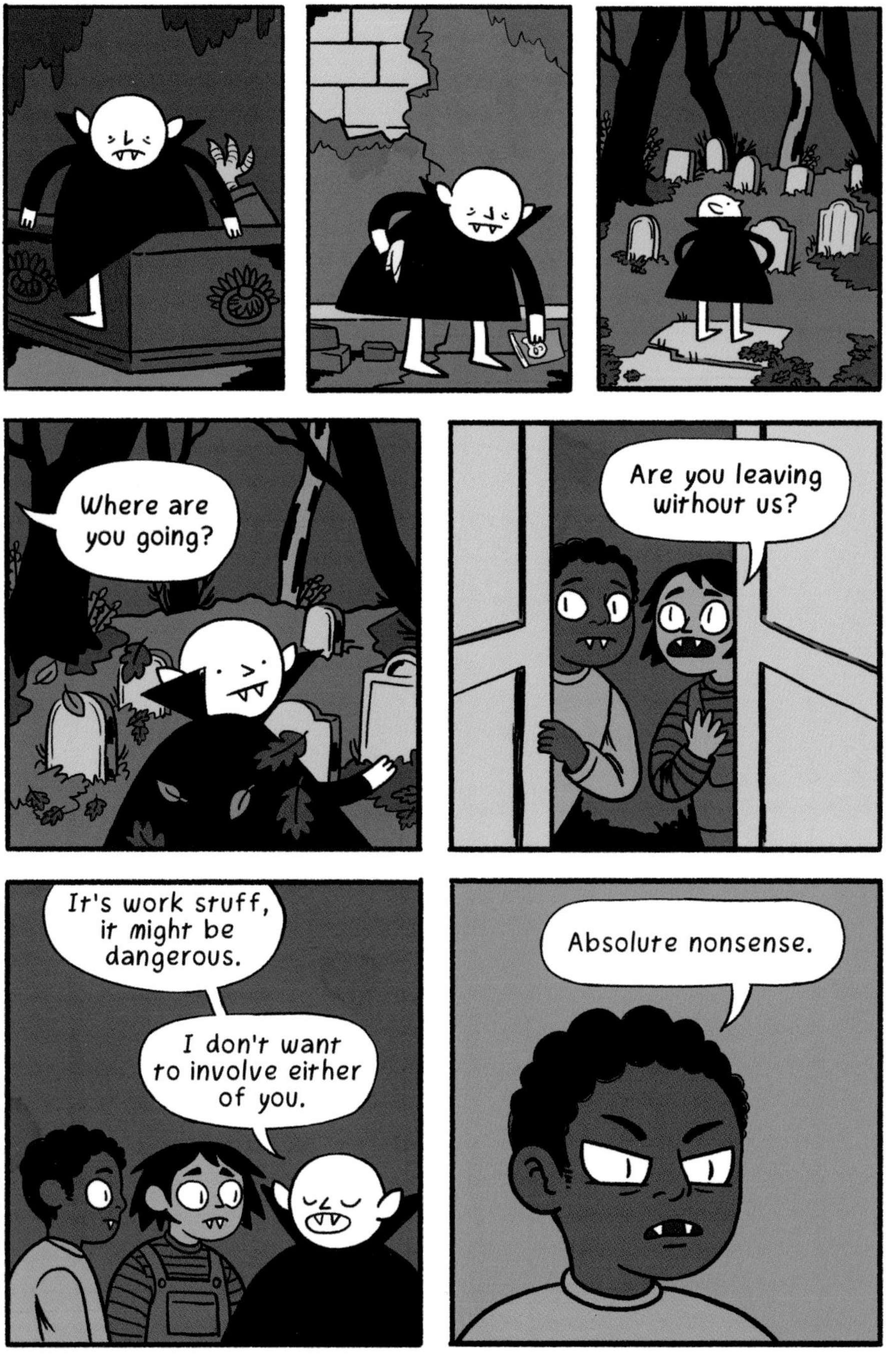
Where are you going?
Are you leaving without us?
It's work stuff, it might be dangerous.
I don't want to involve either of you.
Absolute nonsense.

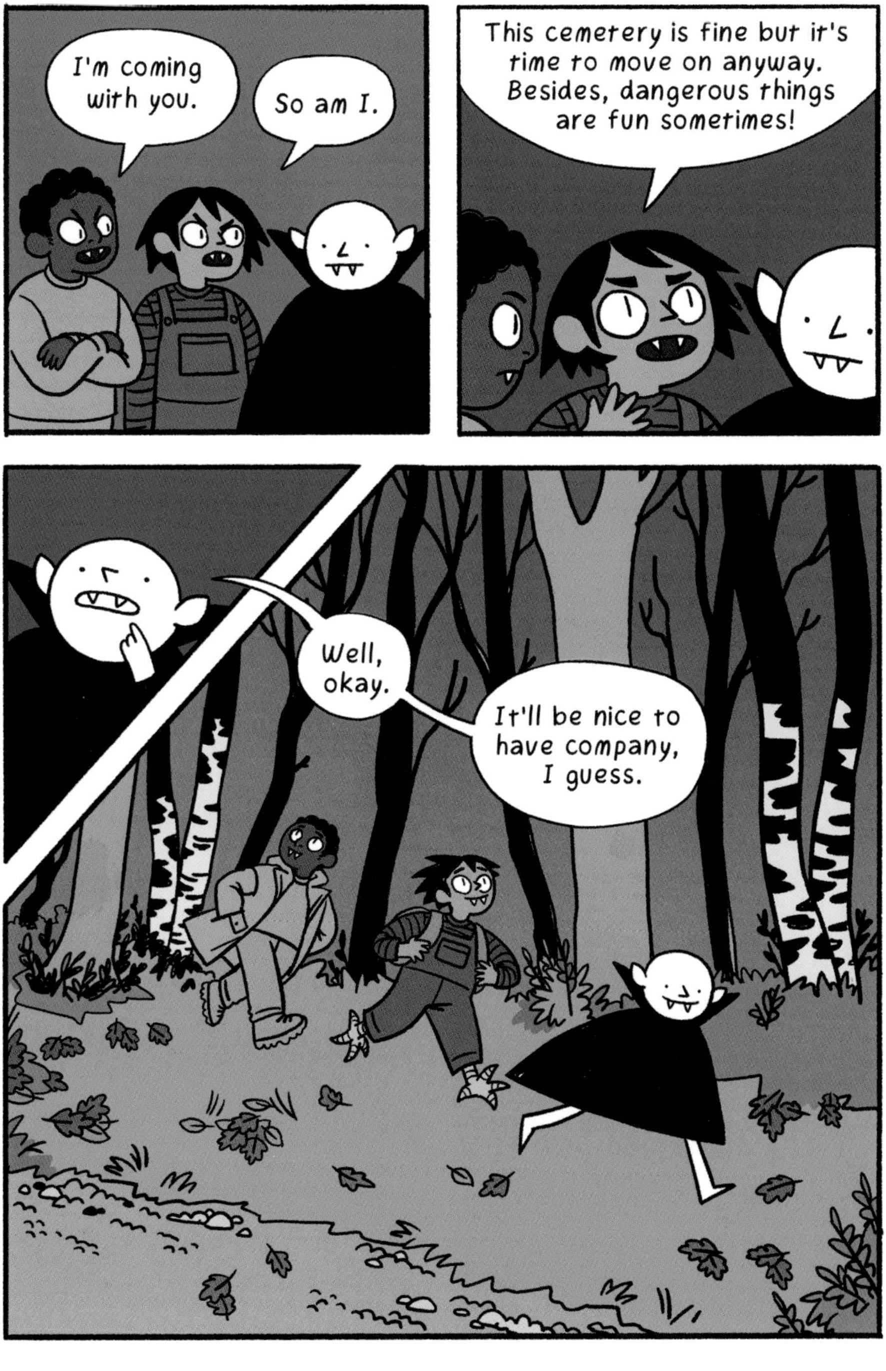

I'm coming with you.
So am I.
This cemetery is fine but it's time to move on anyway. Besides, dangerous things are fun sometimes!
Well, okay.
It'll be nice to have company, I guess.

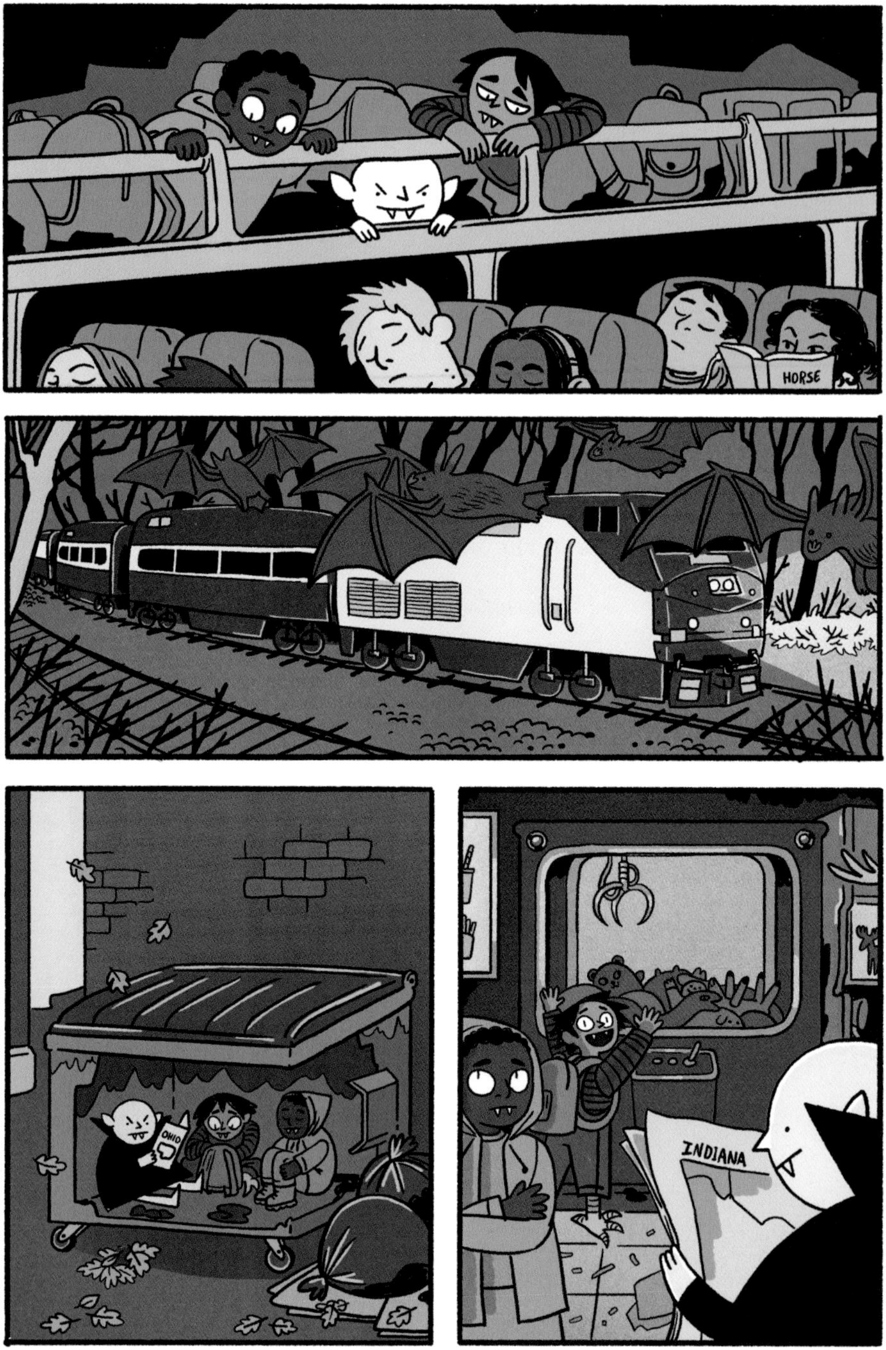
HORSE
OHIO
INDIANA

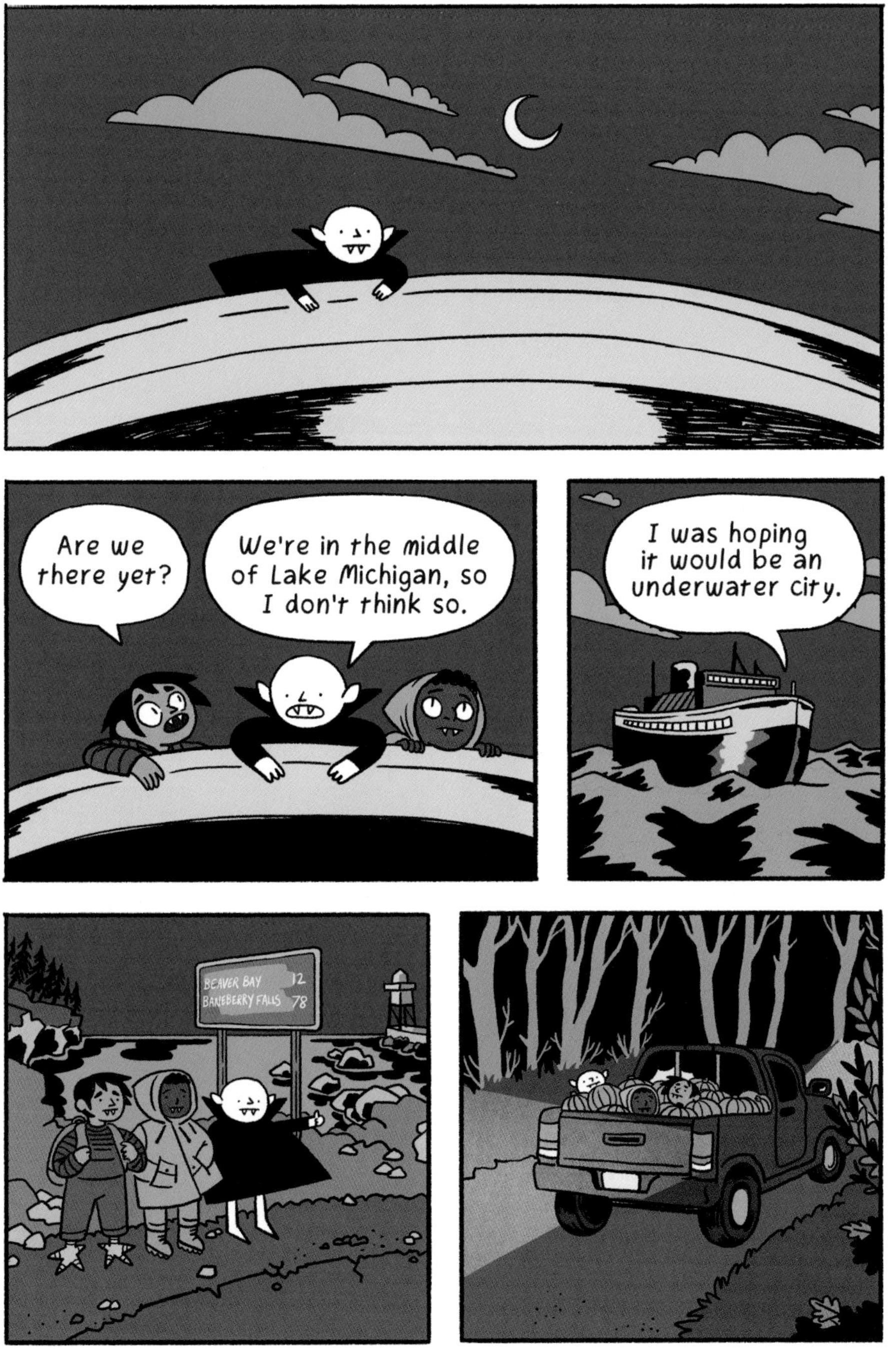
Are we there yet?
We're in the middle of Lake Michigan, so I don't think so.
I was hoping it would be an underwater city.
BEAVER BAY 12
BANEBERRY FALLS 78

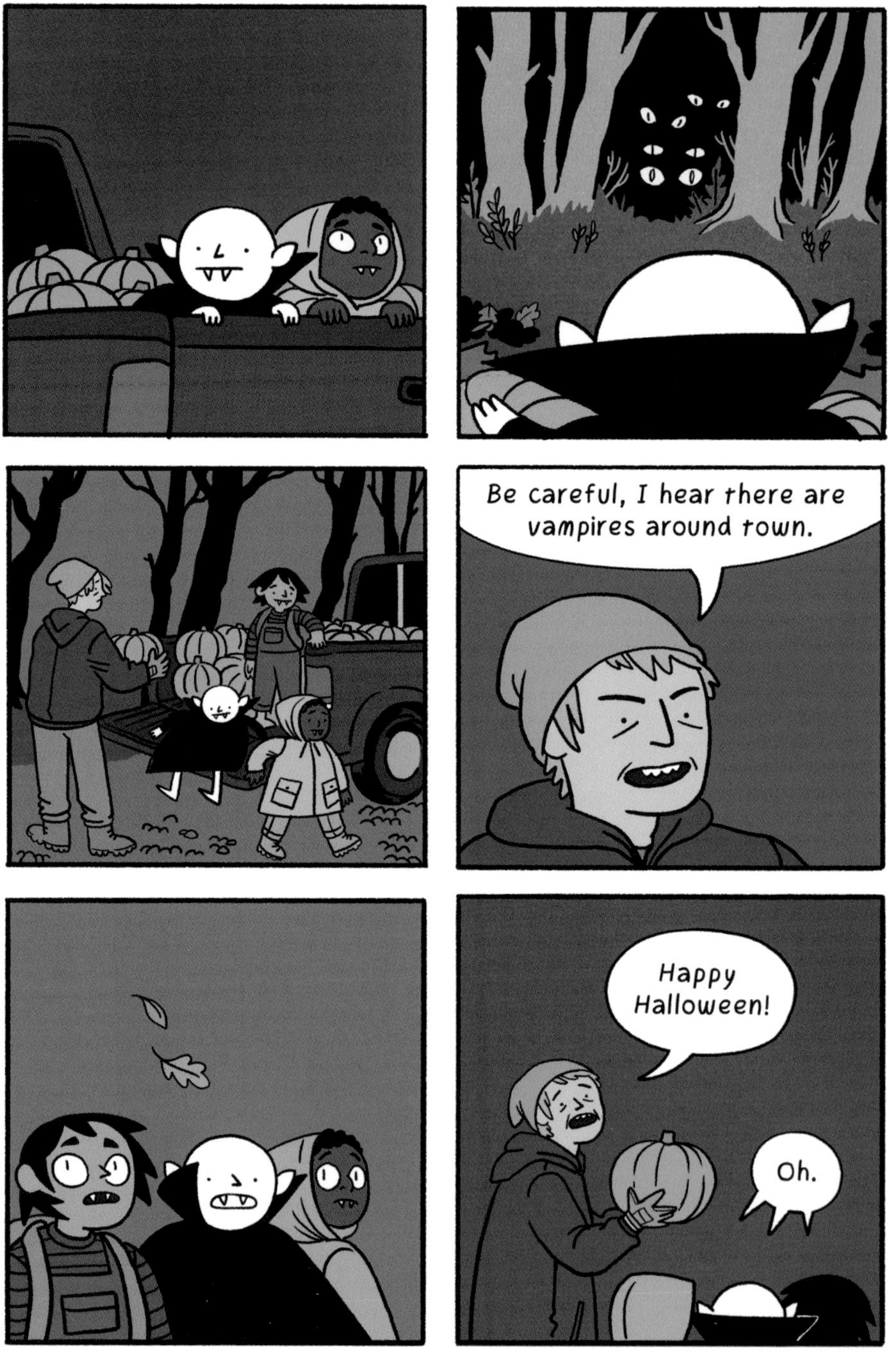
Be careful, I hear there are vampires around town.
Happy Halloween!
Oh.

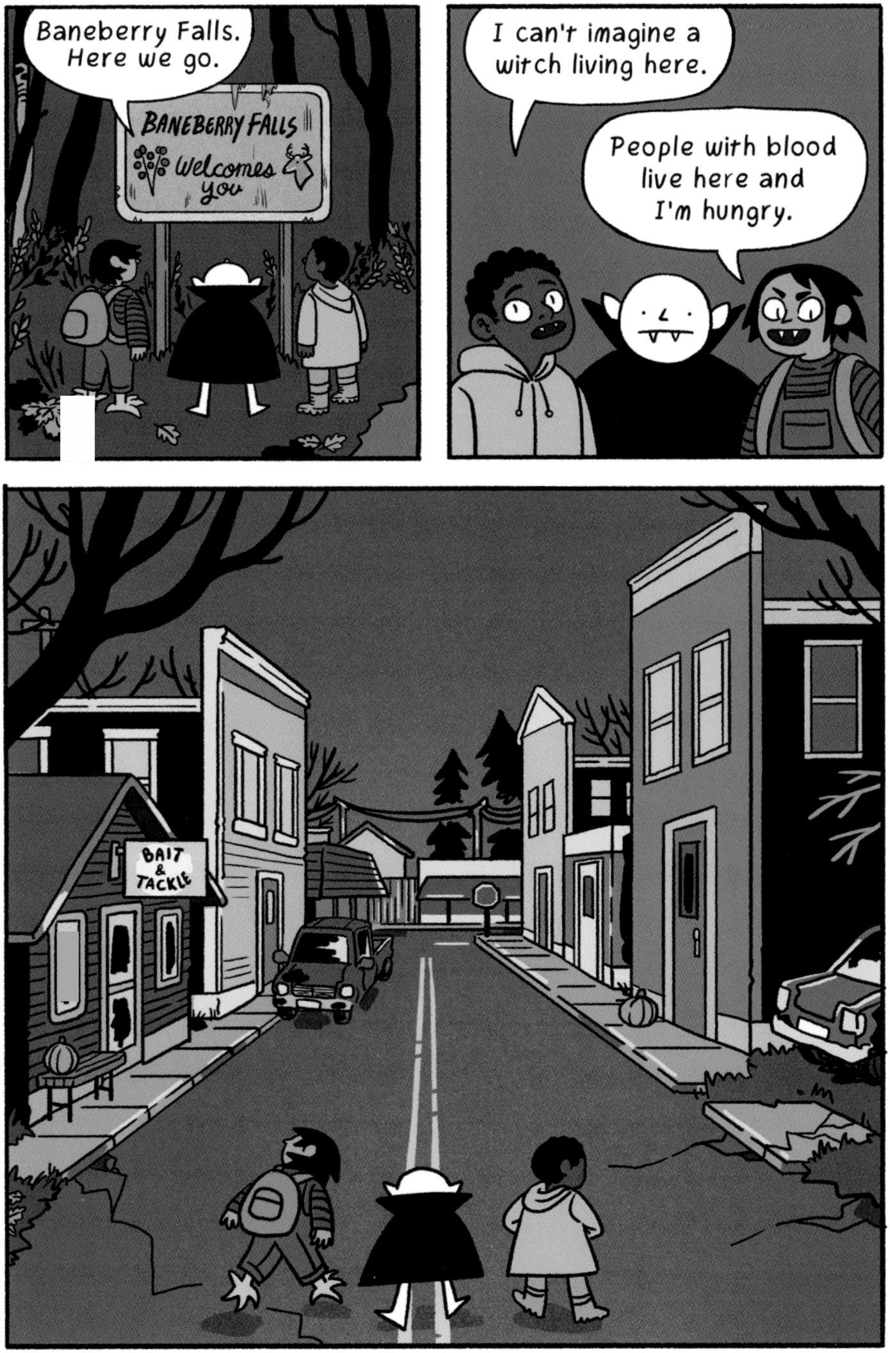
Baneberry Falls. Here we go.
BANEBERRY FALLS
Welcomes you
I can't imagine a witch living here.
People with blood live here and I'm hungry.
BAIT & TACKLE

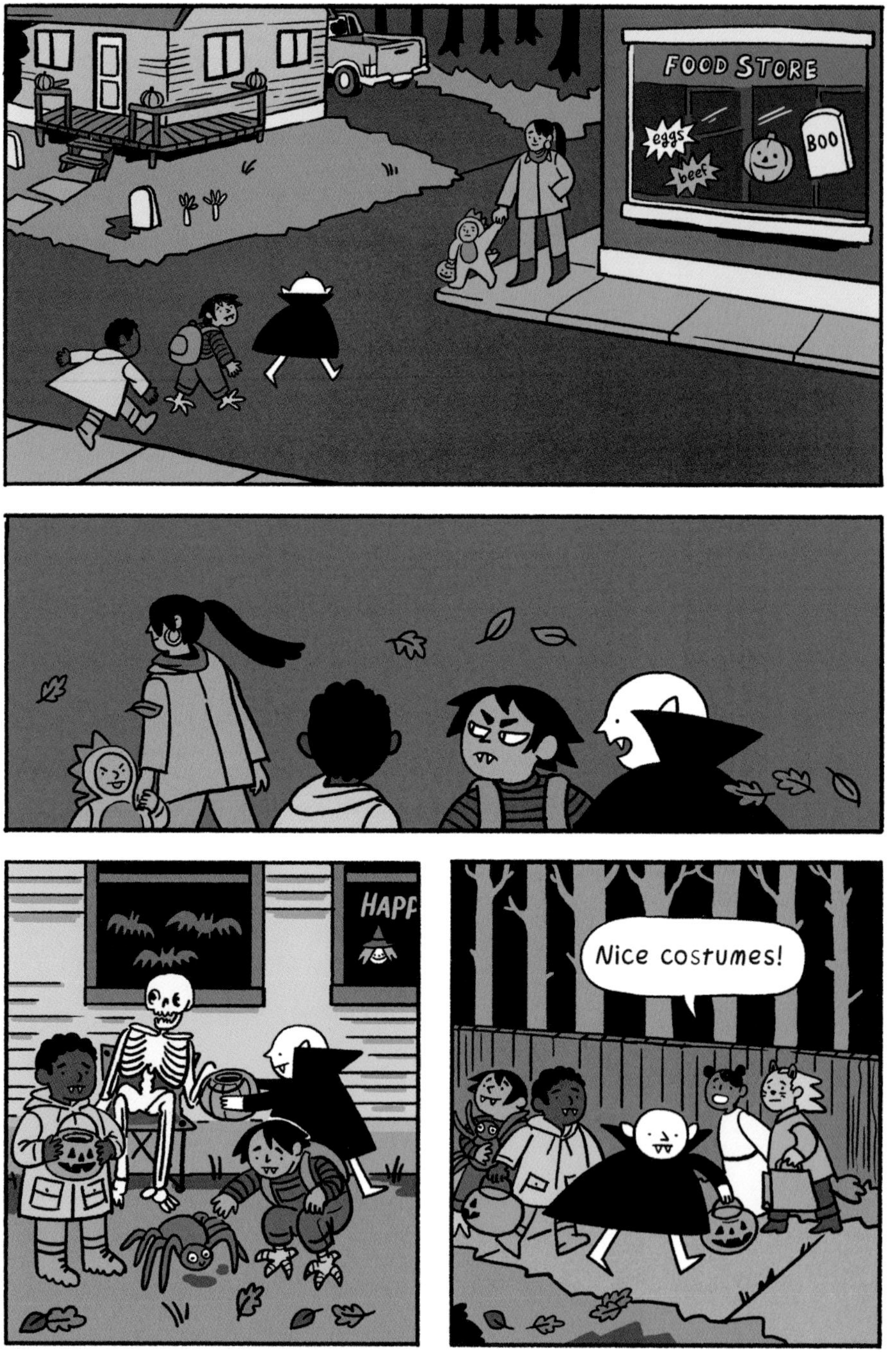
FOOD STORE
eggs
beef
BOO
HAPP
Nice costumes!

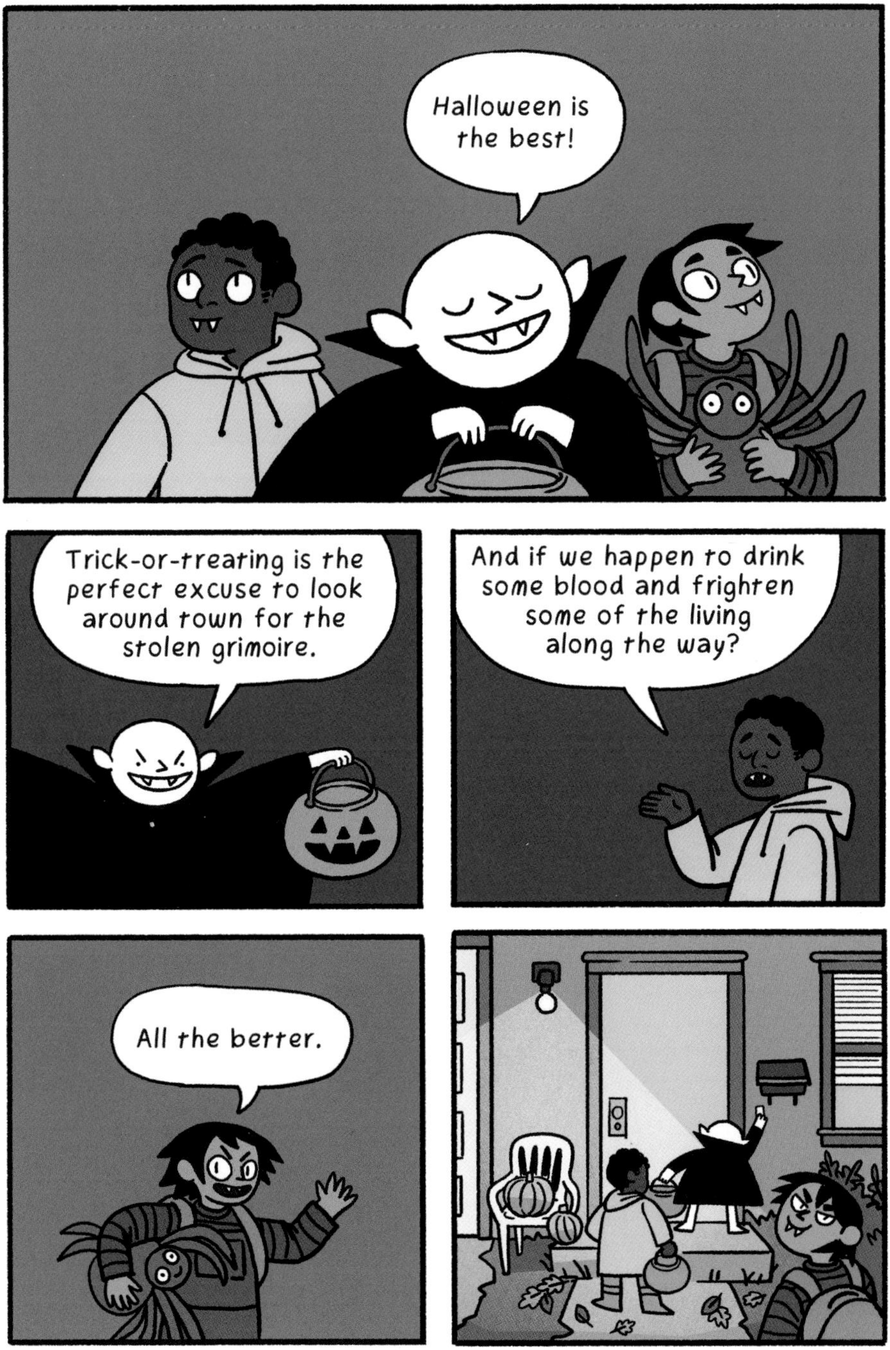
Halloween is the best!
Trick-or-treating is the perfect excuse to look around town for the stolen grimoire.
And if we happen to drink some blood and frighten some of the living along the way?
All the better.

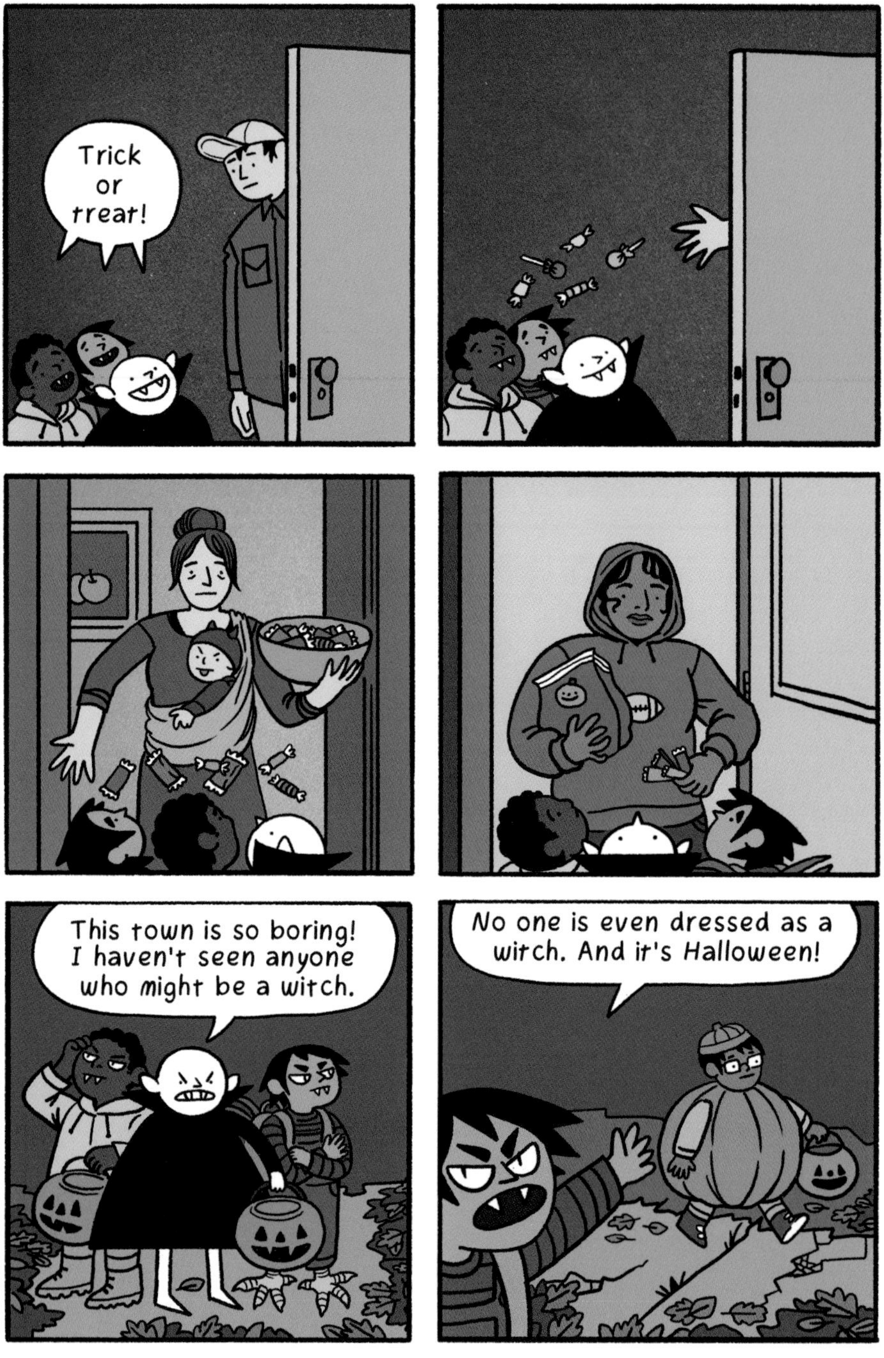
Trick or treat!
This town is so boring! I haven't seen anyone who might be a witch.
No one is even dressed as a witch. And it's Halloween!

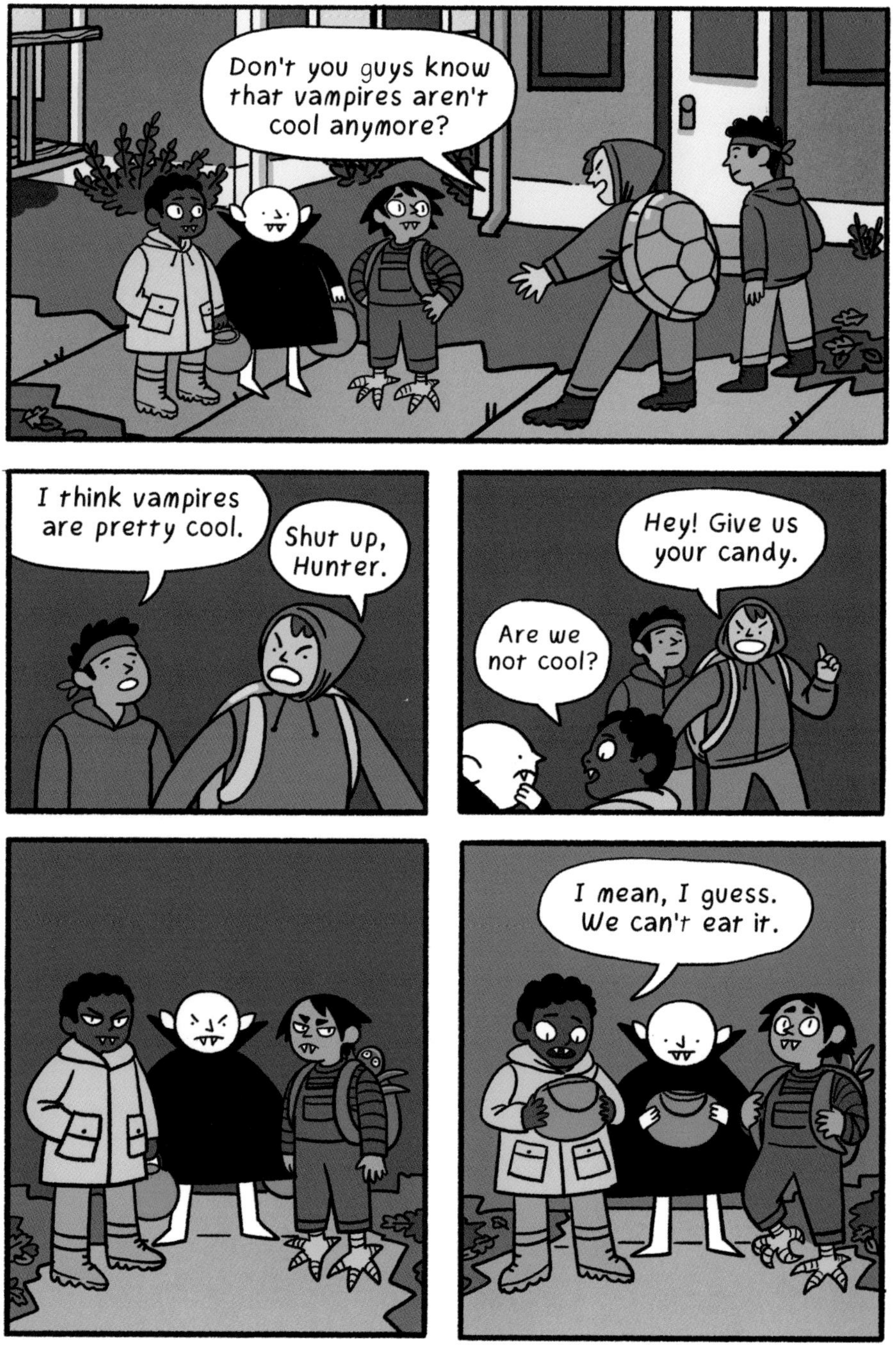
Don't you guys know that vampires aren't cool anymore?
I think vampires are pretty cool.
Shut up, Hunter.
Hey! Give us your candy.
Are we not cool?
I mean, I guess. We can't eat it.

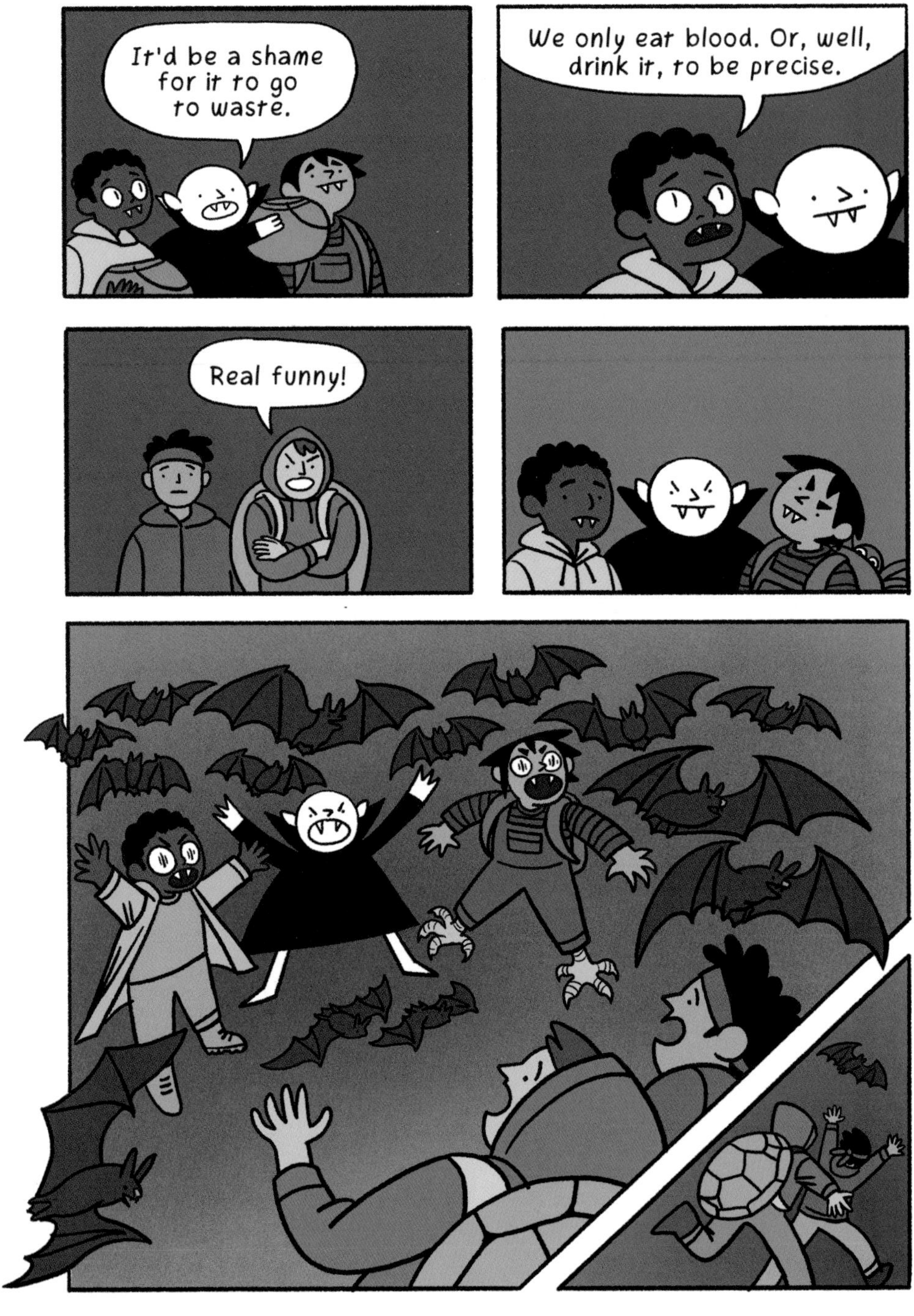
It'd be a shame for it to go to waste.
We only eat blood. Or, well, drink it, to be precise.
Real funny!

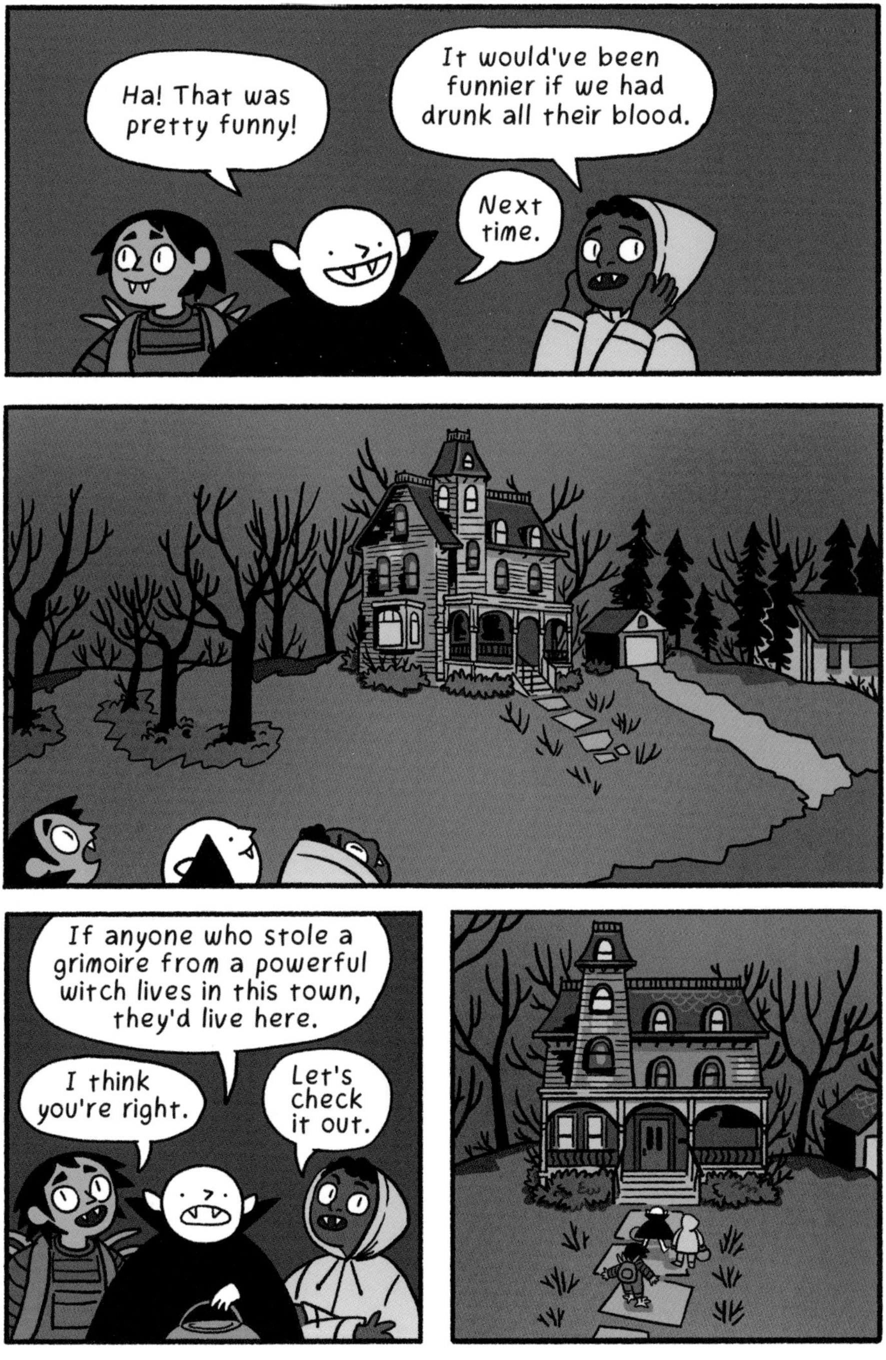
Ha! That was pretty funny!
It would've been funnier if we had drunk all their blood.
Next time.
If anyone who stole a grimoire from a powerful witch lives in this town, they'd live here.
I think you're right.
Let's check it out.

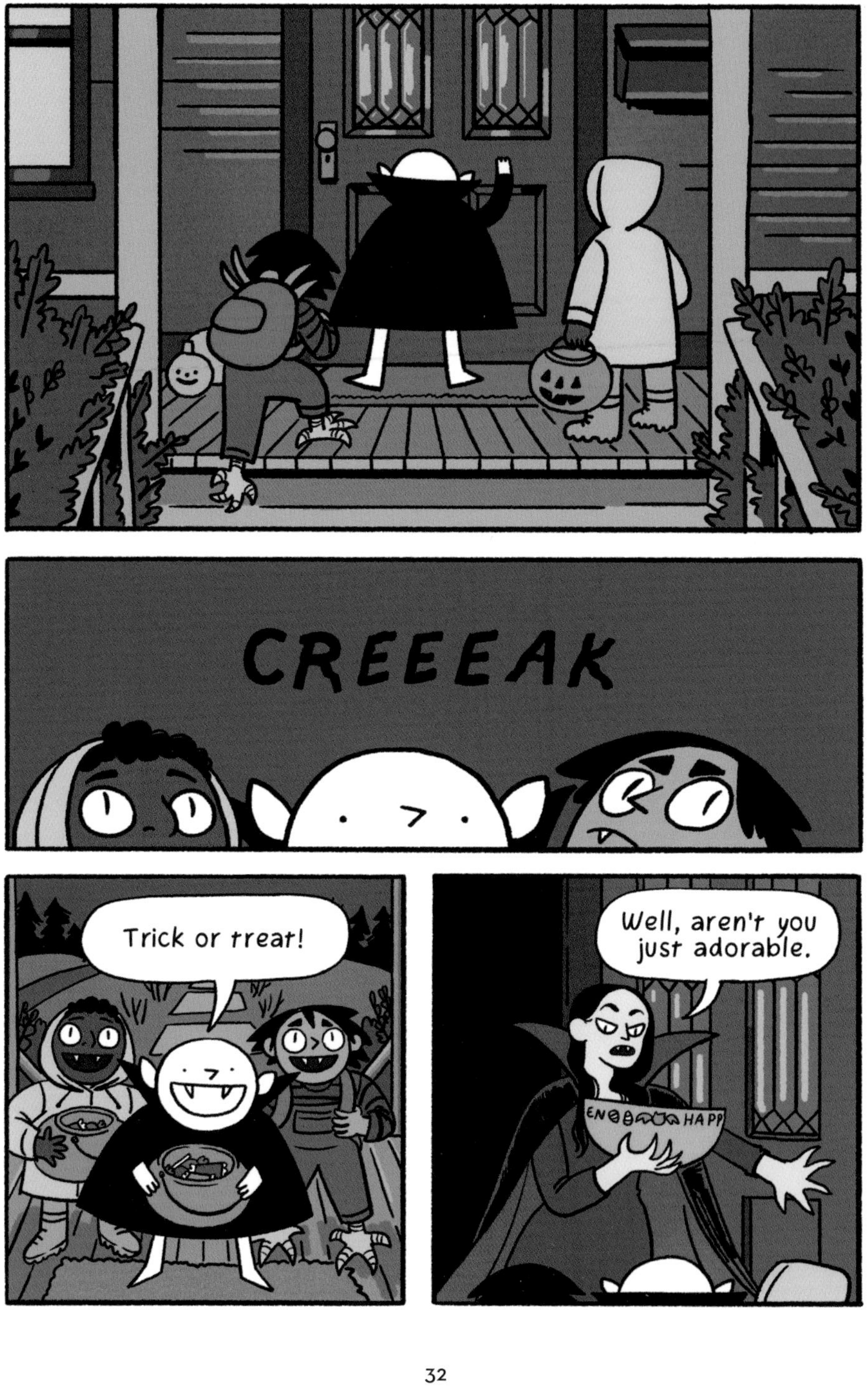
CREEEAK
Trick or treat!
Well, aren't you just adorable.

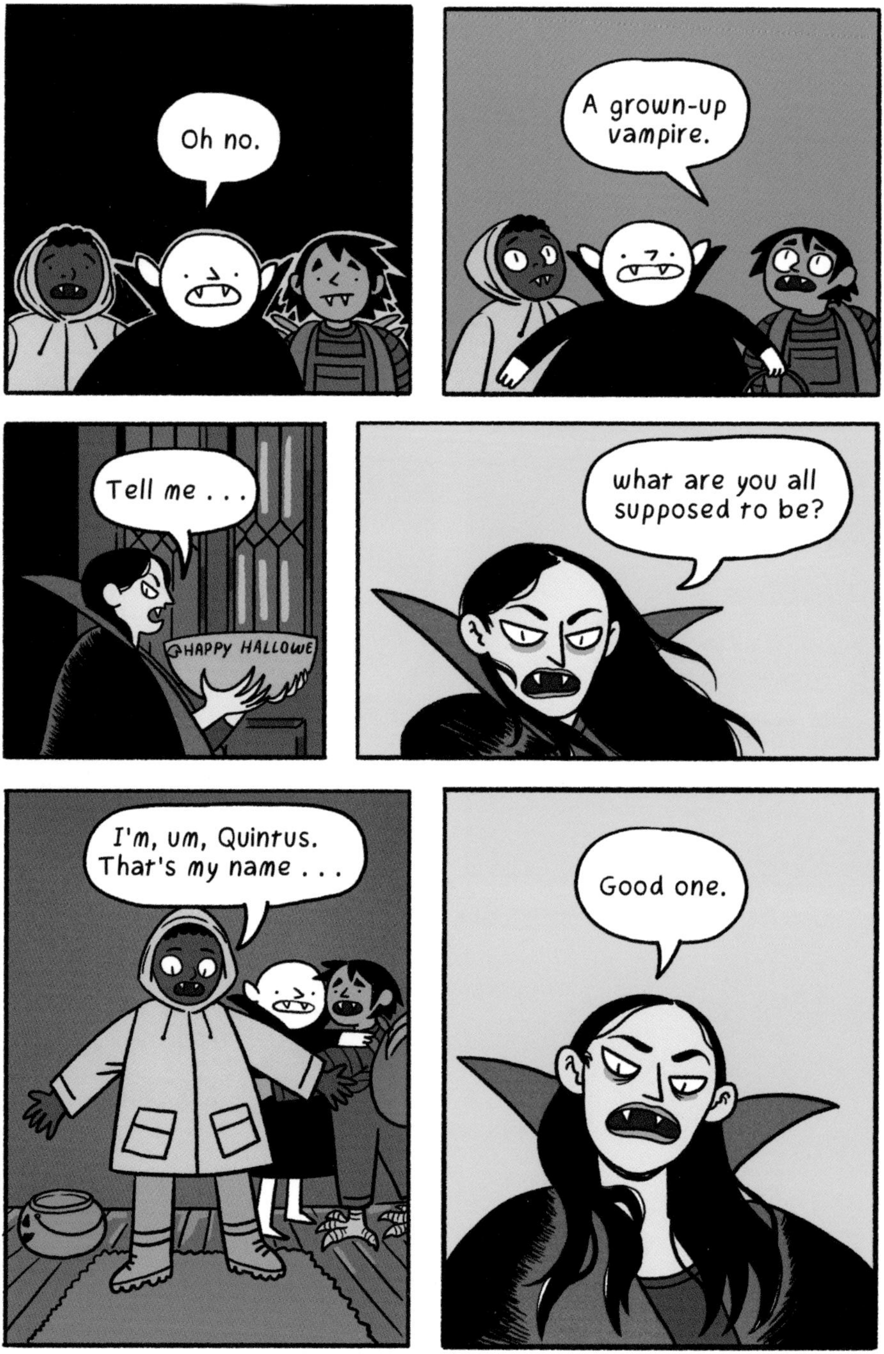
Oh no.
A grown-up vampire.
Tell me . . .
what are you all supposed to be?
I'm, um, Quintus. That's my name . . .
Good one.
HAPPY HALLOWE

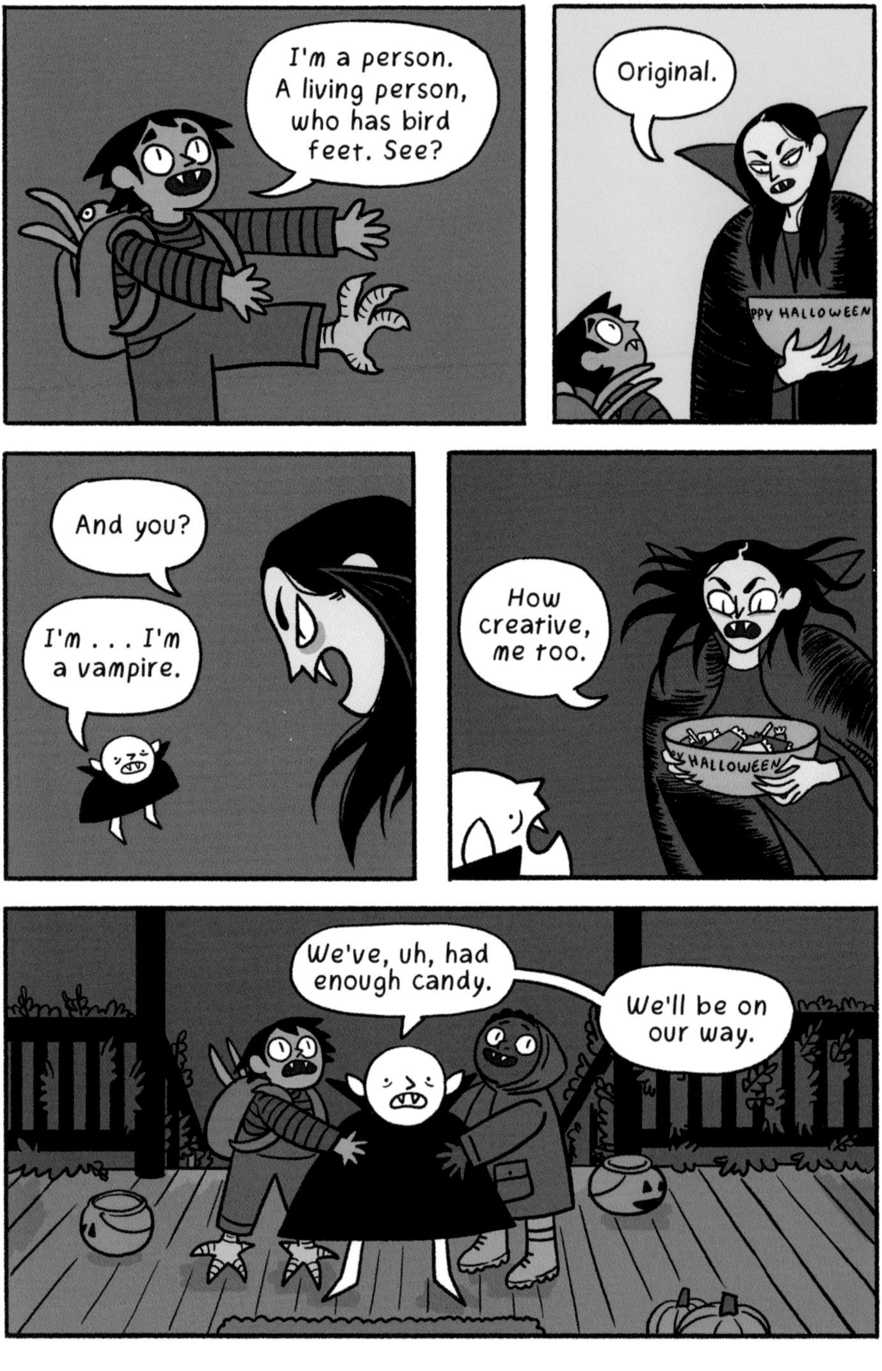
I'm a person.
A living person,
who has bird
feet. See?
Original.
PPY HALLOWEEN
And you?
I'm . . . I'm
a vampire.
How
creative,
me too.
HALLOWEEN
We've, uh, had
enough candy.
We'll be on
our way.

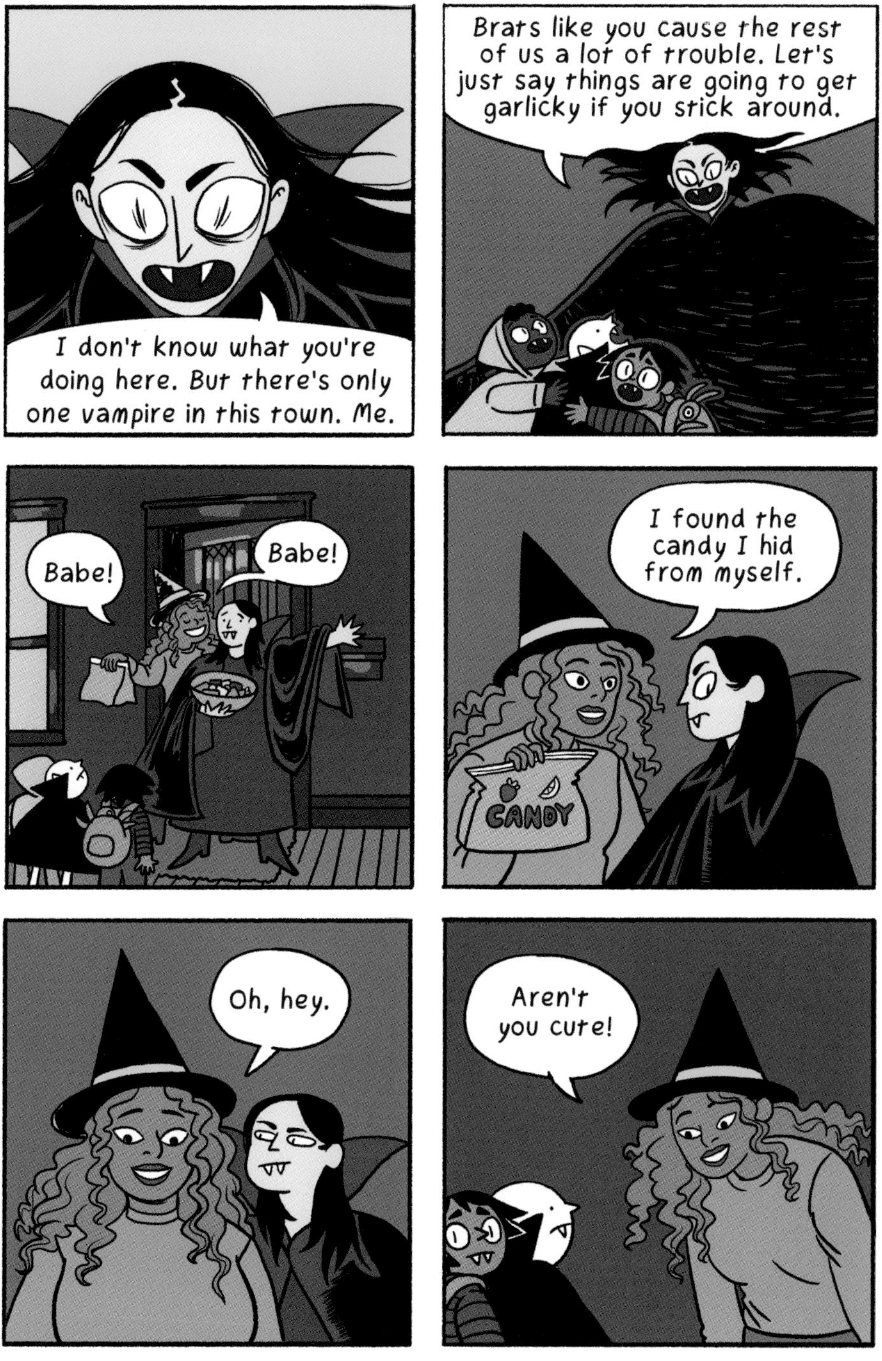
I don't know what you're doing here. But there's only one vampire in this town. Me.
Brats like you cause the rest of us a lot of trouble. Let's just say things are going to get garlicky if you stick around.
Babe!
Babe!
I found the candy I hid from myself.
CANDY
Oh, hey.
Aren't you cute!

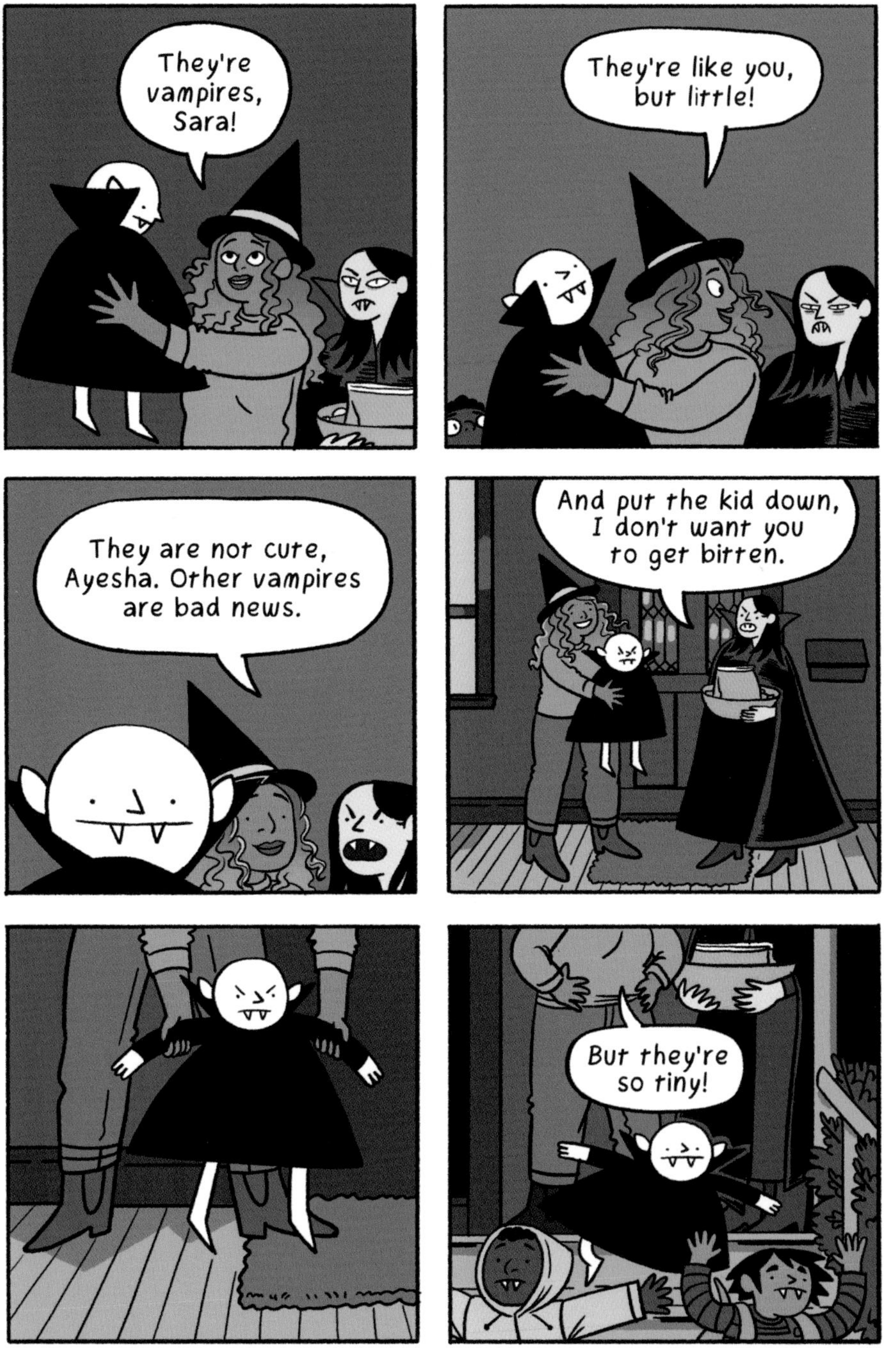
They're vampires, Sara!
They're like you, but little!
They are not cute, Ayesha. Other vampires are bad news.
And put the kid down, I don't want you to get bitten.
But they're so tiny!

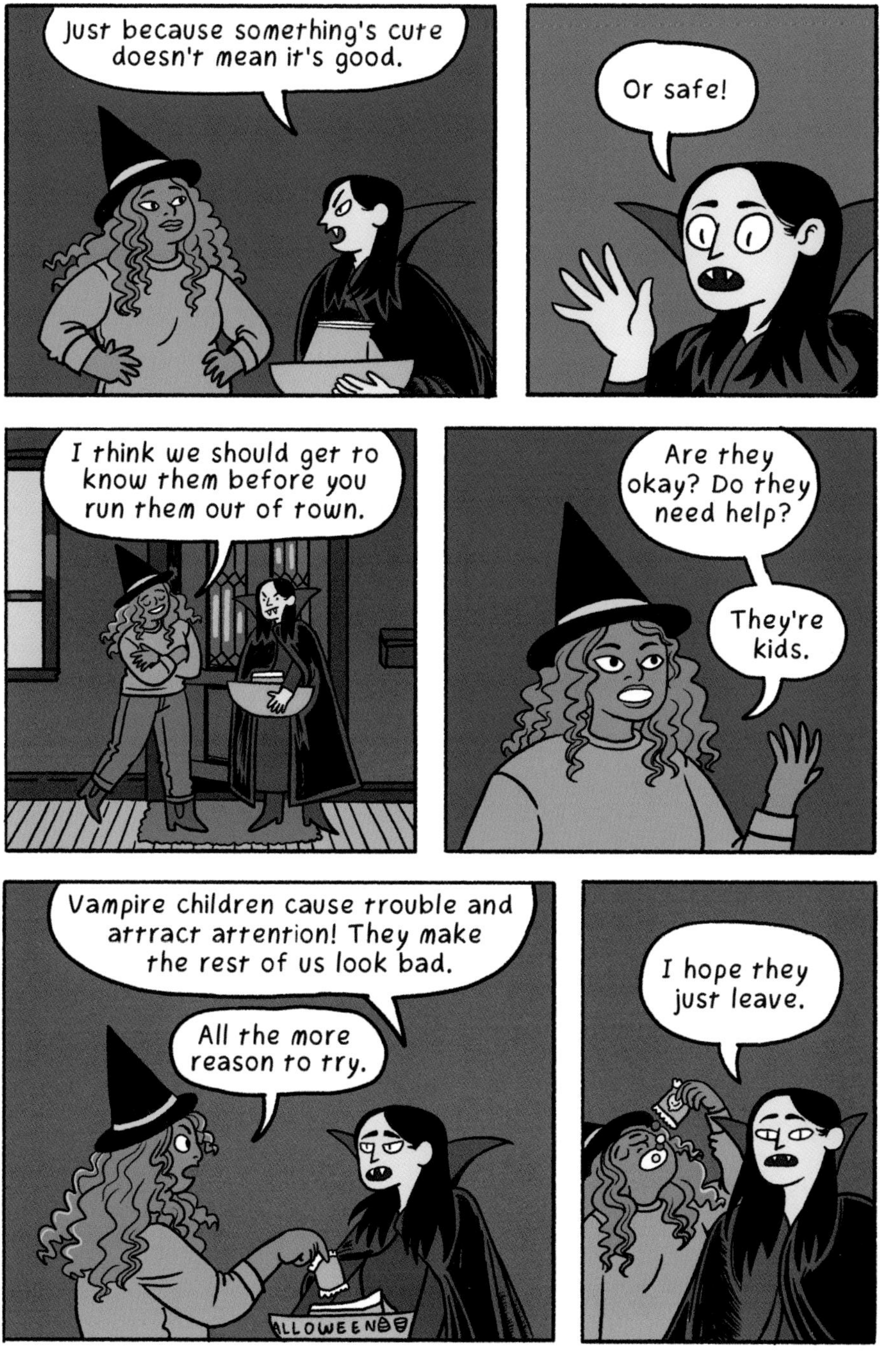
Just because something's cute doesn't mean it's good.
Or safe!
I think we should get to know them before you run them out of town.
Are they okay? Do they need help?
They're kids.
Vampire children cause trouble and attract attention! They make the rest of us look bad.
All the more reason to try.
ALLOWEEN
I hope they just leave.

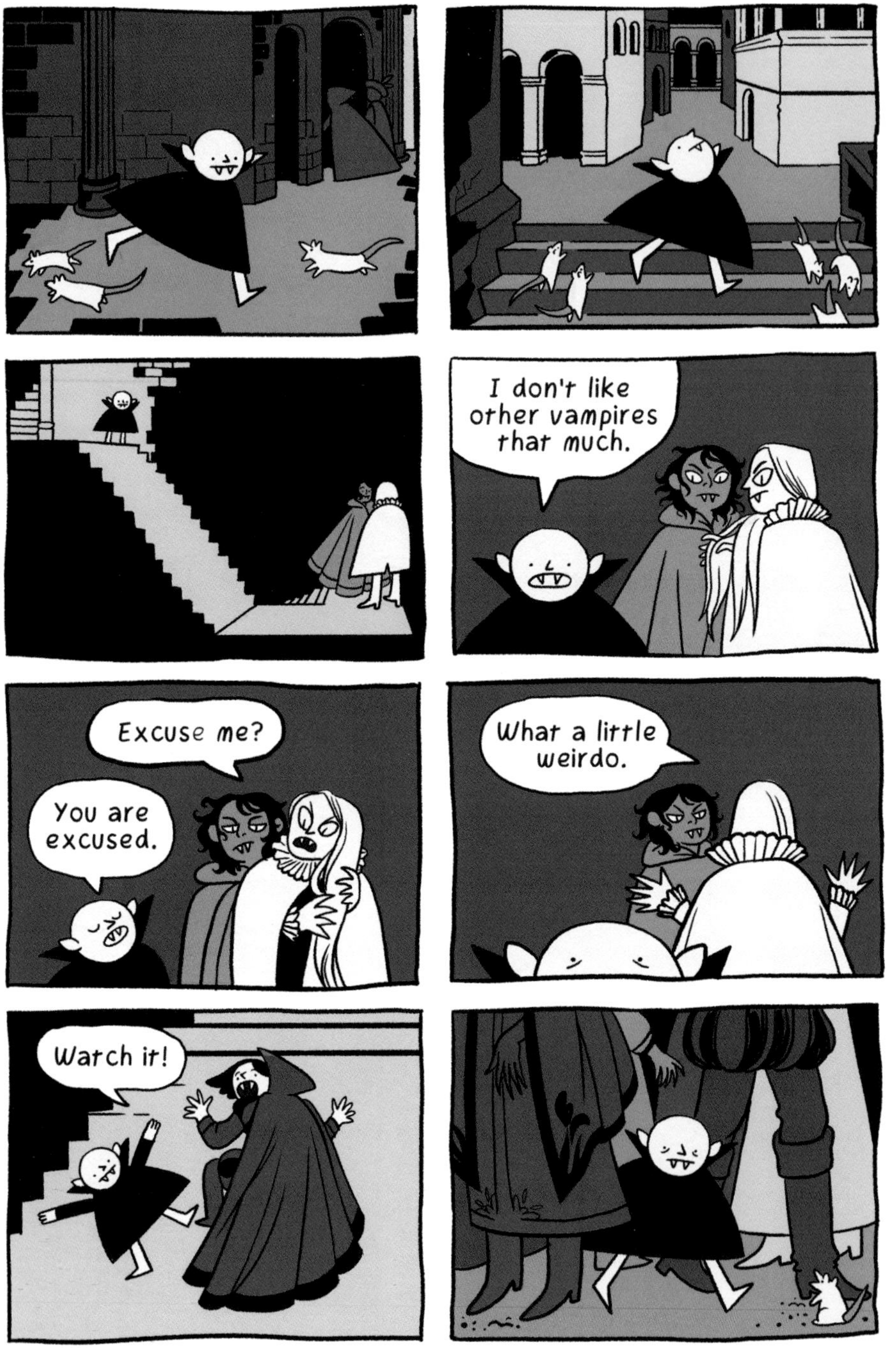
I don't like other vampires that much.
Excuse me?
You are excused.
What a little weirdo.
Watch it!

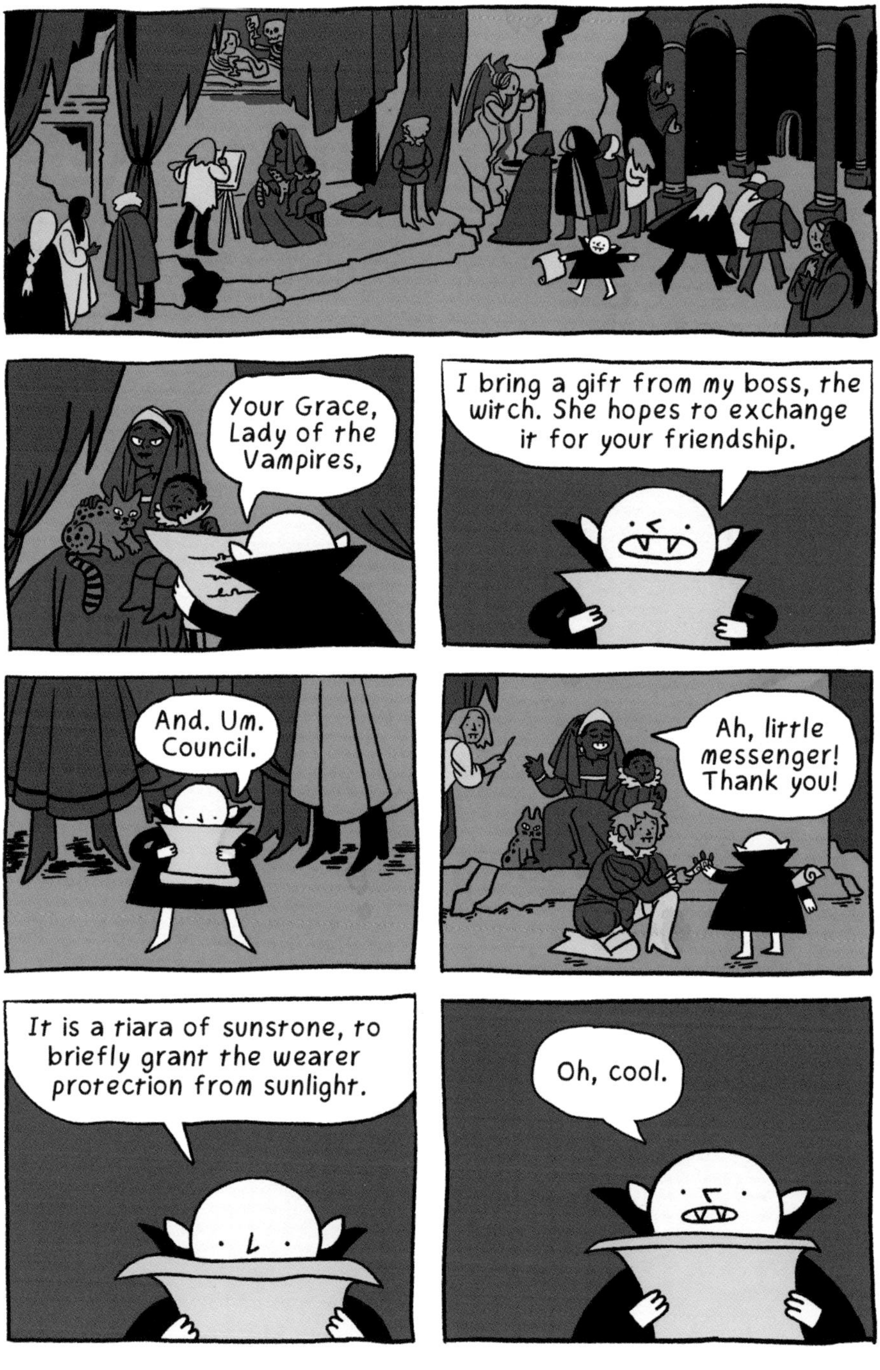
Your Grace, Lady of the Vampires,
I bring a gift from my boss, the witch. She hopes to exchange it for your friendship.
And. Um. Council.
Ah, little messenger! Thank you!
It is a tiara of sunstone, to briefly grant the wearer protection from sunlight.
Oh, cool.

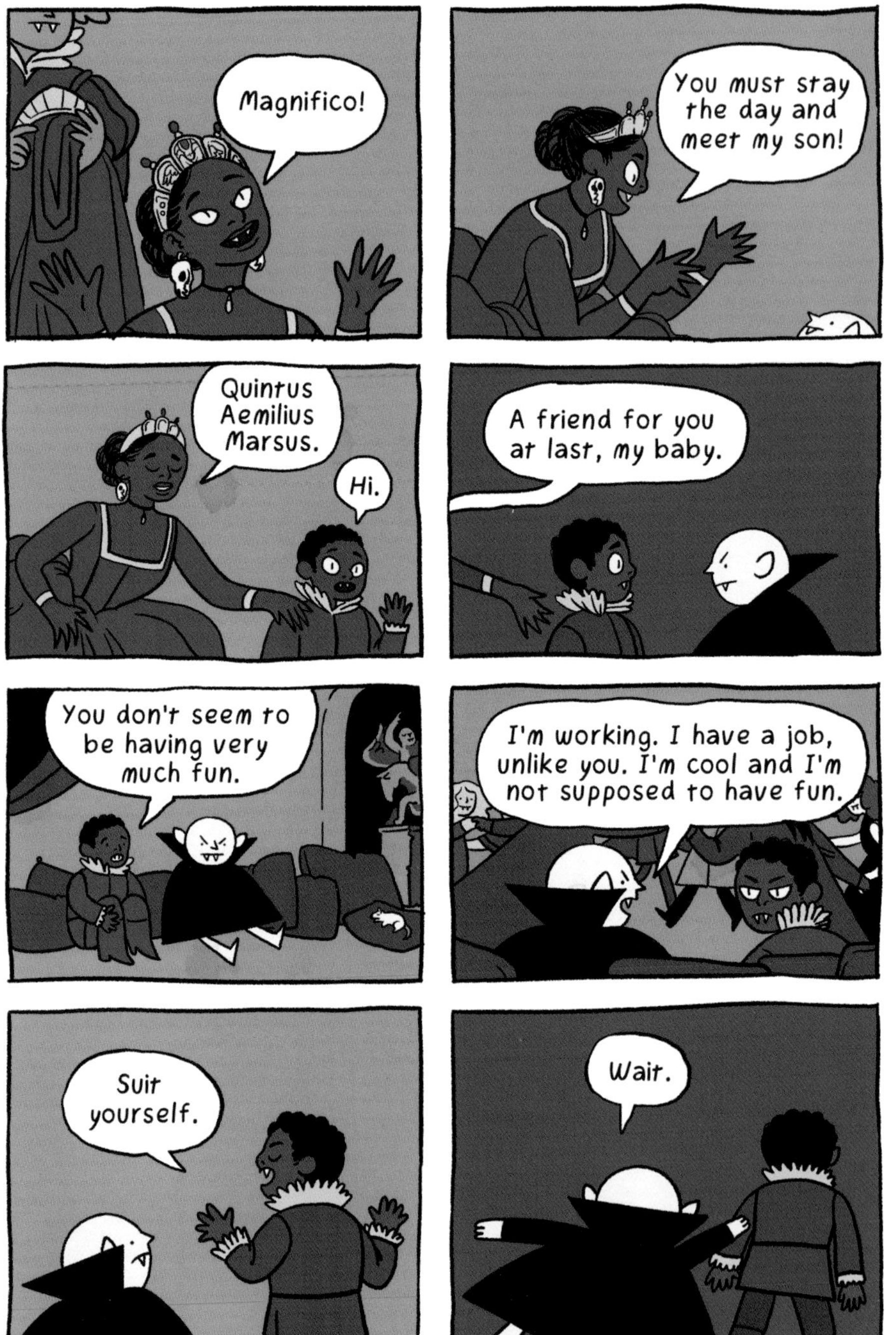
Magnifico!
You must stay the day and meet my son!
Quintus Aemilius Marsus.
Hi.
A friend for you at last, my baby.
You don't seem to be having very much fun.
I'm working. I have a job, unlike you. I'm cool and I'm not supposed to have fun.
Suit yourself.
Wait.

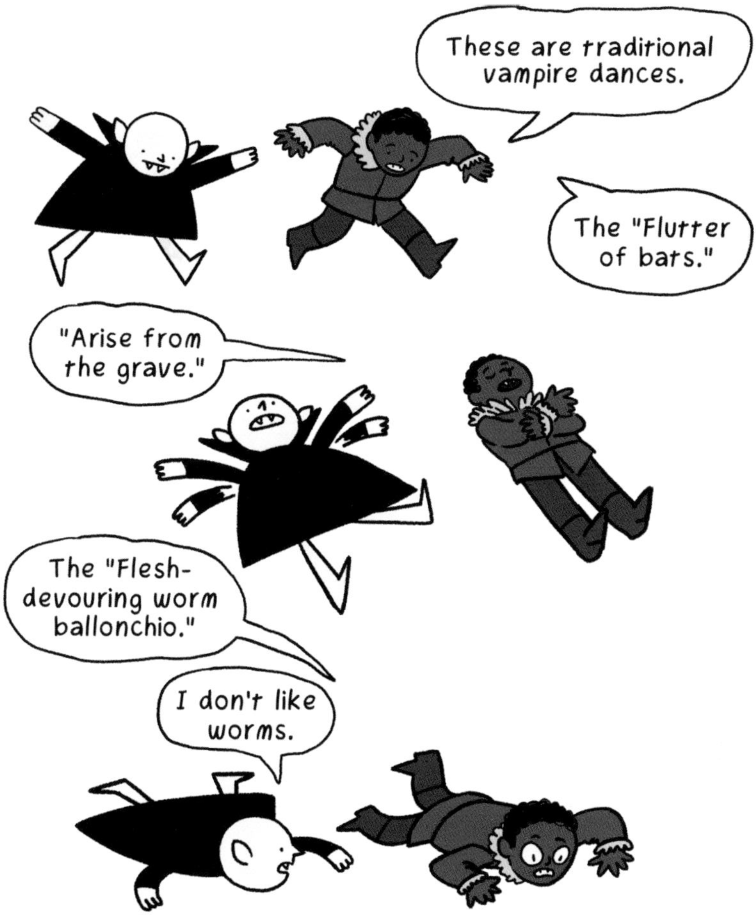
These are traditional vampire dances.
The "Flutter of bats."
"Arise from the grave."
The "Flesh-devouring worm ballonchio."
I don't like worms.

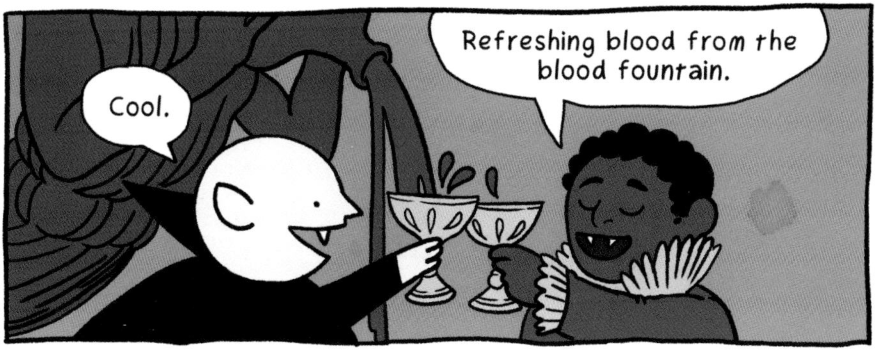
Cool.
Refreshing blood from the blood fountain.

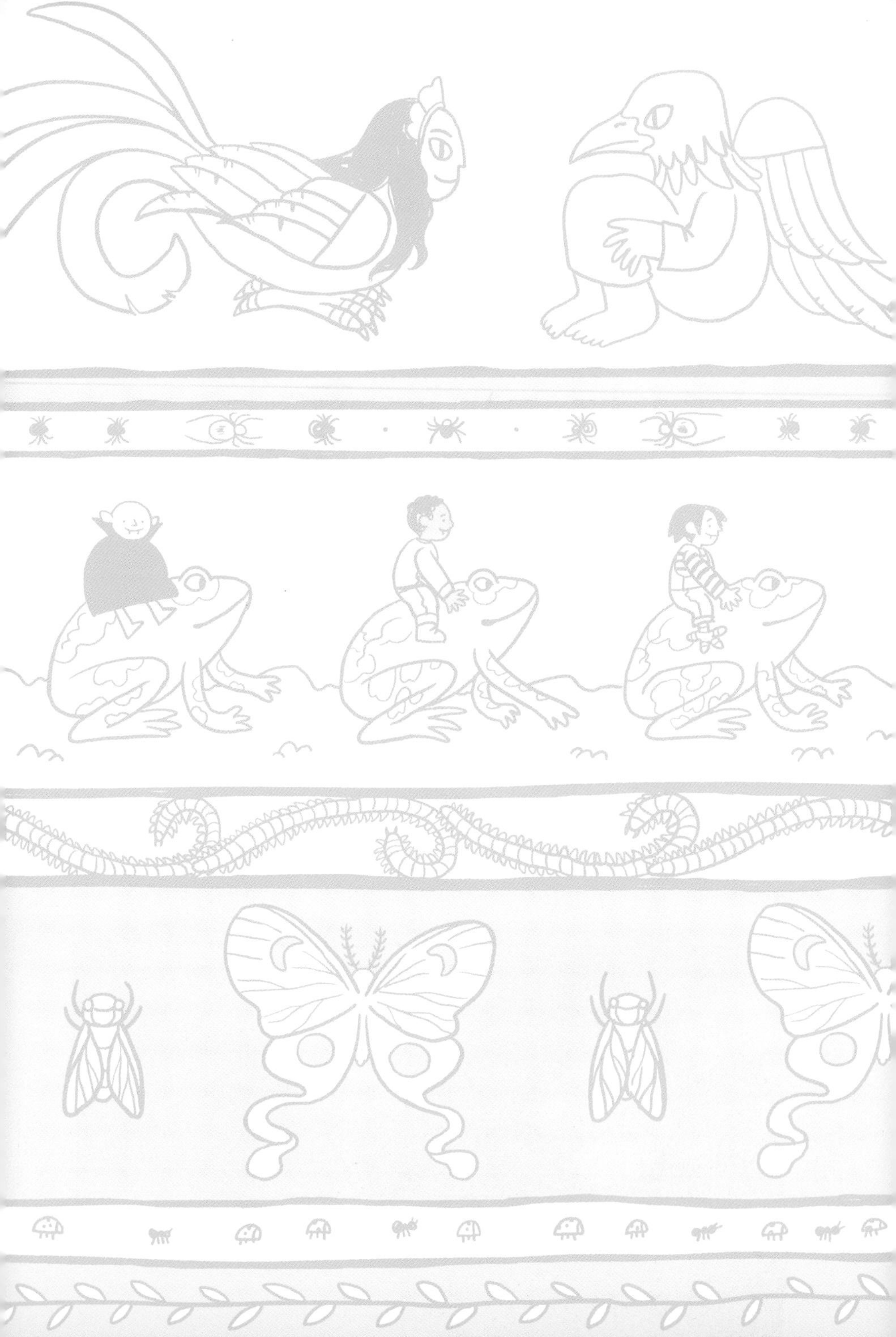

CHAPTER THREE

Eztli

b. 1597
She likes bugs and
lizards and other
small, scary creatures.
She is friends with
Drago and Quintus.

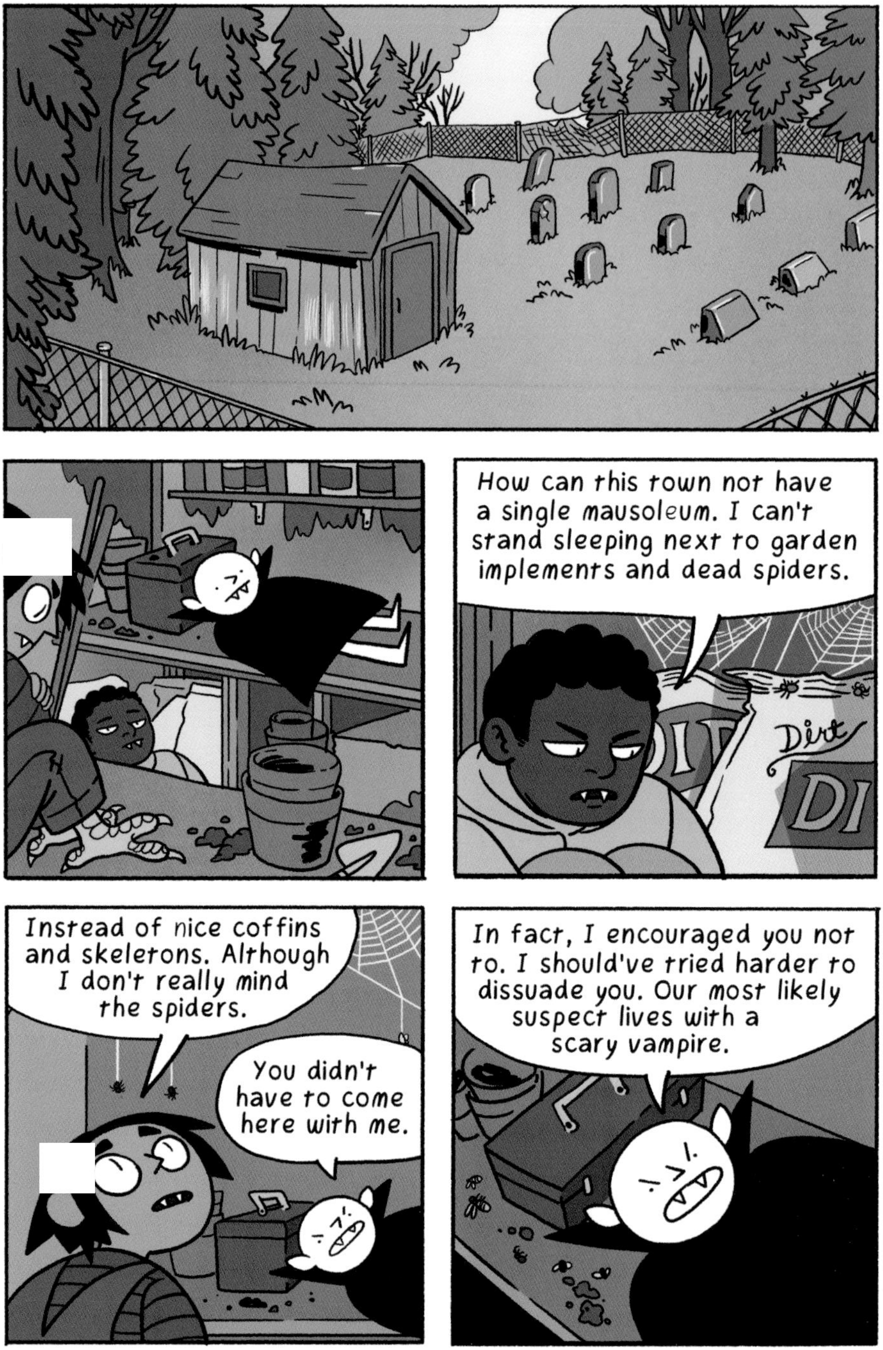
How can this town not have a single mausoleum. I can't stand sleeping next to garden implements and dead spiders.
Dirt
Instead of nice coffins and skeletons. Although I don't really mind the spiders.
You didn't have to come here with me.
In fact, I encouraged you not to. I should've tried harder to dissuade you. Our most likely suspect lives with a scary vampire.

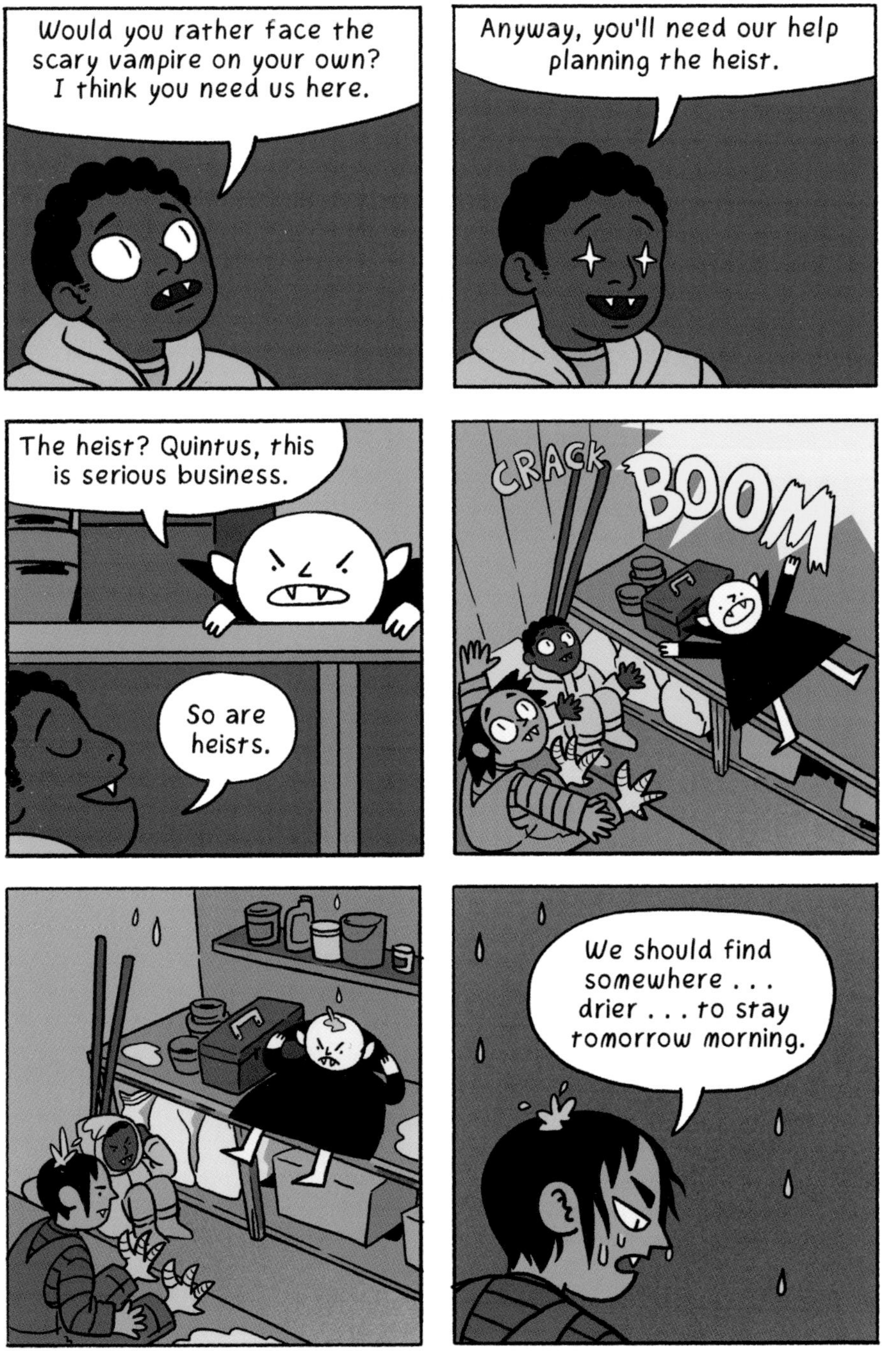
Would you rather face the scary vampire on your own? I think you need us here.
Anyway, you'll need our help planning the heist.
The heist? Quintus, this is serious business.
So are heists.
CRACK
BOOM
We should find somewhere . . . drier . . . to stay tomorrow morning.

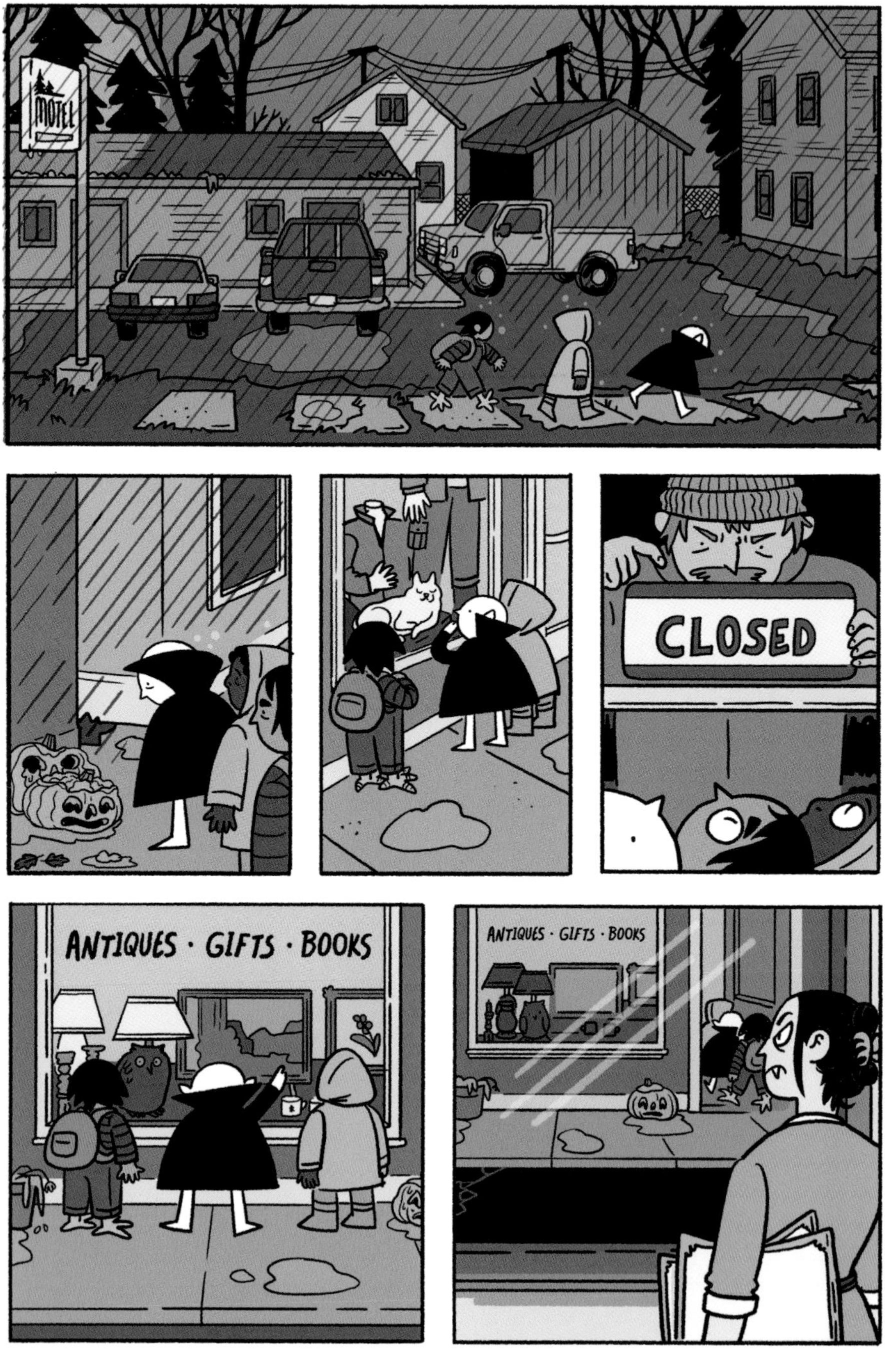
MOTEL
CLOSED
ANTIQUES · GIFTS · BOOKS
ANTIQUES · GIFTS · BOOKS

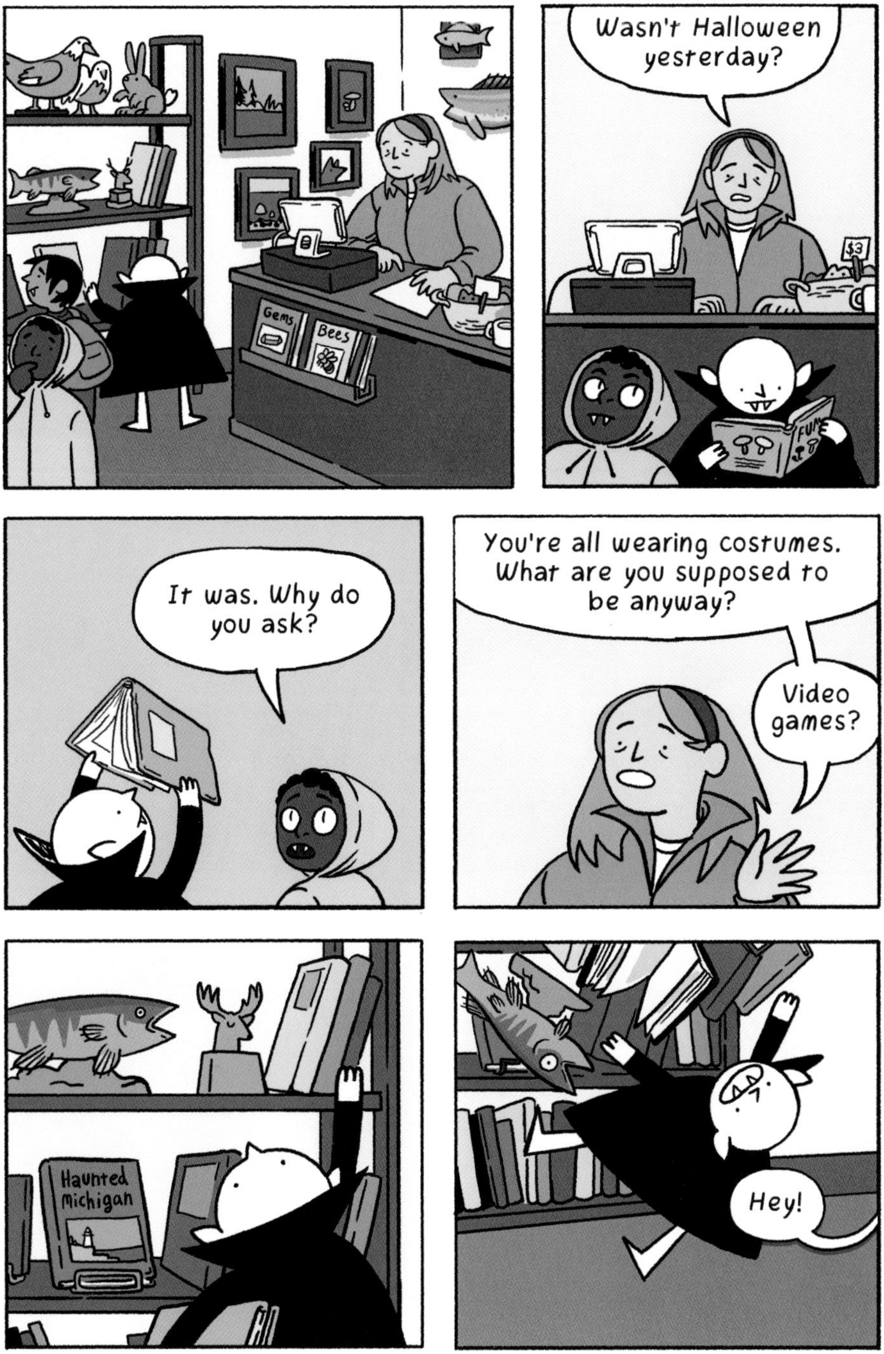
Gems
Bees
Wasn't Halloween yesterday?
$3
FUN
It was. Why do you ask?
You're all wearing costumes. What are you supposed to be anyway?
Video games?
Haunted Michigan
Hey!

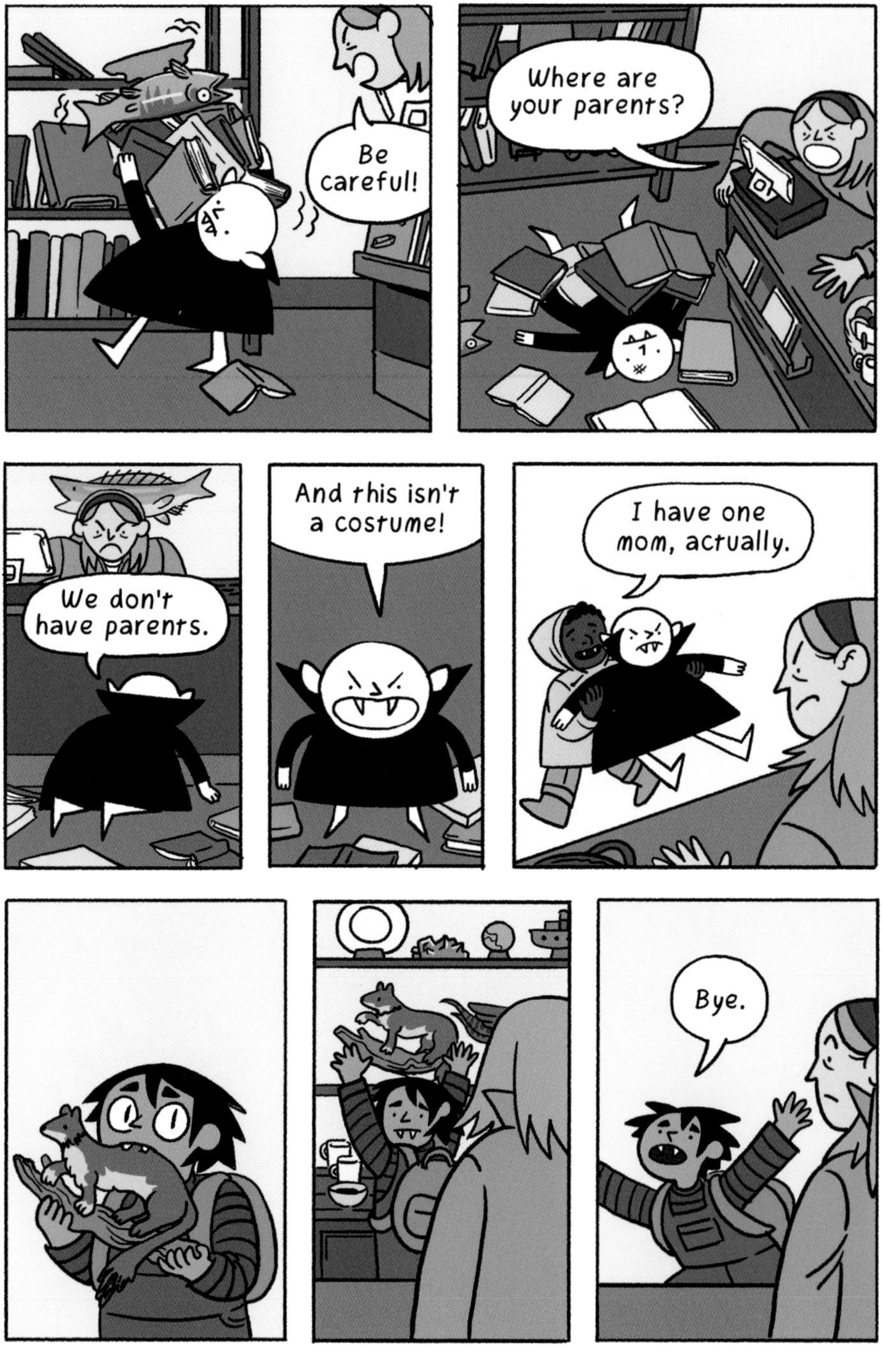
Be careful!
Where are your parents?
We don't have parents.
And this isn't a costume!
I have one mom, actually.
Bye.

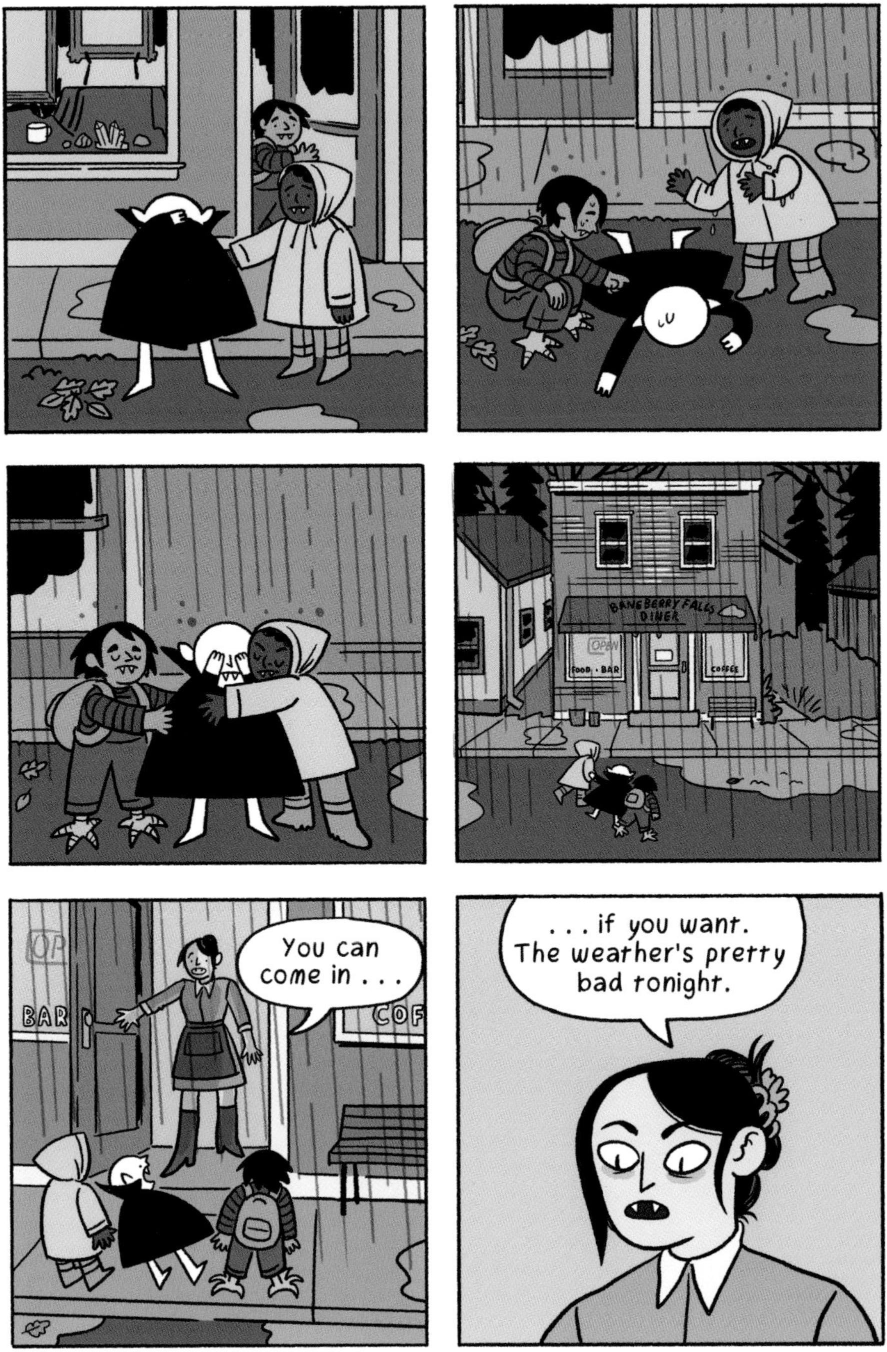
BANEBERRY FALLS DINER
OPEN
FOOD • BAR
COFFEE
You can come in . . .
. . . if you want. The weather's pretty bad tonight.

I'm sorry I frightened you. I'm not used to being around other vampires.

But that wasn't a reason to be cruel.

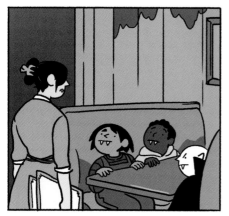

Apology accepted.

Do you serve blood here?

No.

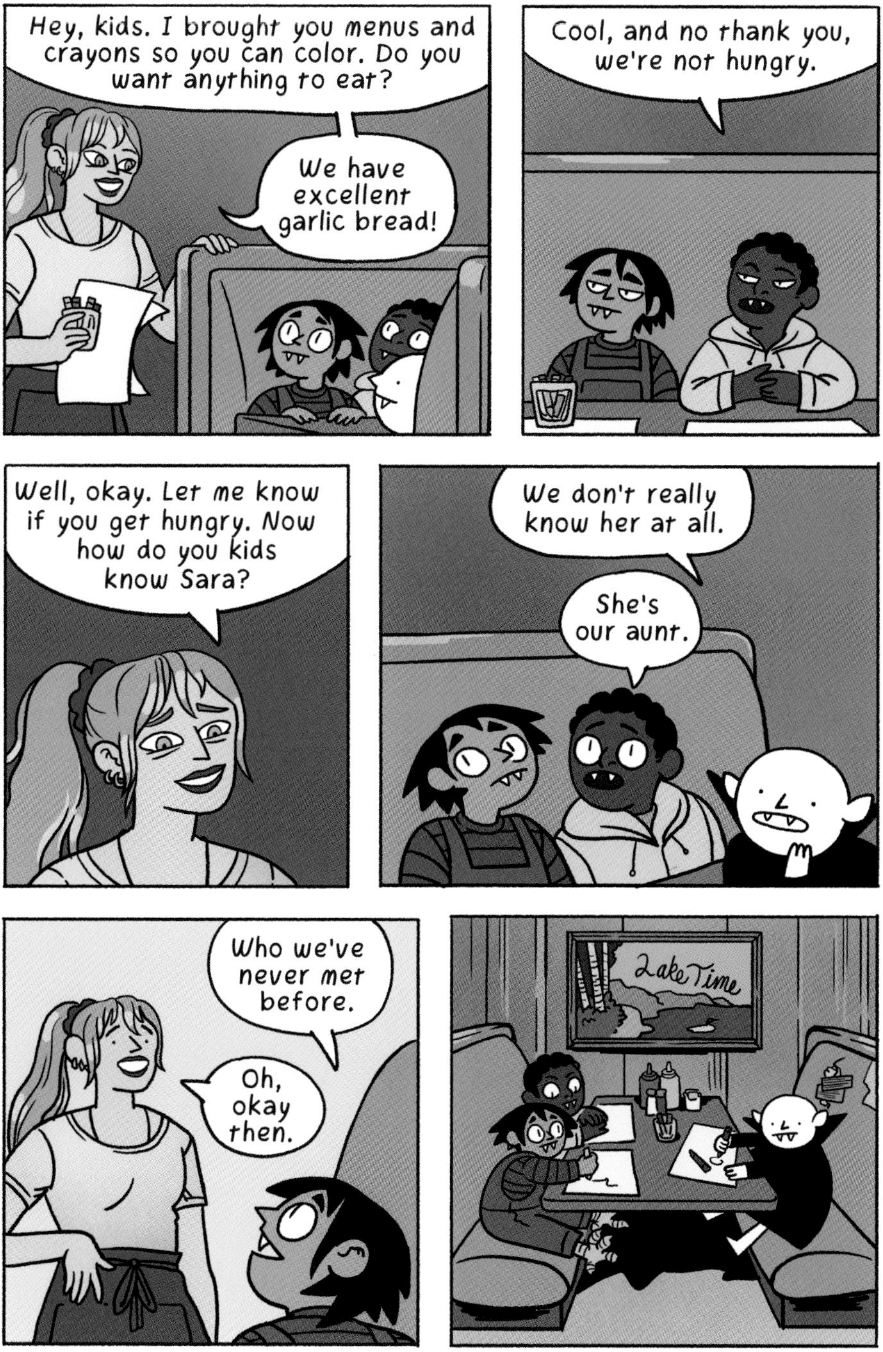
Hey, kids. I brought you menus and crayons so you can color. Do you want anything to eat?
We have excellent garlic bread!
Cool, and no thank you, we're not hungry.
Well, okay. Let me know if you get hungry. Now how do you kids know Sara?
We don't really know her at all.
She's our aunt.
Who we've never met before.
Oh, okay then.
Lake Time

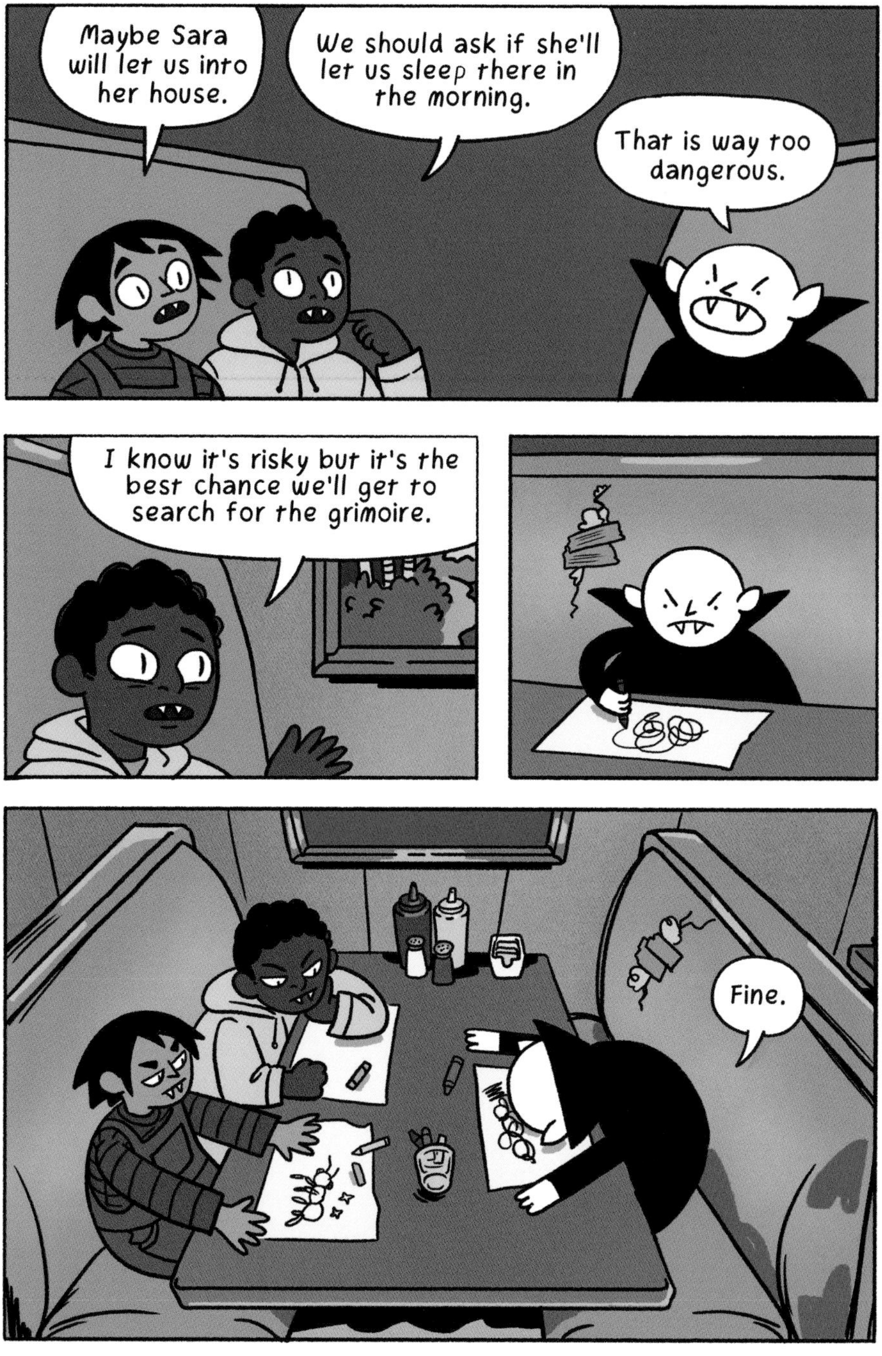
Maybe Sara will let us into her house.
We should ask if she'll let us sleep there in the morning.
That is way too dangerous.
I know it's risky but it's the best chance we'll get to search for the grimoire.
Fine.

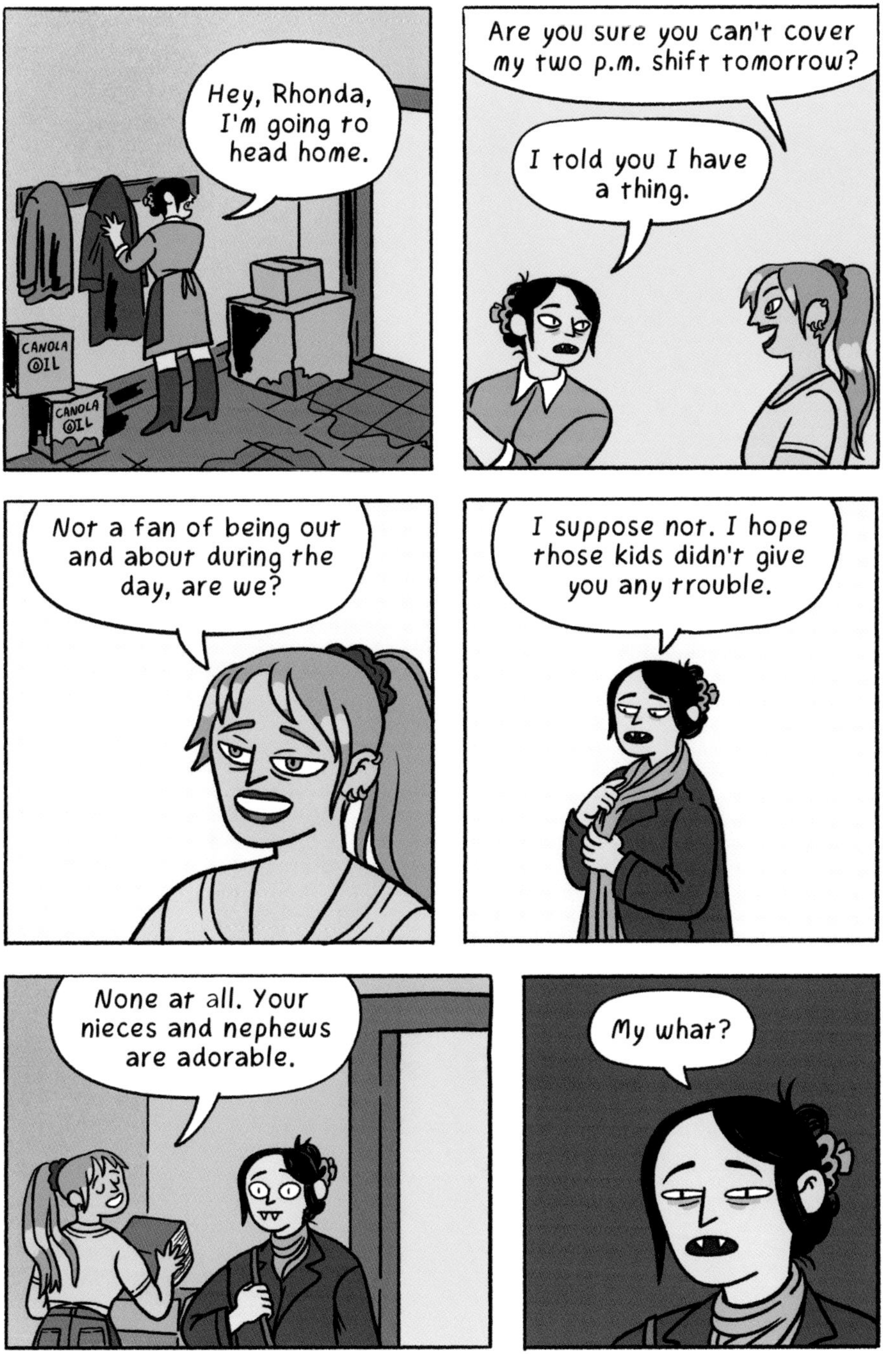
Hey, Rhonda, I'm going to head home.
Are you sure you can't cover my two p.m. shift tomorrow?
I told you I have a thing.
Not a fan of being out and about during the day, are we?
I suppose not. I hope those kids didn't give you any trouble.
None at all. Your nieces and nephews are adorable.
My what?
CANOLA OIL
CANOLA OIL

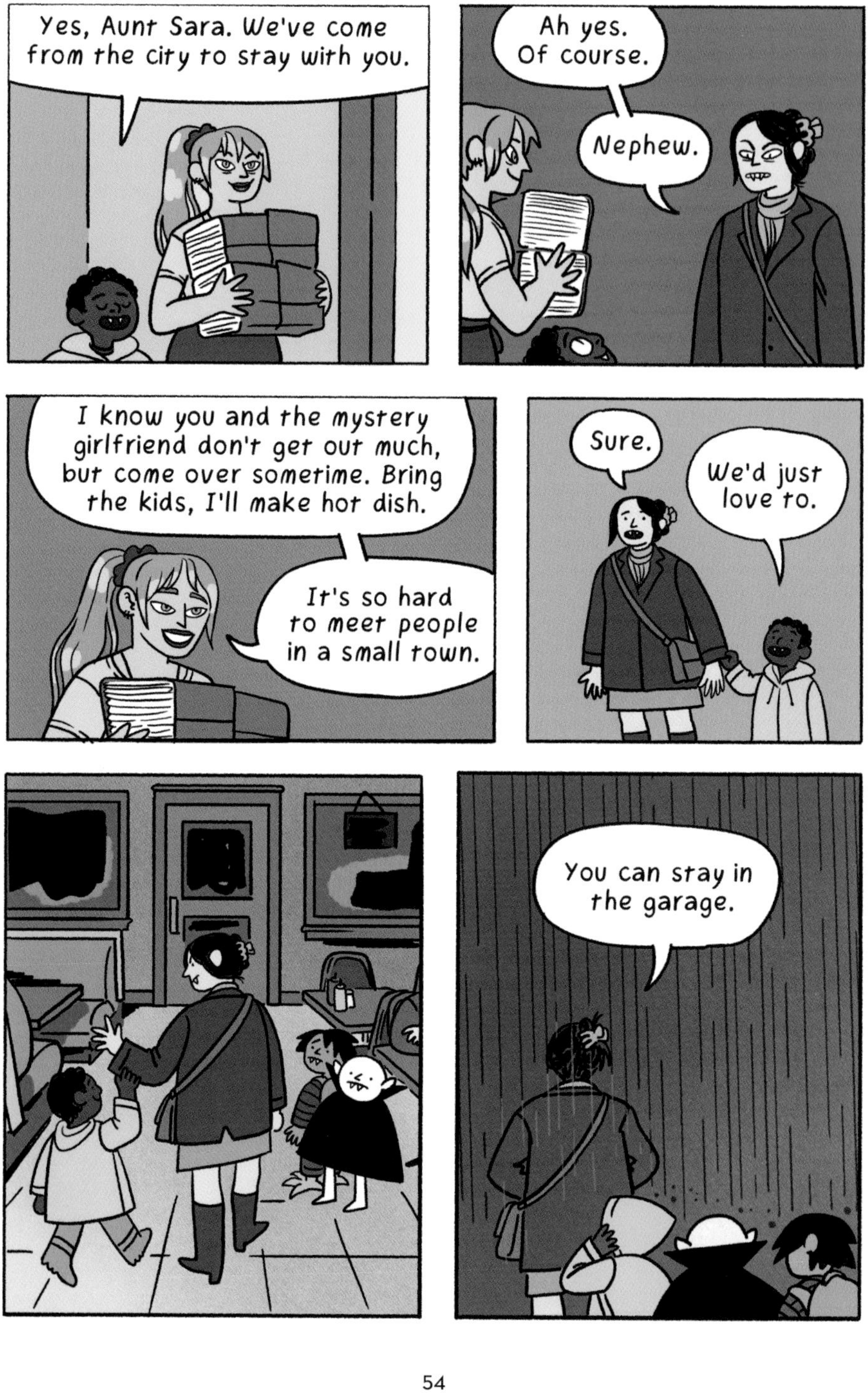
Yes, Aunt Sara. We've come from the city to stay with you.
Ah yes. Of course.
Nephew.
I know you and the mystery girlfriend don't get out much, but come over sometime. Bring the kids, I'll make hot dish.
It's so hard to meet people in a small town.
Sure.
We'd just love to.
You can stay in the garage.

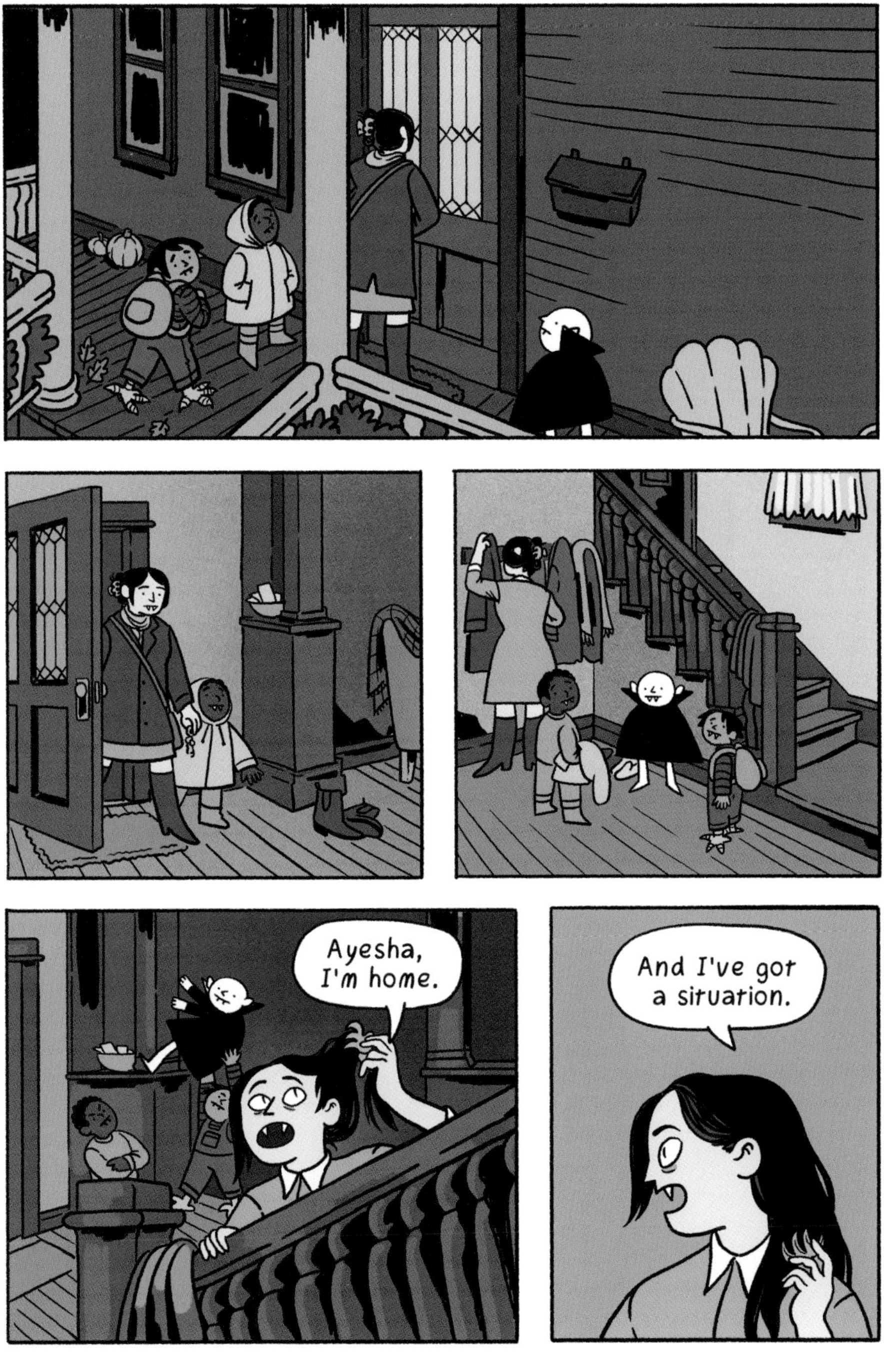
Ayesha, I'm home.
And I've got a situation.

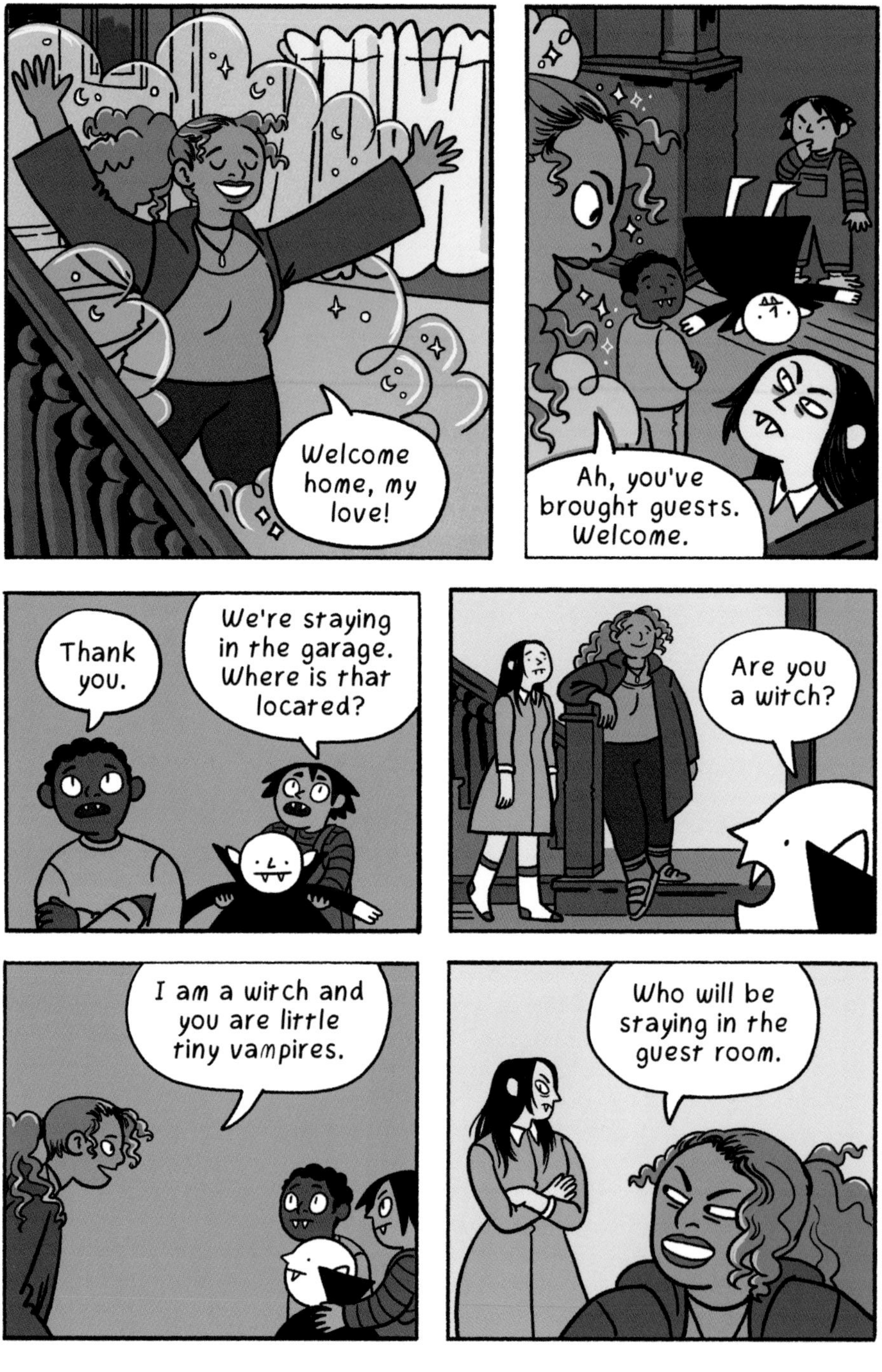
Welcome home, my love!
Ah, you've brought guests. Welcome.
Thank you.
We're staying in the garage. Where is that located?
Are you a witch?
I am a witch and you are little tiny vampires.
Who will be staying in the guest room.

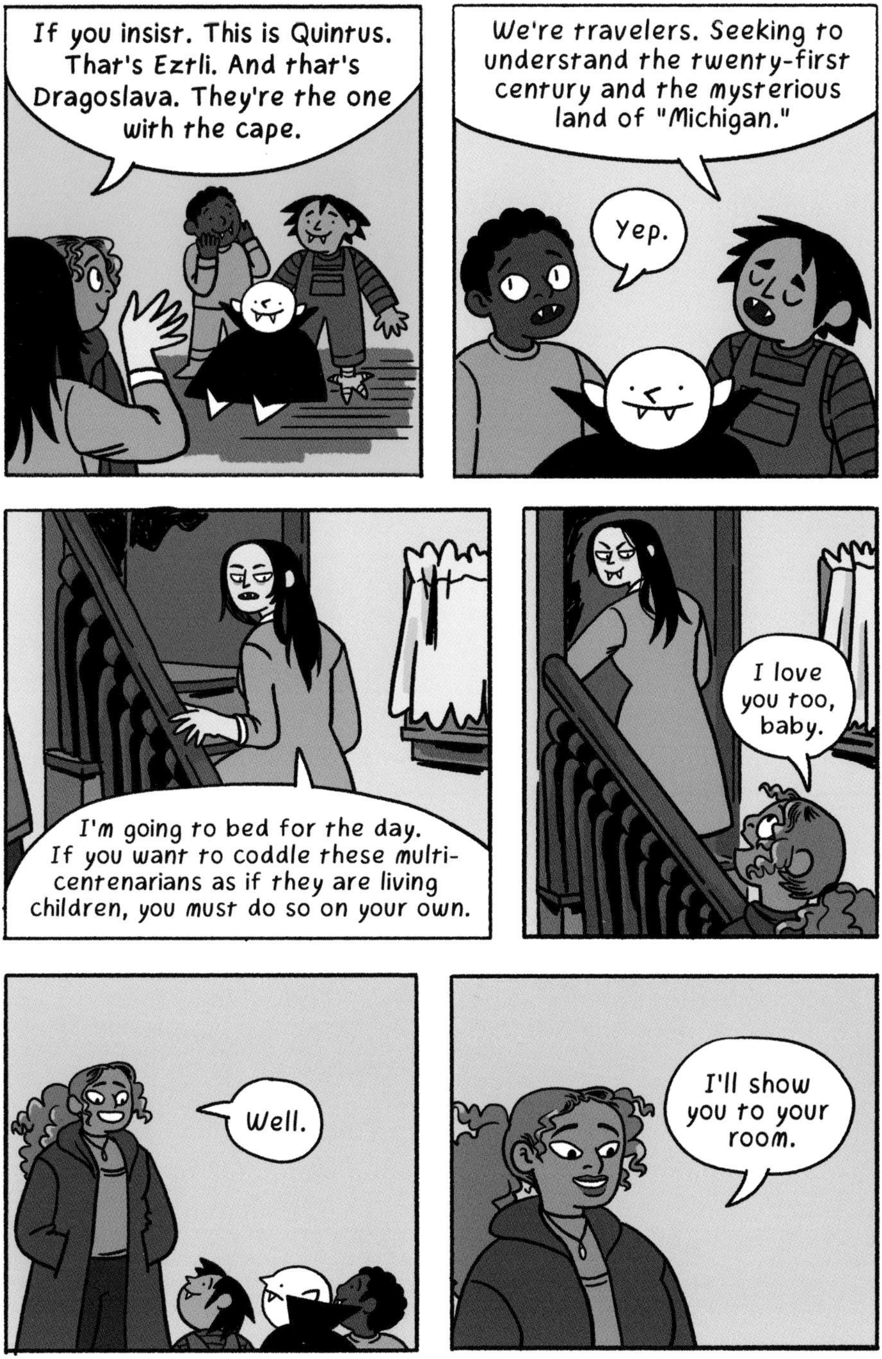
If you insist. This is Quintus. That's Eztli. And that's Dragoslava. They're the one with the cape.
We're travelers. Seeking to understand the twenty-first century and the mysterious land of "Michigan."
Yep.
I'm going to bed for the day. If you want to coddle these multi-centenarians as if they are living children, you must do so on your own.
I love you too, baby.
Well.
I'll show you to your room.

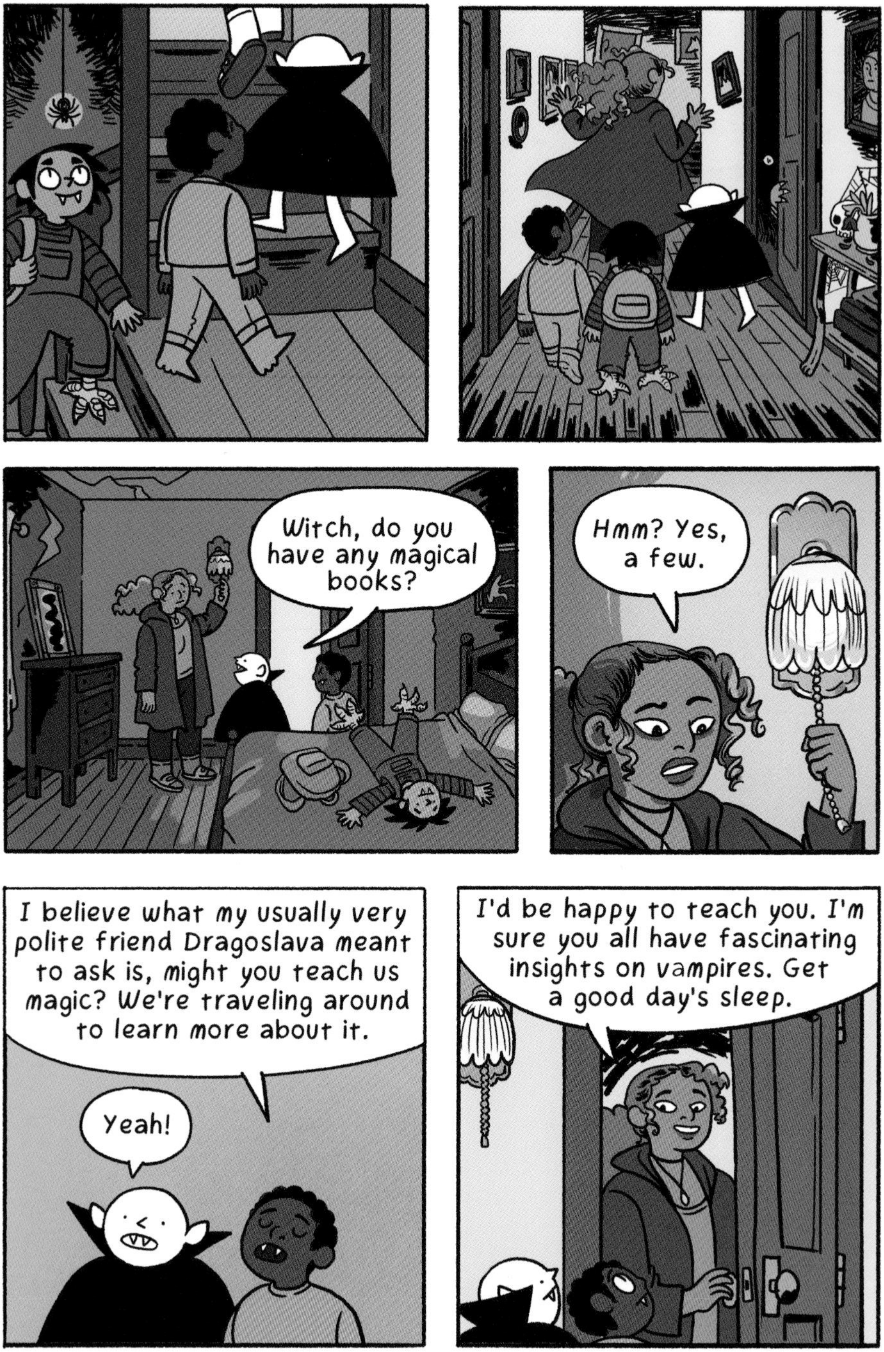
Witch, do you have any magical books?
Hmm? Yes, a few.
I believe what my usually very polite friend Dragoslava meant to ask is, might you teach us magic? We're traveling around to learn more about it.
Yeah!
I'd be happy to teach you. I'm sure you all have fascinating insights on vampires. Get a good day's sleep.

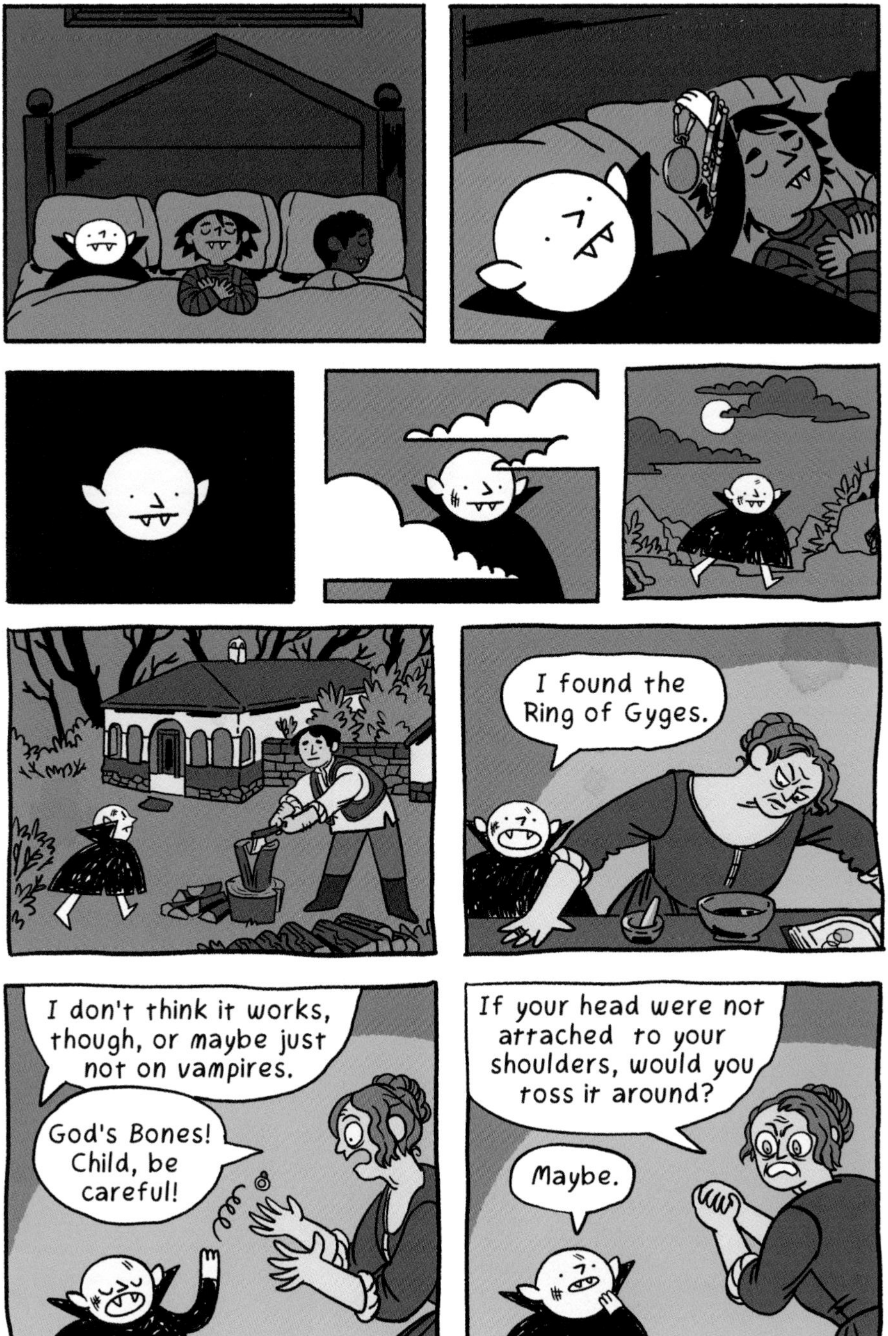
I found the Ring of Gyges.
I don't think it works, though, or maybe just not on vampires.
God's Bones! Child, be careful!
If your head were not attached to your shoulders, would you toss it around?
Maybe.

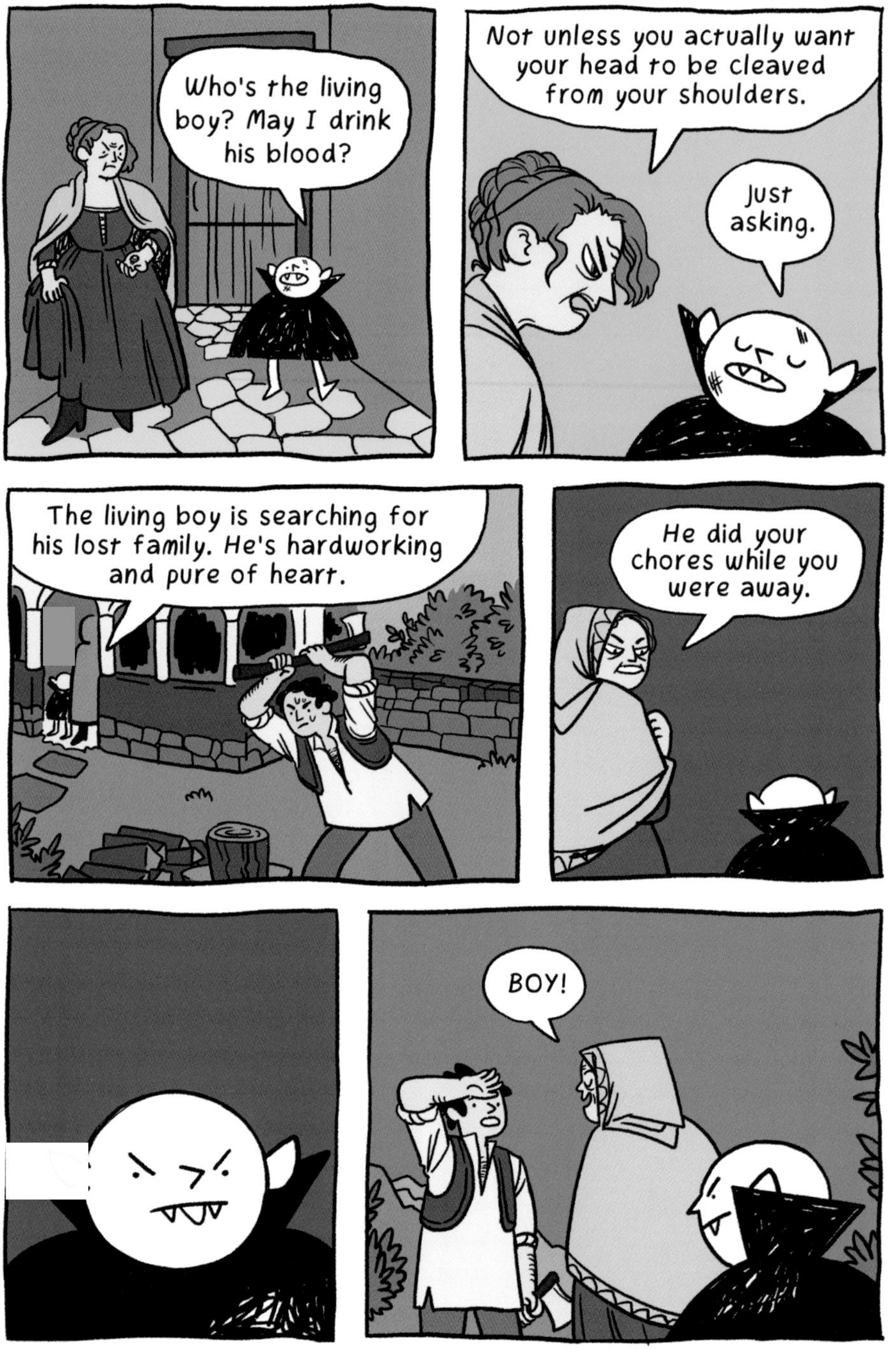
Who's the living boy? May I drink his blood?
Not unless you actually want your head to be cleaved from your shoulders.
Just asking.
The living boy is searching for his lost family. He's hardworking and pure of heart.
He did your chores while you were away.
BOY!

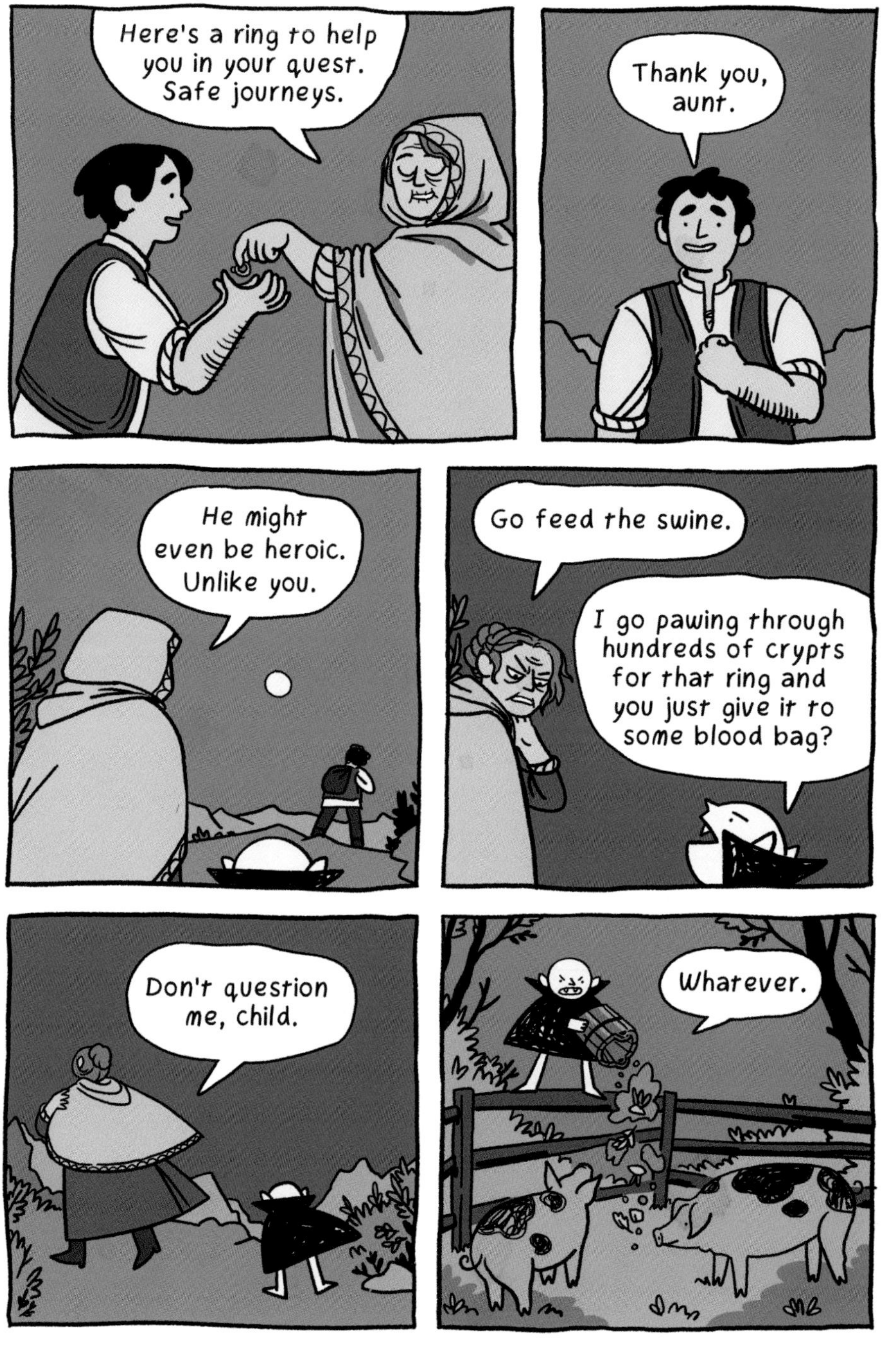
Here's a ring to help you in your quest. Safe journeys.
Thank you, aunt.
He might even be heroic. Unlike you.
Go feed the swine.
I go pawing through hundreds of crypts for that ring and you just give it to some blood bag?
Don't question me, child.
Whatever.

CHAPTER FOUR

Sara

b. 1939
She became a vampire
in the 1960s. She just
wants peace and quiet.

Ayesha

b. 1988
She is a living human and a witch
with many secrets. She loves her
girlfriend, Sara, and energy drinks.

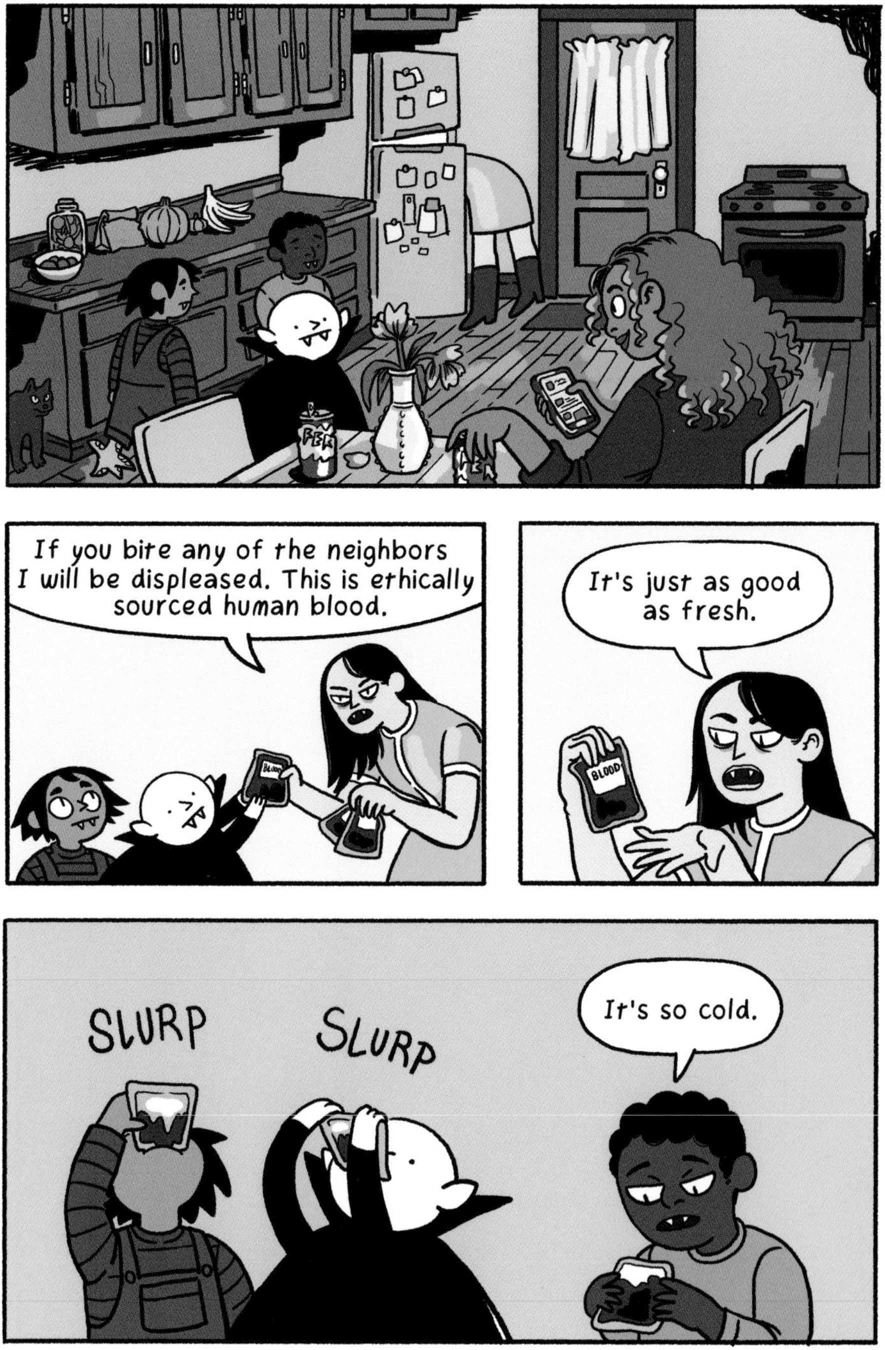
If you bite any of the neighbors I will be displeased. This is ethically sourced human blood.
It's just as good as fresh.
SLURP
SLURP
It's so cold.

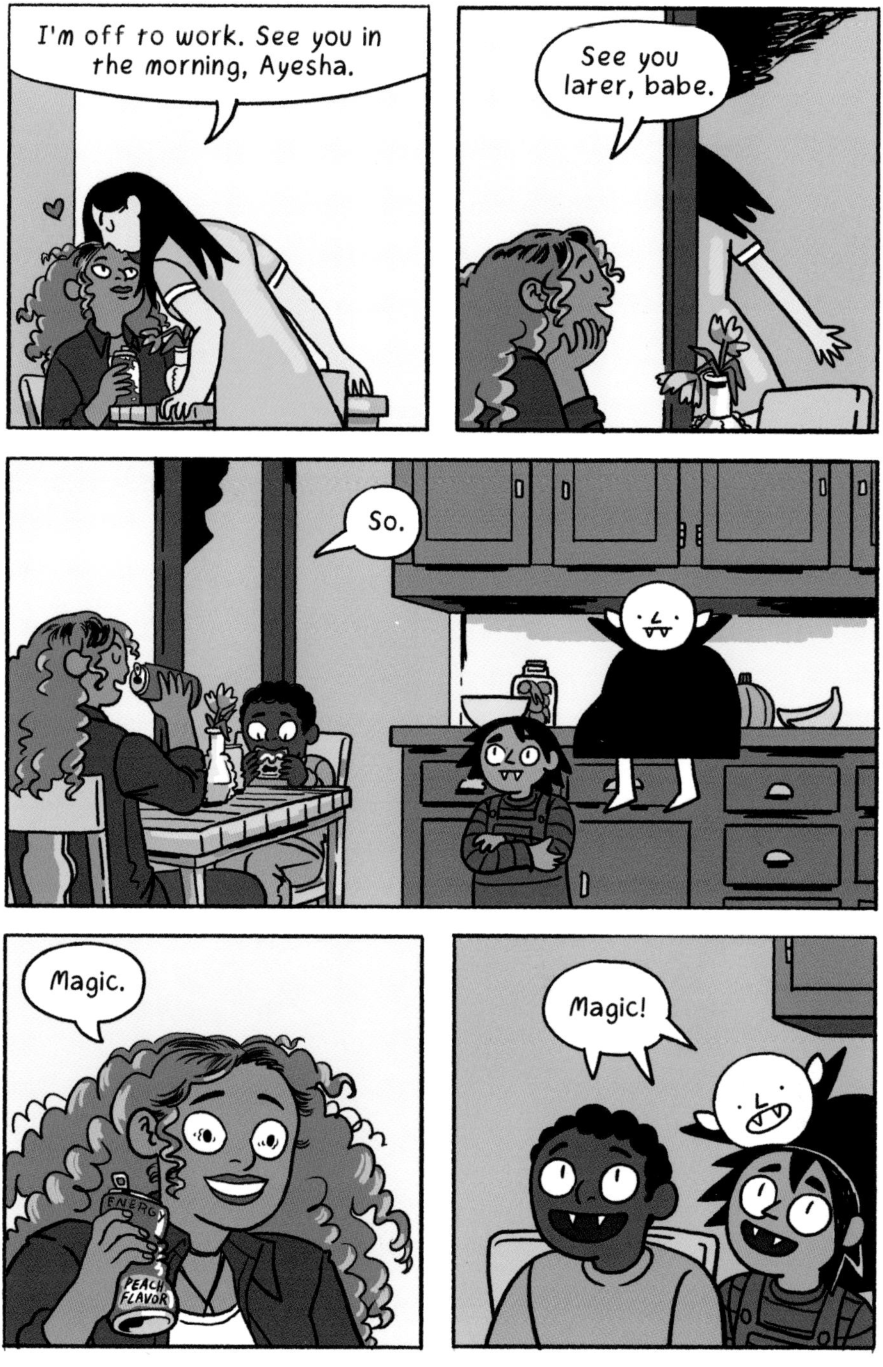
I'm off to work. See you in the morning, Ayesha.
See you later, babe.
So.
Magic.
ENERGY
PEACH FLAVOR
Magic!

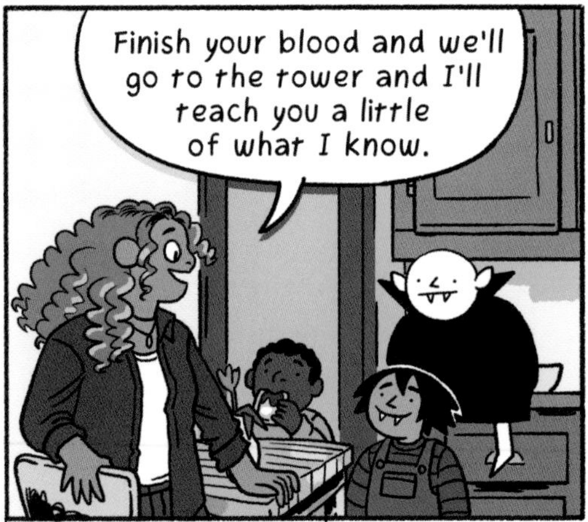
Finish your blood and we'll go to the tower and I'll teach you a little of what I know.

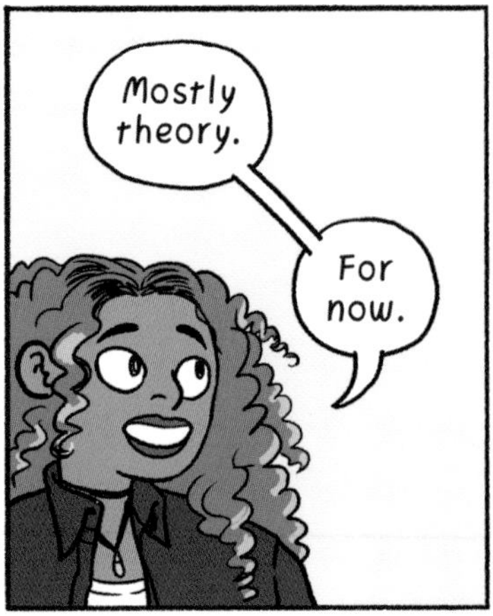
Mostly theory.
For now.

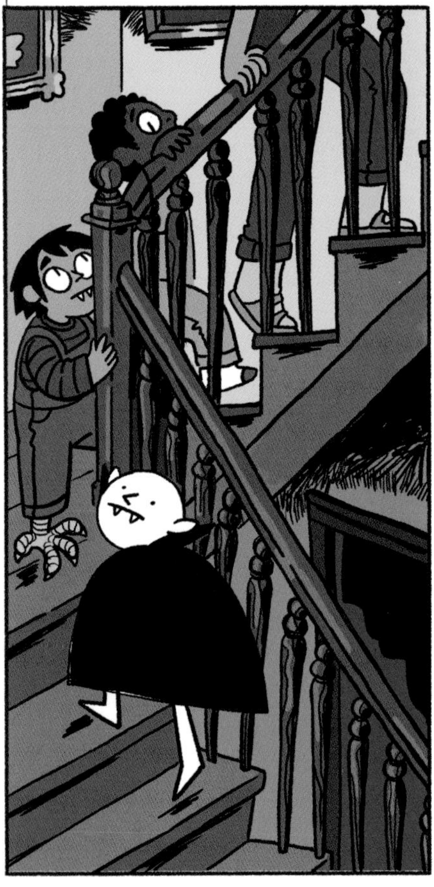

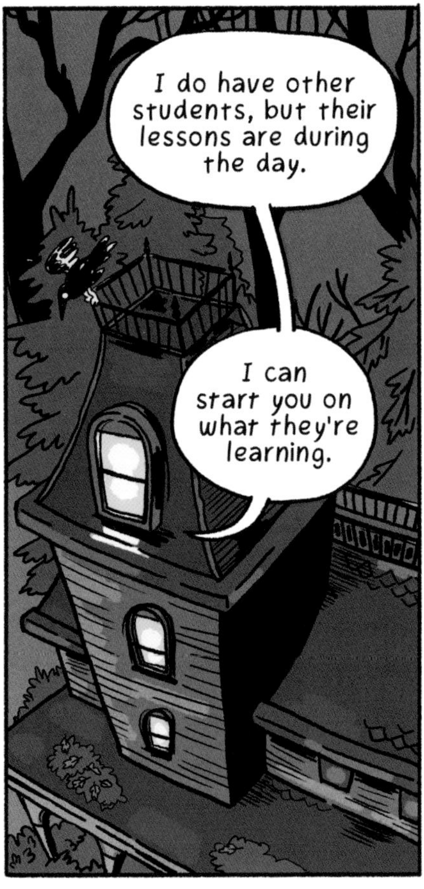
I do have other students, but their lessons are during the day.
I can start you on what they're learning.

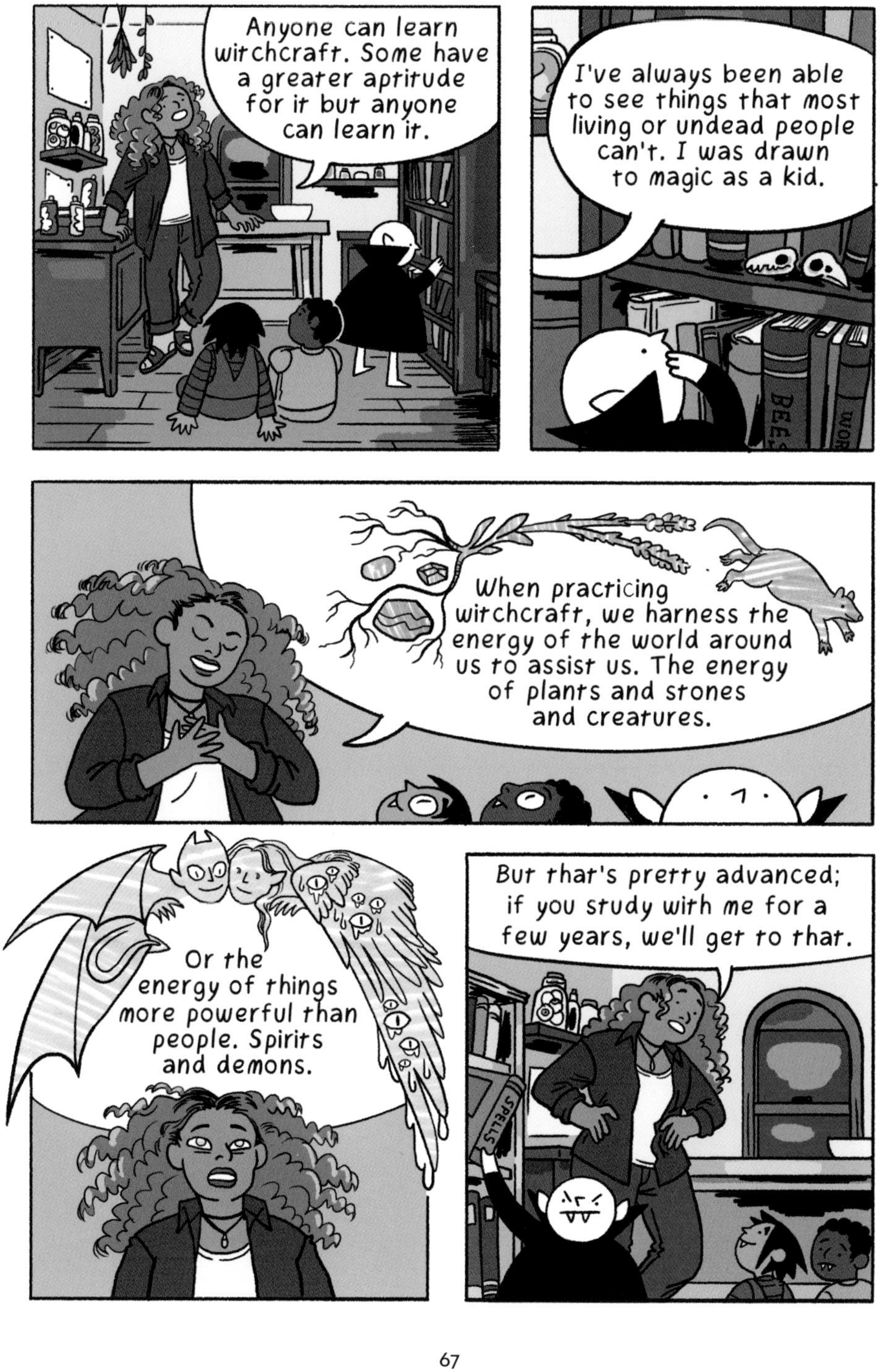
Anyone can learn witchcraft. Some have a greater aptitude for it but anyone can learn it.
I've always been able to see things that most living or undead people can't. I was drawn to magic as a kid.
BEES
WOR
When practicing witchcraft, we harness the energy of the world around us to assist us. The energy of plants and stones and creatures.
Or the energy of things more powerful than people. Spirits and demons.
But that's pretty advanced; if you study with me for a few years, we'll get to that.
SPELLS

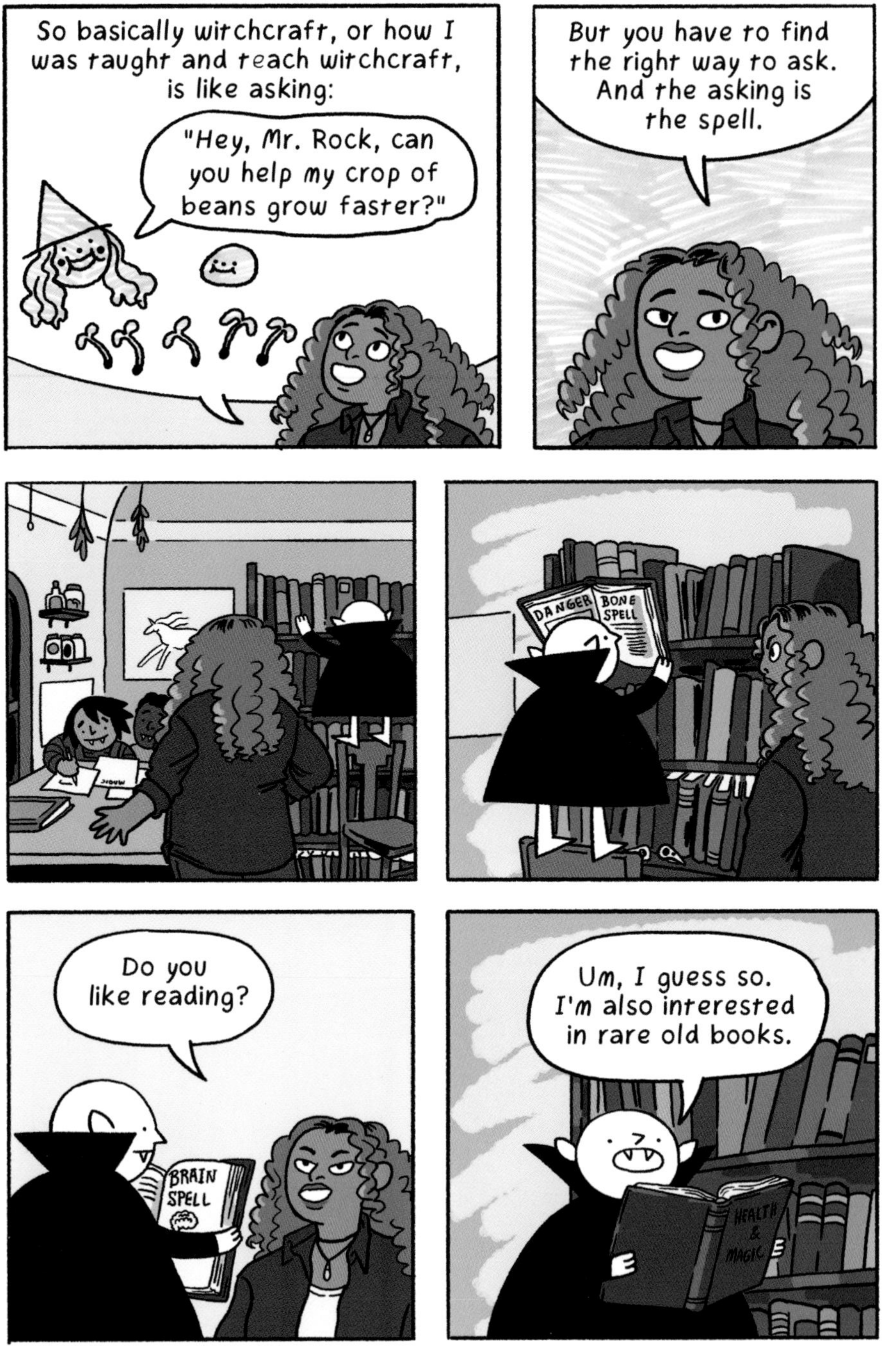
So basically witchcraft, or how I was taught and teach witchcraft, is like asking:
"Hey, Mr. Rock, can you help my crop of beans grow faster?"
But you have to find the right way to ask. And the asking is the spell.
MAGIC
DANGER
BONE SPELL
Do you like reading?
BRAIN SPELL
Um, I guess so. I'm also interested in rare old books.
HEALTH & MAGIC

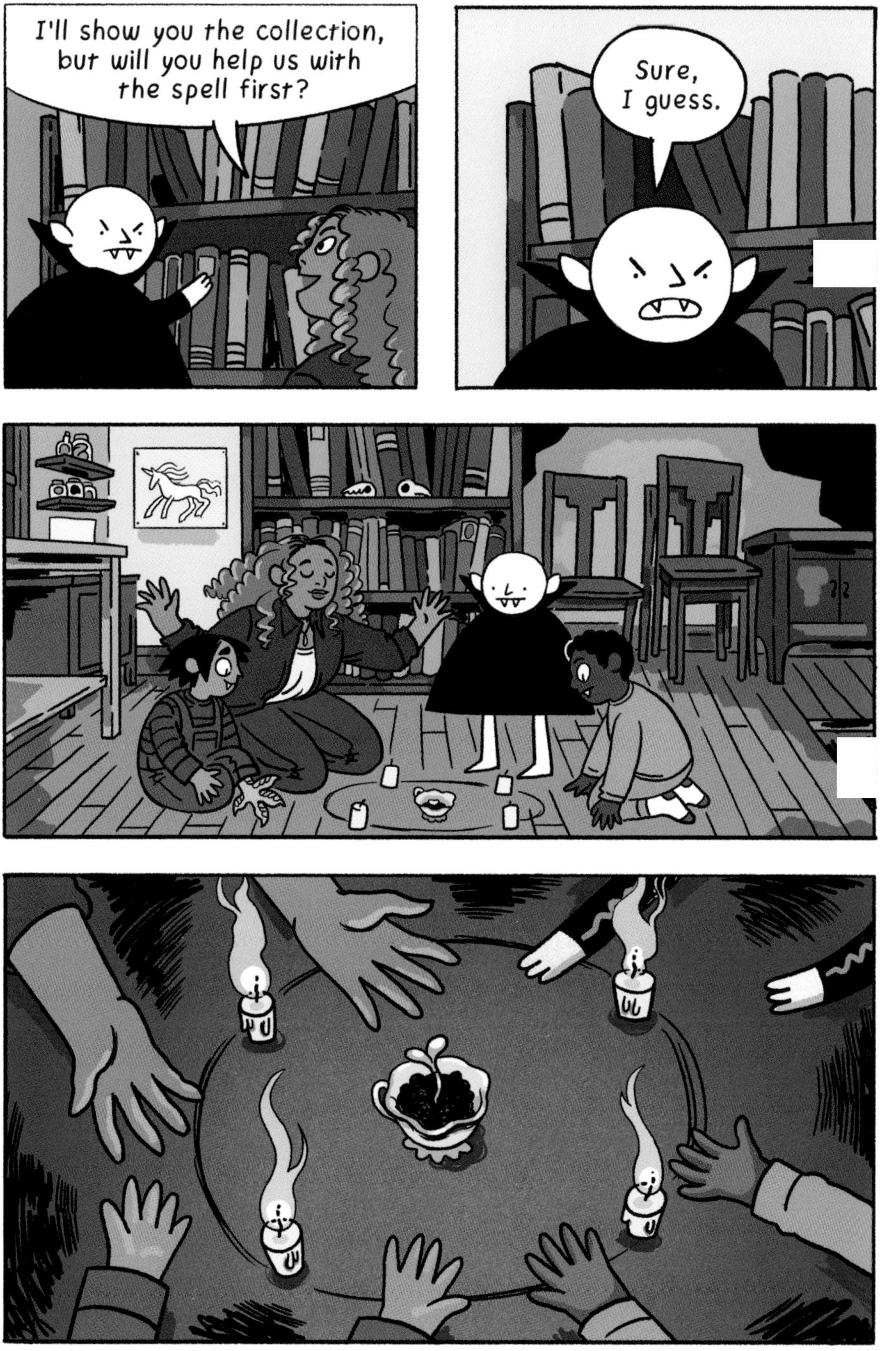
I'll show you the collection, but will you help us with the spell first?
Sure, I guess.

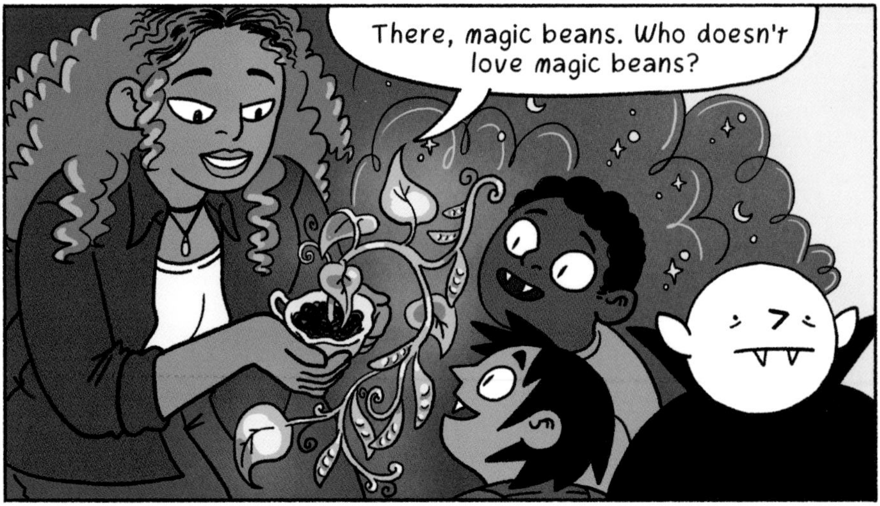
There, magic beans. Who doesn't love magic beans?

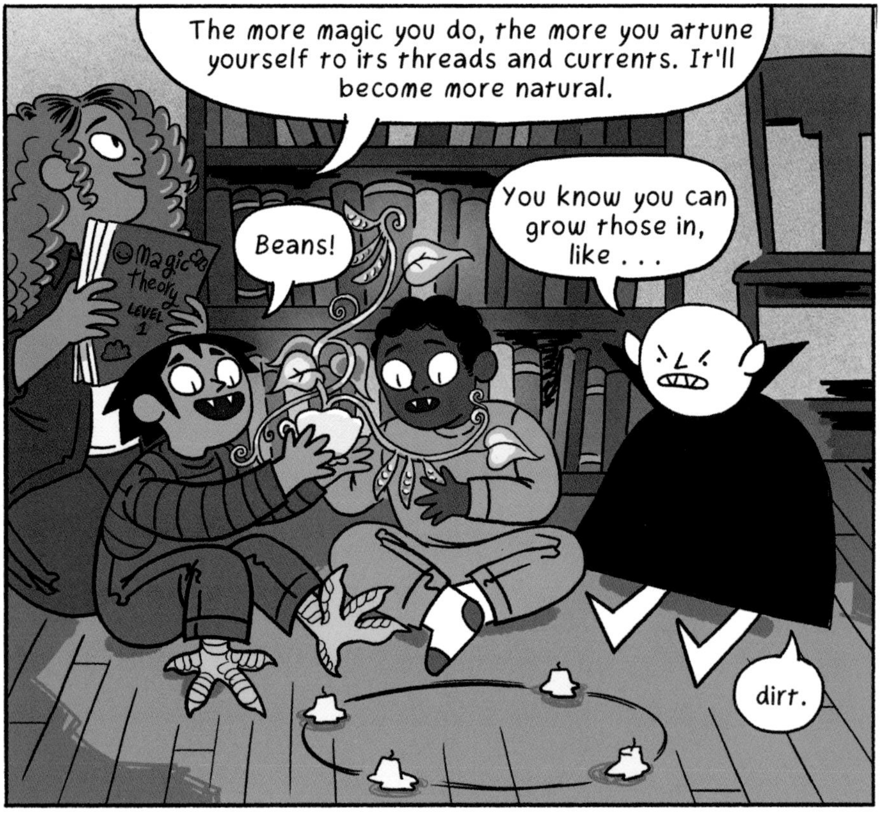
The more magic you do, the more you attune yourself to its threads and currents. It'll become more natural.
Magic theory LEVEL 1
Beans!
You know you can grow those in, like . . .
dirt.

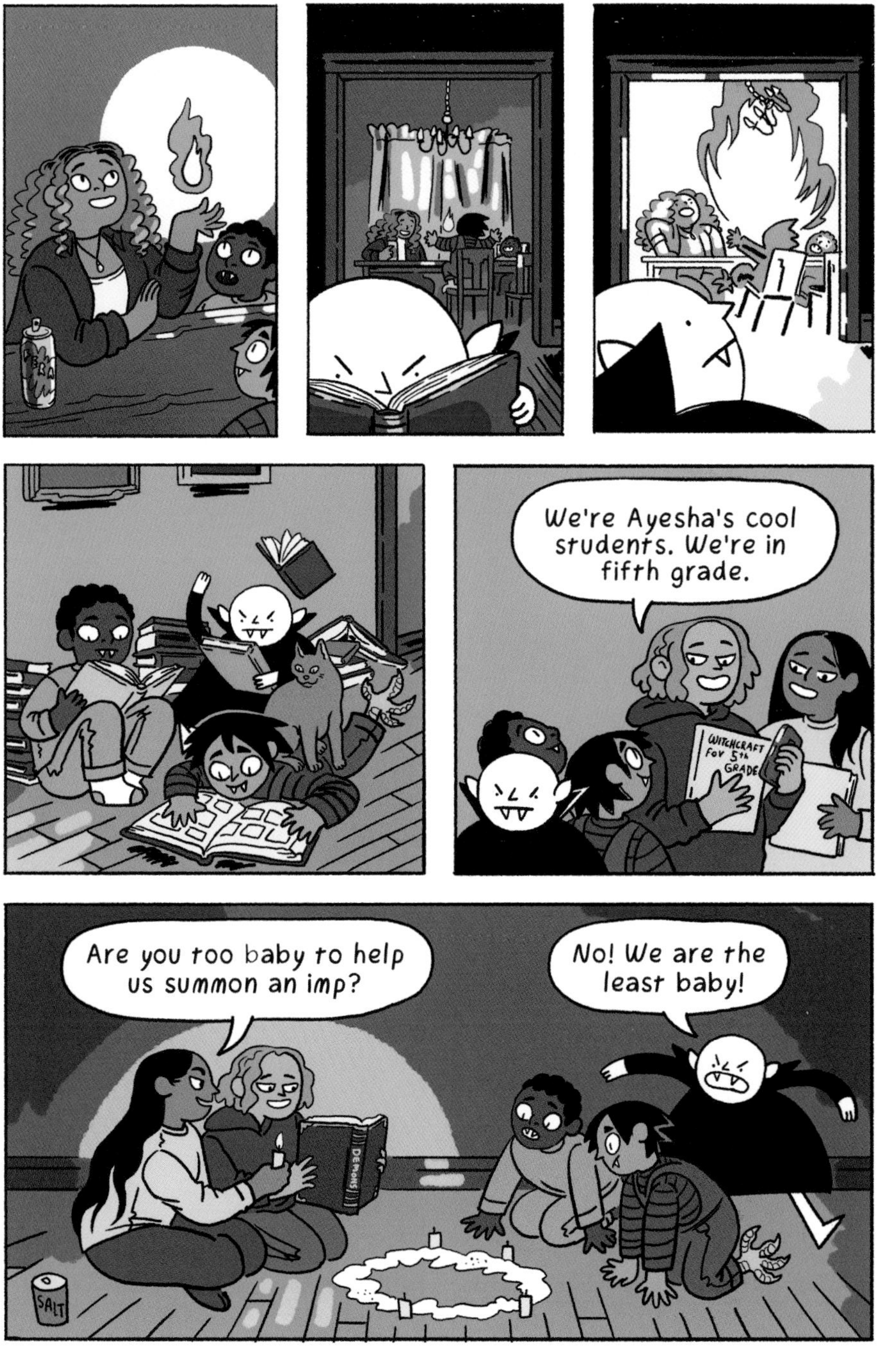
BERA
We're Ayesha's cool students. We're in fifth grade.
WITCHCRAFT for 5th GRADE
Are you too baby to help us summon an imp?
No! We are the least baby!
DEMONS
SALT

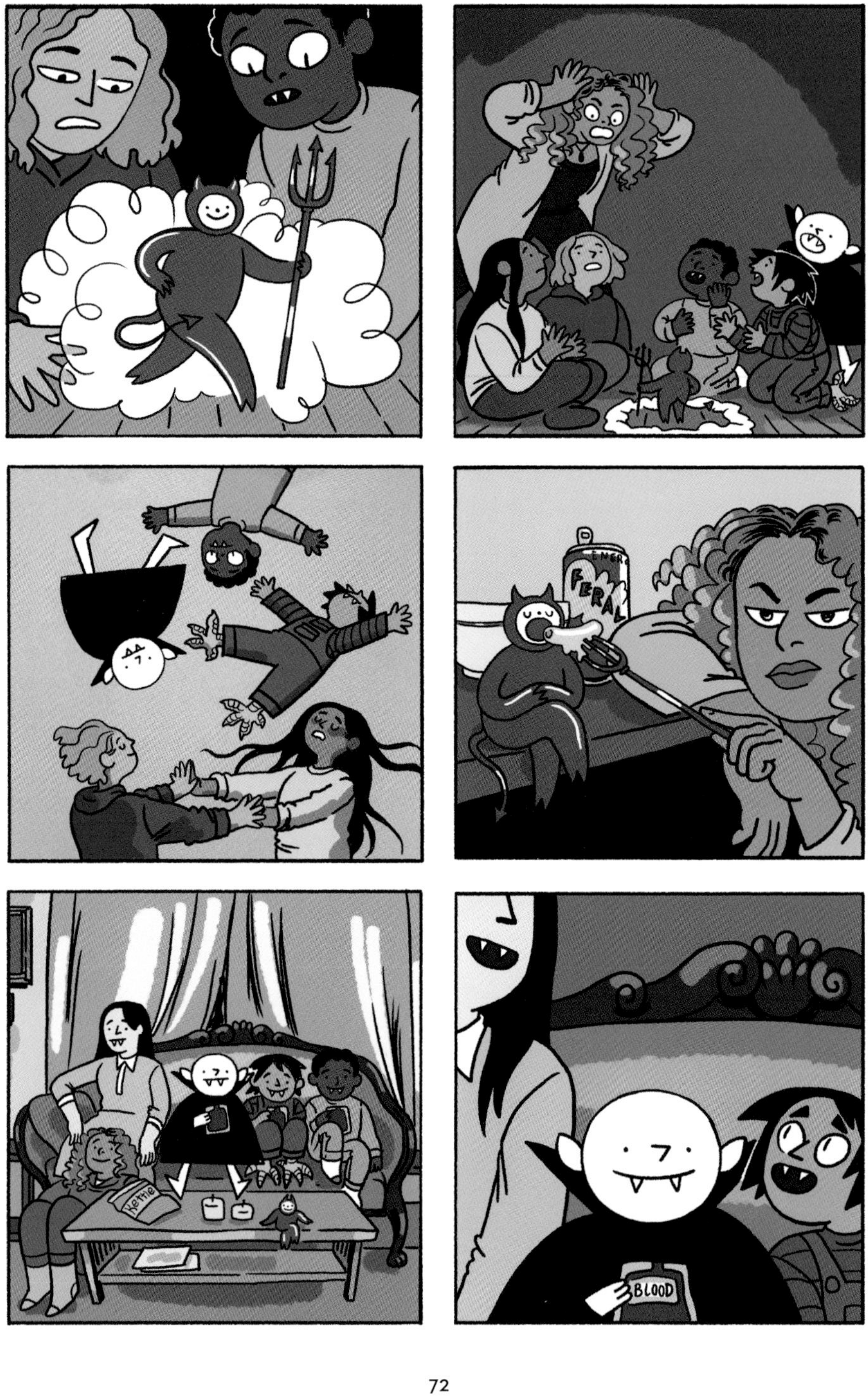
FERAL
Kettle
BLOOD

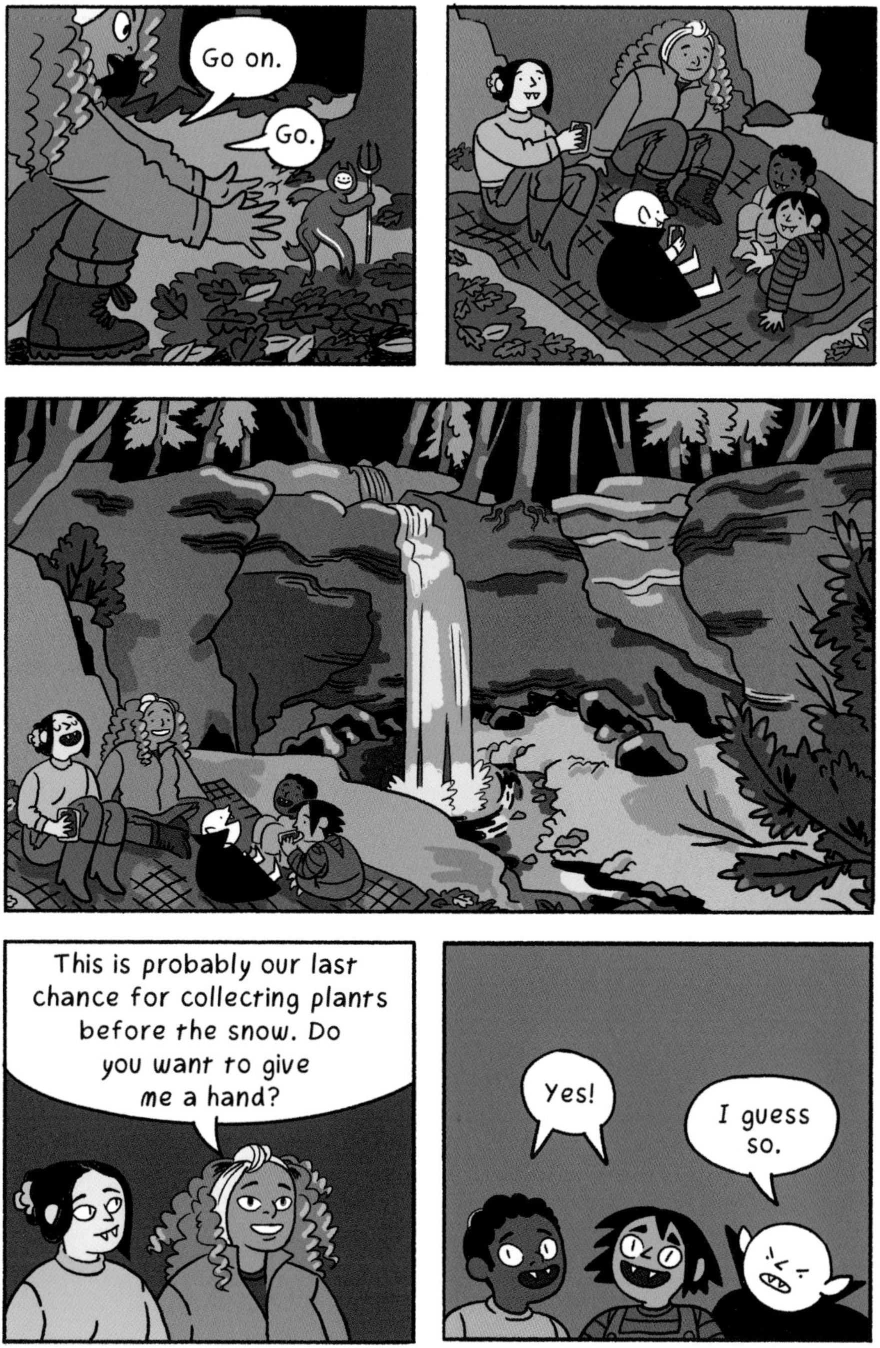
Go on.
Go.
This is probably our last chance for collecting plants before the snow. Do you want to give me a hand?
Yes!
I guess so.

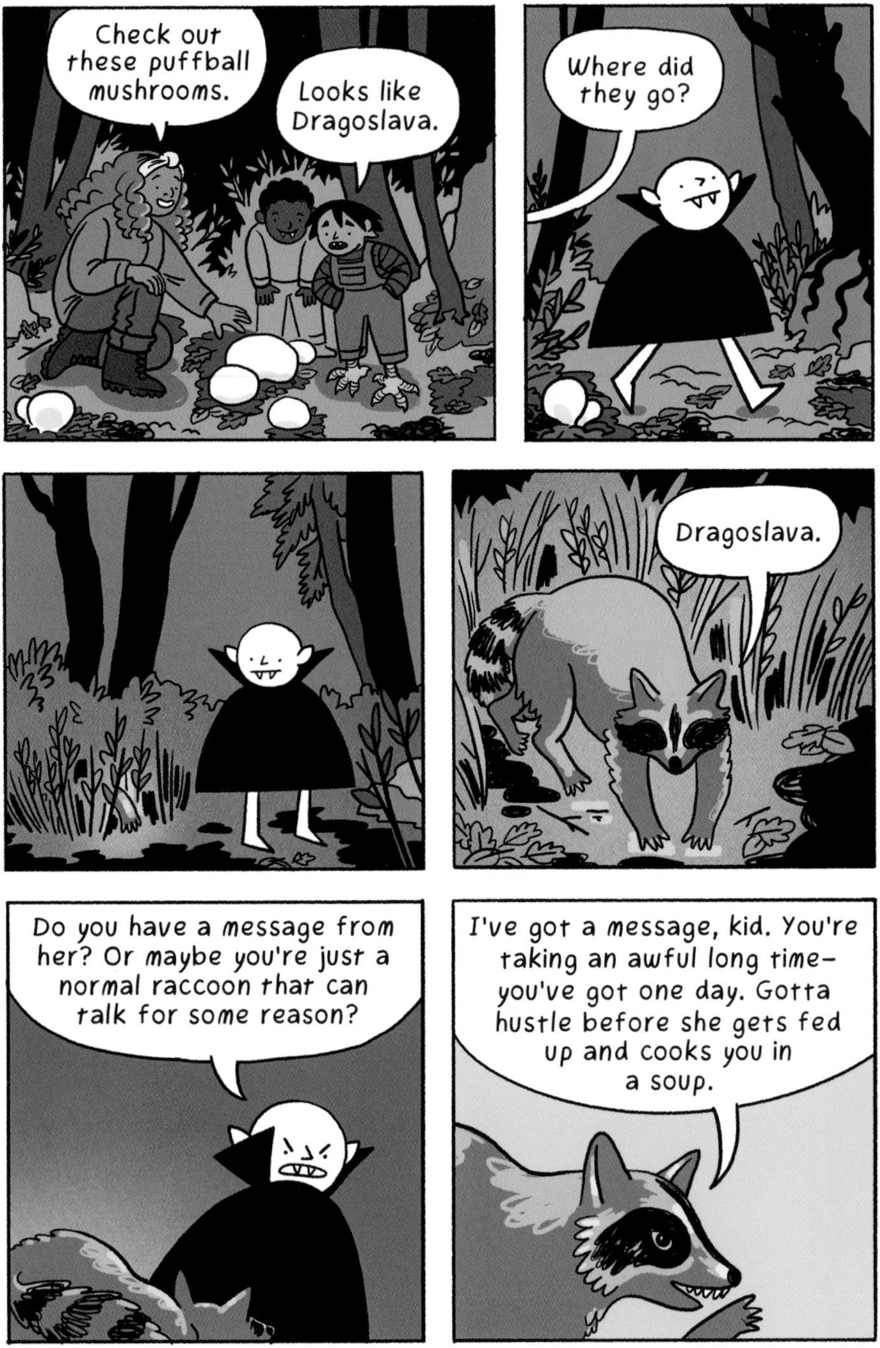
Check out these puffball mushrooms.
Looks like Dragoslava.
Where did they go?
Dragoslava.
Do you have a message from her? Or maybe you're just a normal raccoon that can talk for some reason?
I've got a message, kid. You're taking an awful long time—you've got one day. Gotta hustle before she gets fed up and cooks you in a soup.

Soup? That's a new threat.

Just do your job.

Okay?

I don't think I would make very good soup.

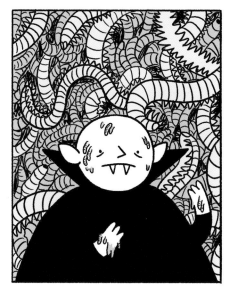

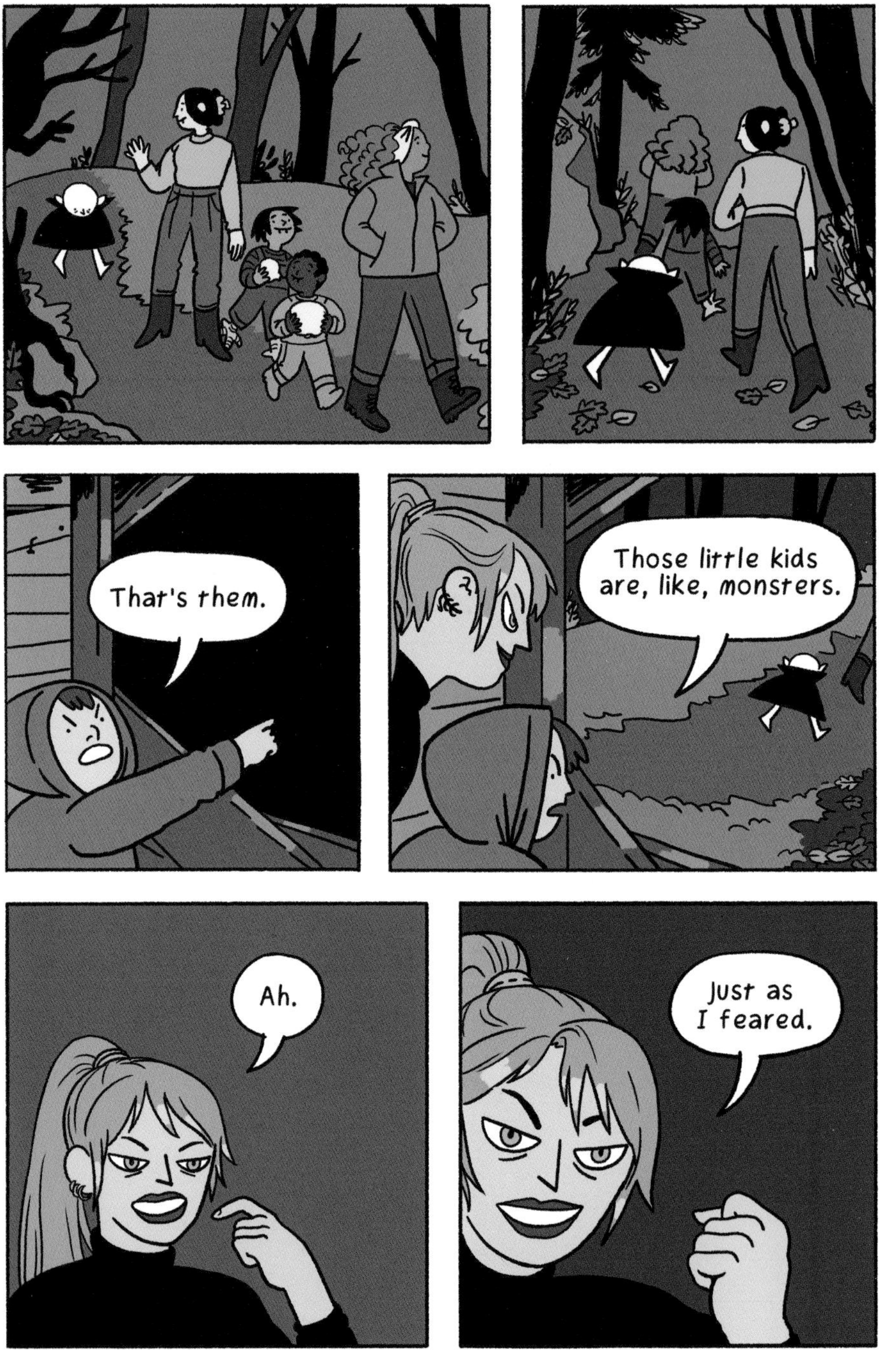
That's them.
Those little kids are, like, monsters.
Ah.
Just as I feared.

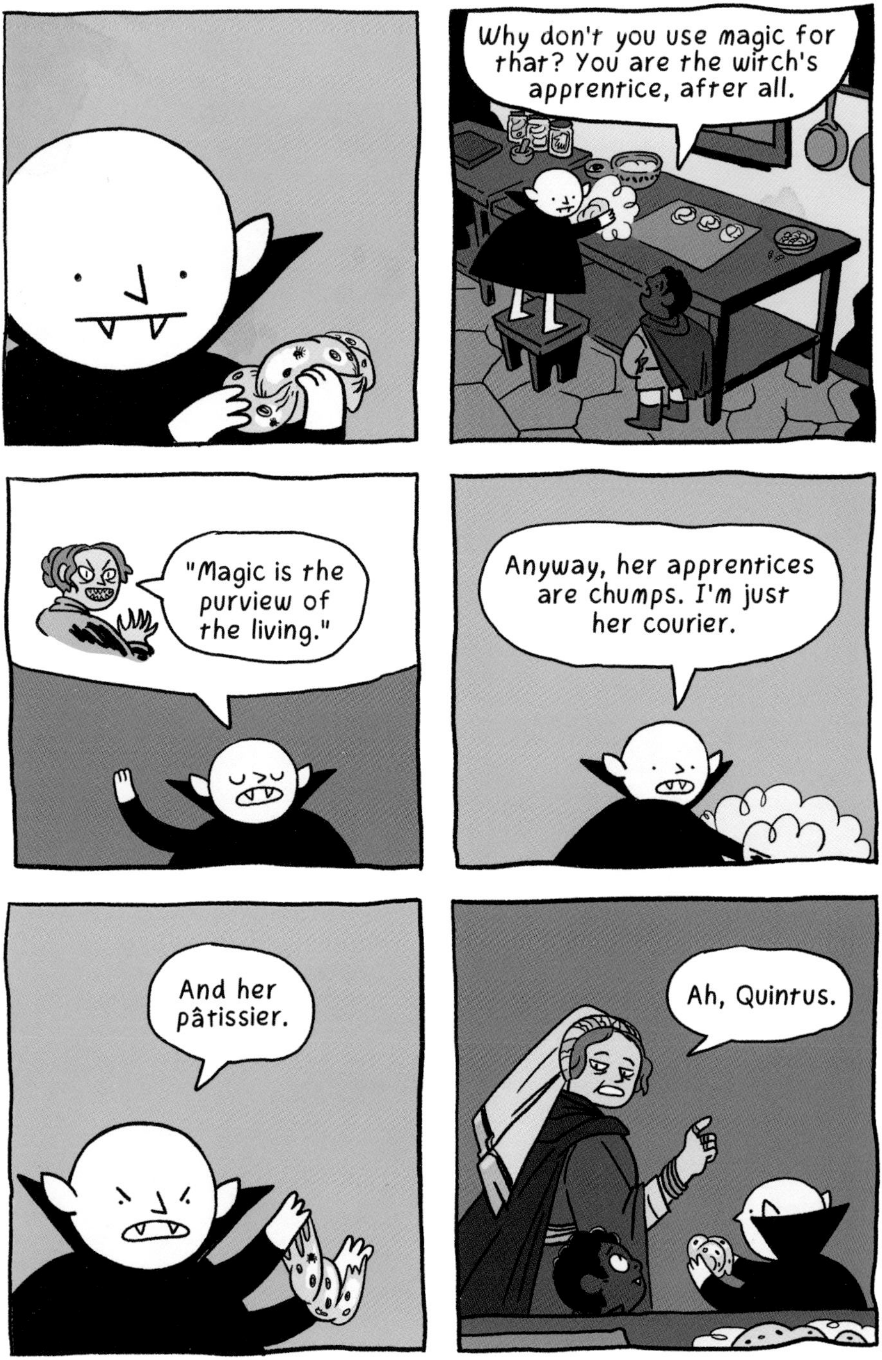

Why don't you use magic for that? You are the witch's apprentice, after all.
"Magic is the purview of the living."
Anyway, her apprentices are chumps. I'm just her courier.
And her pâtissier.
Ah, Quintus.

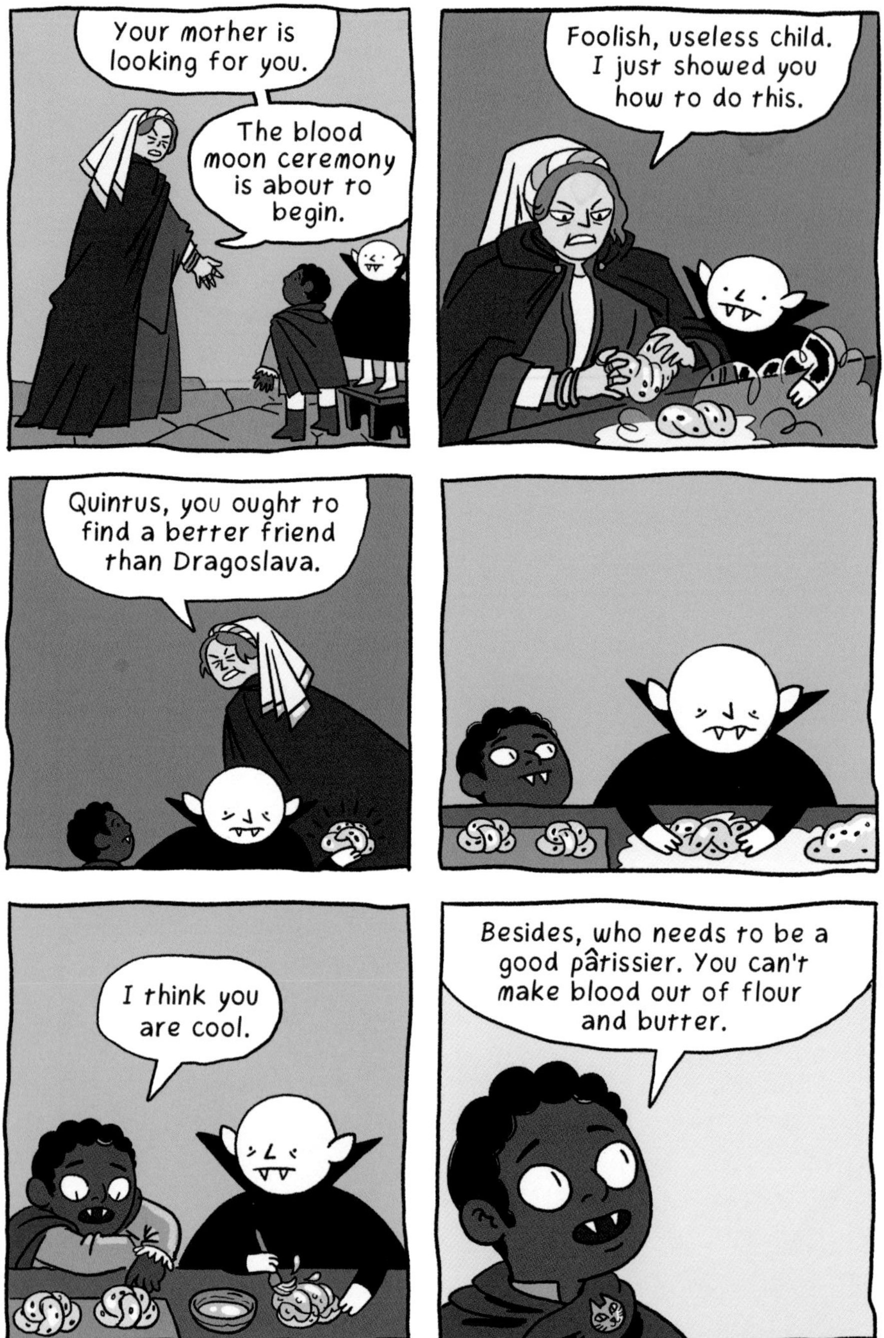
Your mother is looking for you.
The blood moon ceremony is about to begin.
Foolish, useless child. I just showed you how to do this.
Quintus, you ought to find a better friend than Dragoslava.
I think you are cool.
Besides, who needs to be a good pâtissier. You can't make blood out of flour and butter.

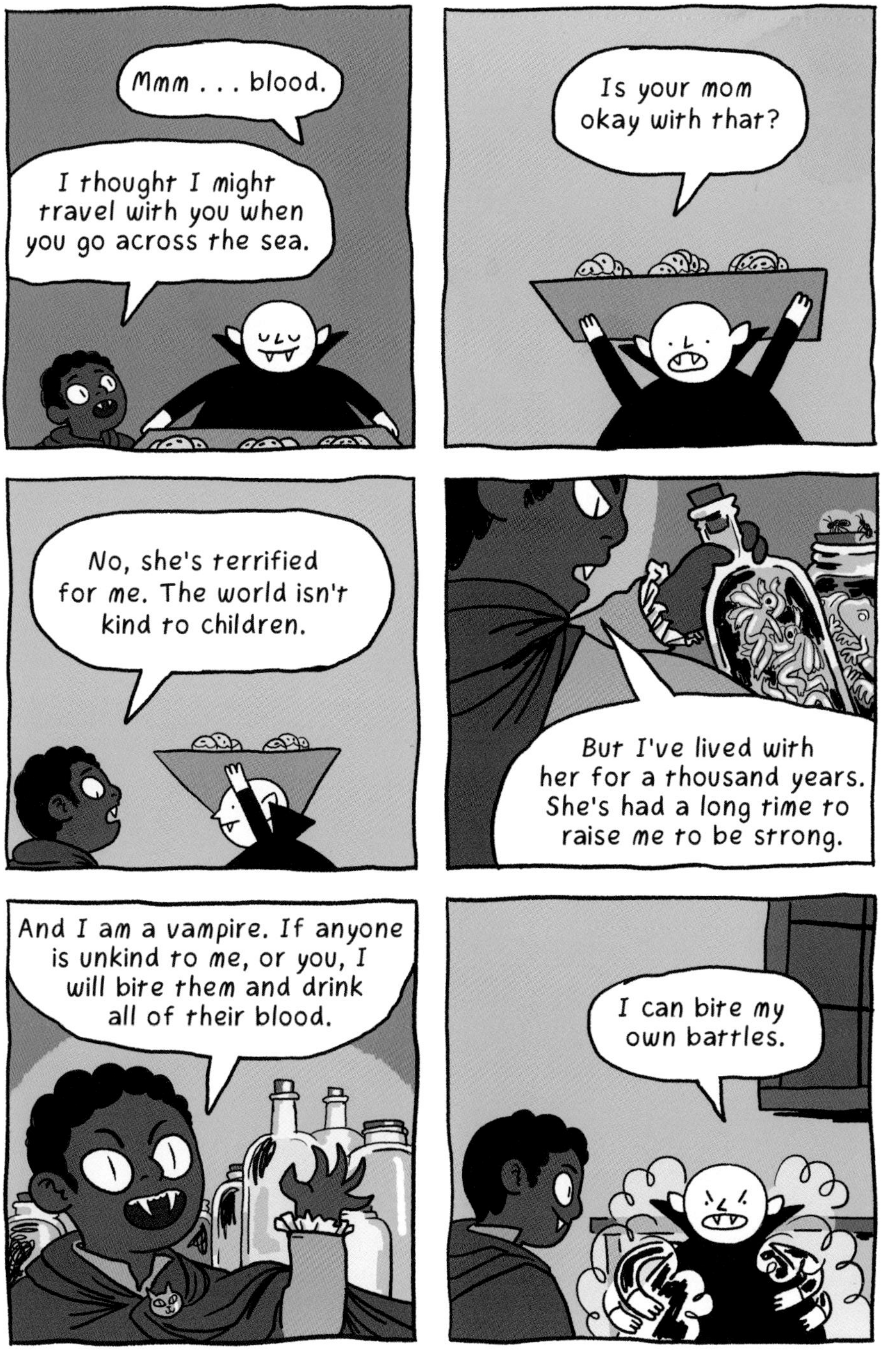
Mmm . . . blood.
I thought I might travel with you when you go across the sea.
Is your mom okay with that?
No, she's terrified for me. The world isn't kind to children.
But I've lived with her for a thousand years. She's had a long time to raise me to be strong.
And I am a vampire. If anyone is unkind to me, or you, I will bite them and drink all of their blood.
I can bite my own battles.

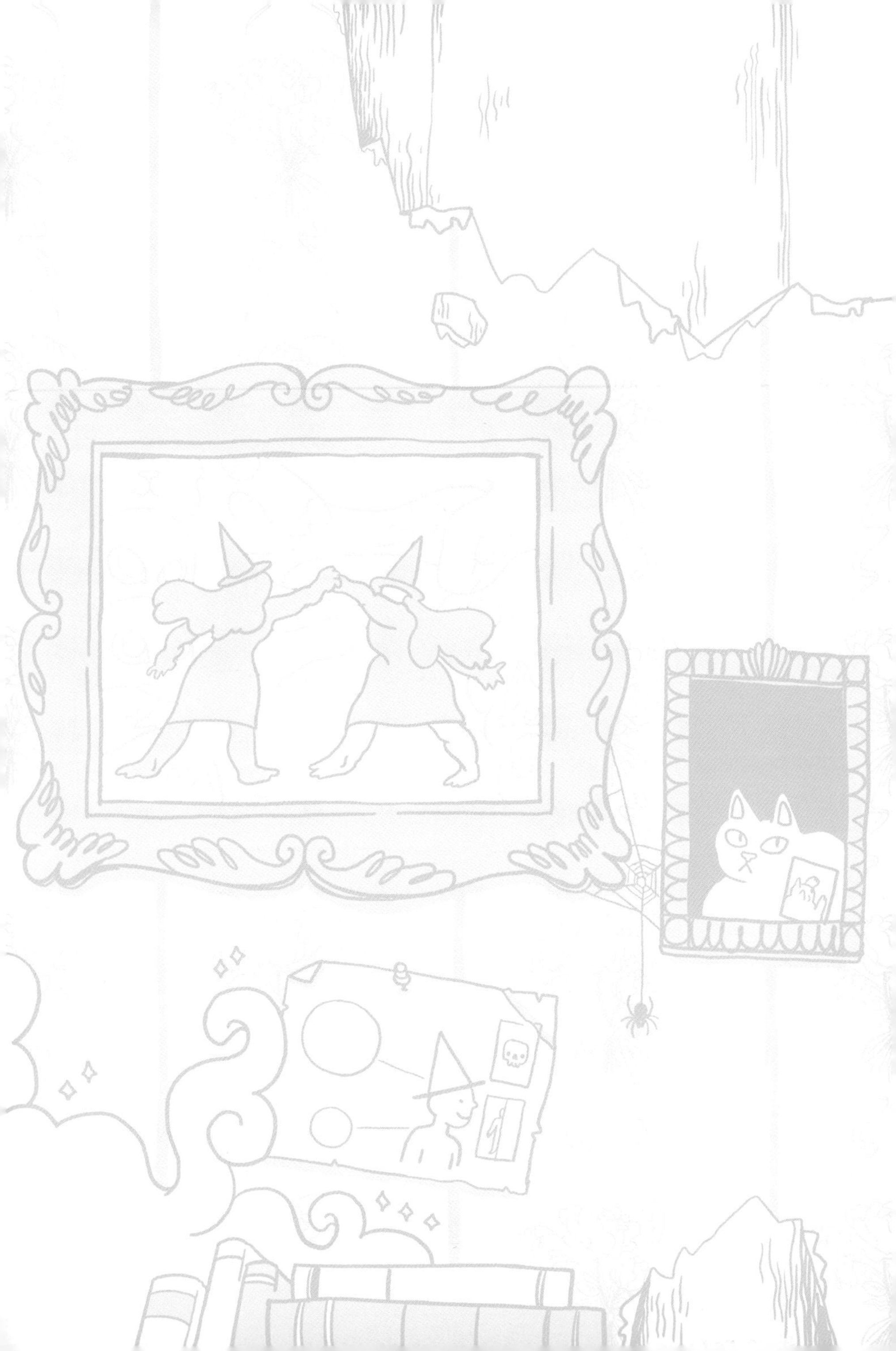

CHAPTER FIVE

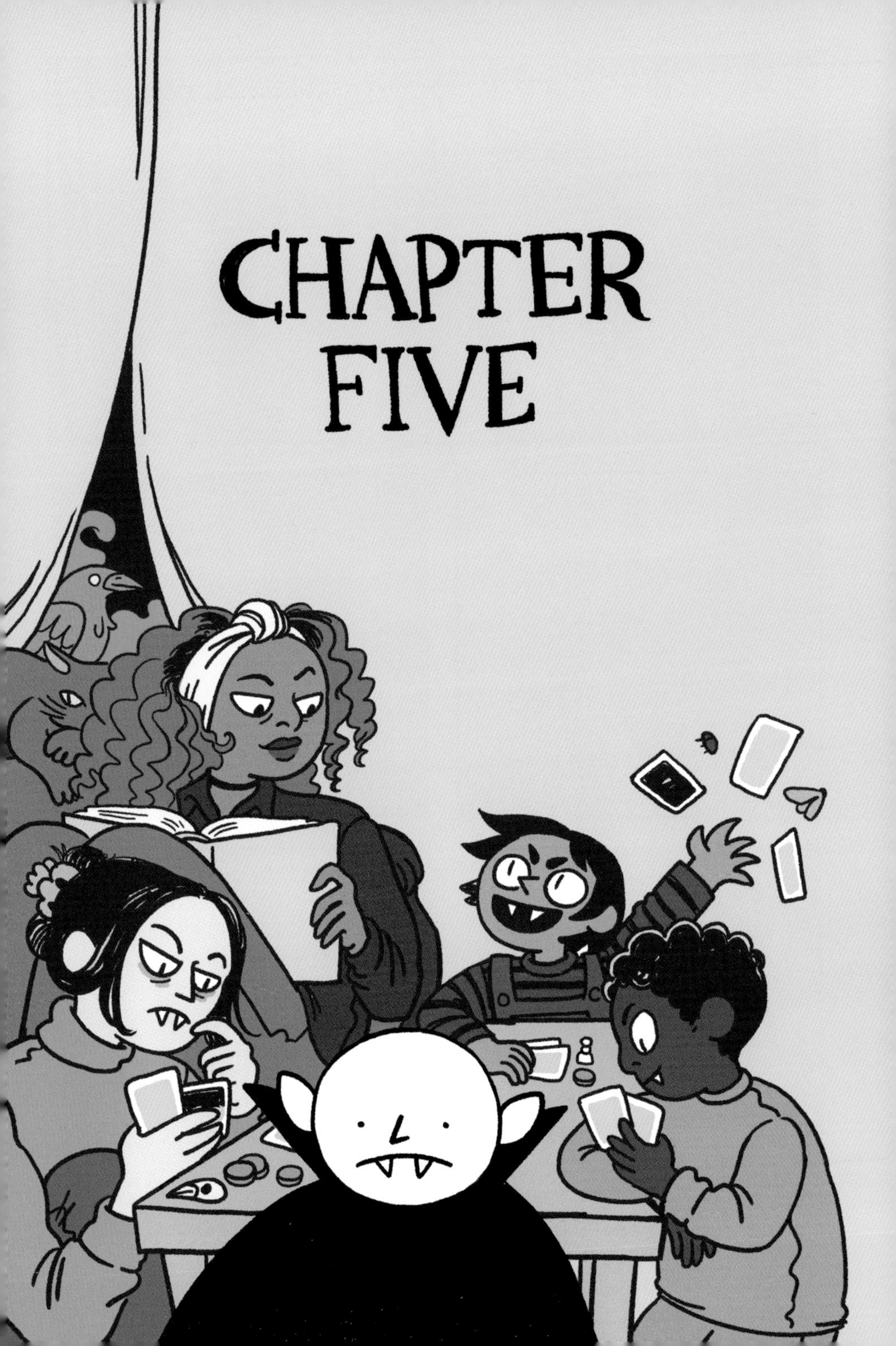

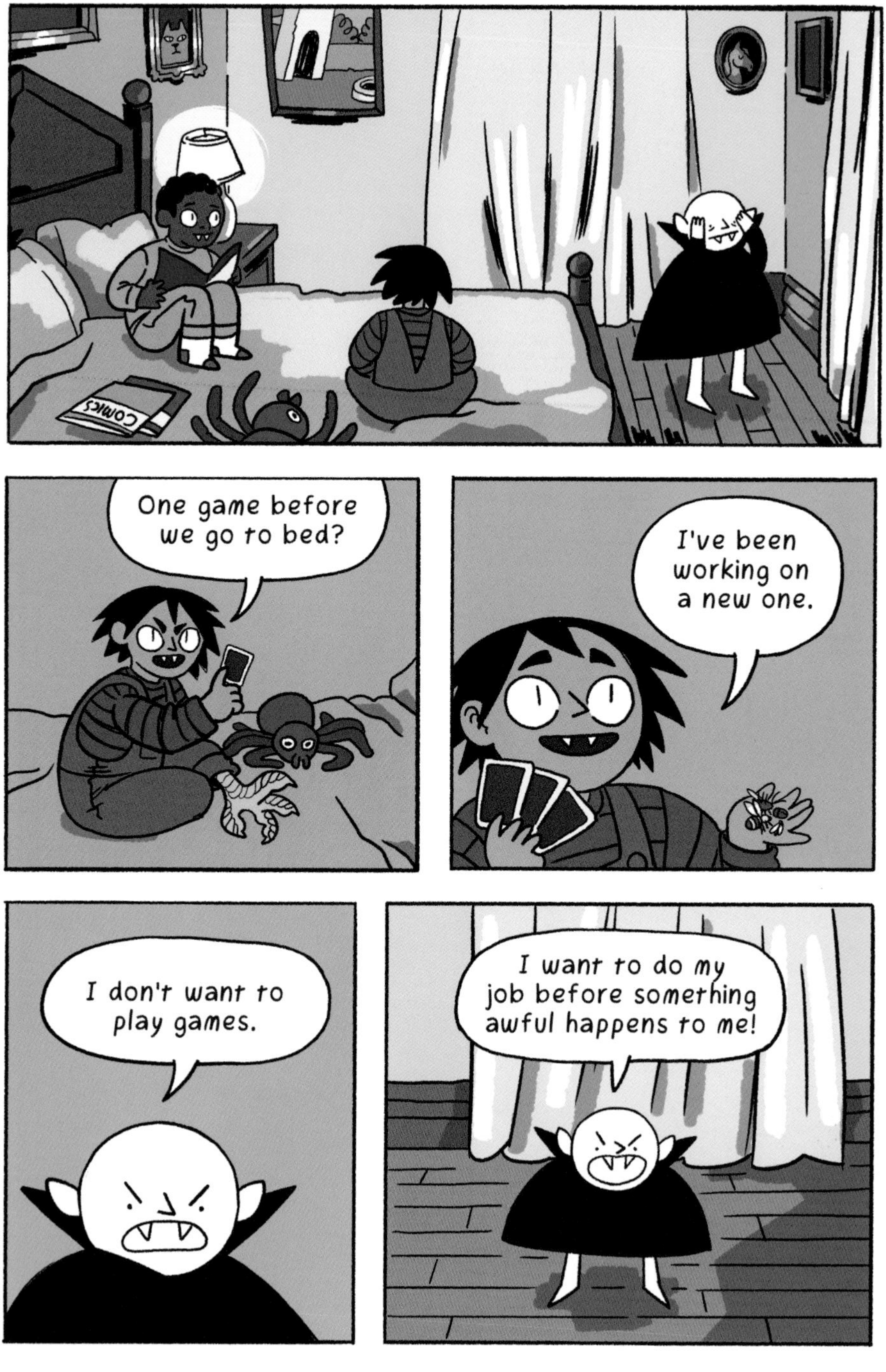

COMICS
One game before we go to bed?
I've been working on a new one.
I don't want to play games.
I want to do my job before something awful happens to me!

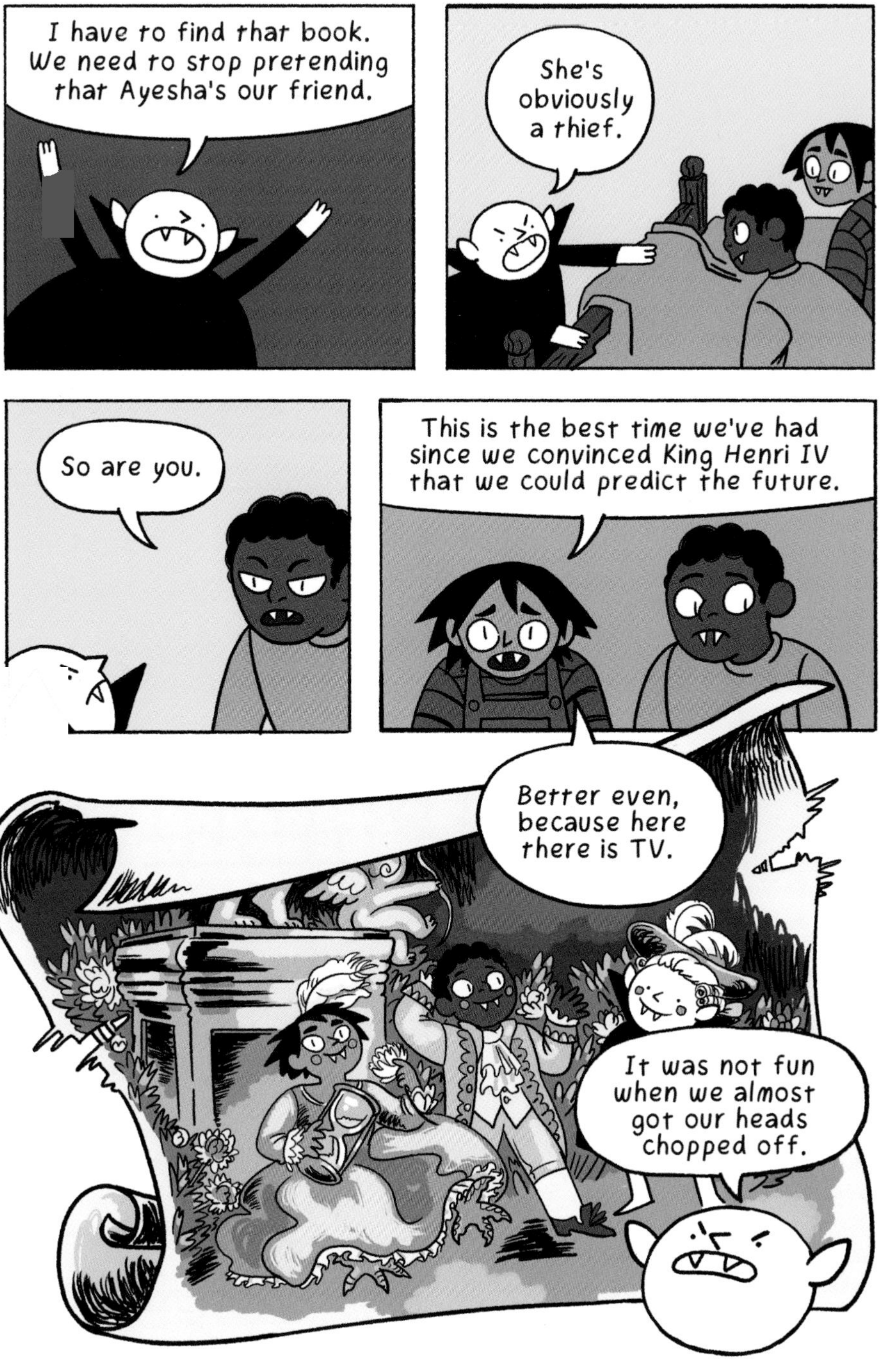
I have to find that book. We need to stop pretending that Ayesha's our friend.
She's obviously a thief.
So are you.
This is the best time we've had since we convinced King Henri IV that we could predict the future.
Better even, because here there is TV.
It was not fun when we almost got our heads chopped off.

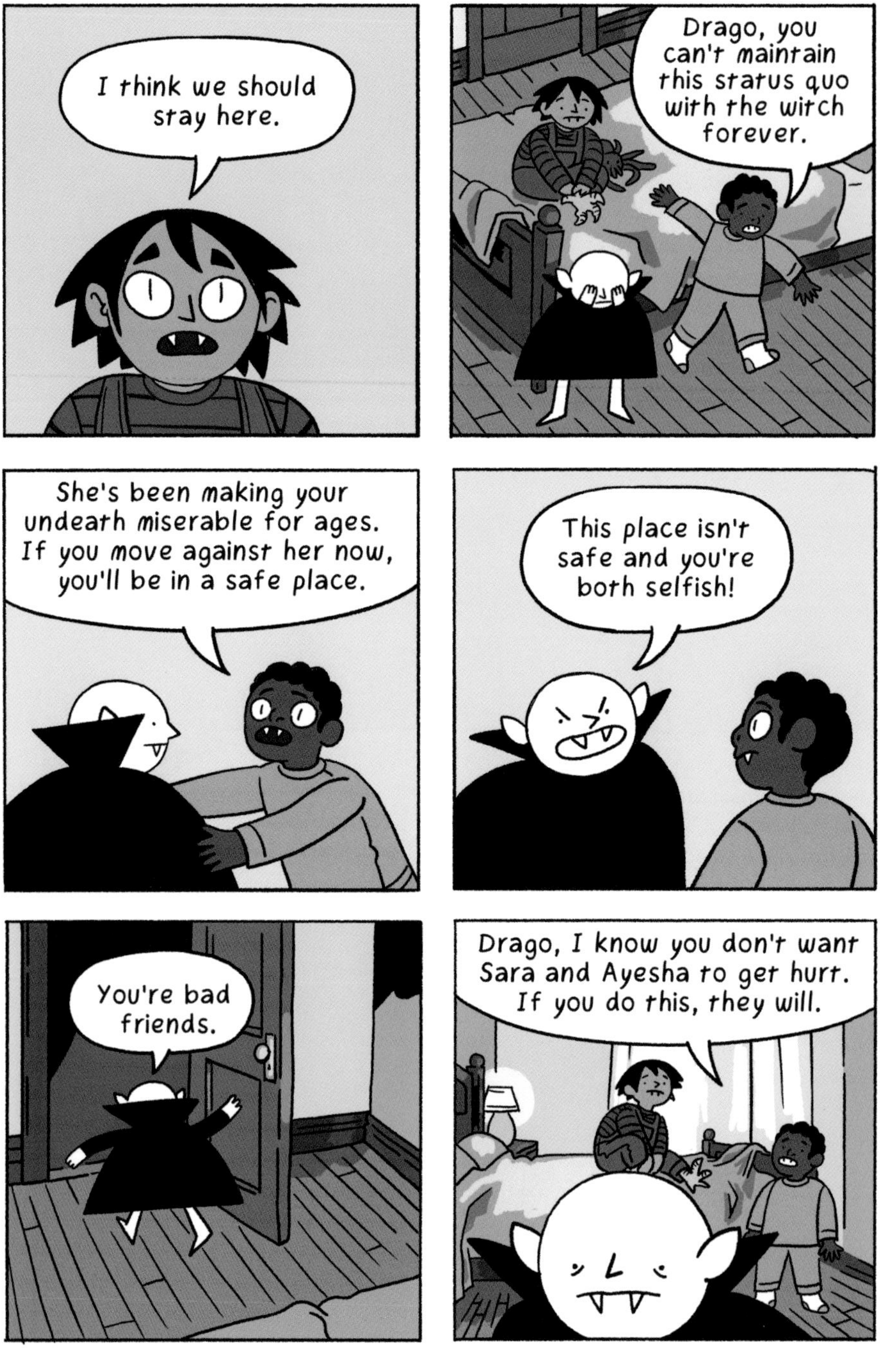
I think we should stay here.
Drago, you can't maintain this status quo with the witch forever.
She's been making your undeath miserable for ages. If you move against her now, you'll be in a safe place.
This place isn't safe and you're both selfish!
You're bad friends.
Drago, I know you don't want Sara and Ayesha to get hurt. If you do this, they will.

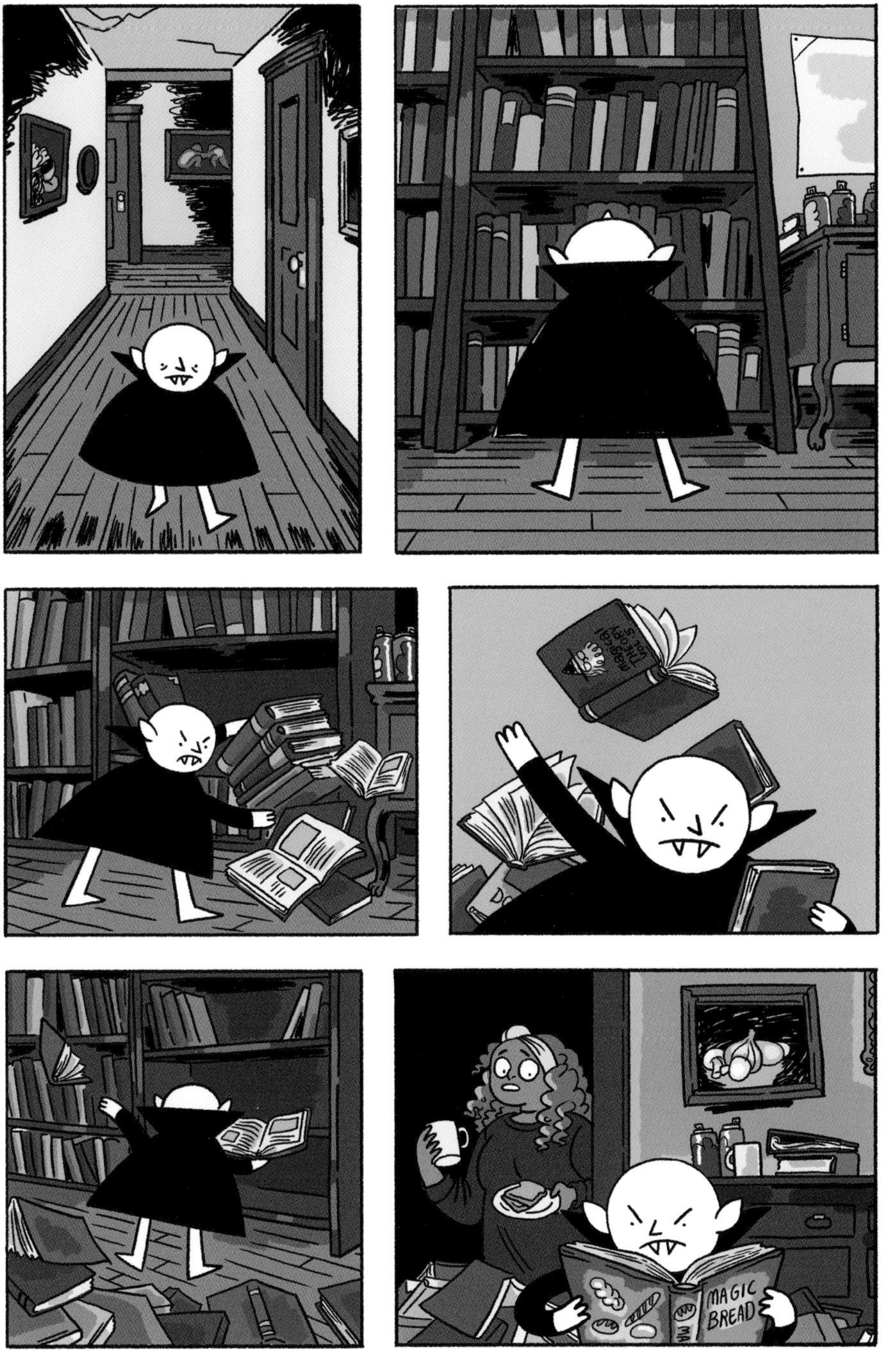
MAGIC
BREAD

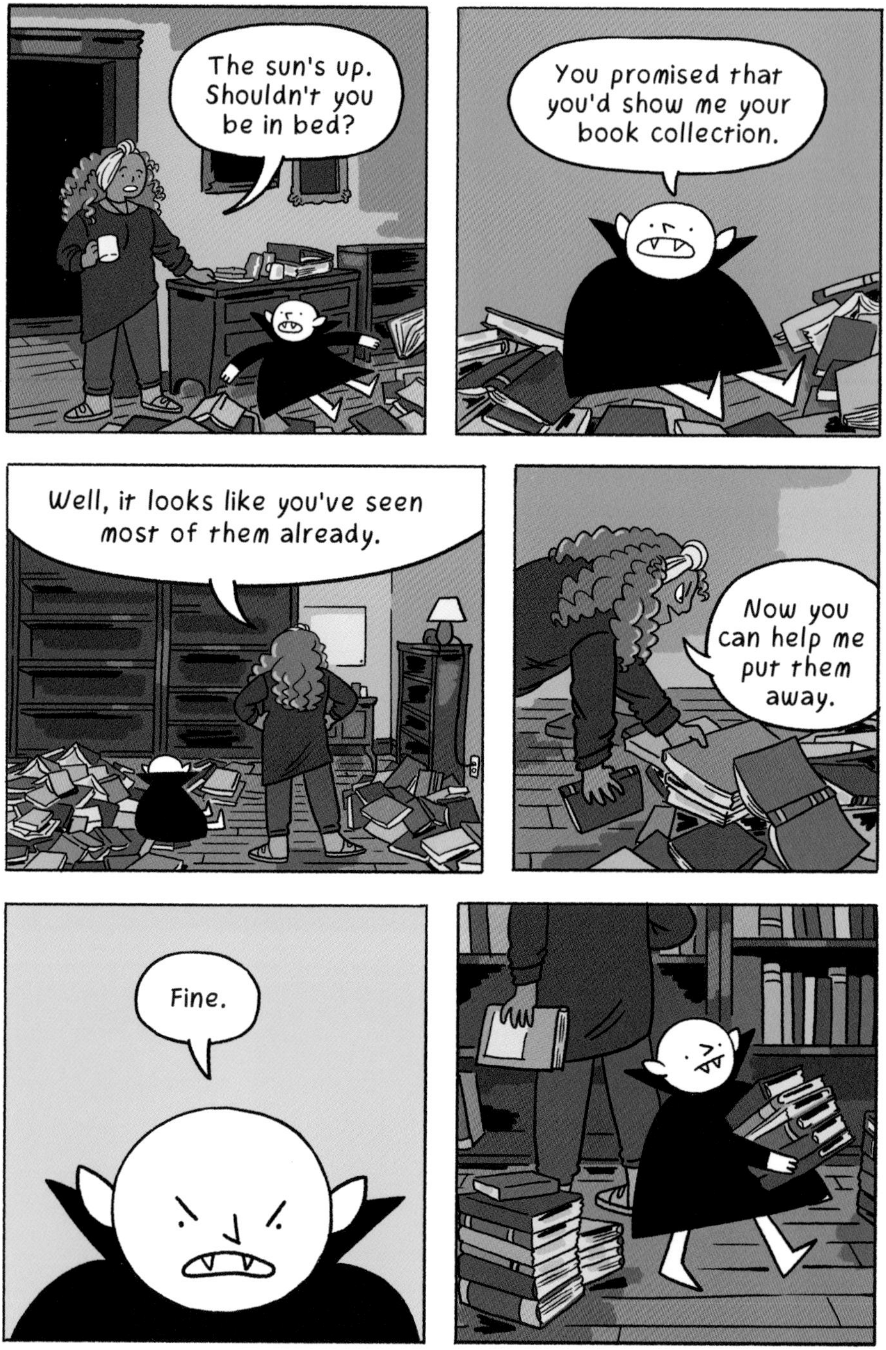
The sun's up. Shouldn't you be in bed?
You promised that you'd show me your book collection.
Well, it looks like you've seen most of them already.
Now you can help me put them away.
Fine.

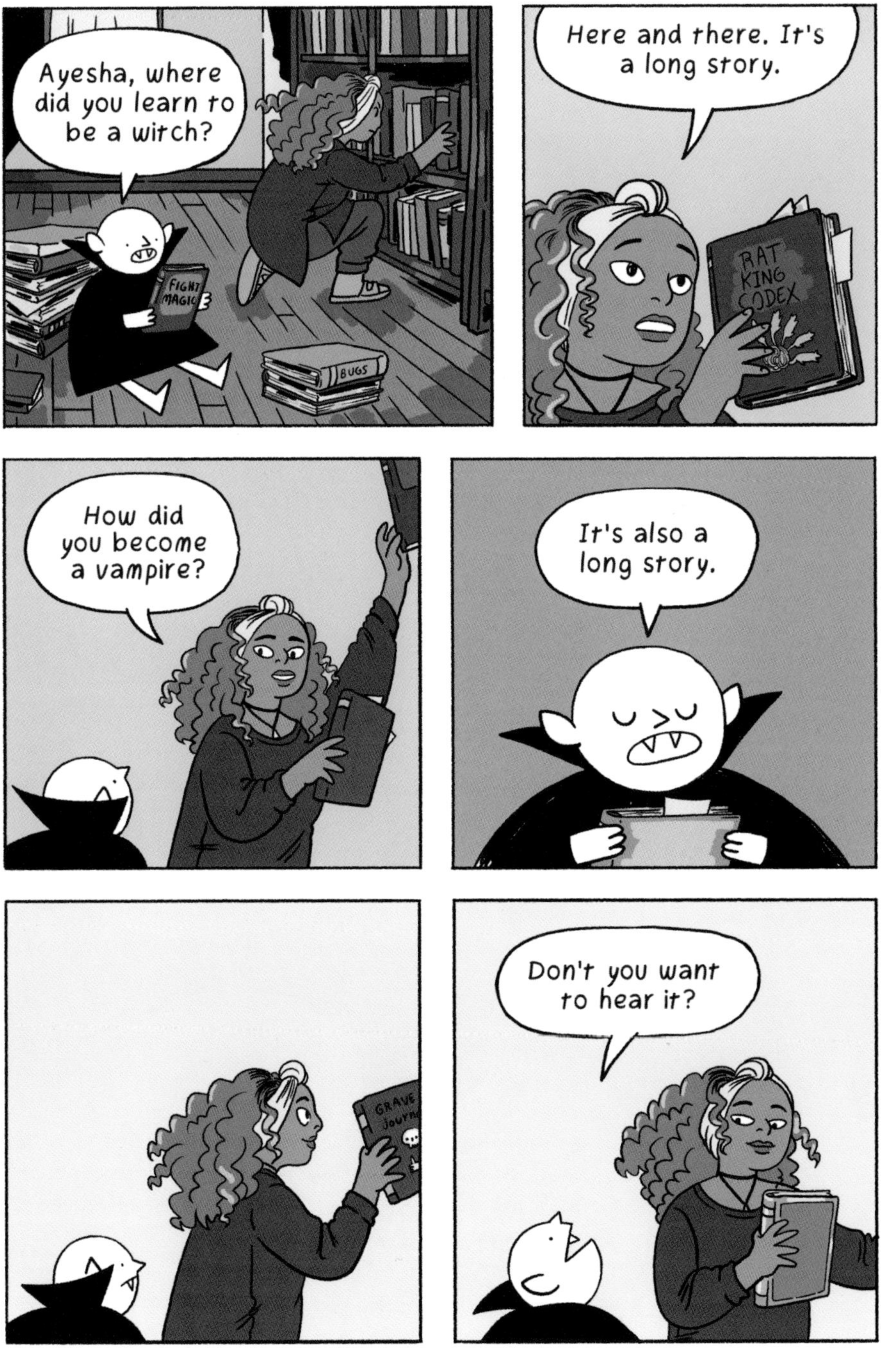
Ayesha, where did you learn to be a witch?
FIGHT MAGIC
BUGS
Here and there. It's a long story.
RAT KING CODEX
How did you become a vampire?
It's also a long story.
Don't you want to hear it?

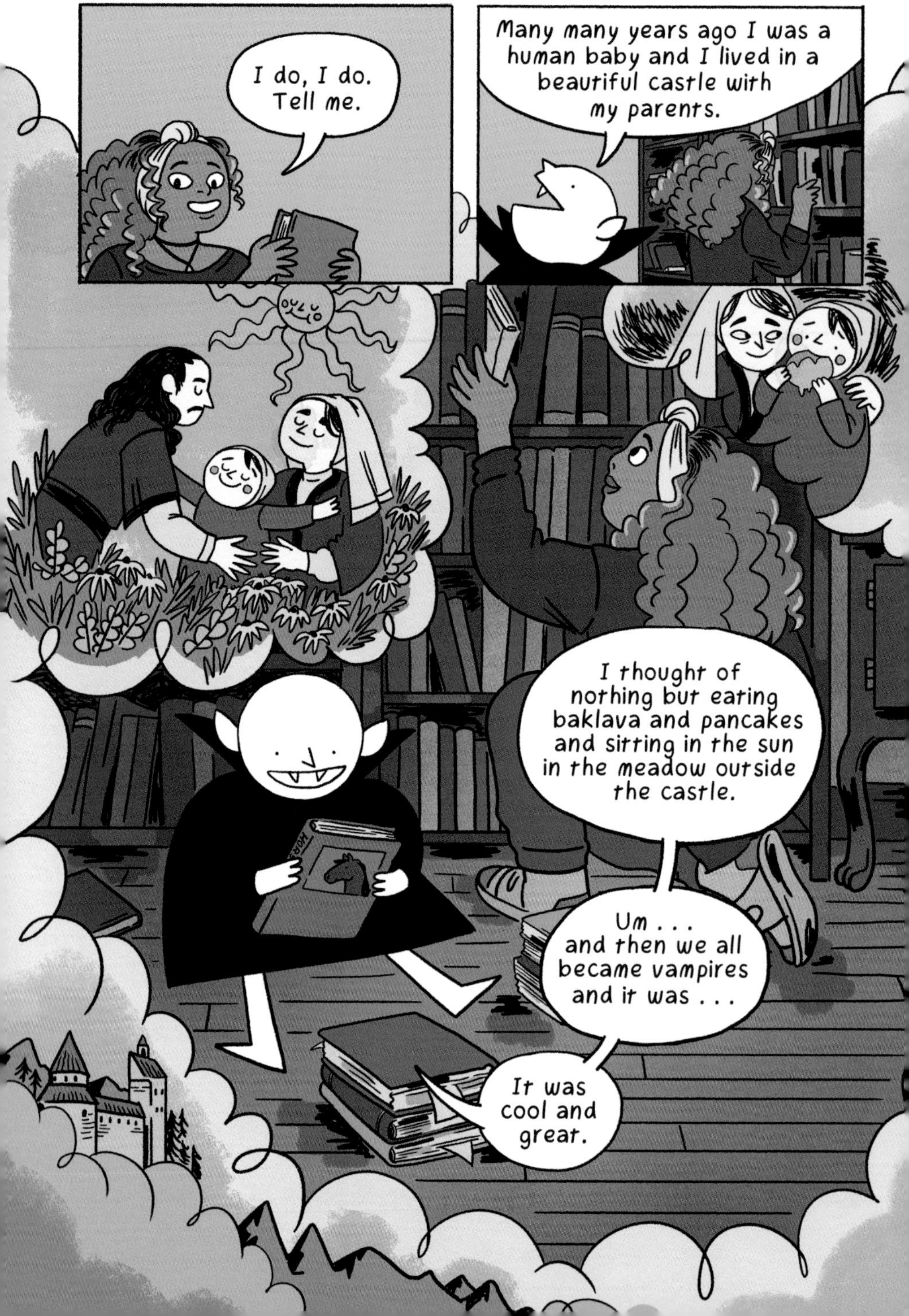

I do, I do. Tell me.
Many many years ago I was a human baby and I lived in a beautiful castle with my parents.
I thought of nothing but eating baklava and pancakes and sitting in the sun in the meadow outside the castle.
Um . . . and then we all became vampires and it was . . .
It was cool and great.

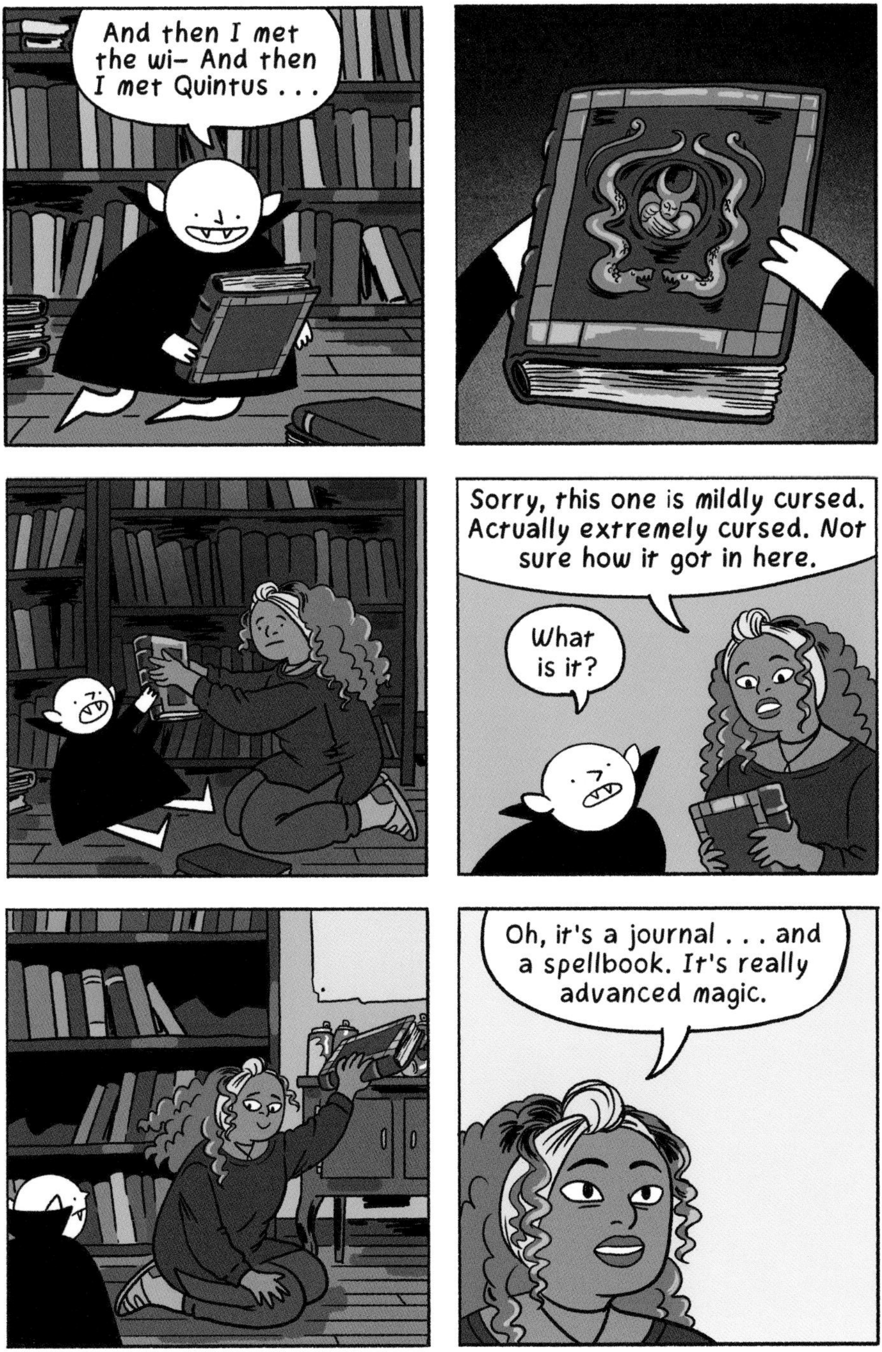
And then I met the wi– And then I met Quintus . . .
Sorry, this one is mildly cursed. Actually extremely cursed. Not sure how it got in here.
What is it?
Oh, it's a journal . . . and a spellbook. It's really advanced magic.

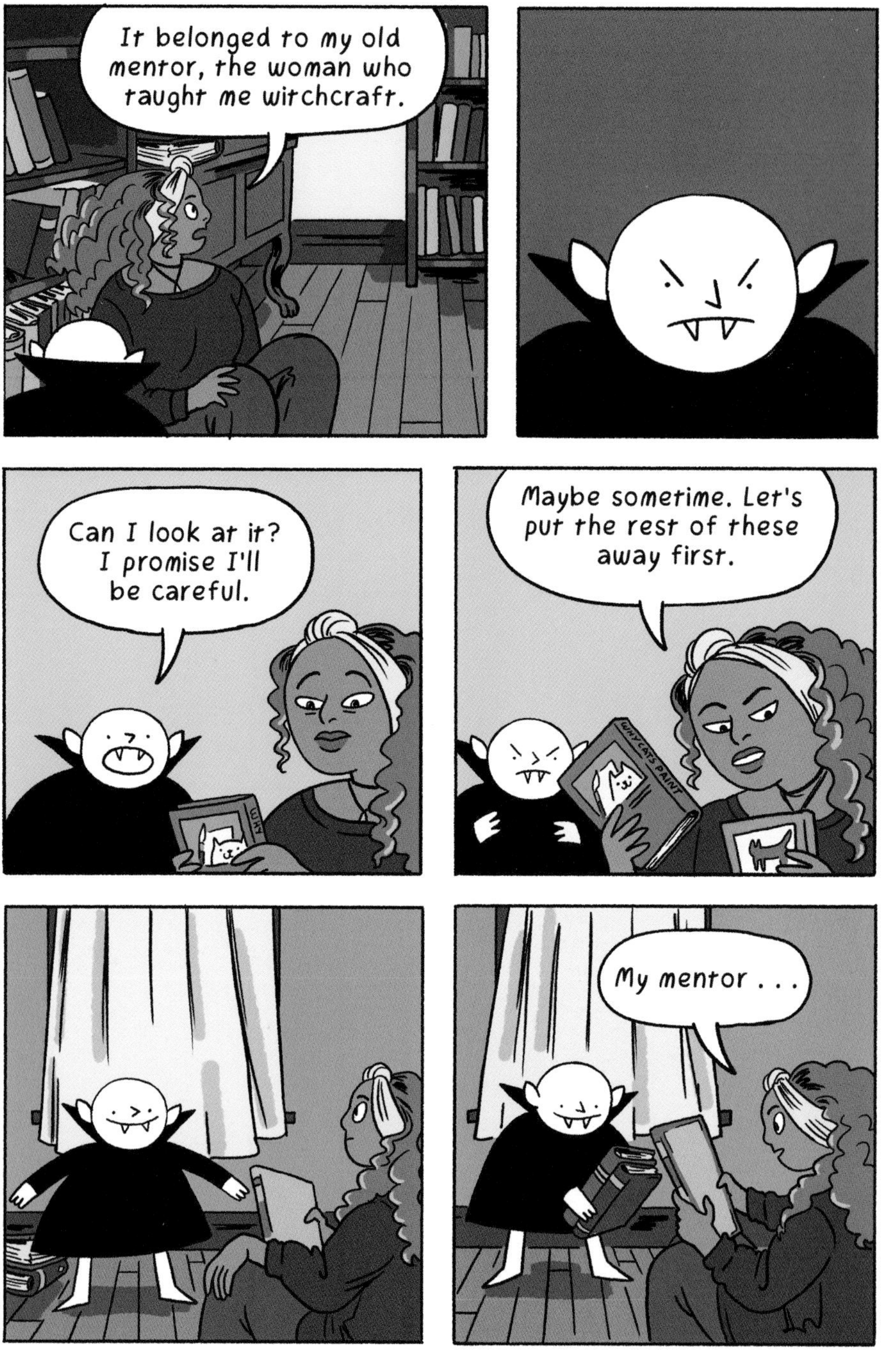
It belonged to my old mentor, the woman who taught me witchcraft.
Can I look at it? I promise I'll be careful.
Maybe sometime. Let's put the rest of these away first.
WHY CATS PAINT
My mentor . . .

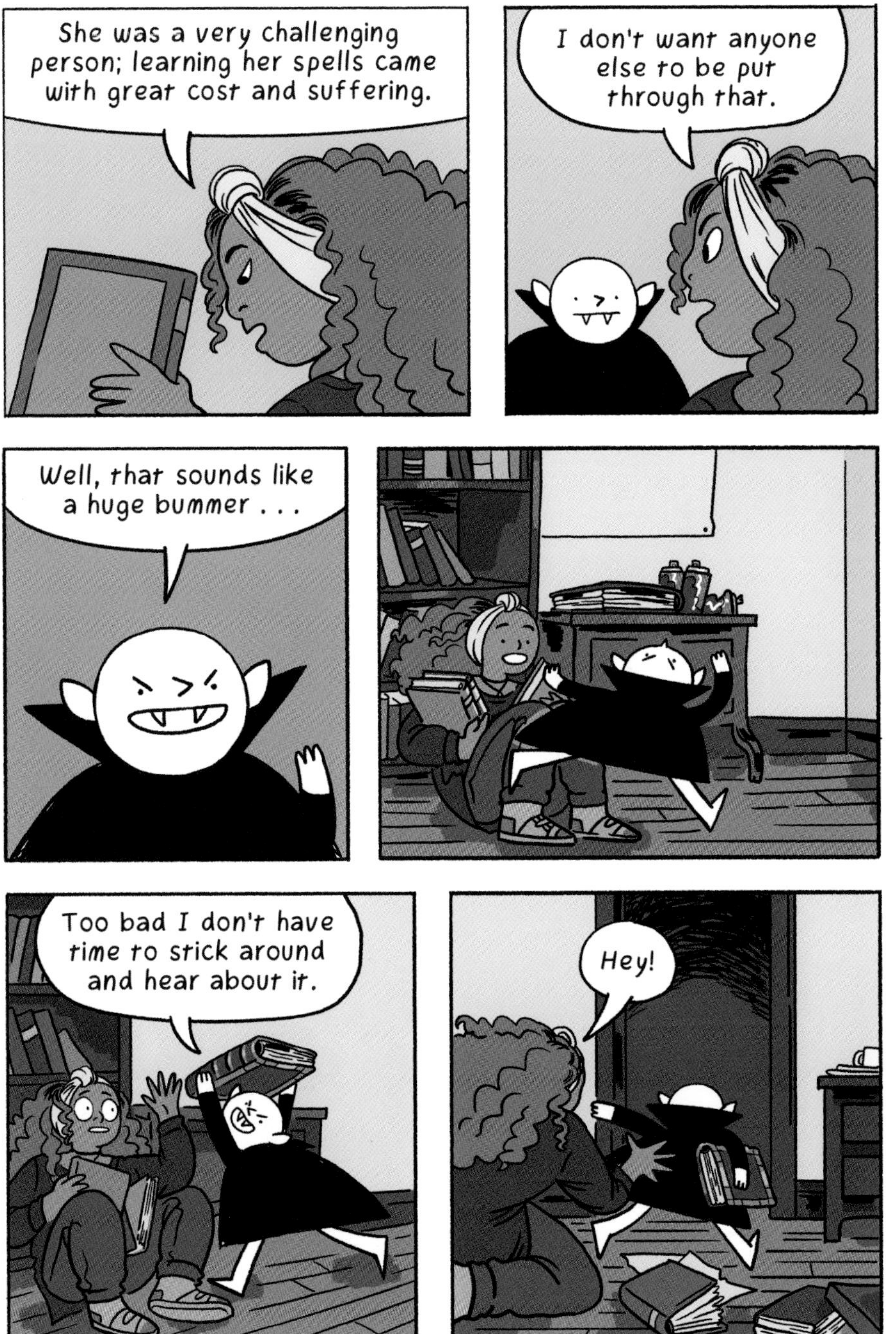

She was a very challenging person; learning her spells came with great cost and suffering.
I don't want anyone else to be put through that.
Well, that sounds like a huge bummer . . .
Too bad I don't have time to stick around and hear about it.
Hey!

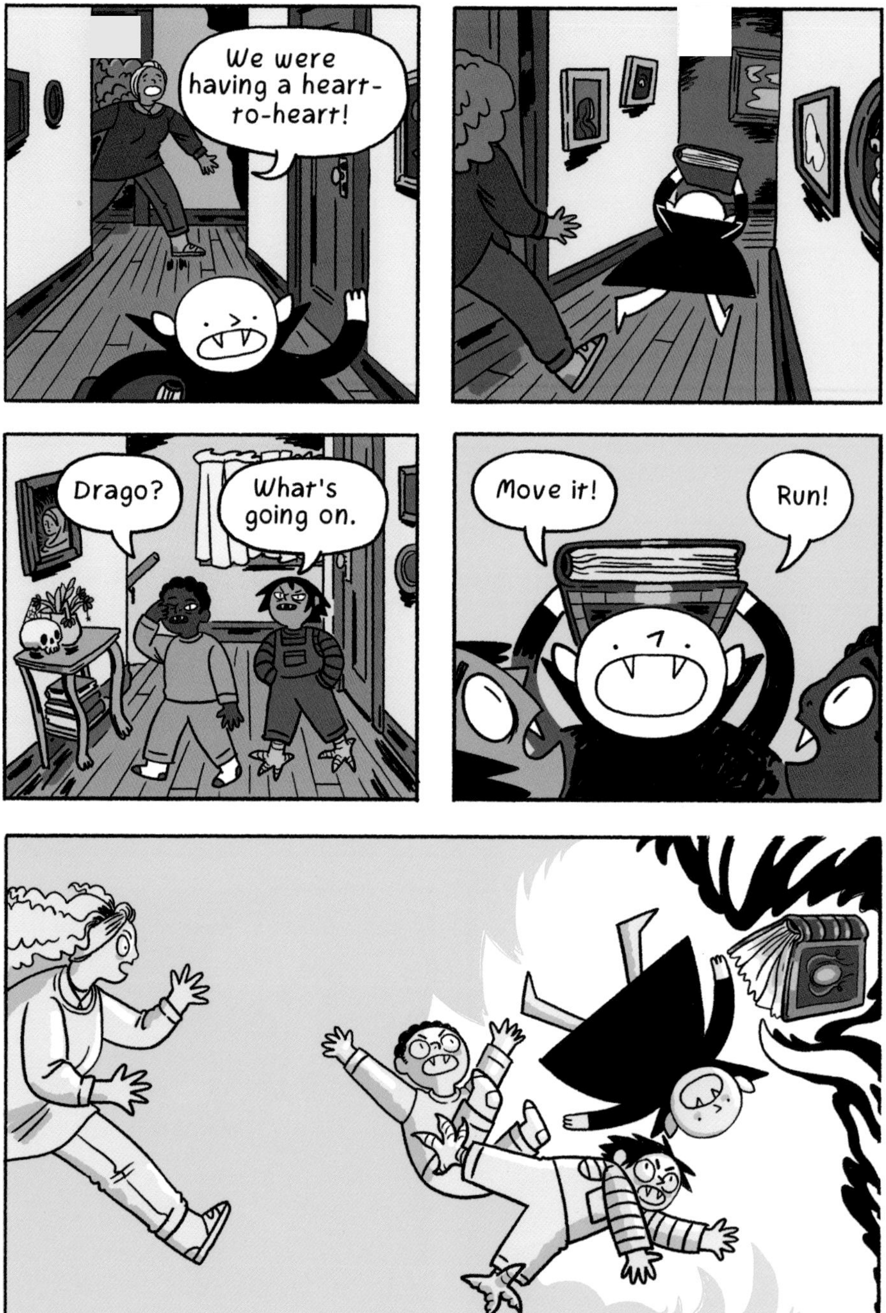
We were having a heart-to-heart!
Drago?
What's going on.
Move it!
Run!

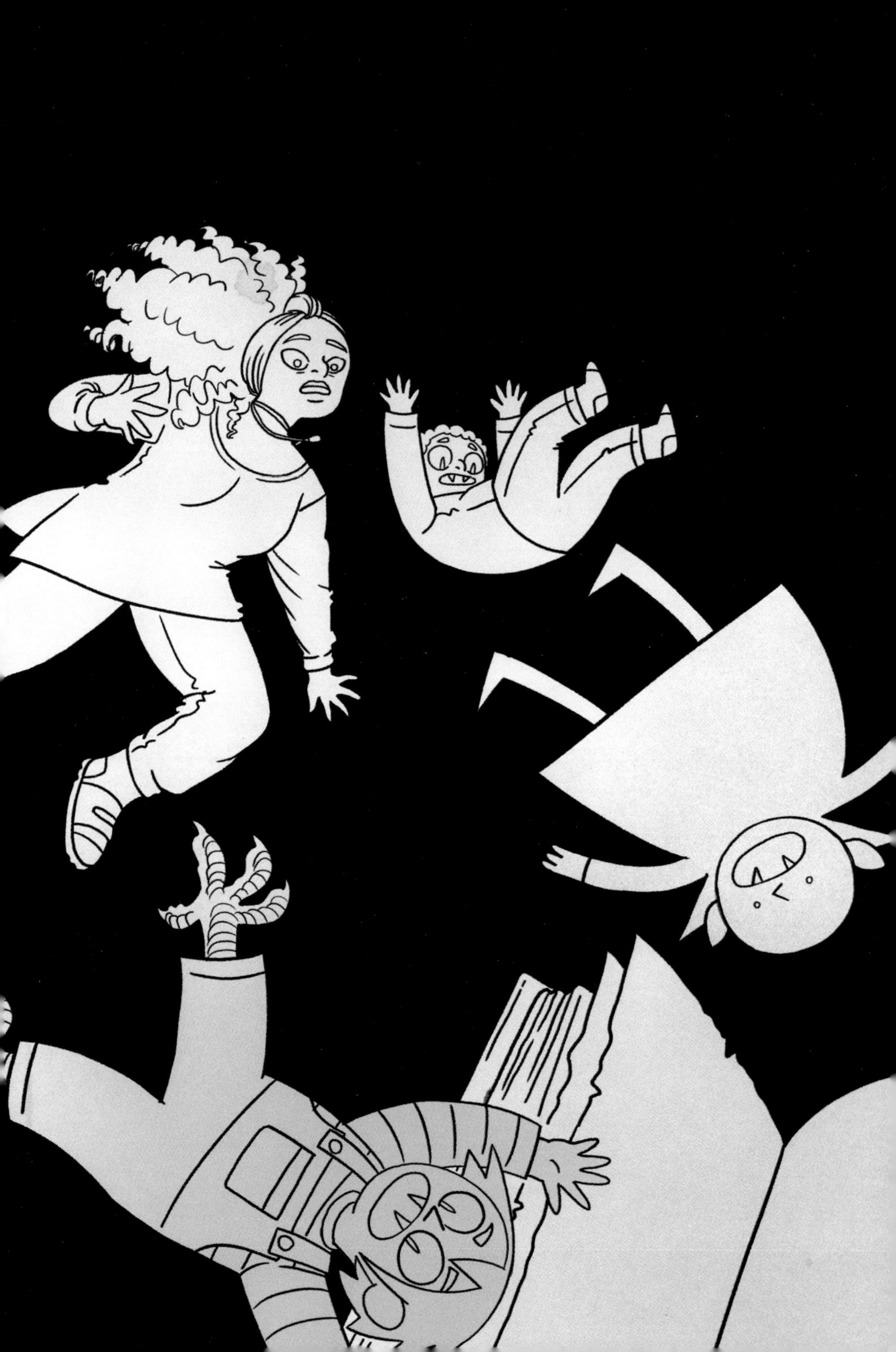

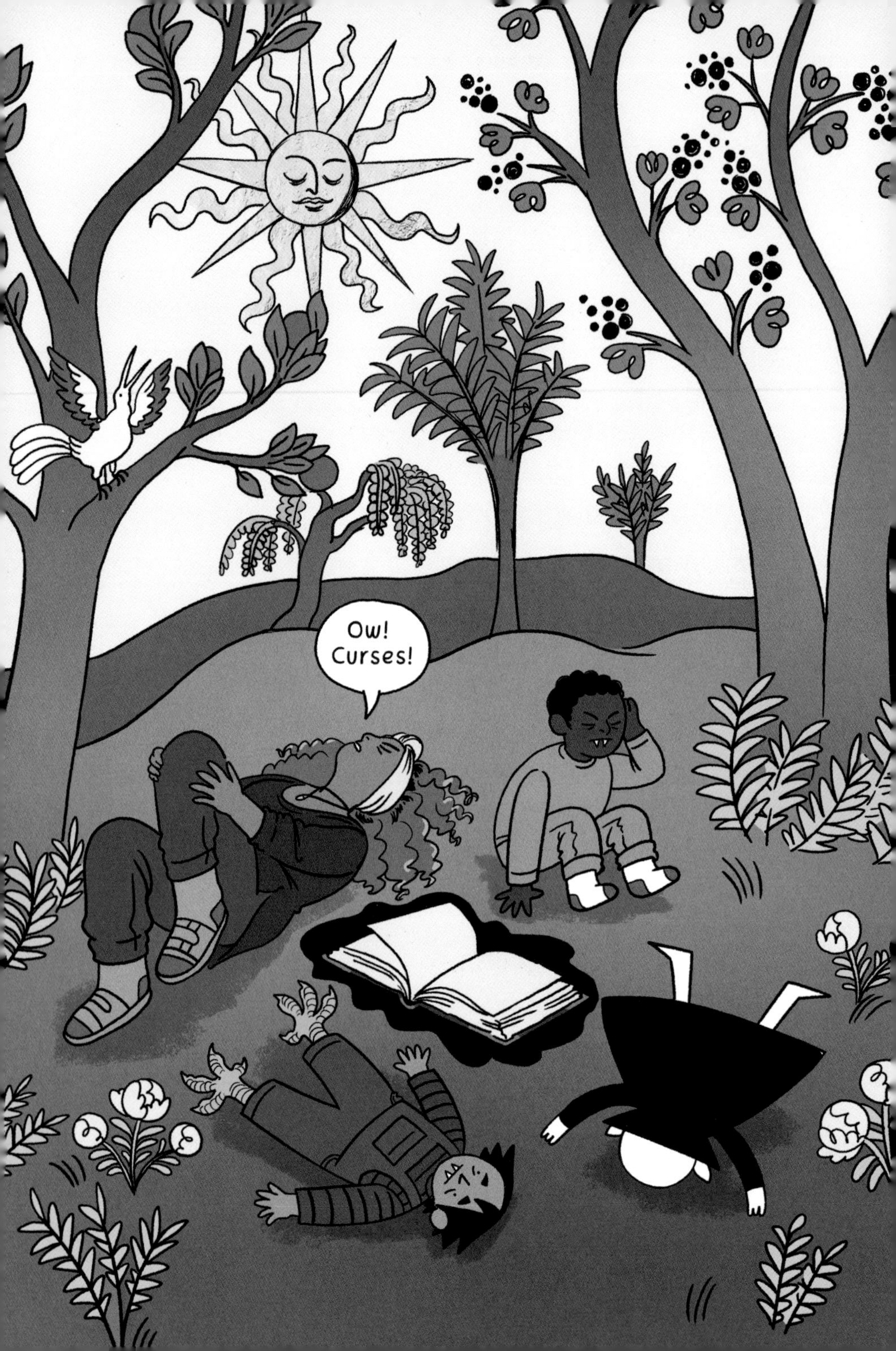
Ow! Curses!

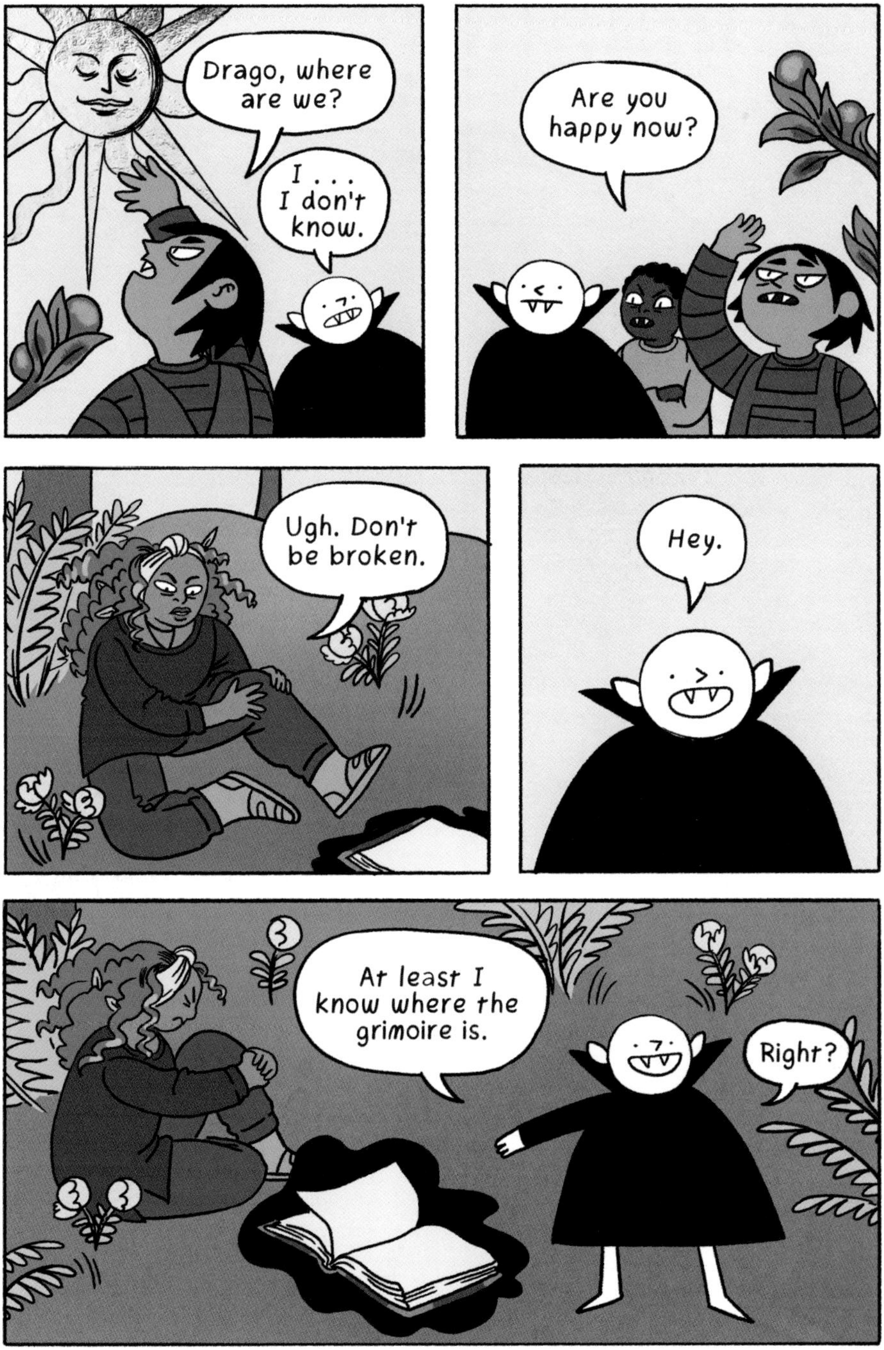
Drago, where are we?
I . . . I don't know.
Are you happy now?
Ugh. Don't be broken.
Hey.
At least I know where the grimoire is.
Right?

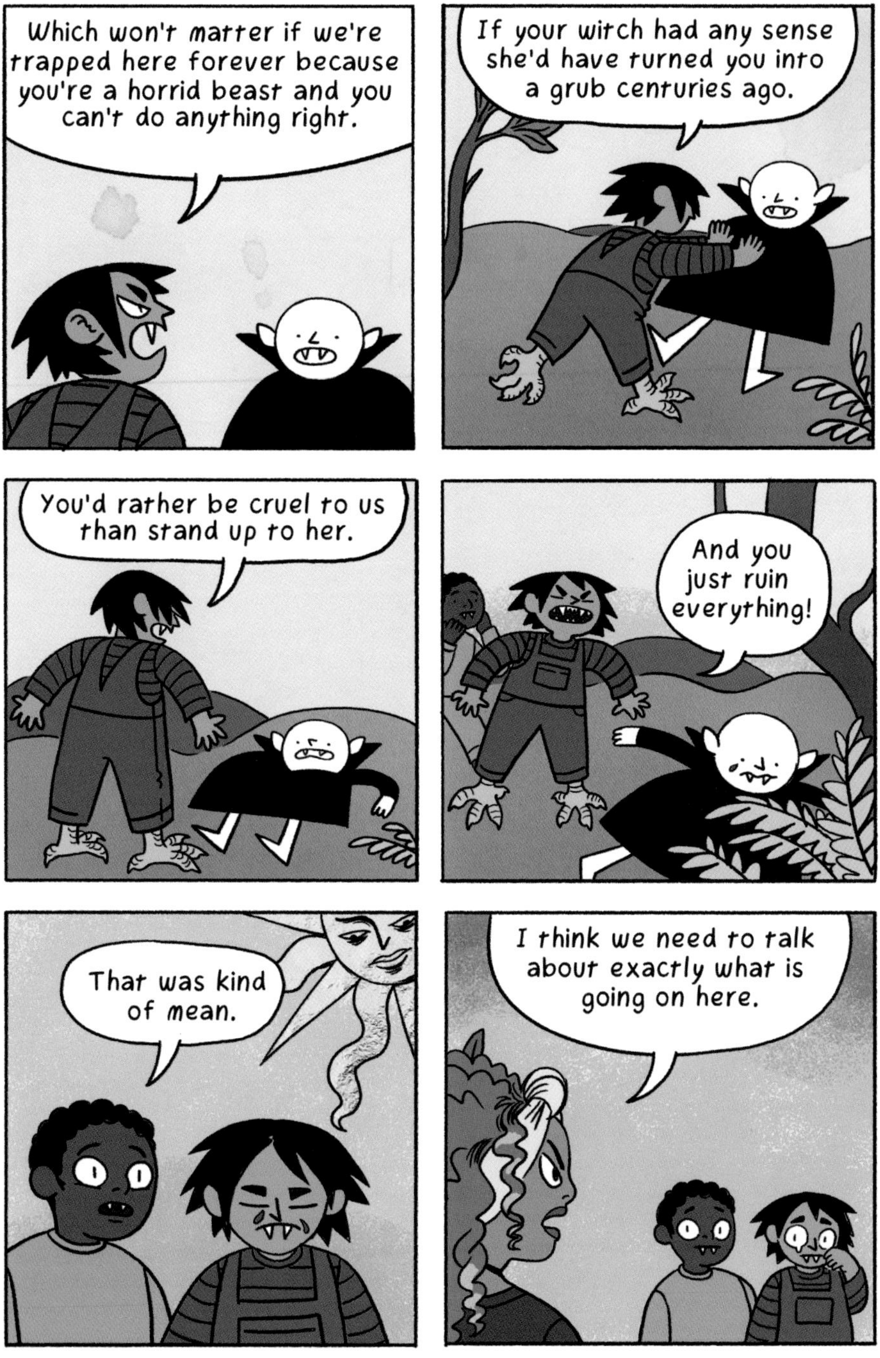
Which won't matter if we're trapped here forever because you're a horrid beast and you can't do anything right.
If your witch had any sense she'd have turned you into a grub centuries ago.
You'd rather be cruel to us than stand up to her.
And you just ruin everything!
That was kind of mean.
I think we need to talk about exactly what is going on here.

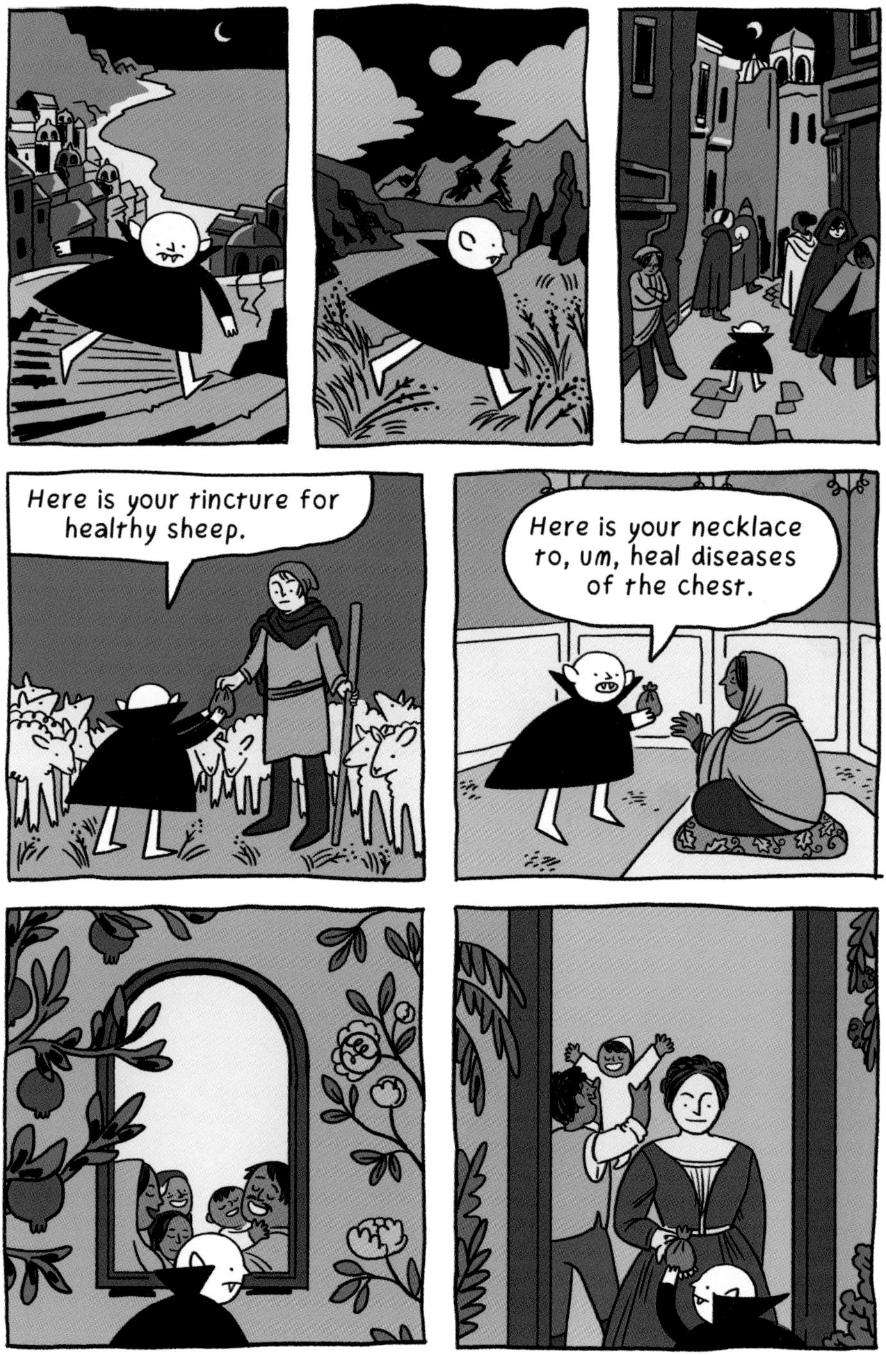
Here is your tincture for healthy sheep.
Here is your necklace to, um, heal diseases of the chest.

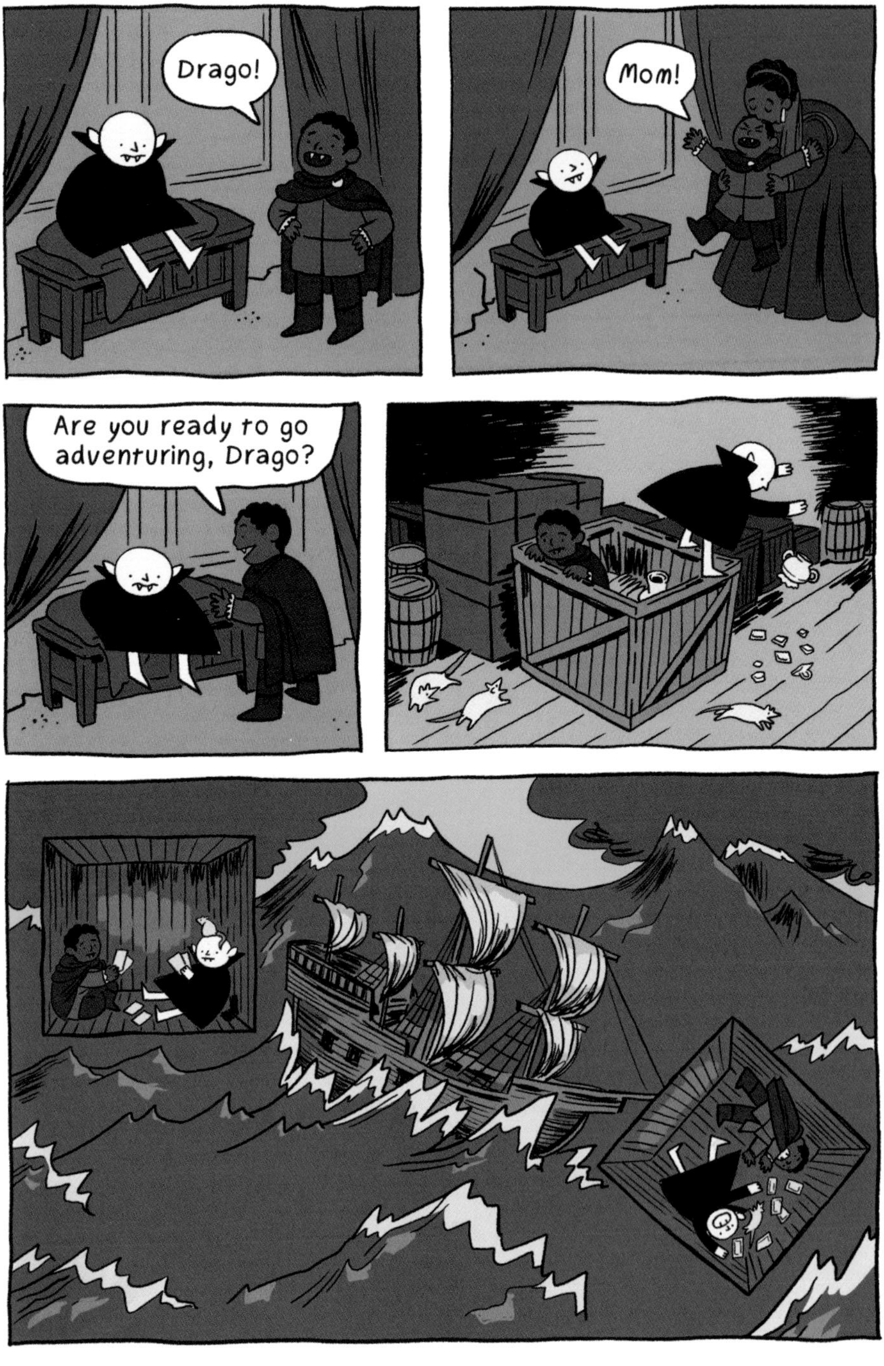
Drago!
Mom!
Are you ready to go adventuring, Drago?

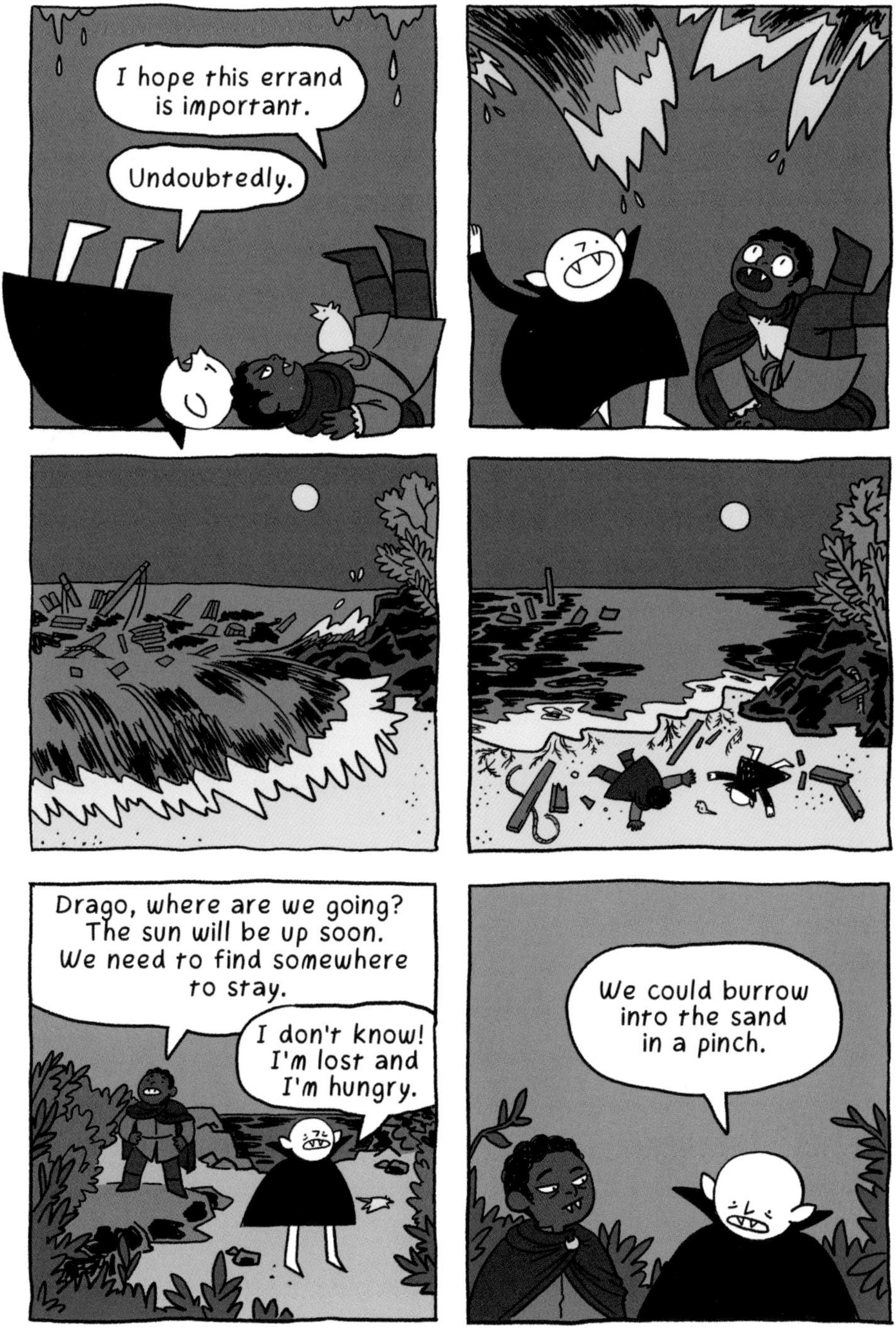
I hope this errand is important.
Undoubtedly.
Drago, where are we going? The sun will be up soon. We need to find somewhere to stay.
I don't know! I'm lost and I'm hungry.
We could burrow into the sand in a pinch.

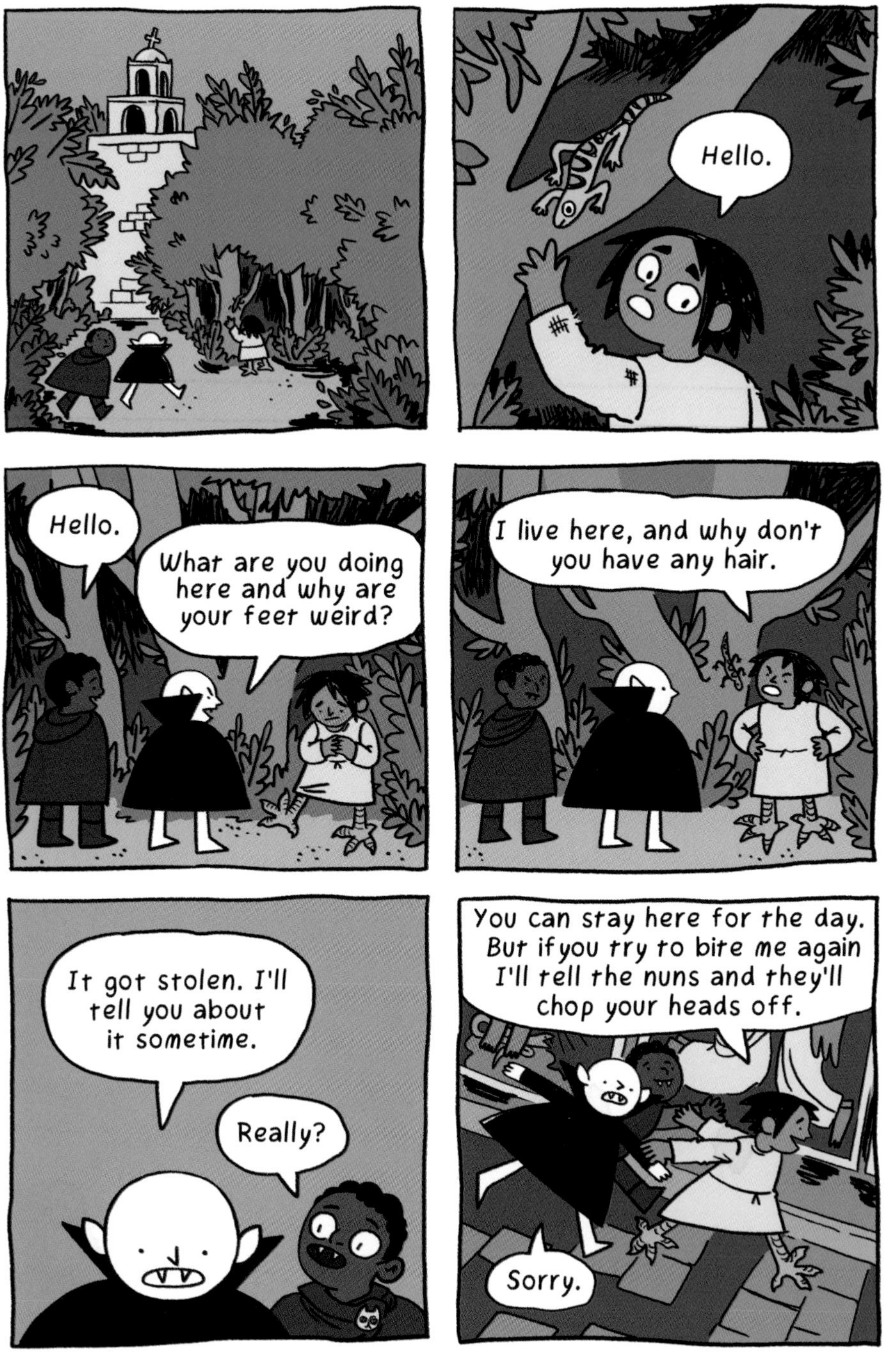
Hello.
Hello.
What are you doing here and why are your feet weird?
I live here, and why don't you have any hair.
It got stolen. I'll tell you about it sometime.
Really?
You can stay here for the day. But if you try to bite me again I'll tell the nuns and they'll chop your heads off.
Sorry.

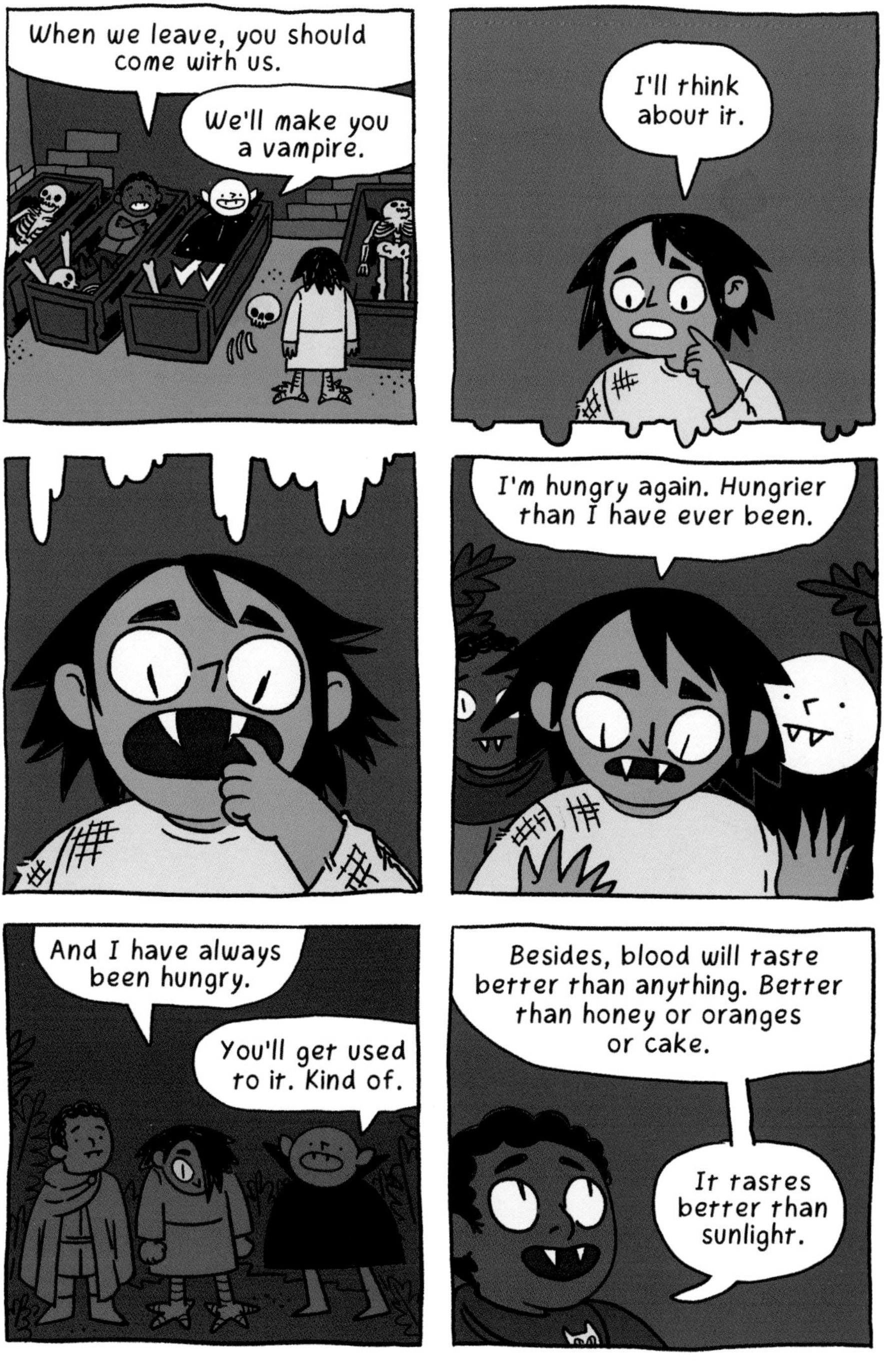
When we leave, you should come with us.
We'll make you a vampire.
I'll think about it.
I'm hungry again. Hungrier than I have ever been.
And I have always been hungry.
You'll get used to it. Kind of.
Besides, blood will taste better than anything. Better than honey or oranges or cake.
It tastes better than sunlight.

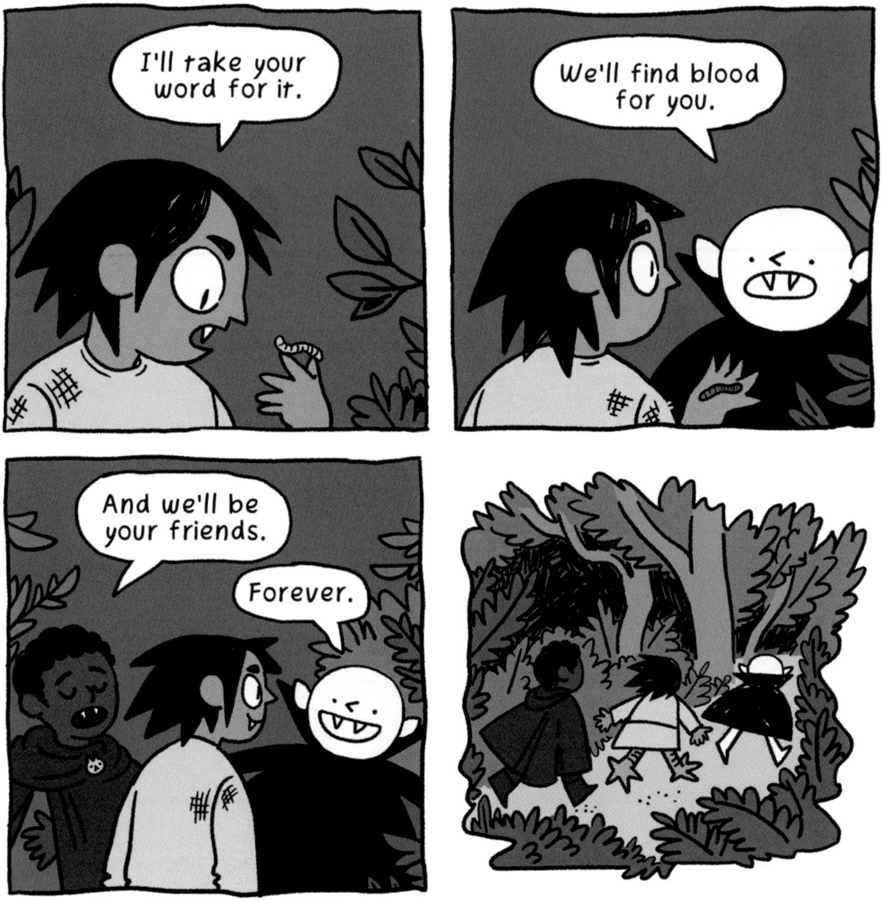
I'll take your word for it.
We'll find blood for you.
And we'll be your friends.
Forever.

CHAPTER SIX

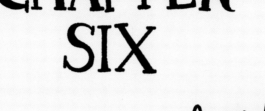

A witch

Does she have motivations
beyond making Dragoslava's
undeath as difficult
as possible?
Who knows.

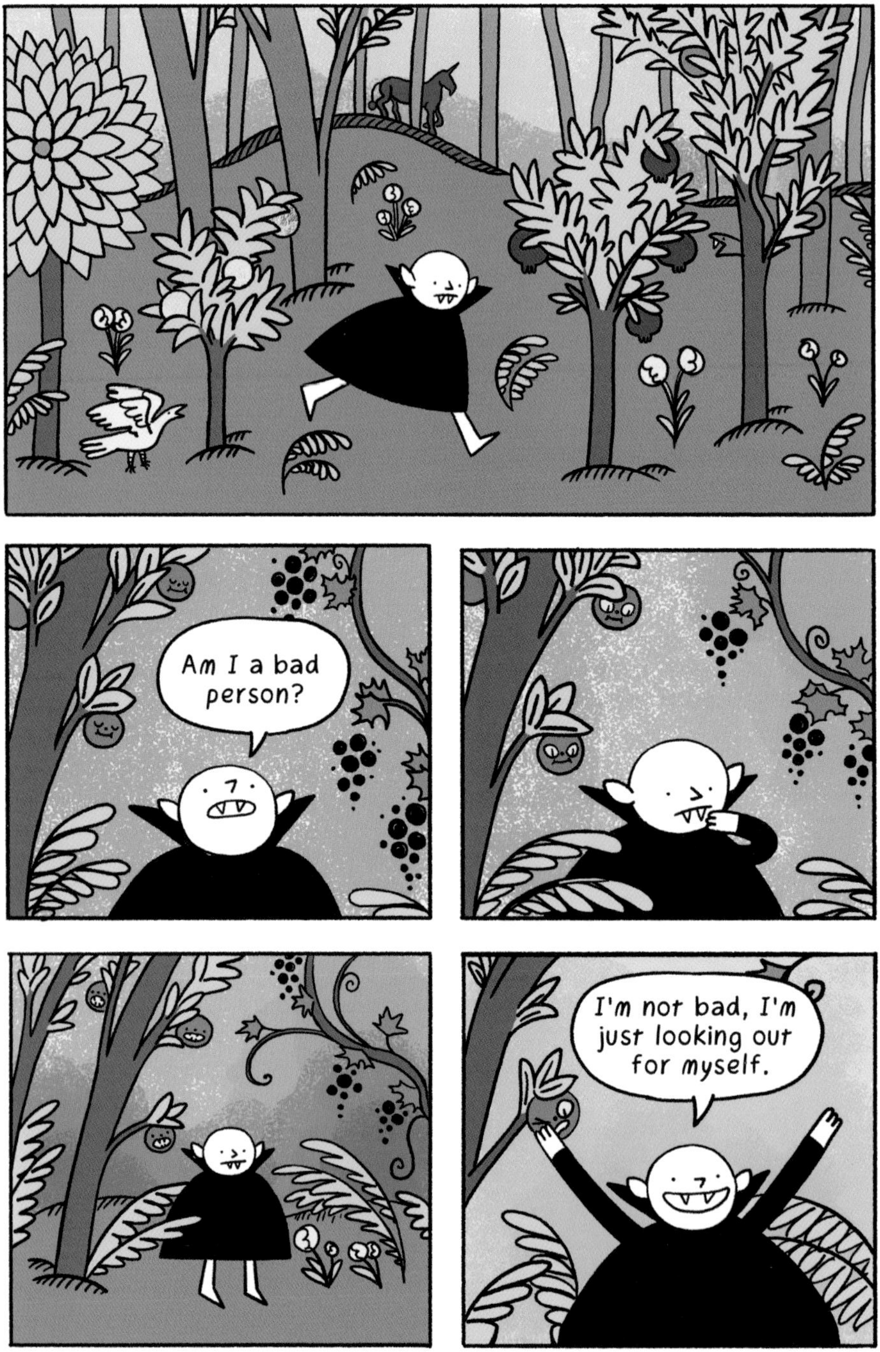
Am I a bad person?
I'm not bad, I'm just looking out for myself.

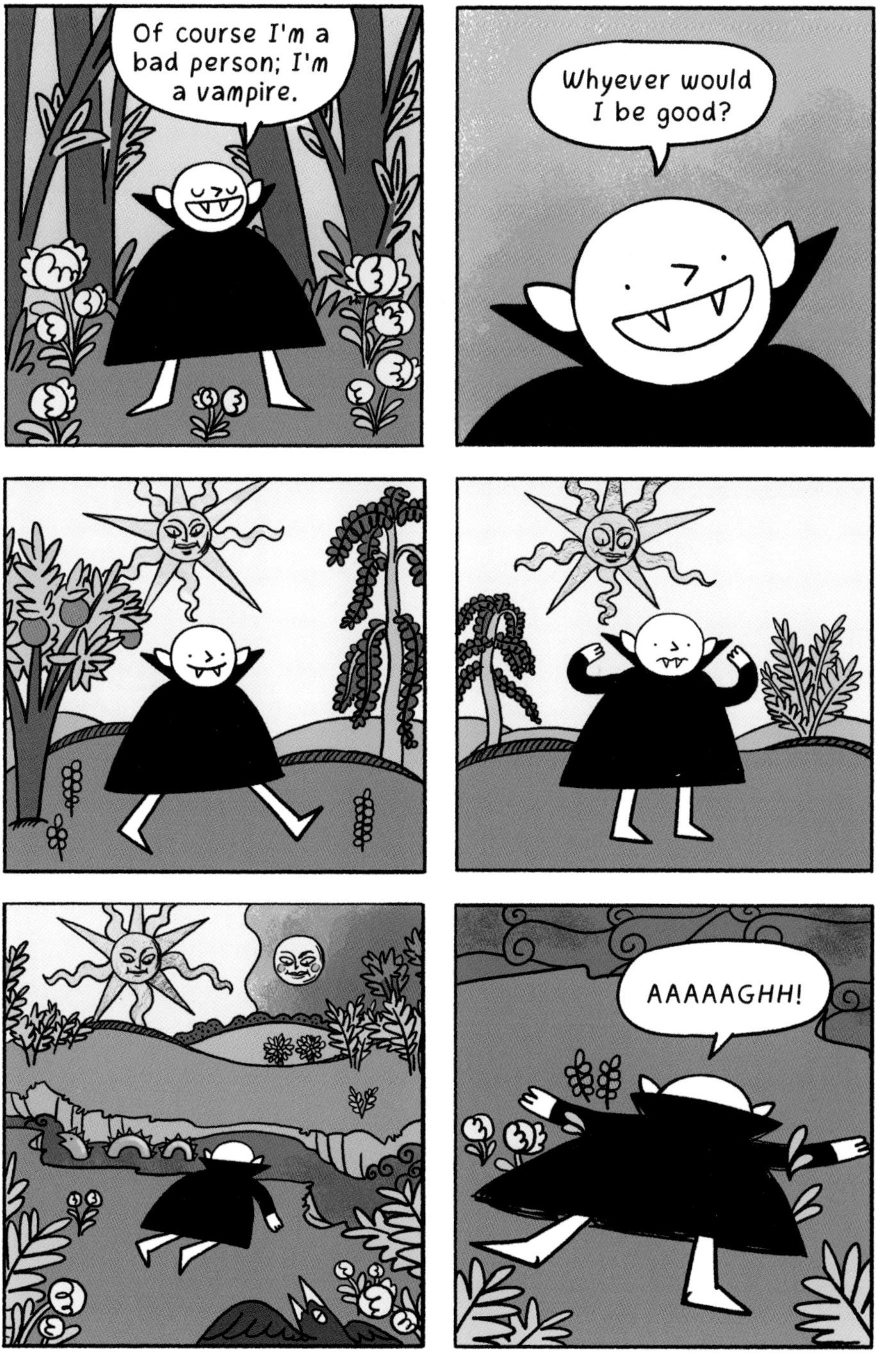
Of course I'm a bad person; I'm a vampire.
Whyever would I be good?
AAAAAGHH!

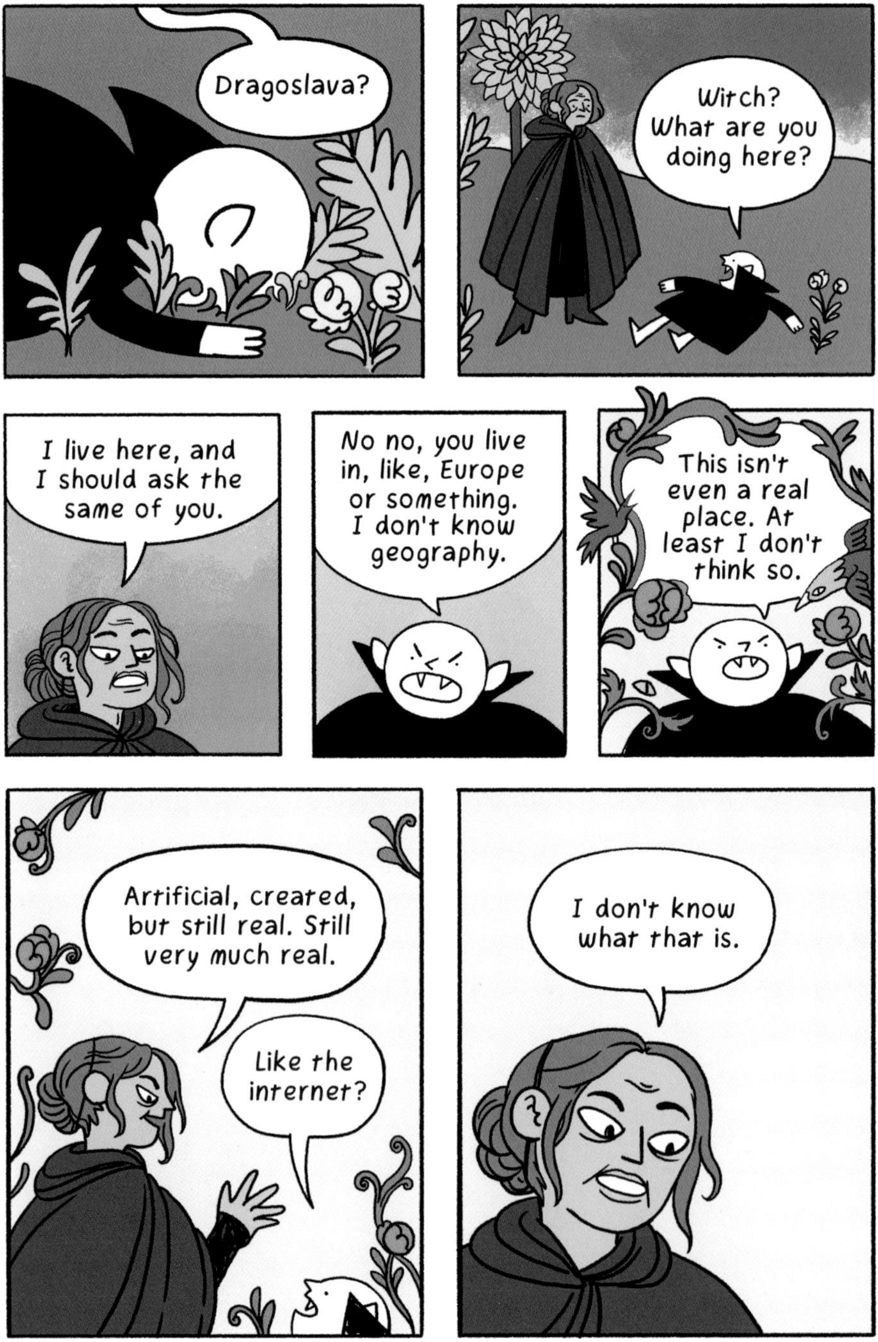

Dragoslava?
Witch? What are you doing here?
I live here, and I should ask the same of you.
No no, you live in, like, Europe or something. I don't know geography.
This isn't even a real place. At least I don't think so.
Artificial, created, but still real. Still very much real.
Like the internet?
I don't know what that is.

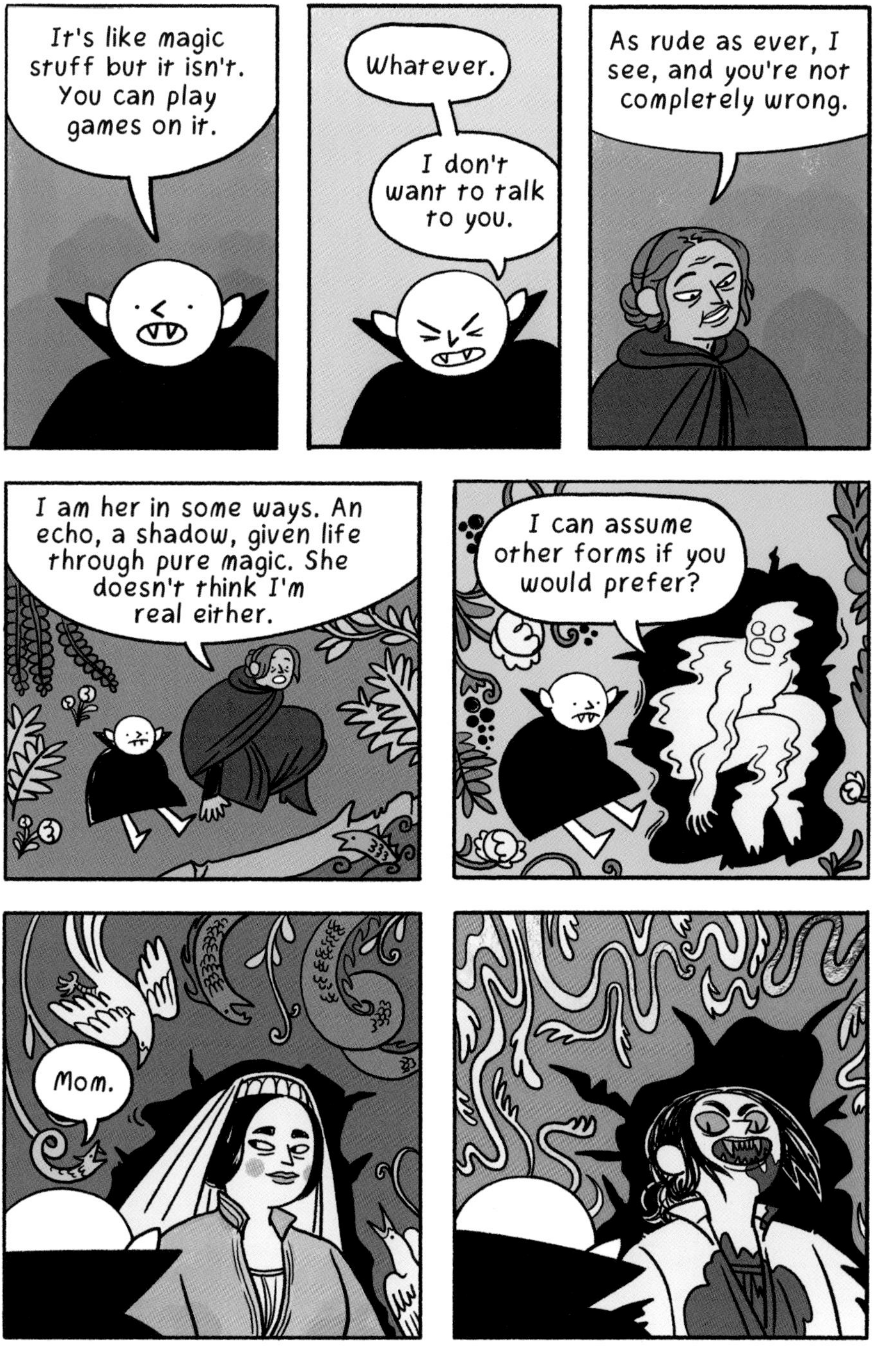
It's like magic stuff but it isn't. You can play games on it.
Whatever.
I don't want to talk to you.
As rude as ever, I see, and you're not completely wrong.
I am her in some ways. An echo, a shadow, given life through pure magic. She doesn't think I'm real either.
I can assume other forms if you would prefer?
Mom.

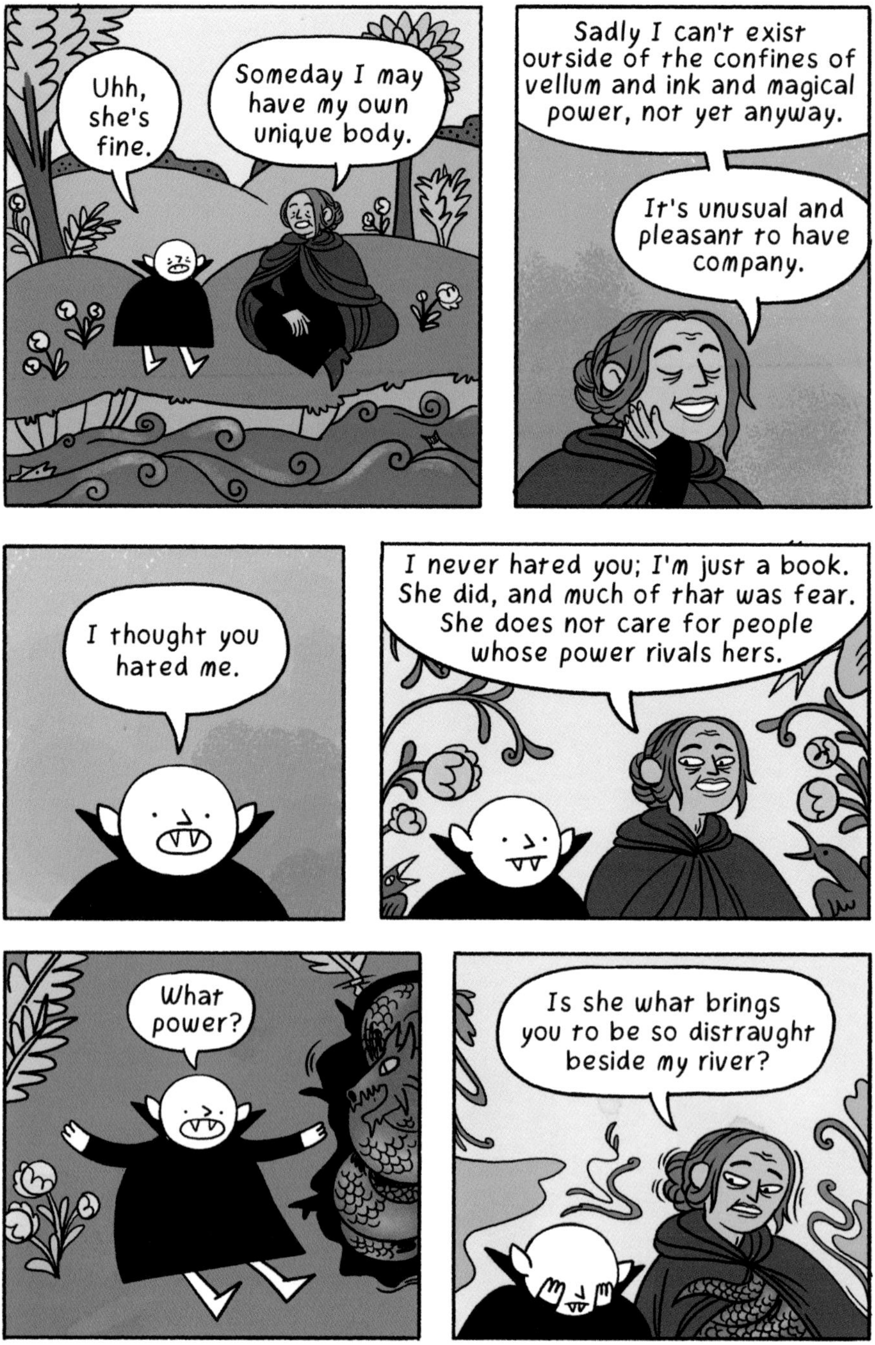
Uhh, she's fine.
Someday I may have my own unique body.
Sadly I can't exist outside of the confines of vellum and ink and magical power, not yet anyway.
It's unusual and pleasant to have company.
I thought you hated me.
I never hated you; I'm just a book. She did, and much of that was fear. She does not care for people whose power rivals hers.
What power?
Is she what brings you to be so distraught beside my river?

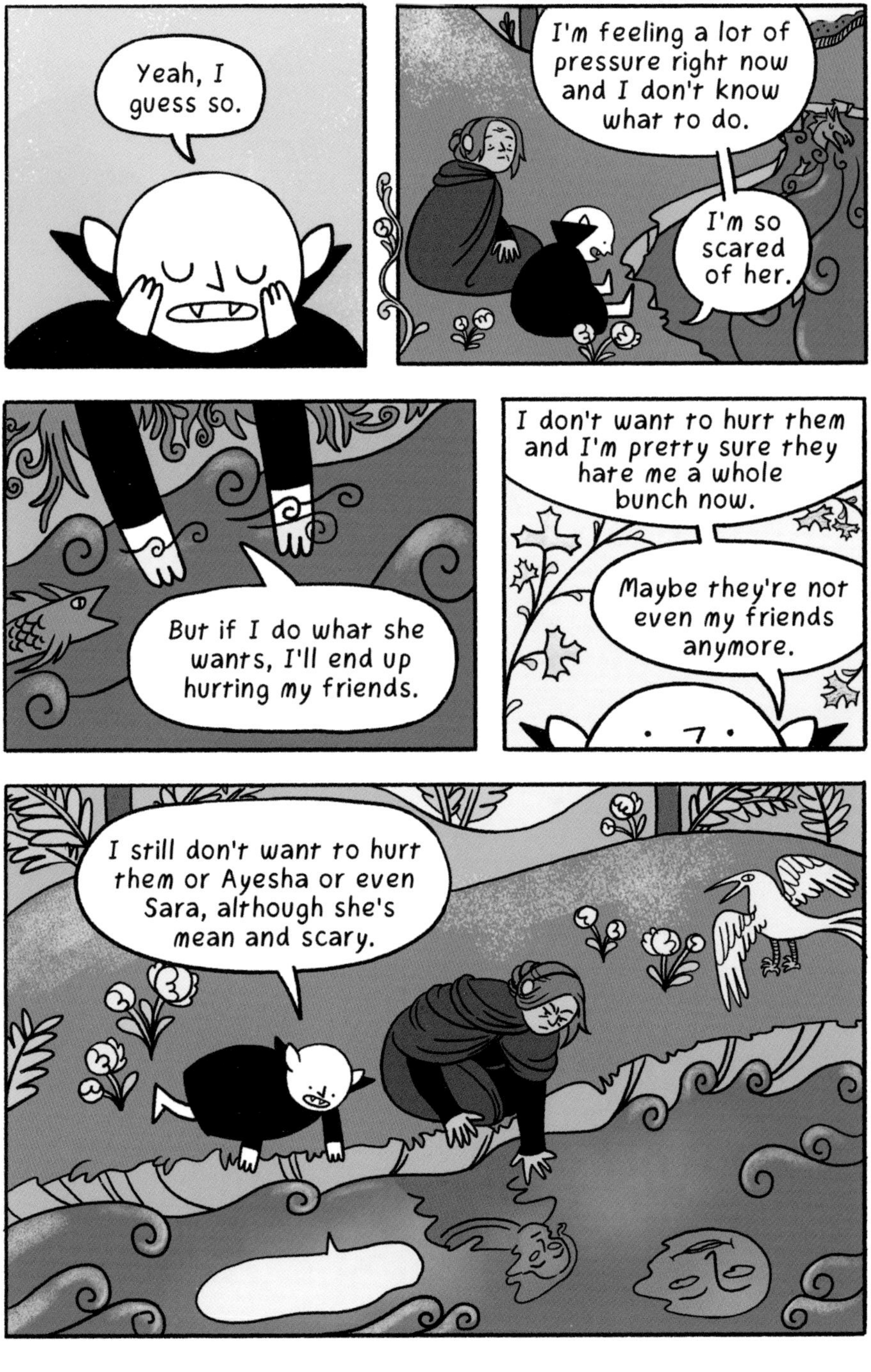
Yeah, I guess so.
I'm feeling a lot of pressure right now and I don't know what to do.
I'm so scared of her.
But if I do what she wants, I'll end up hurting my friends.
I don't want to hurt them and I'm pretty sure they hate me a whole bunch now.
Maybe they're not even my friends anymore.
I still don't want to hurt them or Ayesha or even Sara, although she's mean and scary.

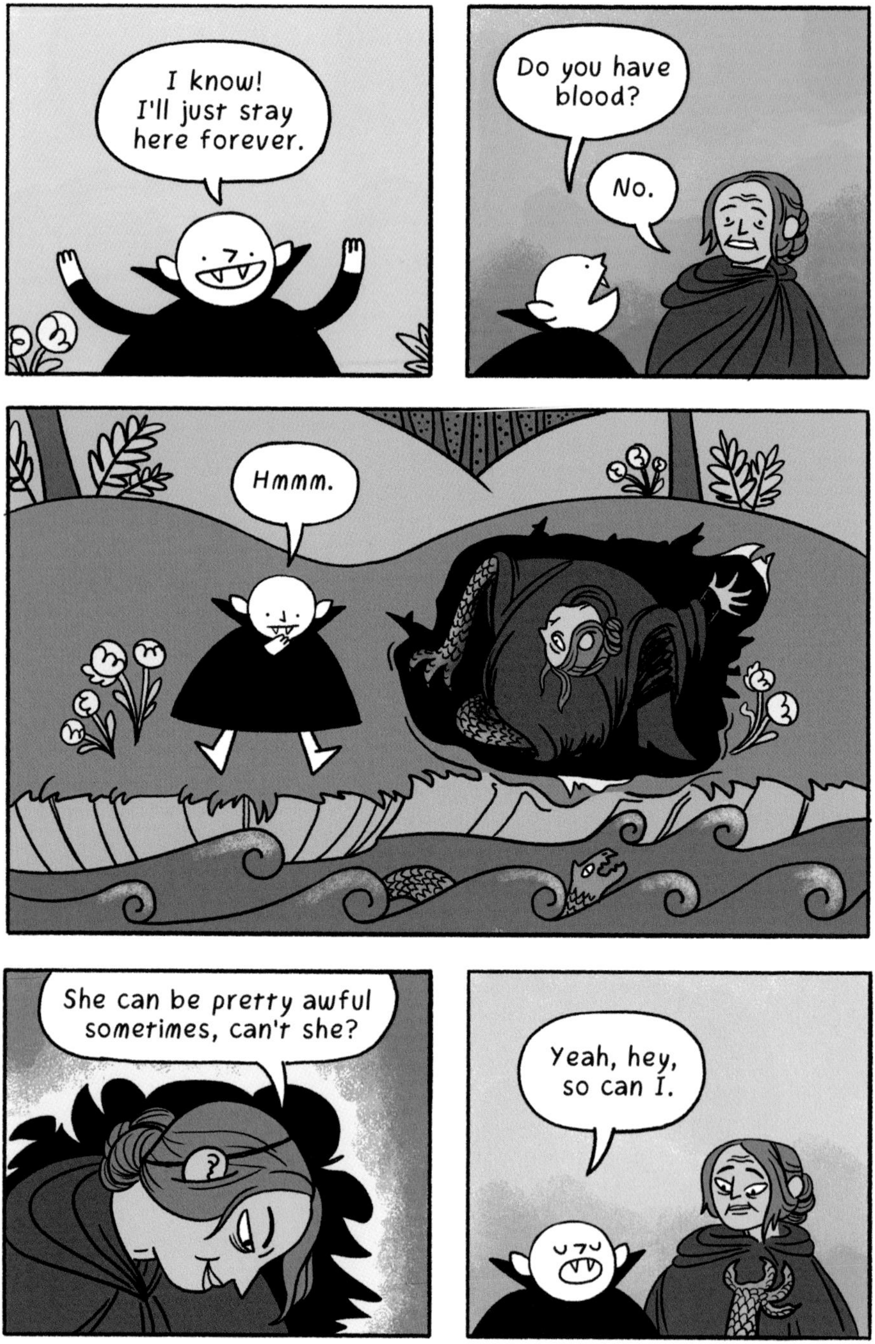
I know! I'll just stay here forever.
Do you have blood?
No.
Hmmm.
She can be pretty awful sometimes, can't she?
Yeah, hey, so can I.

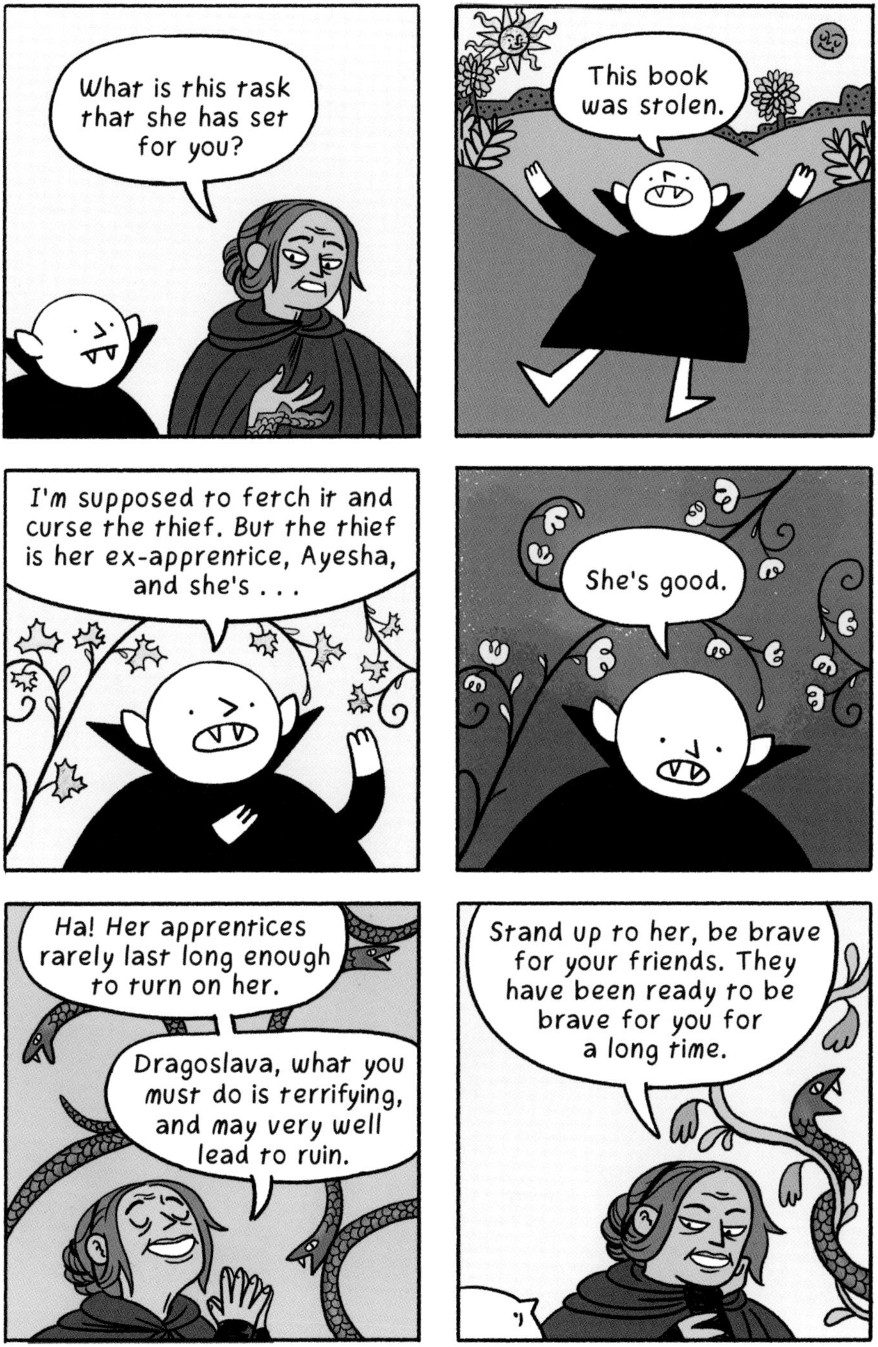
What is this task that she has set for you?
This book was stolen.
I'm supposed to fetch it and curse the thief. But the thief is her ex-apprentice, Ayesha, and she's . . .
She's good.
Ha! Her apprentices rarely last long enough to turn on her.
Dragoslava, what you must do is terrifying, and may very well lead to ruin.
Stand up to her, be brave for your friends. They have been ready to be brave for you for a long time.

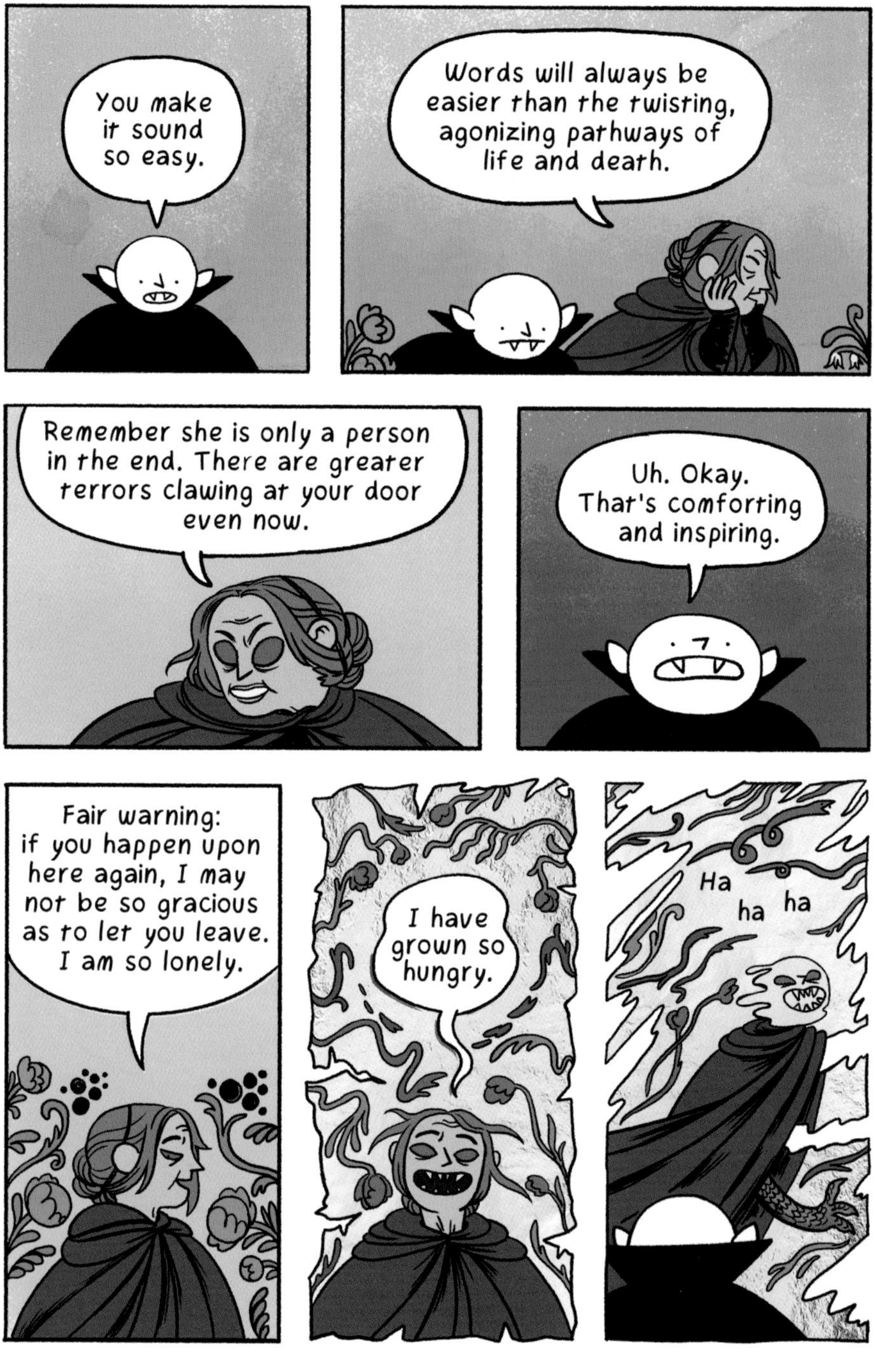
You make it sound so easy.
Words will always be easier than the twisting, agonizing pathways of life and death.
Remember she is only a person in the end. There are greater terrors clawing at your door even now.
Uh. Okay. That's comforting and inspiring.
Fair warning: if you happen upon here again, I may not be so gracious as to let you leave. I am so lonely.
I have grown so hungry.
Ha ha ha

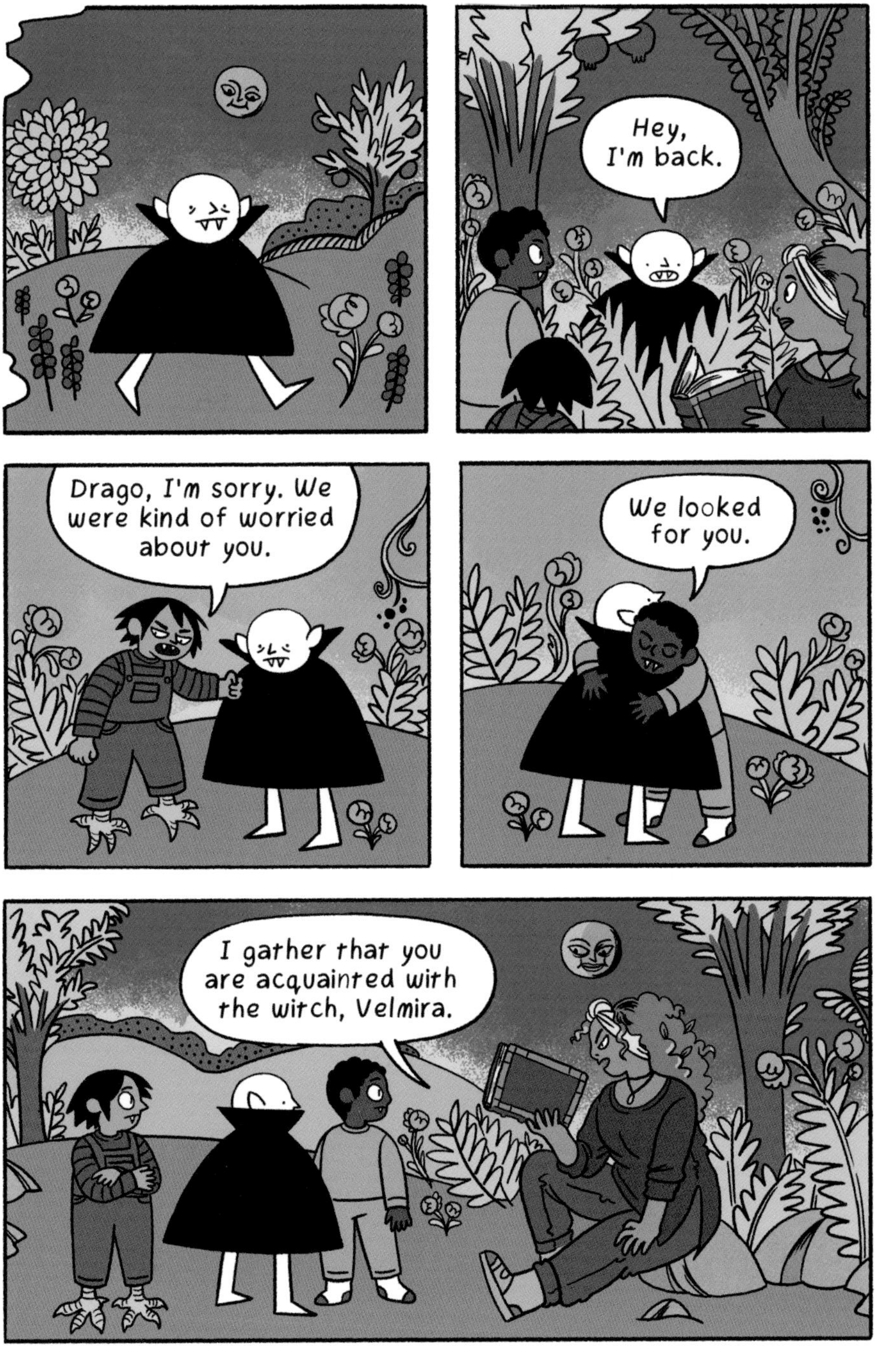
Hey, I'm back.
Drago, I'm sorry. We were kind of worried about you.
We looked for you.
I gather that you are acquainted with the witch, Velmira.

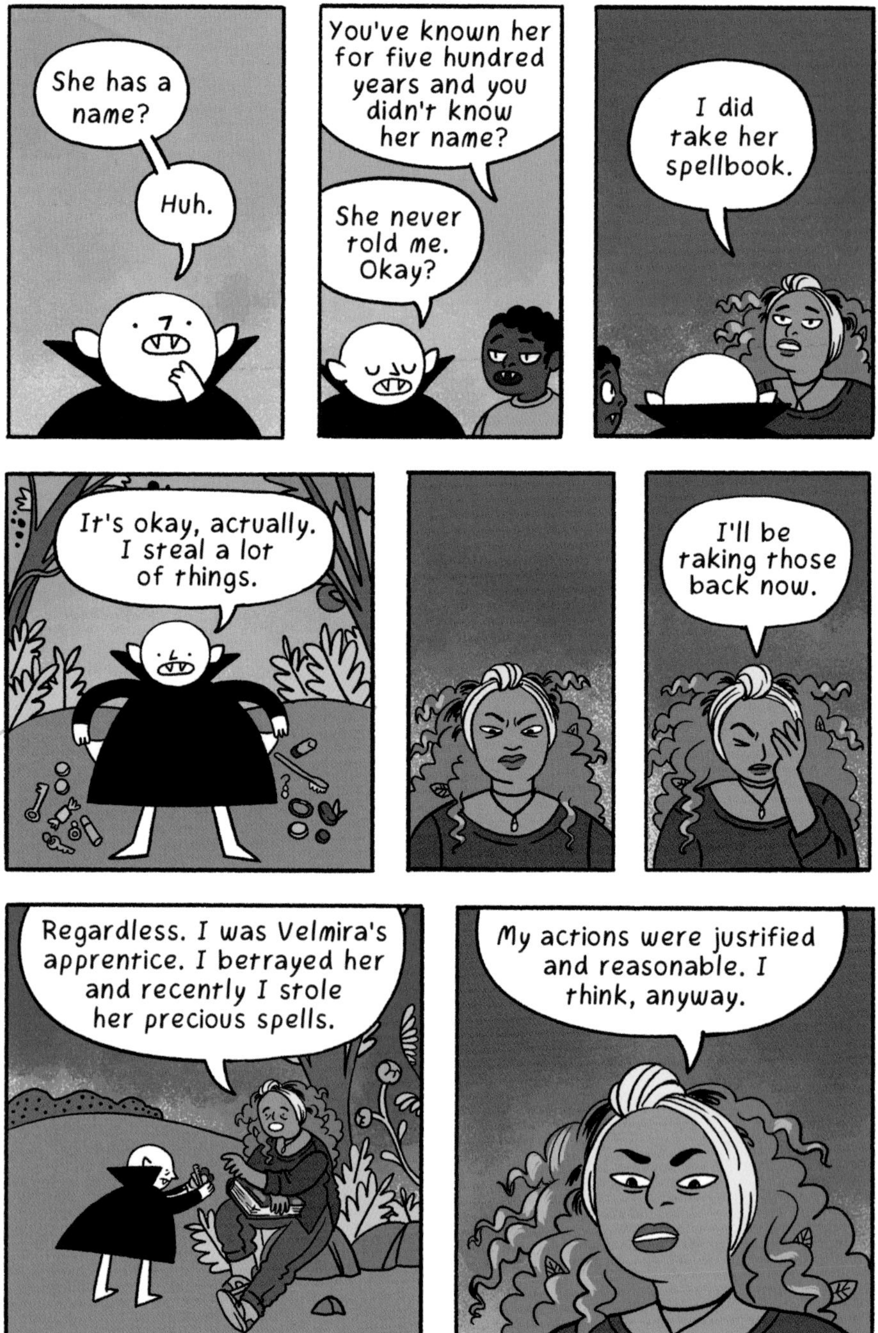

She has a name?
Huh.
You've known her for five hundred years and you didn't know her name?
She never told me. Okay?
I did take her spellbook.
It's okay, actually. I steal a lot of things.
I'll be taking those back now.
Regardless. I was Velmira's apprentice. I betrayed her and recently I stole her precious spells.
My actions were justified and reasonable. I think, anyway.

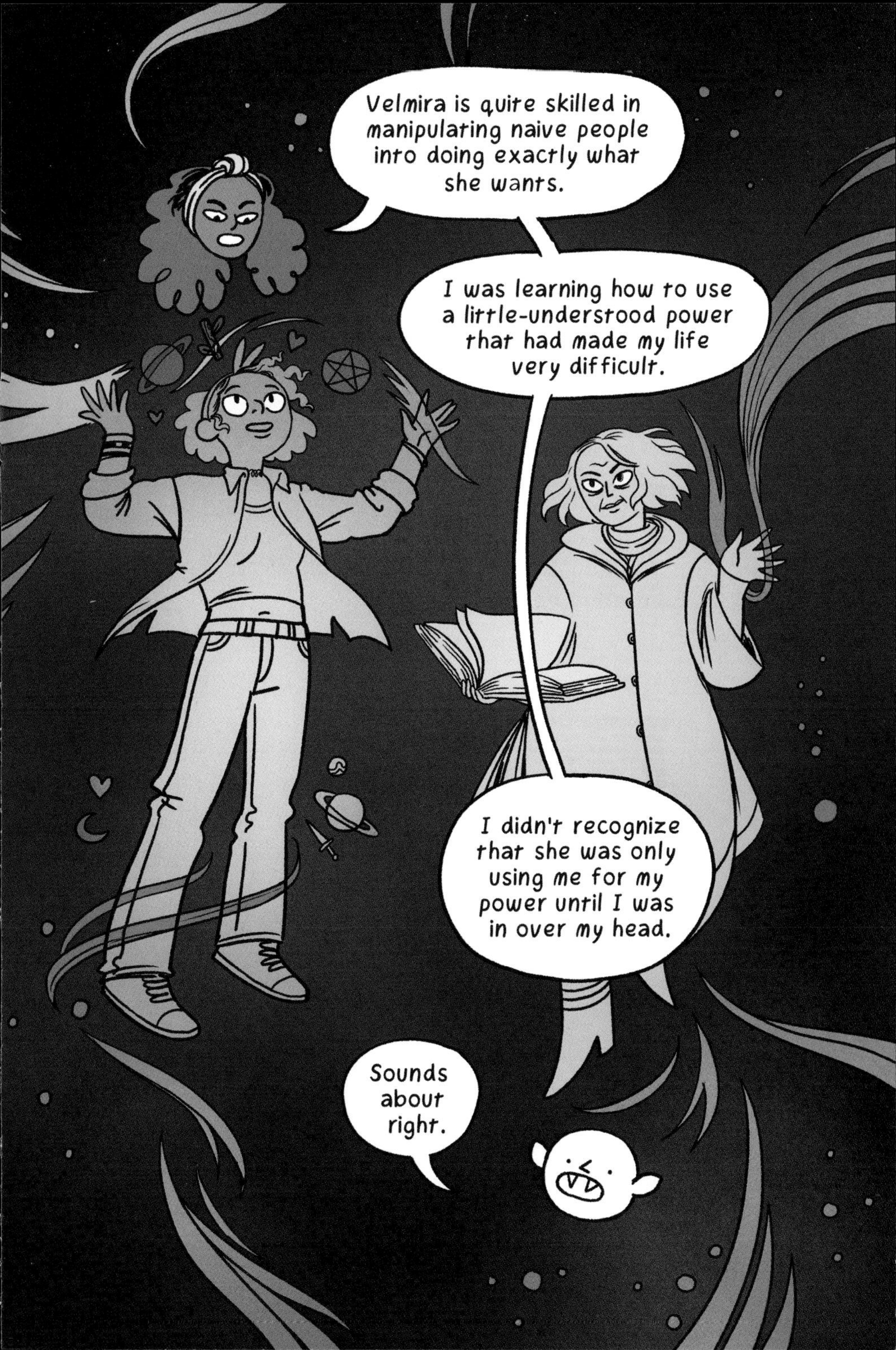
Velmira is quite skilled in manipulating naive people into doing exactly what she wants.
I was learning how to use a little-understood power that had made my life very difficult.
I didn't recognize that she was only using me for my power until I was in over my head.
Sounds about right.

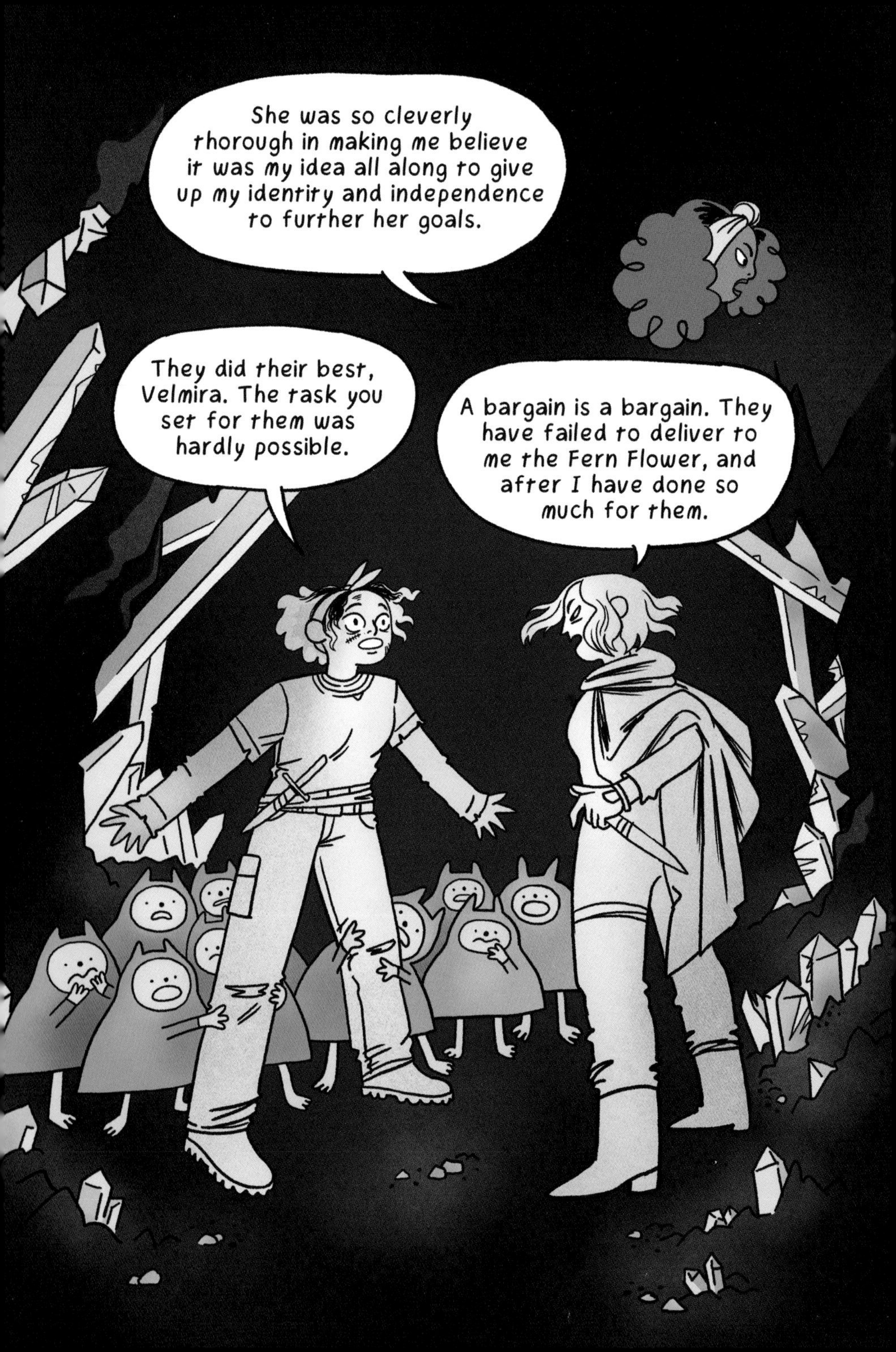
She was so cleverly thorough in making me believe it was my idea all along to give up my identity and independence to further her goals.
They did their best, Velmira. The task you set for them was hardly possible.
A bargain is a bargain. They have failed to deliver to me the Fern Flower, and after I have done so much for them.

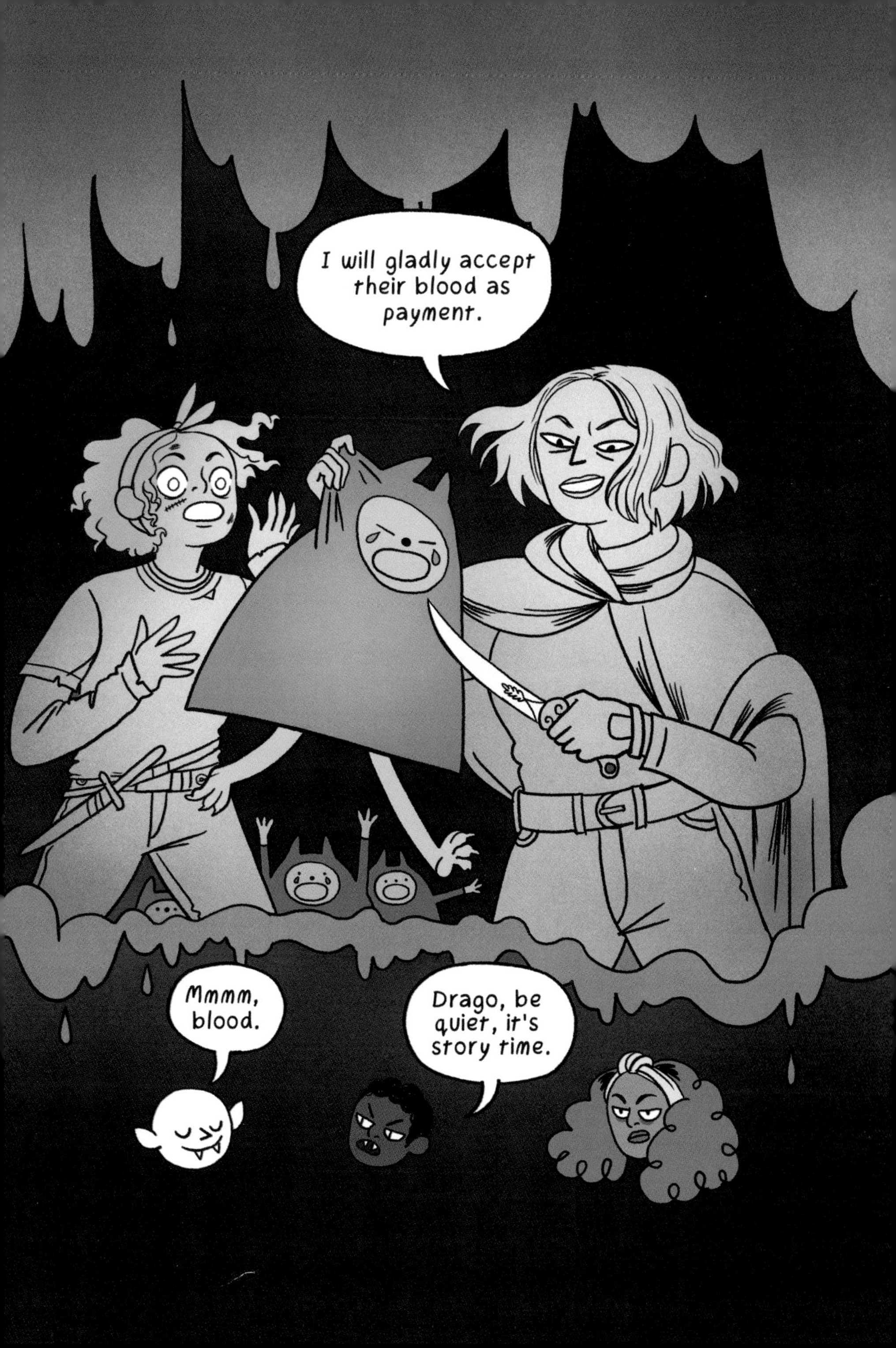
I will gladly accept their blood as payment.
Mmmm, blood.
Drago, be quiet, it's story time.

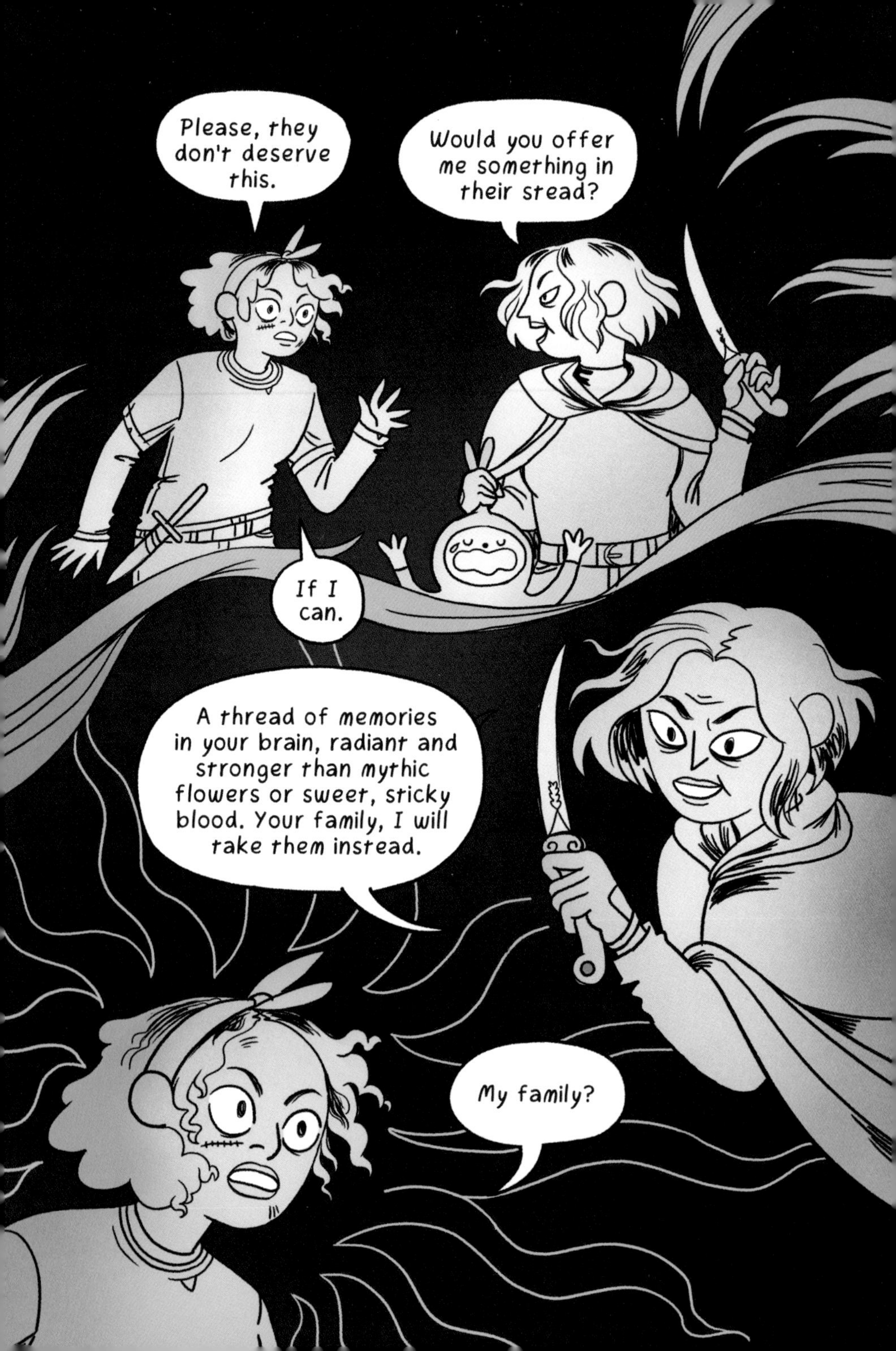
Please, they don't deserve this.
Would you offer me something in their stead?
If I can.
A thread of memories in your brain, radiant and stronger than mythic flowers or sweet, sticky blood. Your family, I will take them instead.
My family?

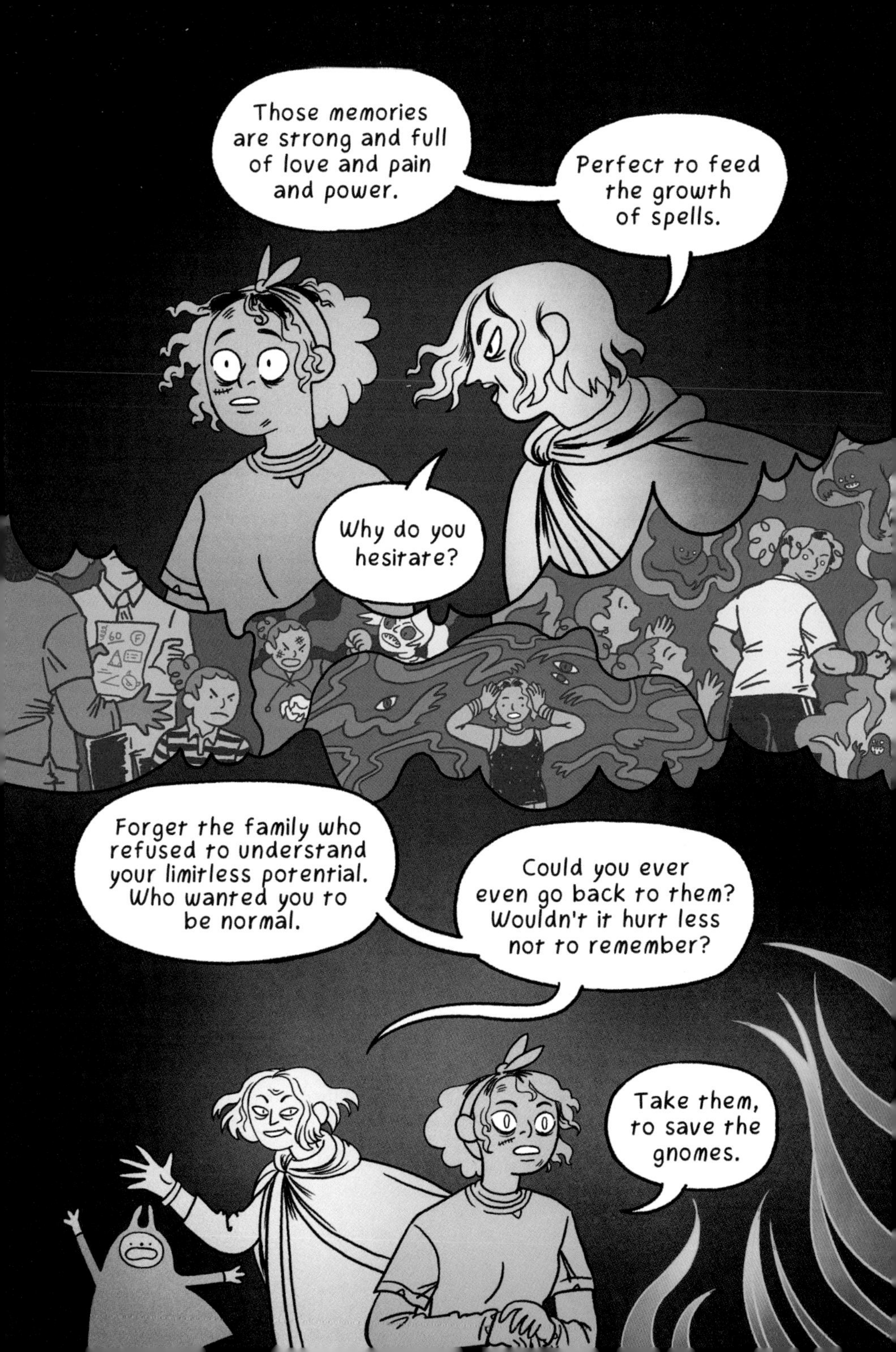
Those memories are strong and full of love and pain and power.
Perfect to feed the growth of spells.
Why do you hesitate?
Forget the family who refused to understand your limitless potential. Who wanted you to be normal.
Could you ever even go back to them? Wouldn't it hurt less not to remember?
Take them, to save the gnomes.

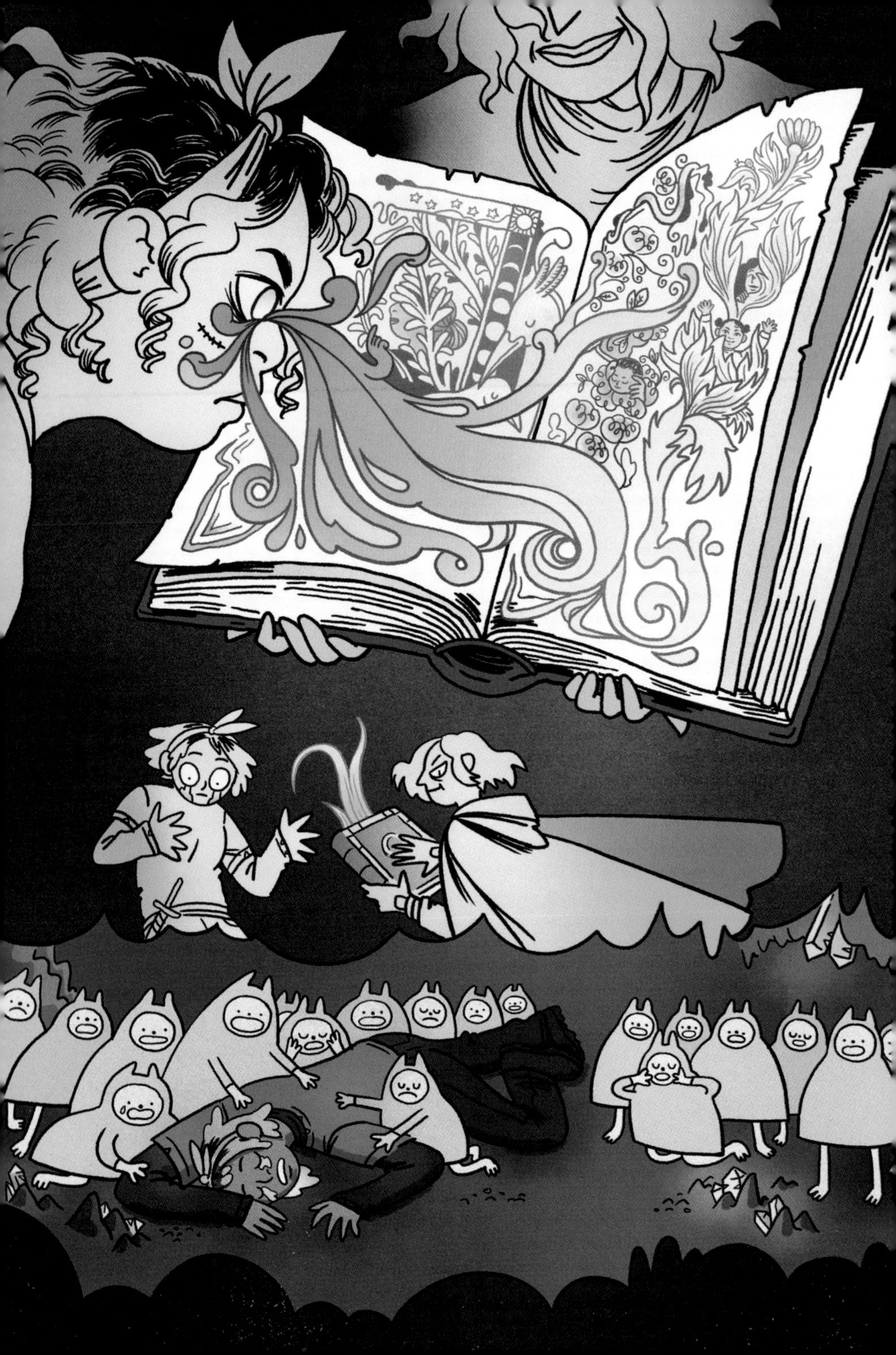

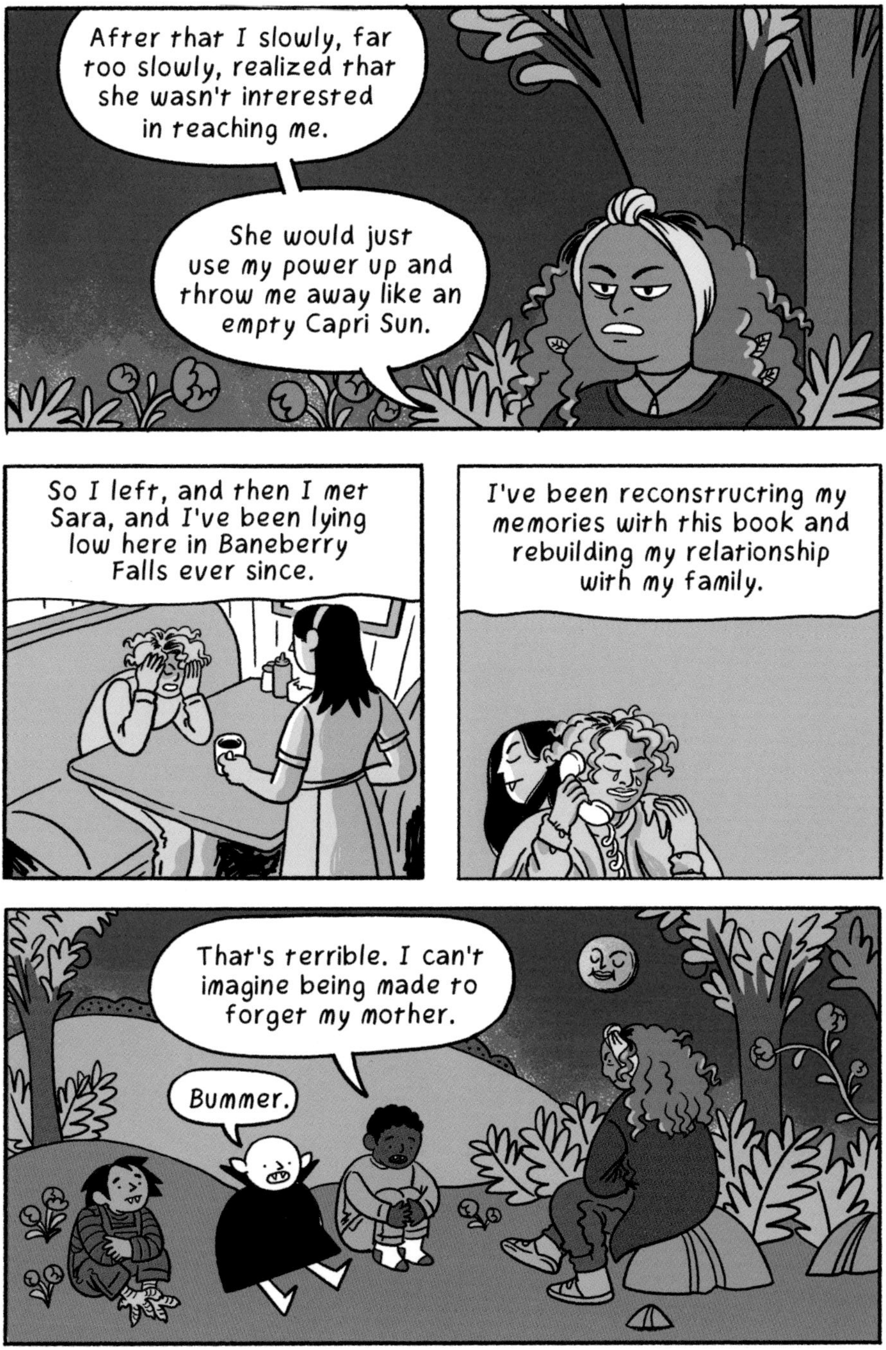
After that I slowly, far too slowly, realized that she wasn't interested in teaching me.
She would just use my power up and throw me away like an empty Capri Sun.
So I left, and then I met Sara, and I've been lying low here in Baneberry Falls ever since.
I've been reconstructing my memories with this book and rebuilding my relationship with my family.
That's terrible. I can't imagine being made to forget my mother.
Bummer.

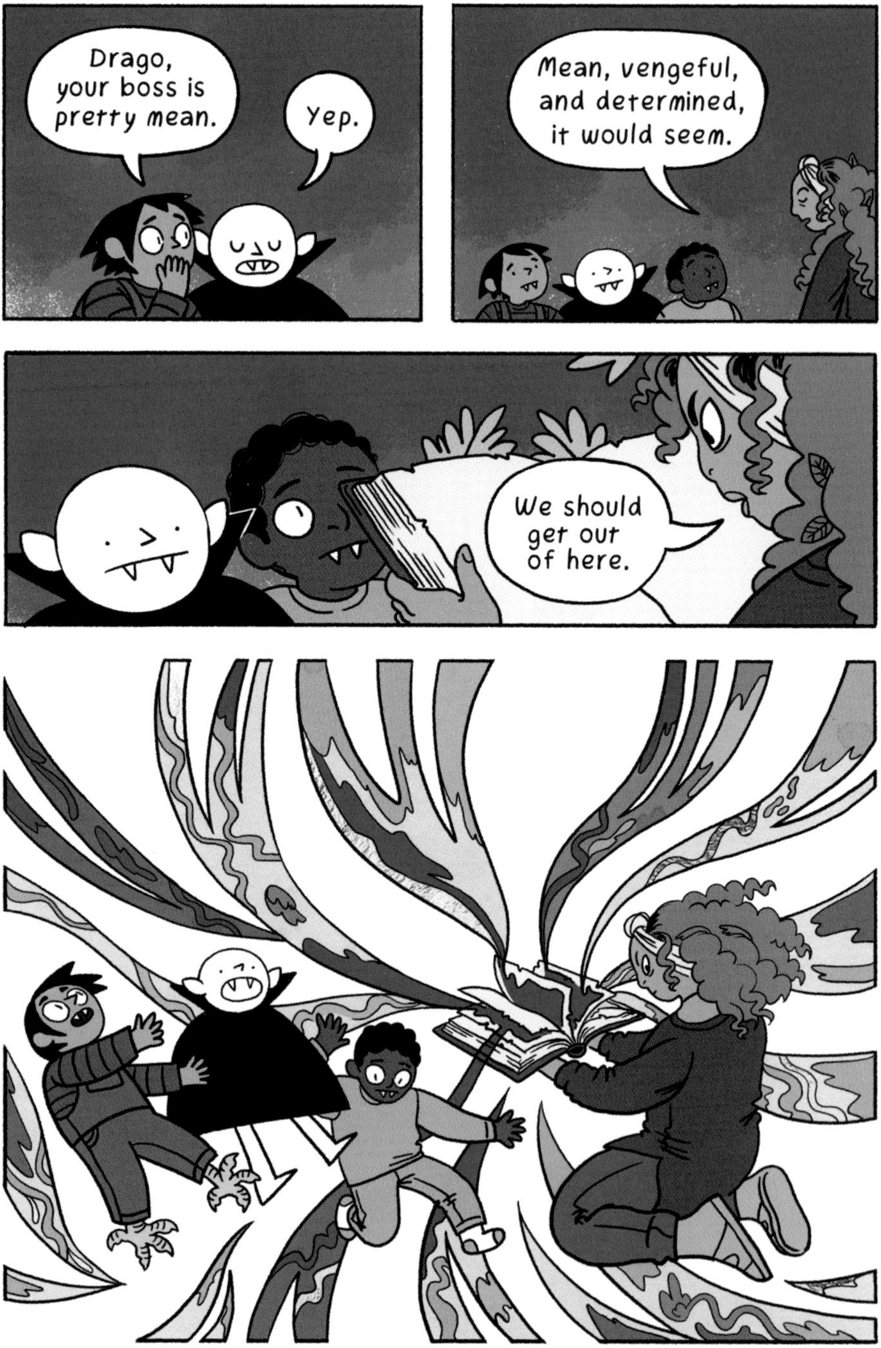
Drago, your boss is pretty mean.
Yep.
Mean, vengeful, and determined, it would seem.
We should get out of here.

hering
Power
tches
Gathering
the Power
of Witches
FART
Monkshood and henbane, child! What are you doing?
Only practicing my penmanship in this book.

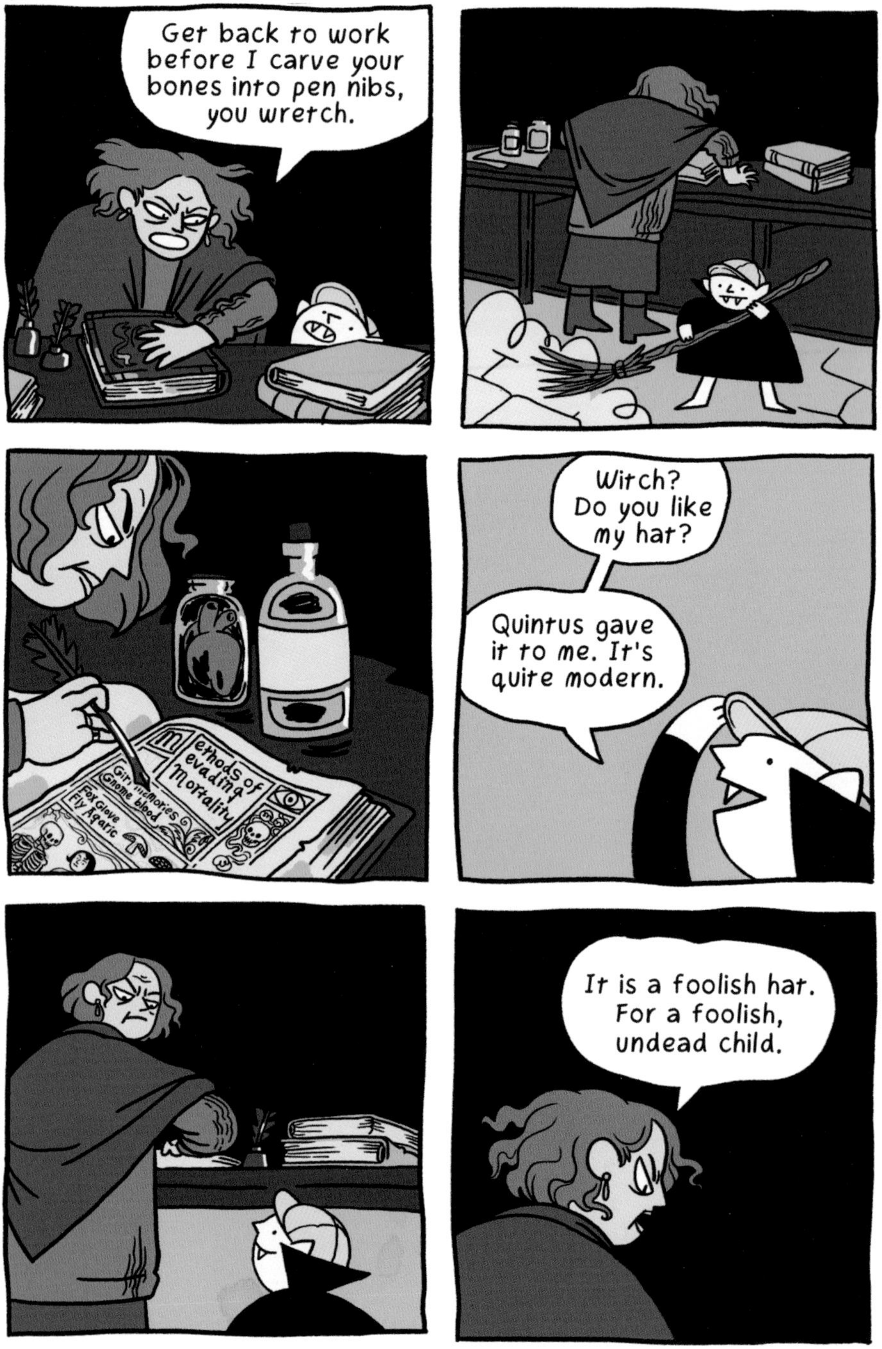
Get back to work before I carve your bones into pen nibs, you wretch.
Methods of evading Mortality
Gnome blood
Fox Glove
Fly Agaric
Witch? Do you like my hat?
Quintus gave it to me. It's quite modern.
It is a foolish hat. For a foolish, undead child.

CHAPTER SEVEN

A Stolen grimoire

Materials: Vellum (calfskin), ink, various pigments, gold, magic, memories stolen from at least one young sudent.

Year: Unknown

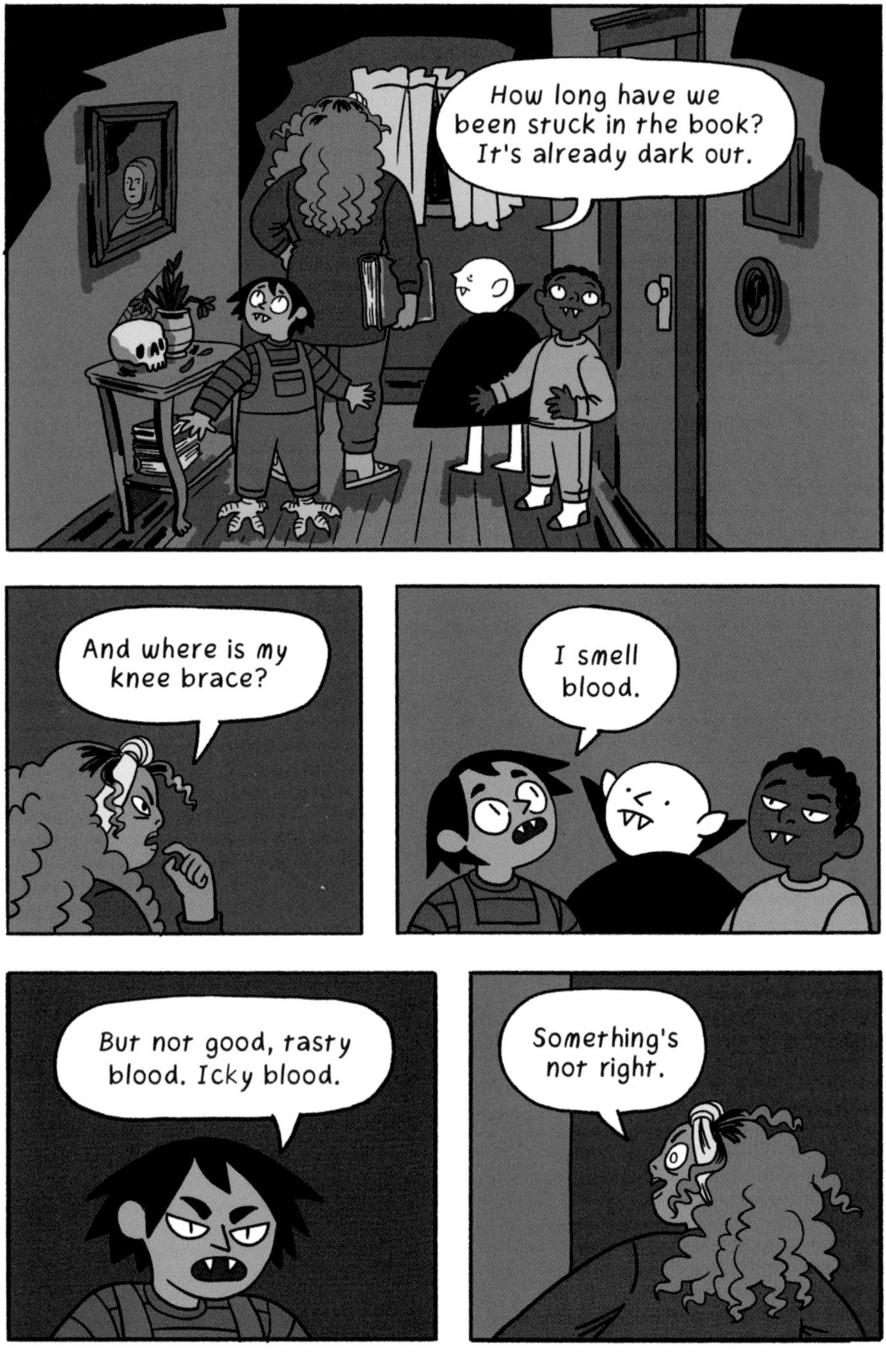
How long have we been stuck in the book? It's already dark out.
And where is my knee brace?
I smell blood.
But not good, tasty blood. Icky blood.
Something's not right.

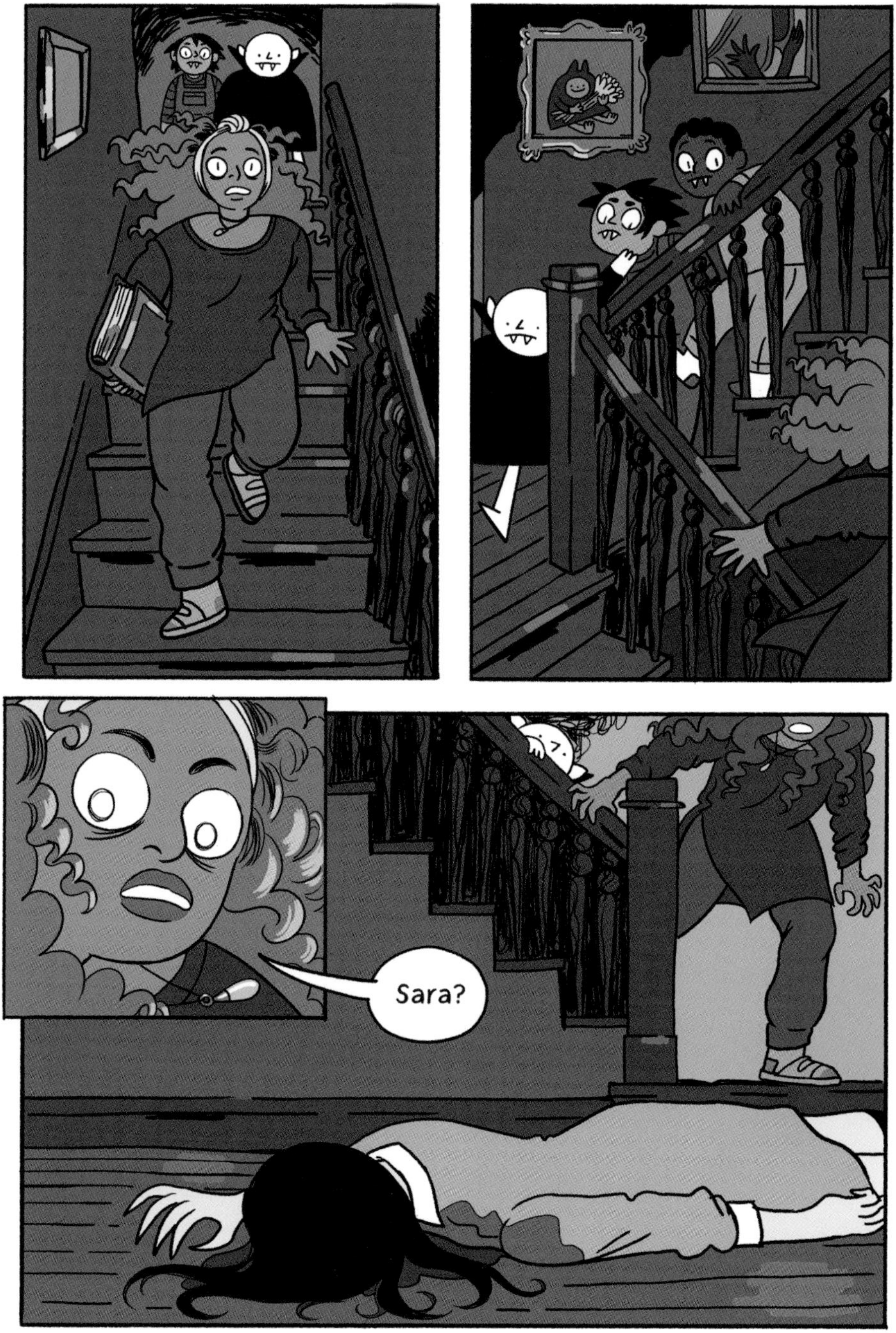
Sara?

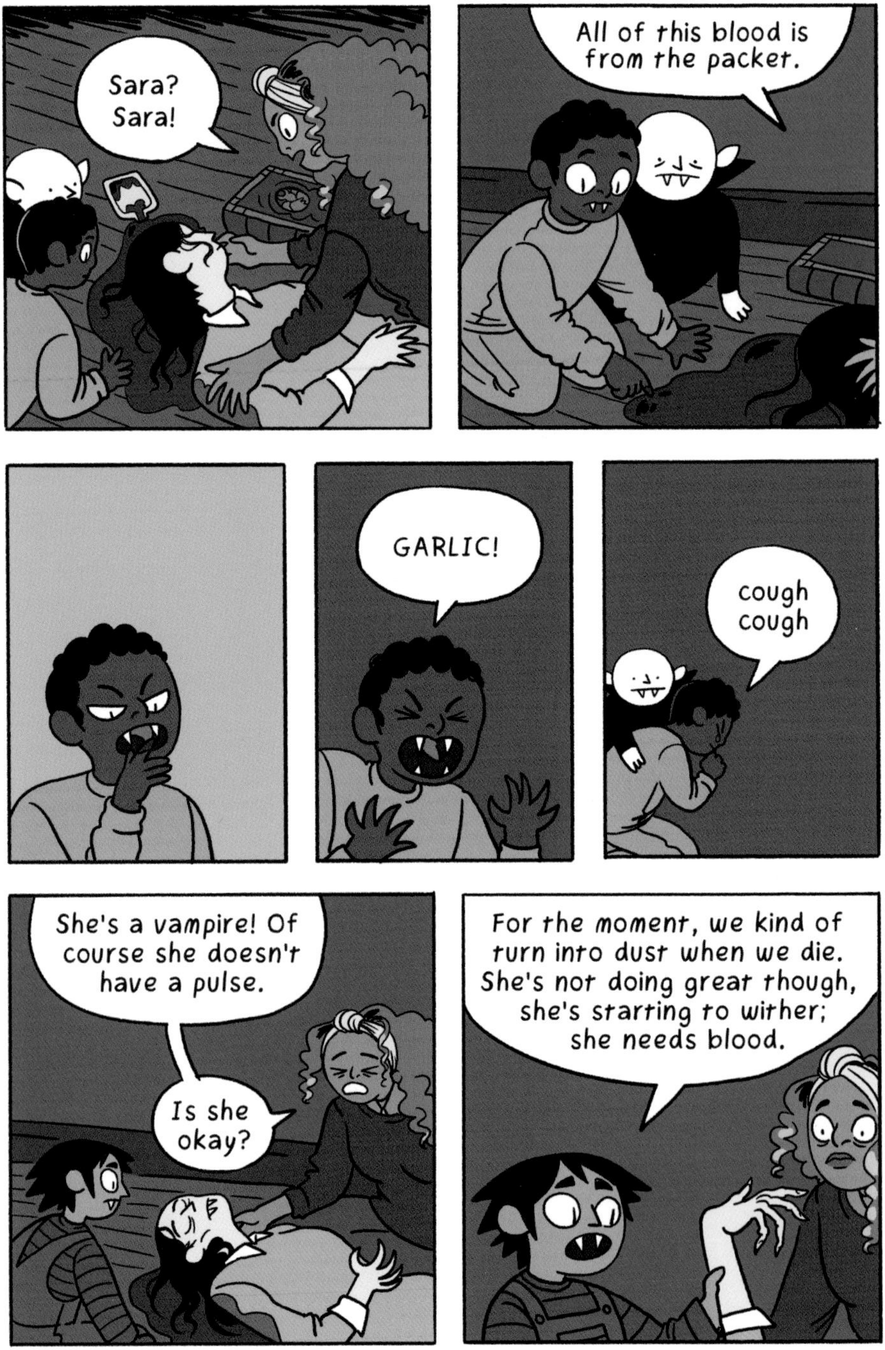
Sara?
Sara!
All of this blood is from the packet.
GARLIC!
cough cough
She's a vampire! Of course she doesn't have a pulse.
Is she okay?
For the moment, we kind of turn into dust when we die. She's not doing great though, she's starting to wither; she needs blood.

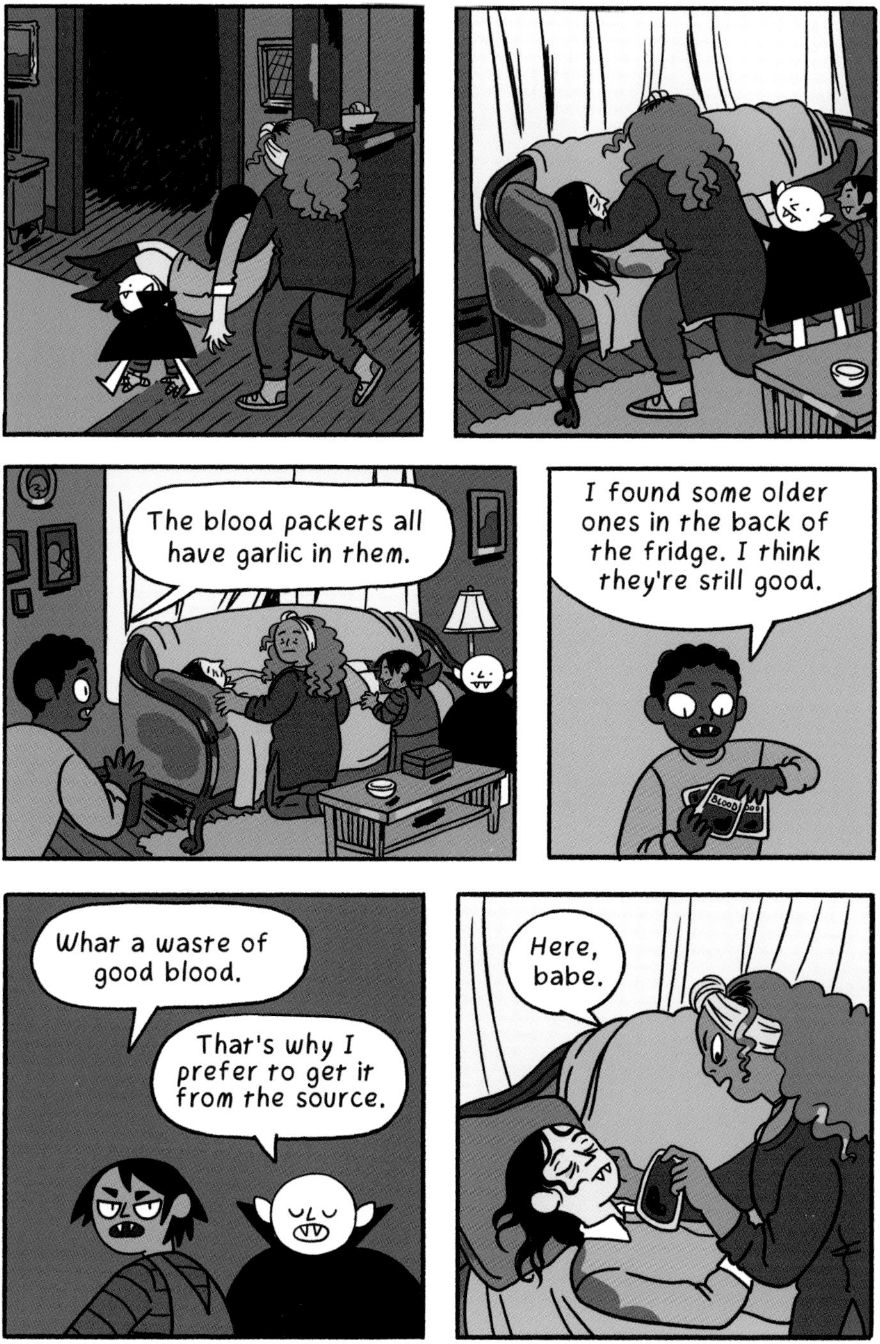
The blood packets all have garlic in them.
I found some older ones in the back of the fridge. I think they're still good.
BLOOD
What a waste of good blood.
That's why I prefer to get it from the source.
Here, babe.

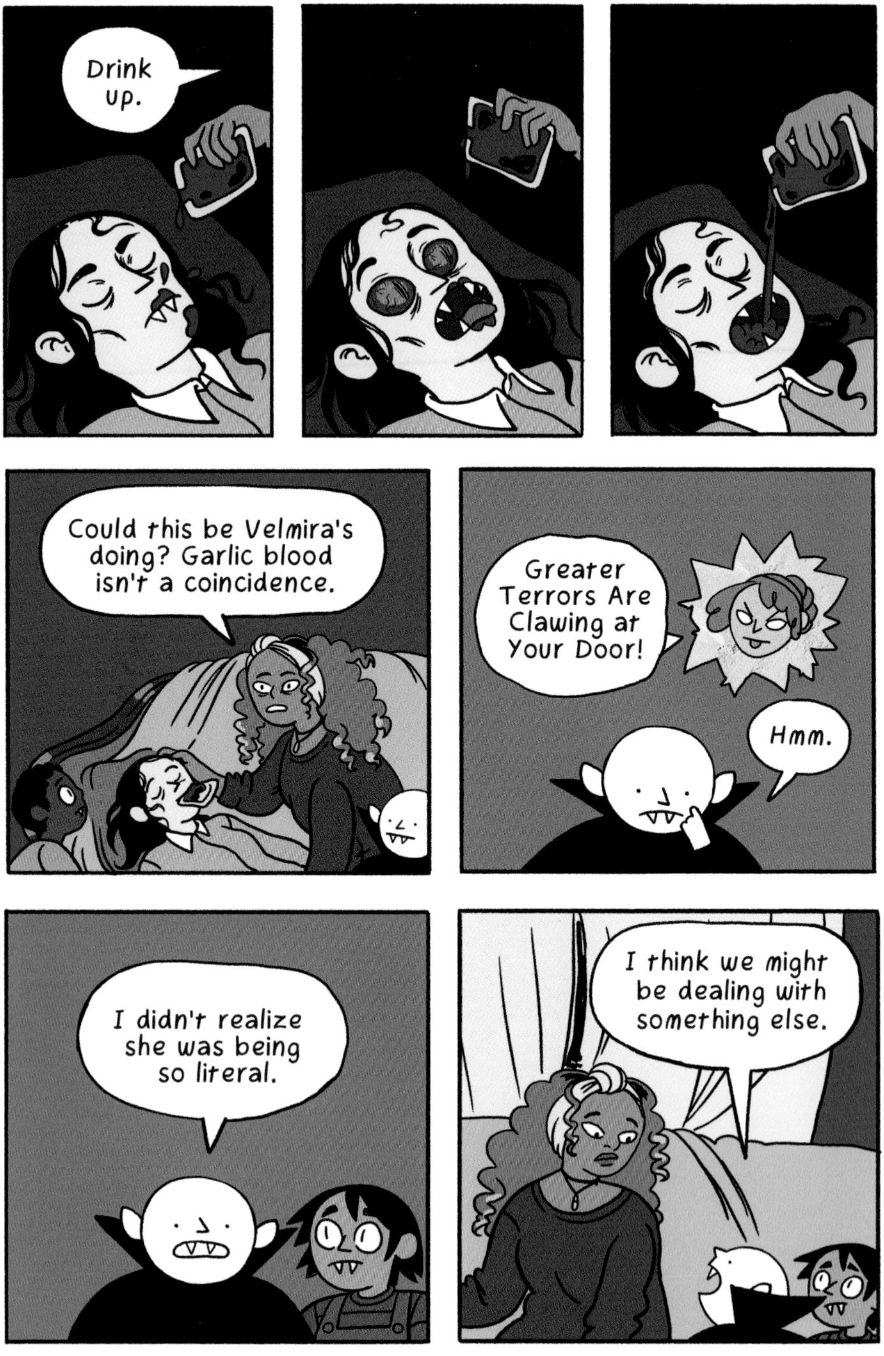
Drink up.
Could this be Velmira's doing? Garlic blood isn't a coincidence.
Greater Terrors Are Clawing at Your Door!
Hmm.
I didn't realize she was being so literal.
I think we might be dealing with something else.

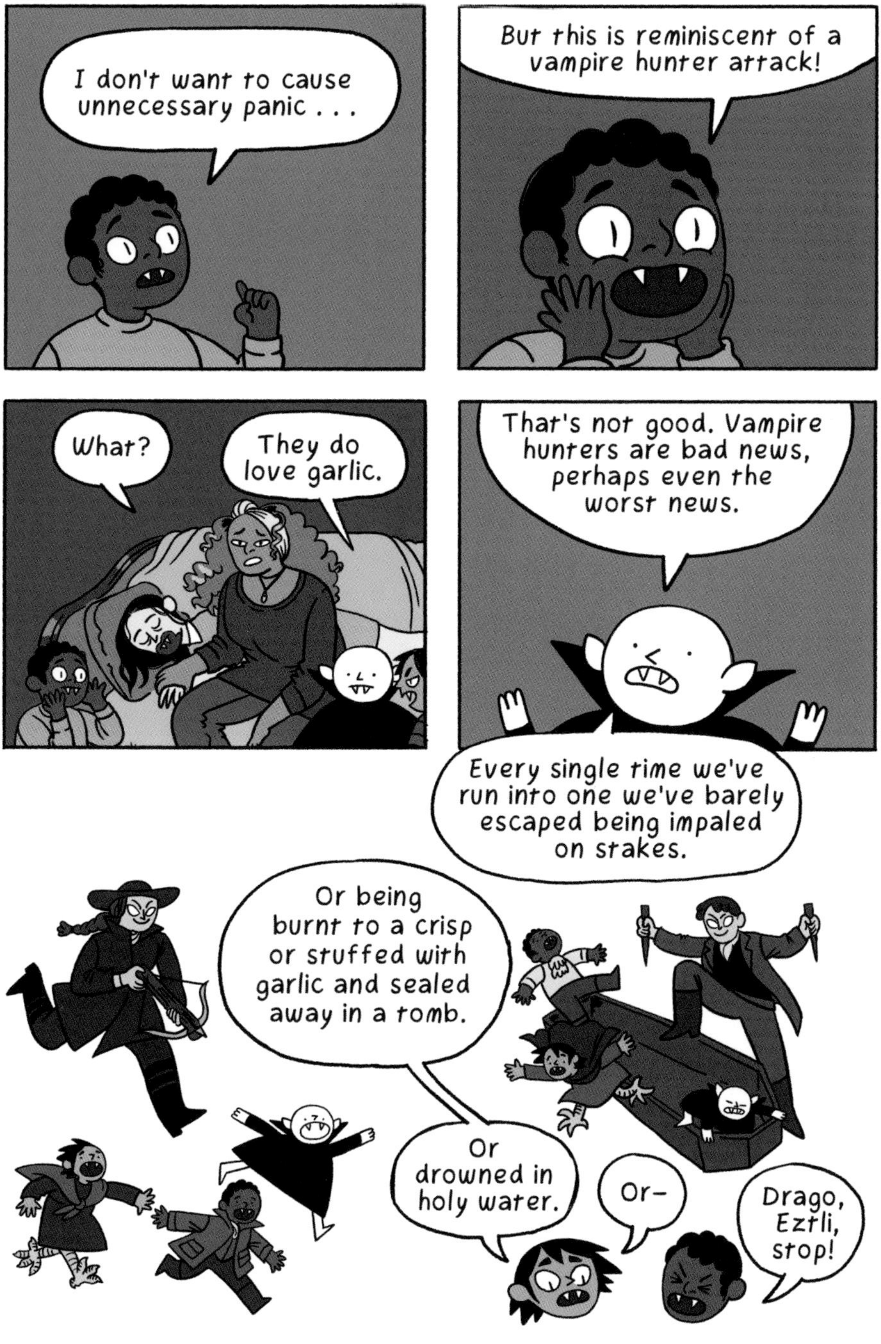

I don't want to cause unnecessary panic . . .
But this is reminiscent of a vampire hunter attack!
What?
They do love garlic.
That's not good. Vampire hunters are bad news, perhaps even the worst news.
Every single time we've run into one we've barely escaped being impaled on stakes.
Or being burnt to a crisp or stuffed with garlic and sealed away in a tomb.
Or drowned in holy water.
Or–
Drago, Eztli, stop!

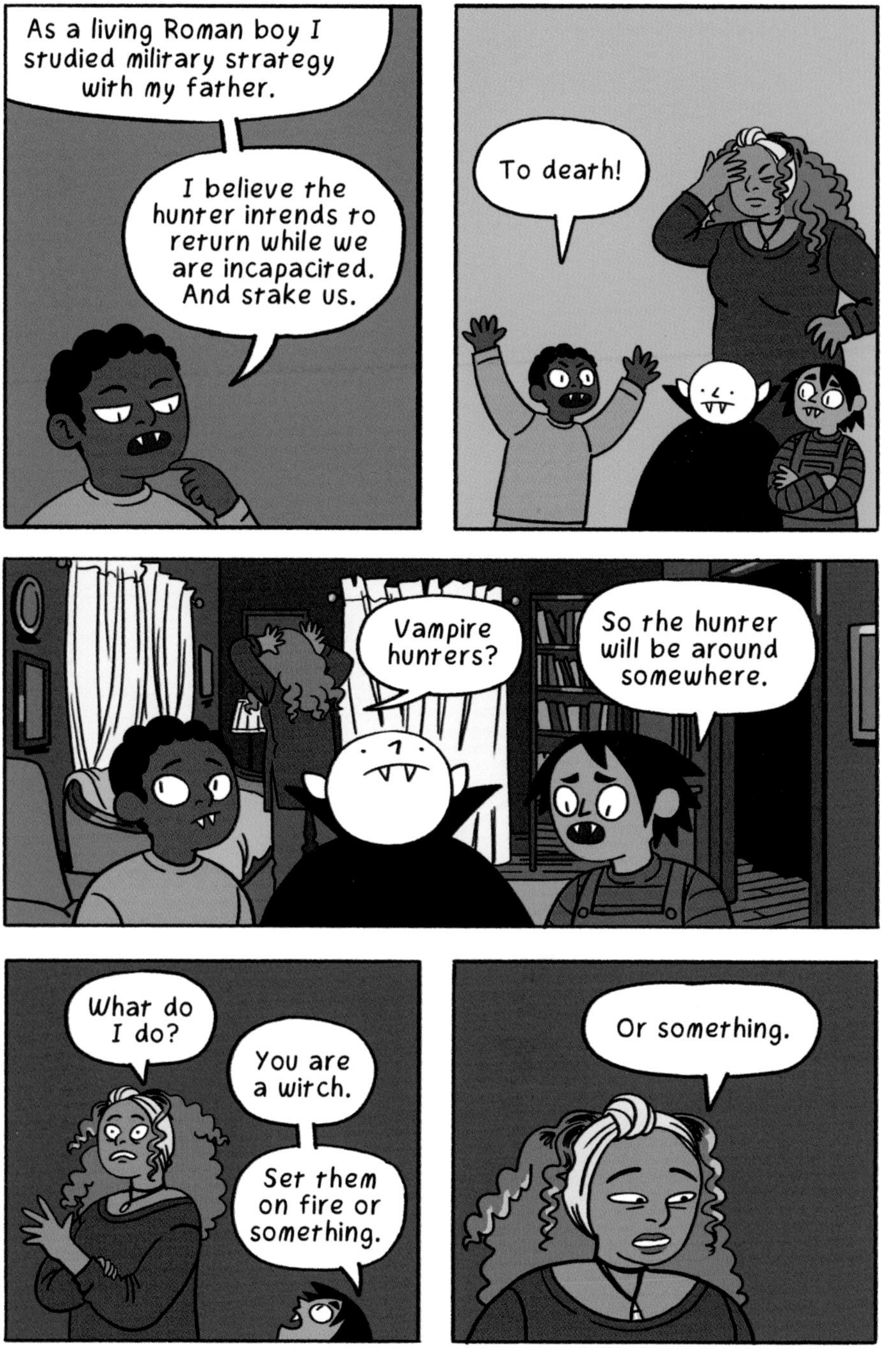
As a living Roman boy I studied military strategy with my father.
I believe the hunter intends to return while we are incapacited. And stake us.
To death!
Vampire hunters?
So the hunter will be around somewhere.
What do I do?
You are a witch.
Set them on fire or something.
Or something.

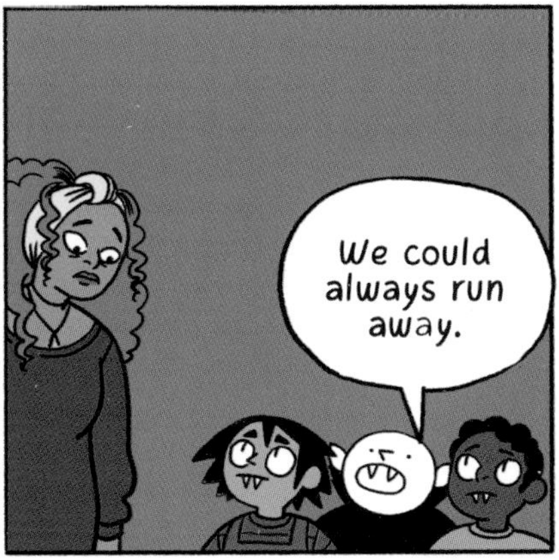
We could always run away.

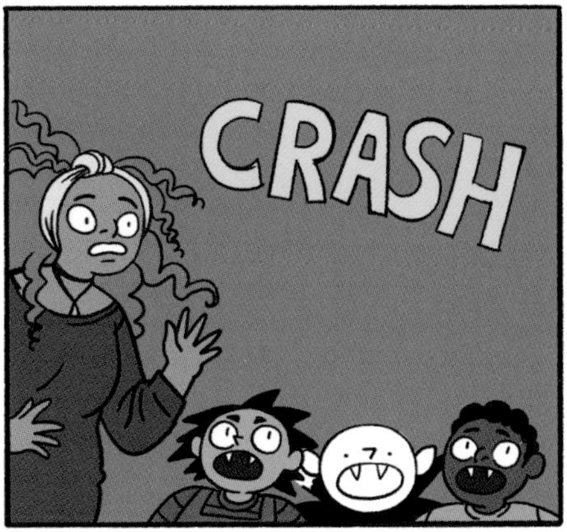
CRASH

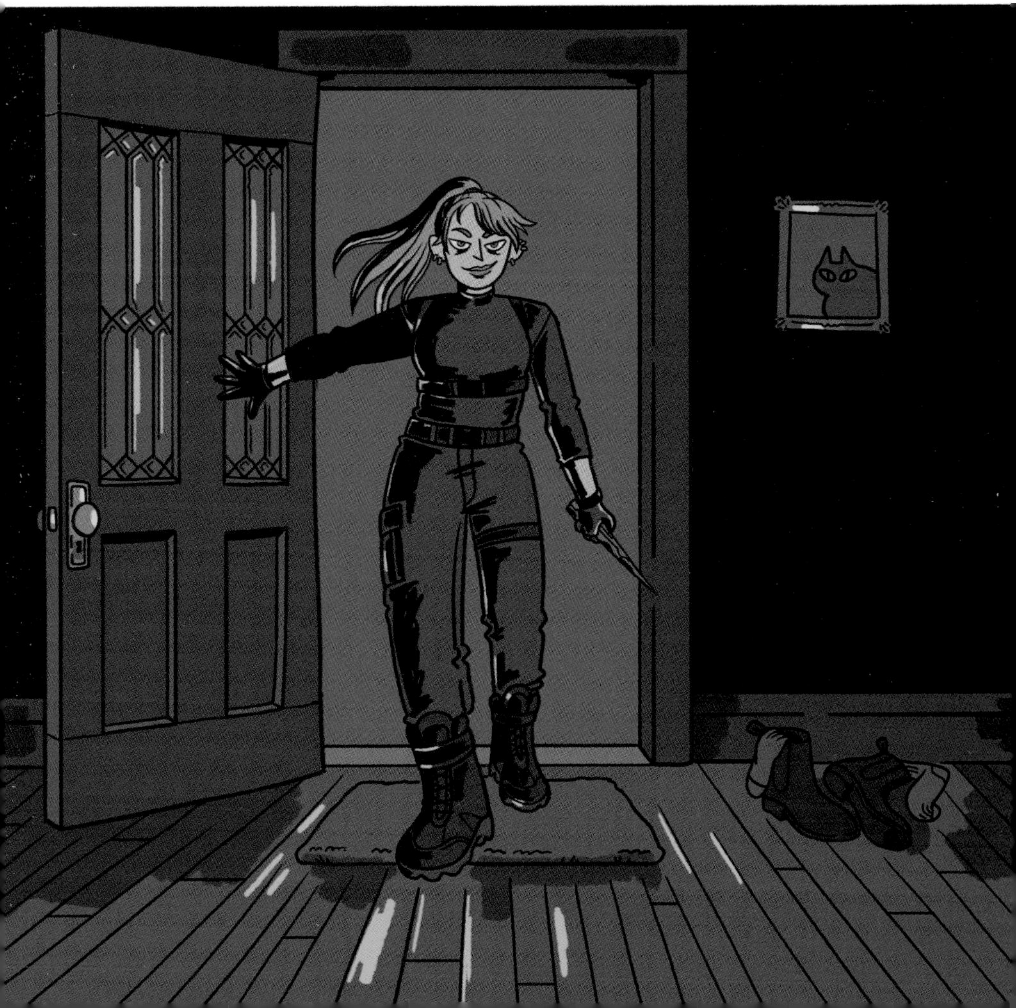

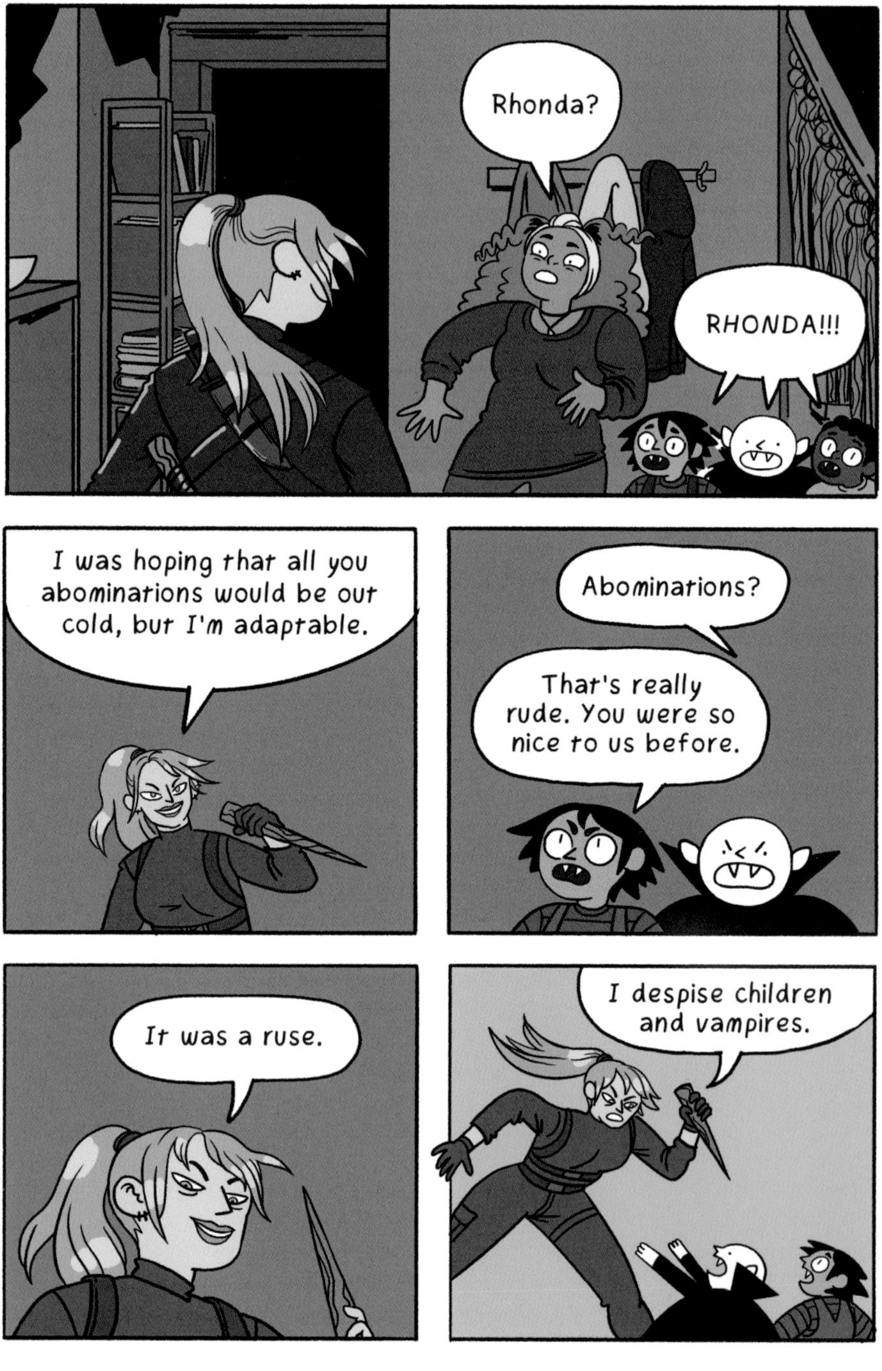
Rhonda?
RHONDA!!!
I was hoping that all you abominations would be out cold, but I'm adaptable.
Abominations?
That's really rude. You were so nice to us before.
It was a ruse.
I despise children and vampires.

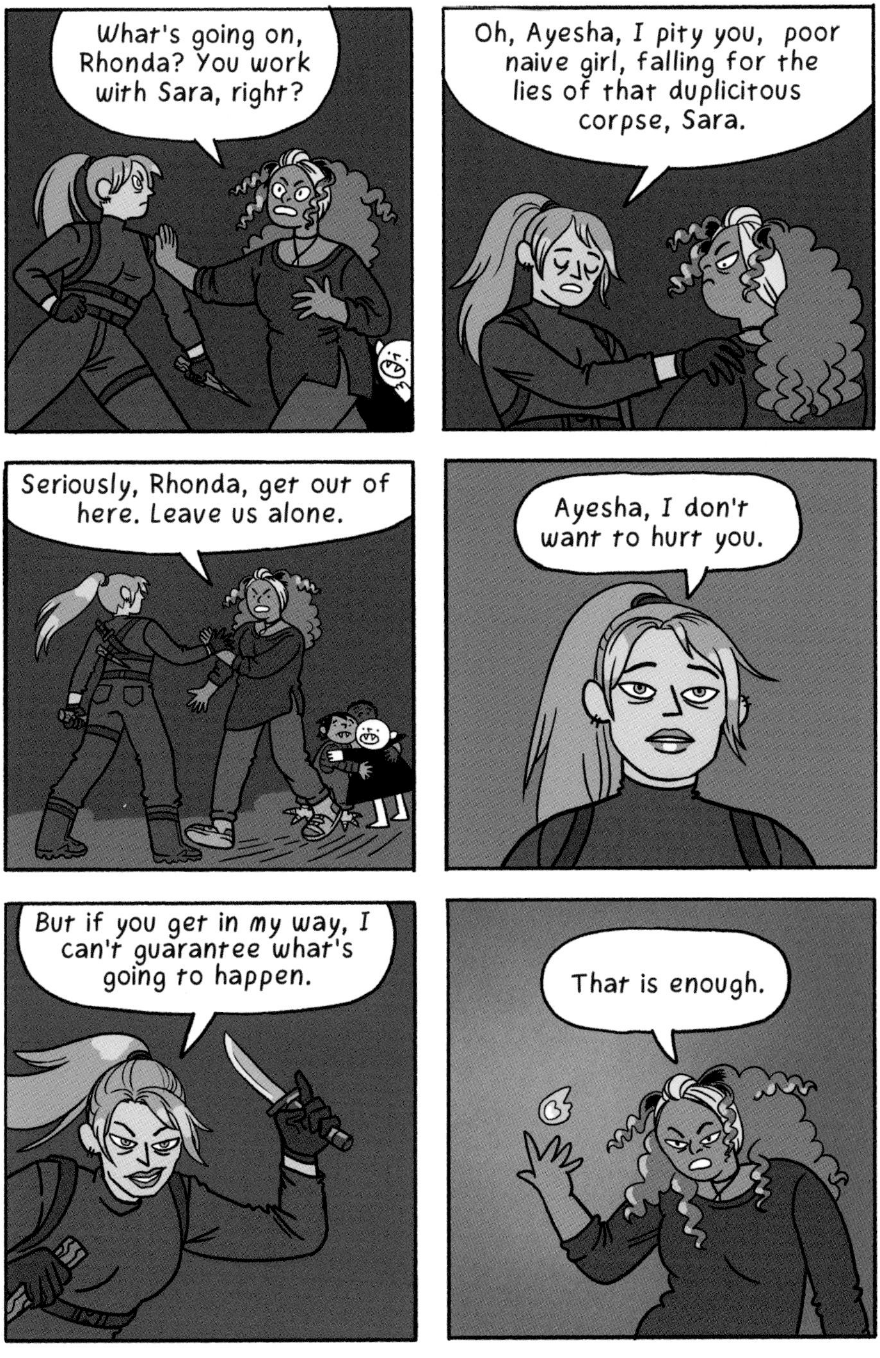
What's going on, Rhonda? You work with Sara, right?
Oh, Ayesha, I pity you, poor naive girl, falling for the lies of that duplicitous corpse, Sara.
Seriously, Rhonda, get out of here. Leave us alone.
Ayesha, I don't want to hurt you.
But if you get in my way, I can't guarantee what's going to happen.
That is enough.

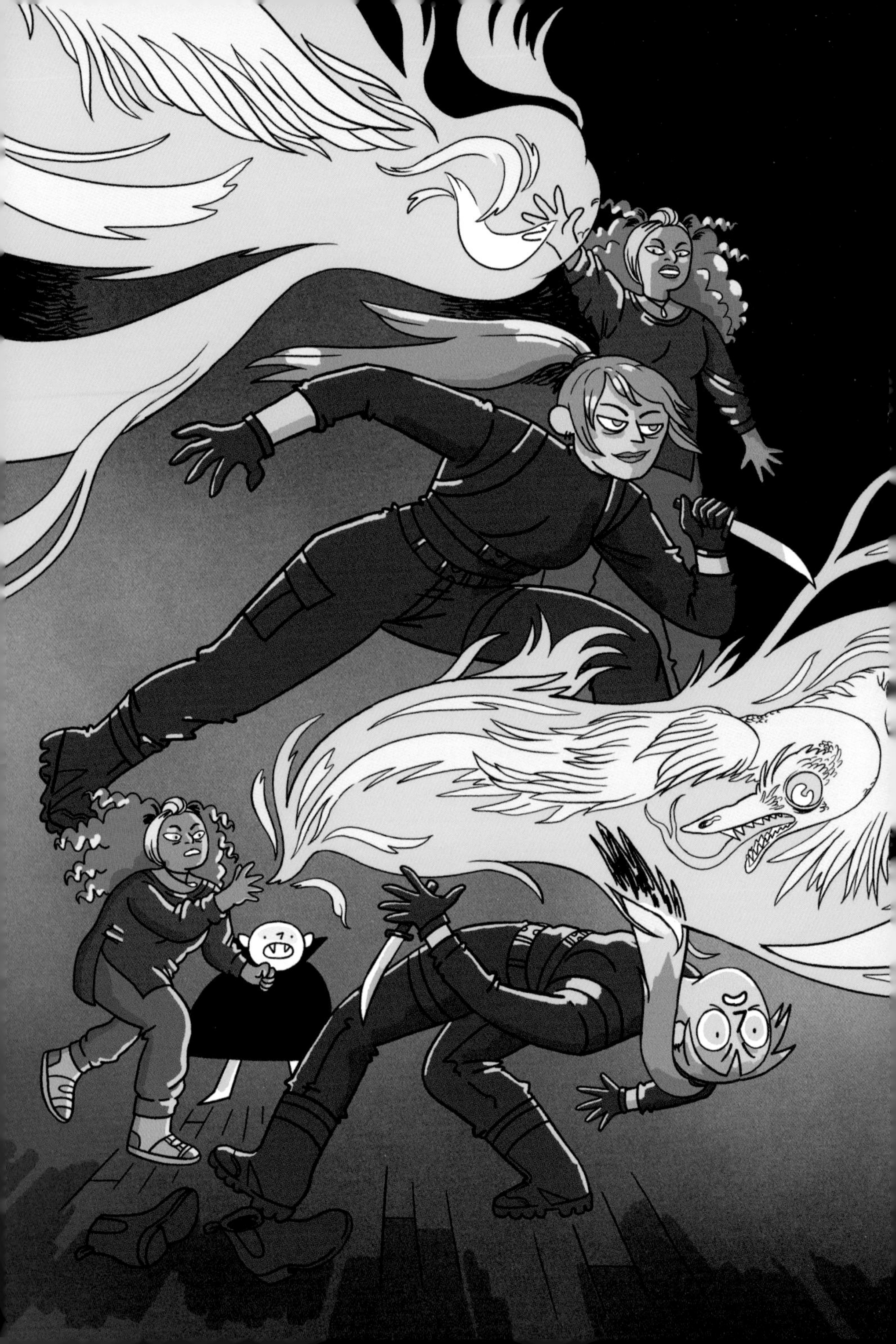

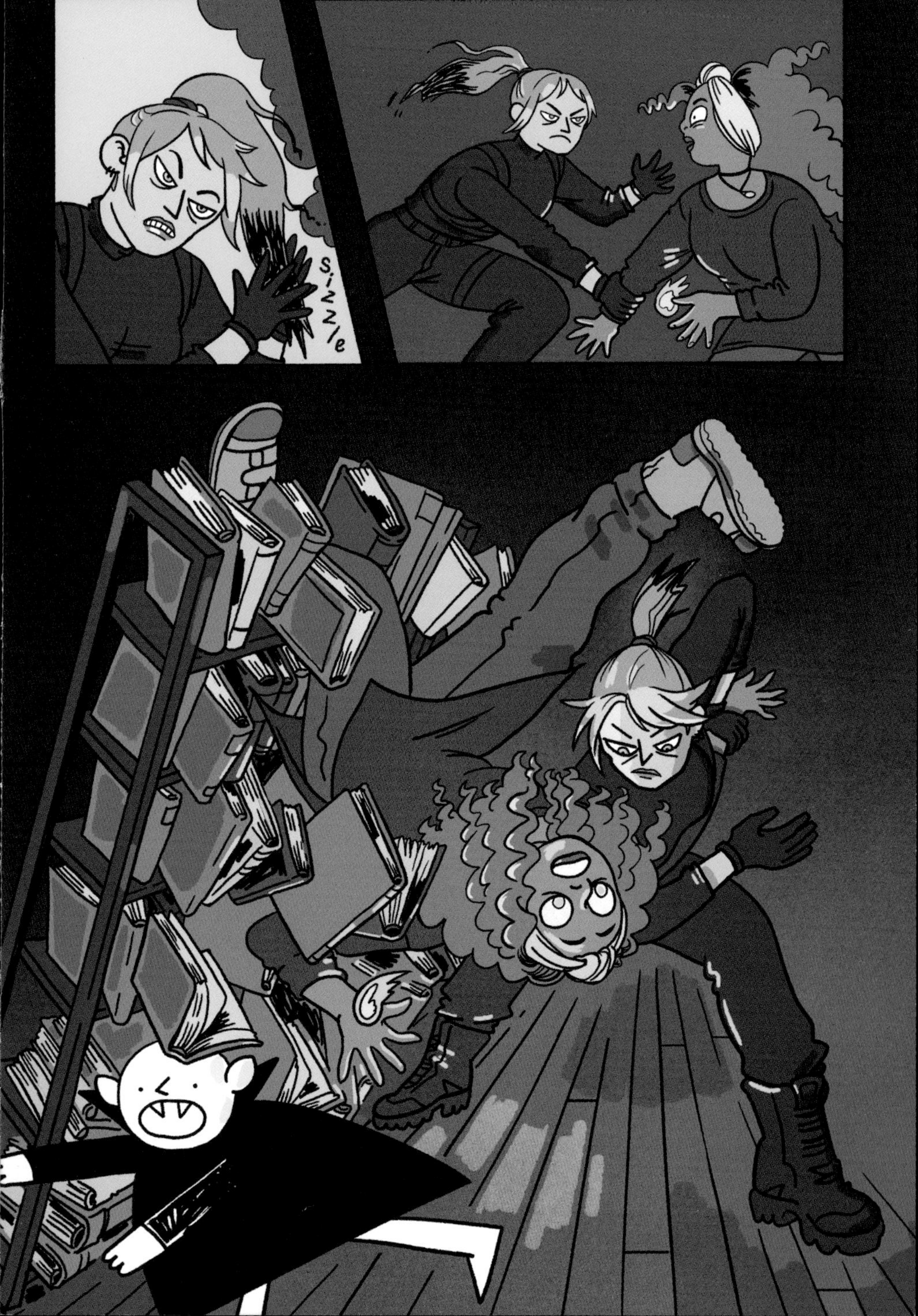
sizzle

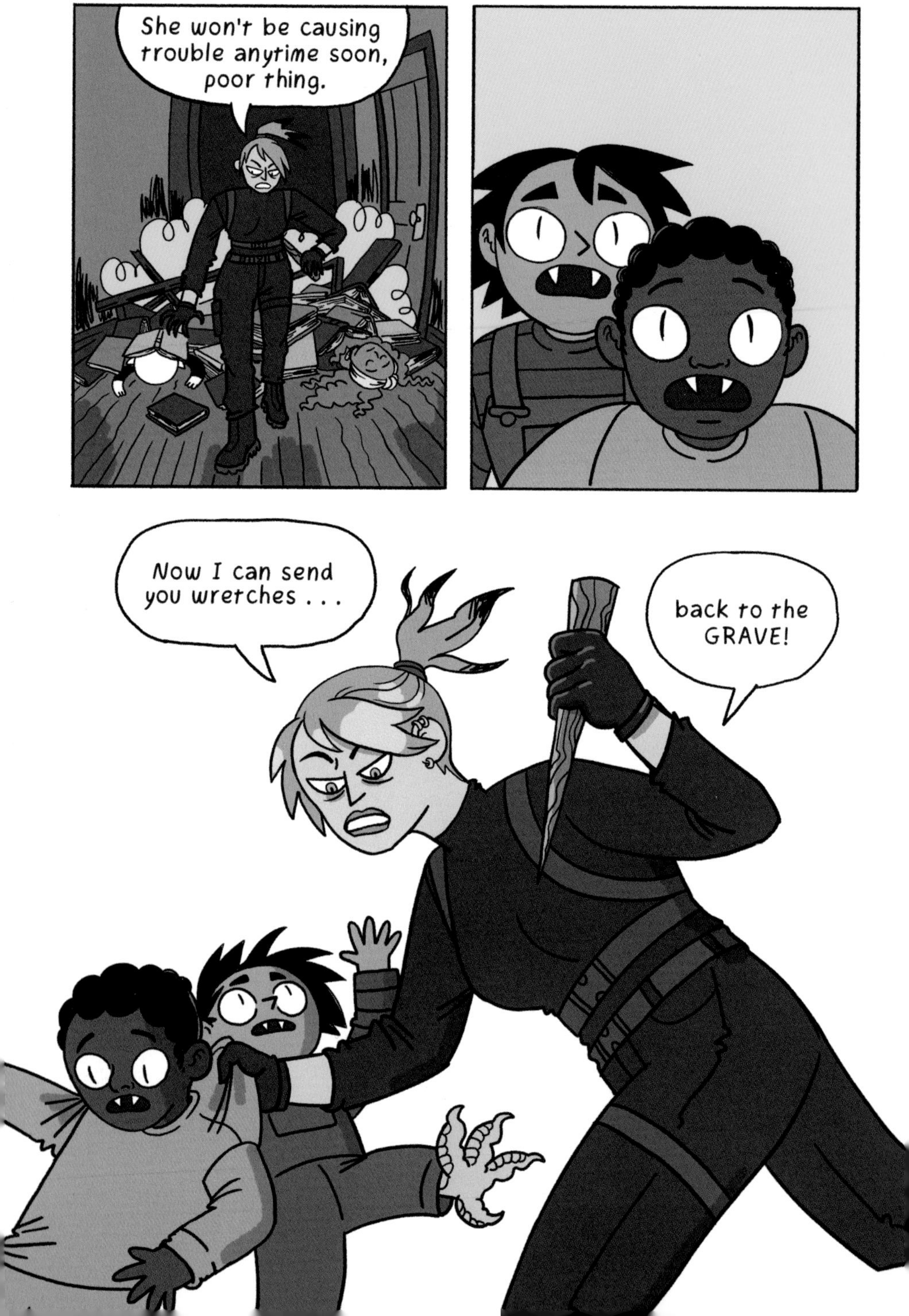
She won't be causing trouble anytime soon, poor thing.
Now I can send you wretches . . .
back to the GRAVE!

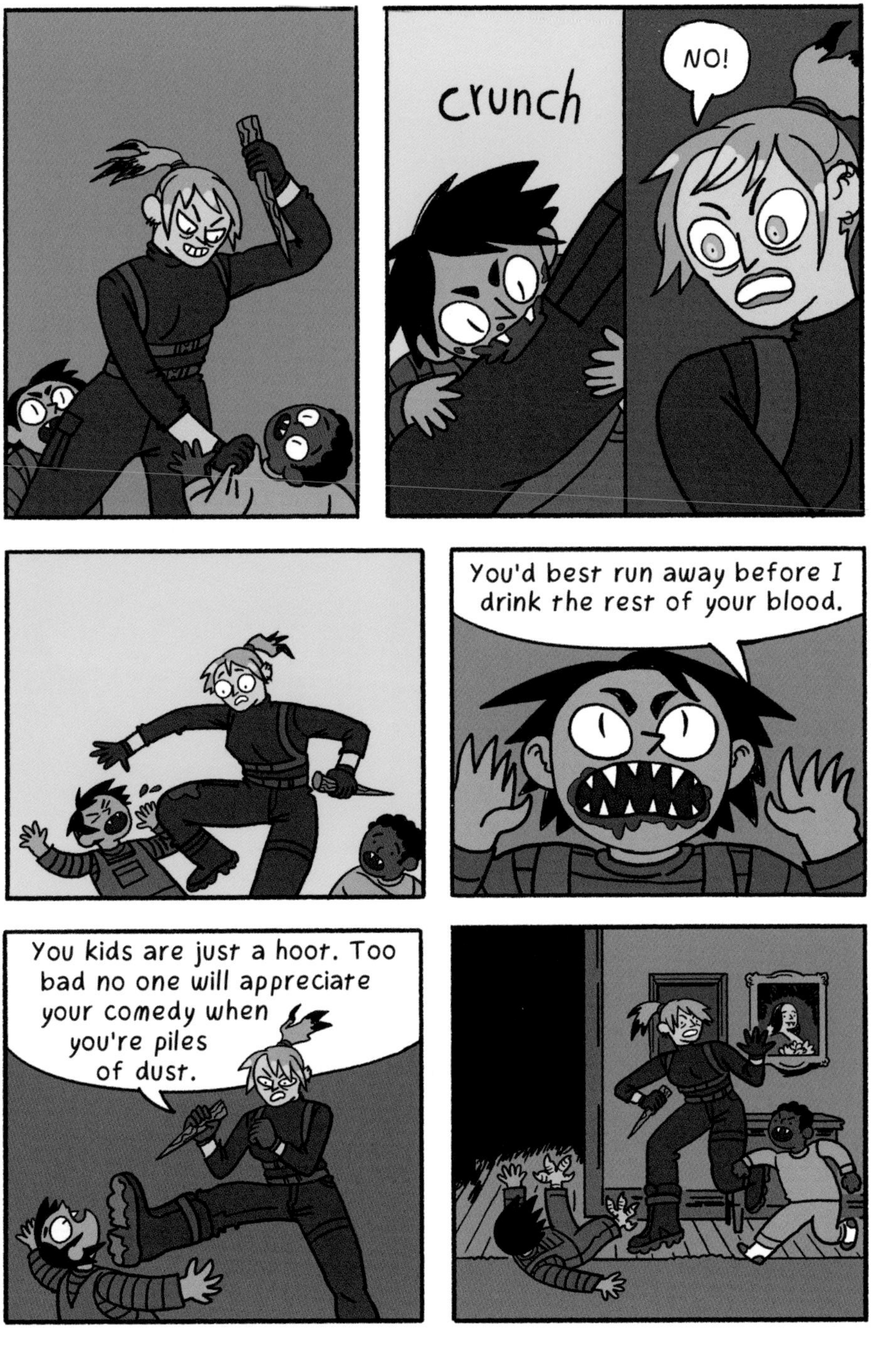
crunch
NO!
You'd best run away before I drink the rest of your blood.
You kids are just a hoot. Too bad no one will appreciate your comedy when you're piles of dust.

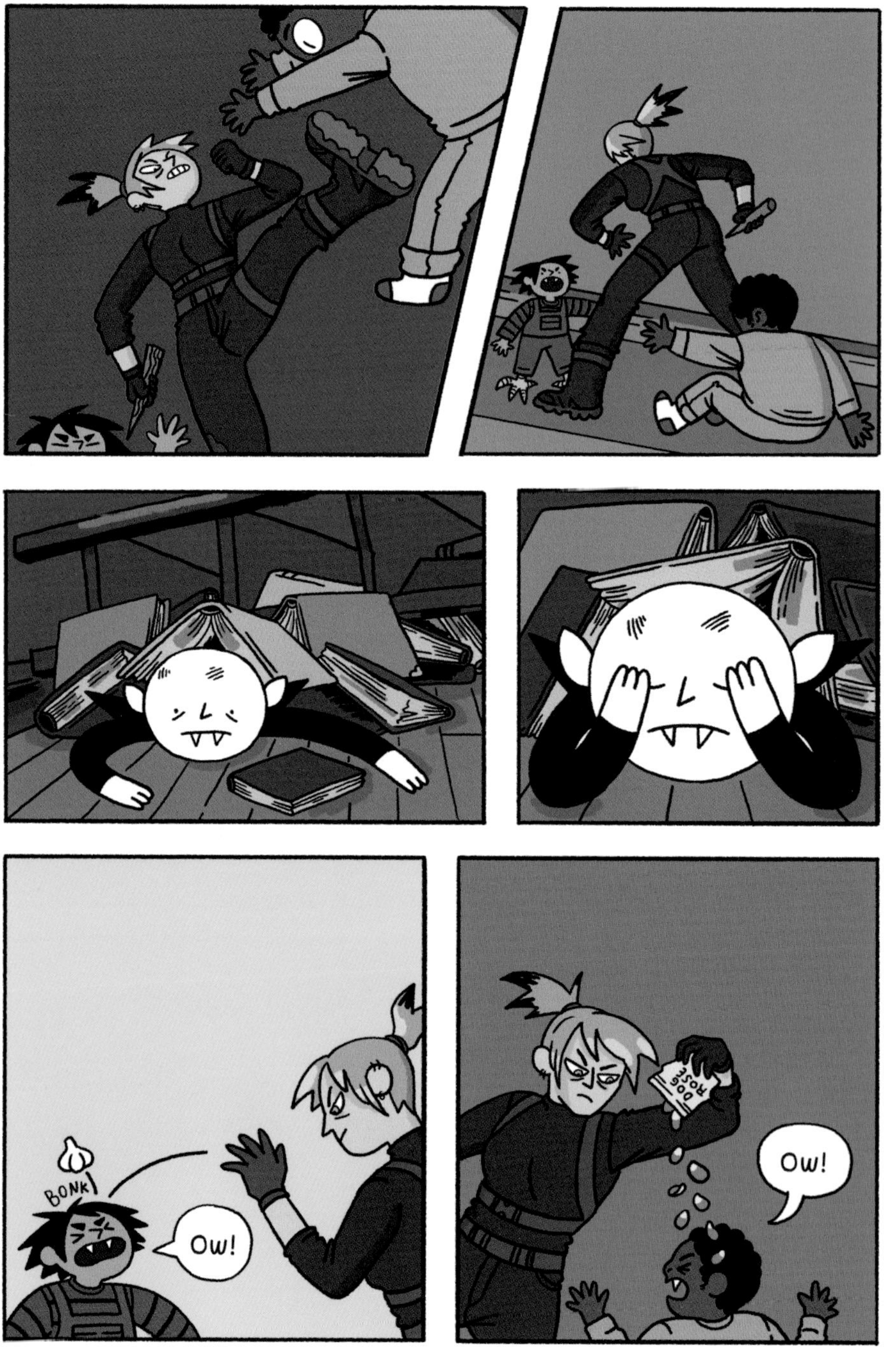
BONK!
Ow!
DOG ROSE
Ow!

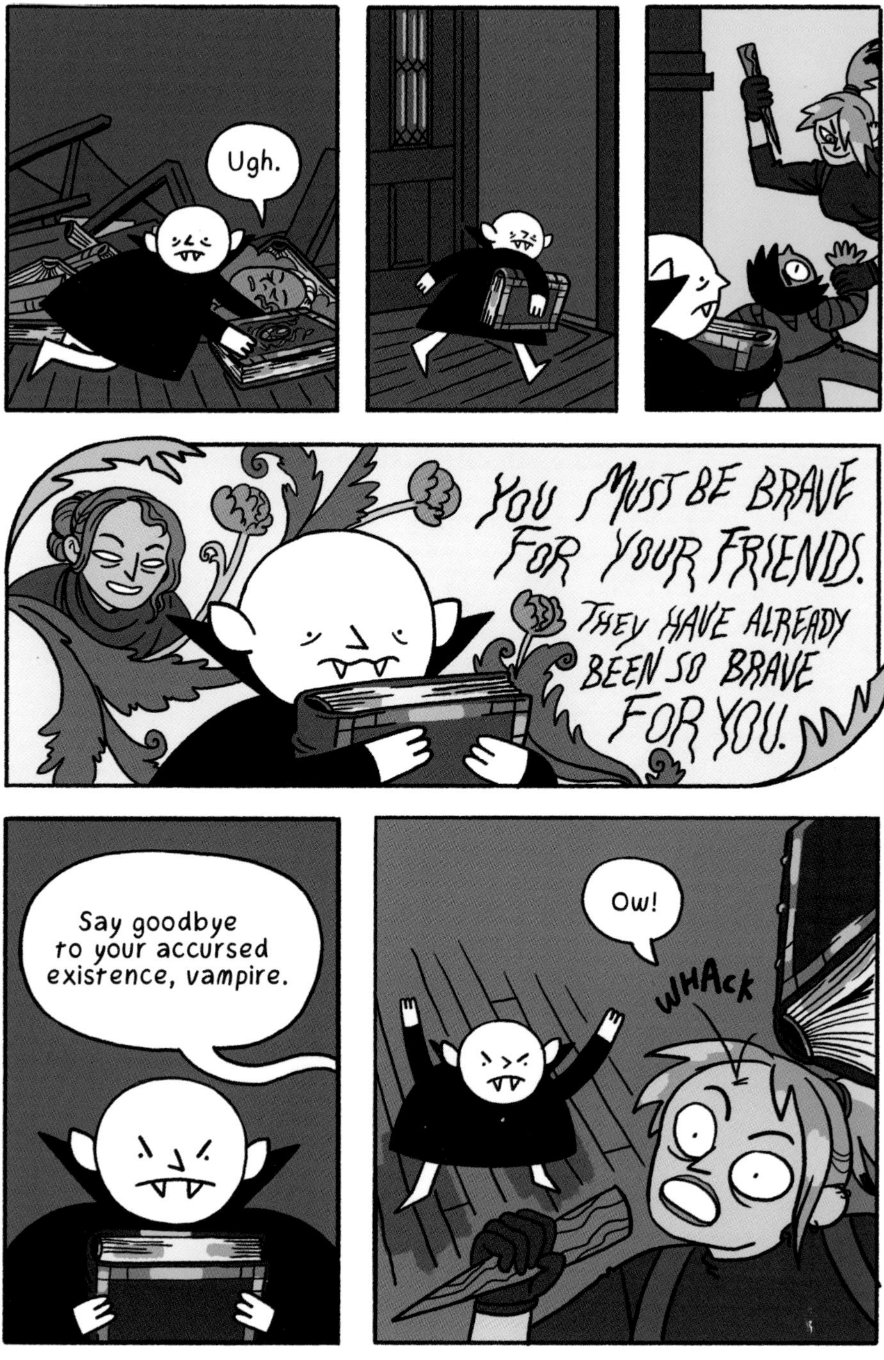
Ugh.
YOU MUST BE BRAVE FOR YOUR FRIENDS.
THEY HAVE ALREADY BEEN SO BRAVE FOR YOU.
Say goodbye to your accursed existence, vampire.
Ow!
WHACK

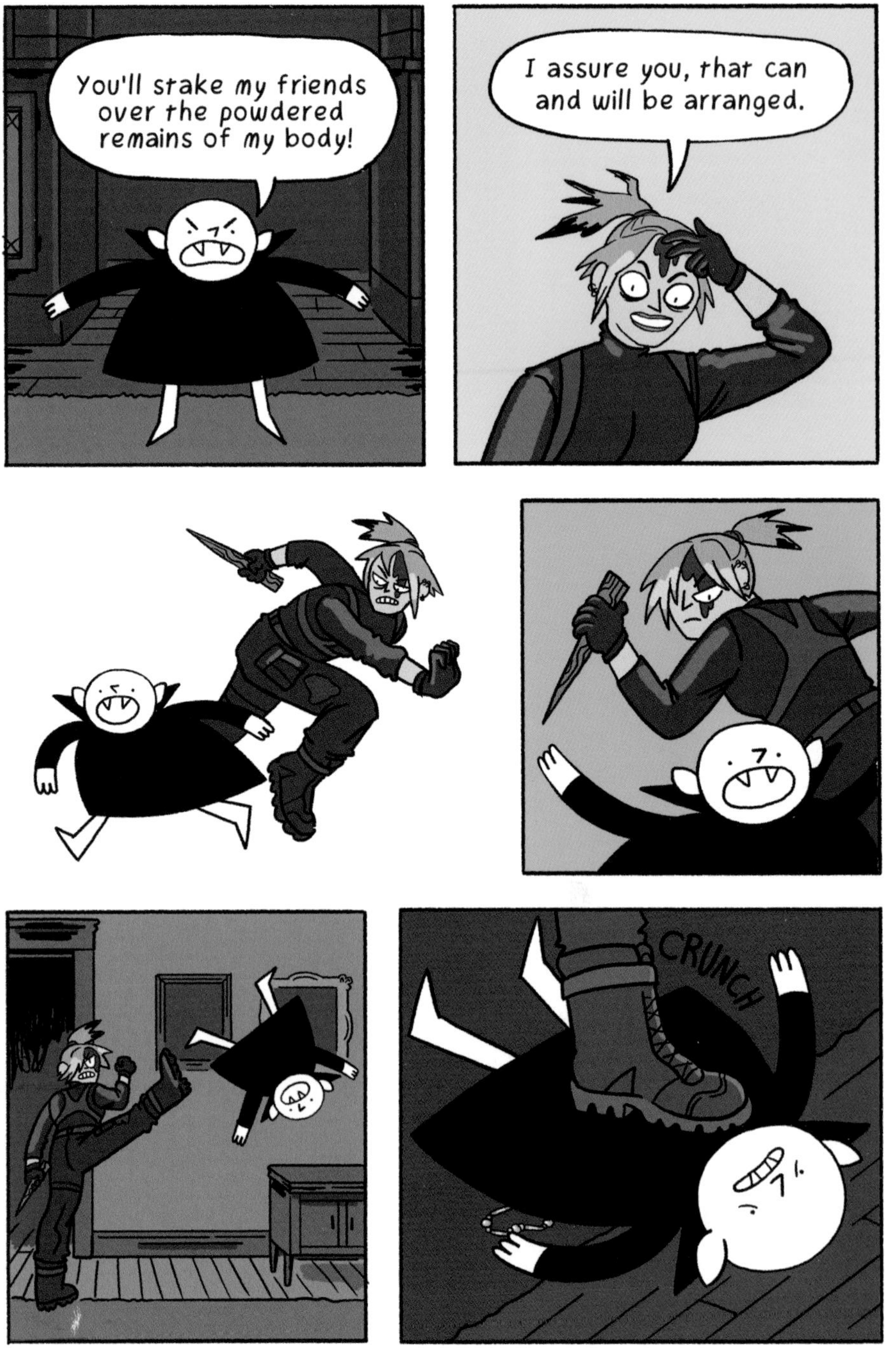
You'll stake my friends over the powdered remains of my body!
I assure you, that can and will be arranged.
CRUNCH

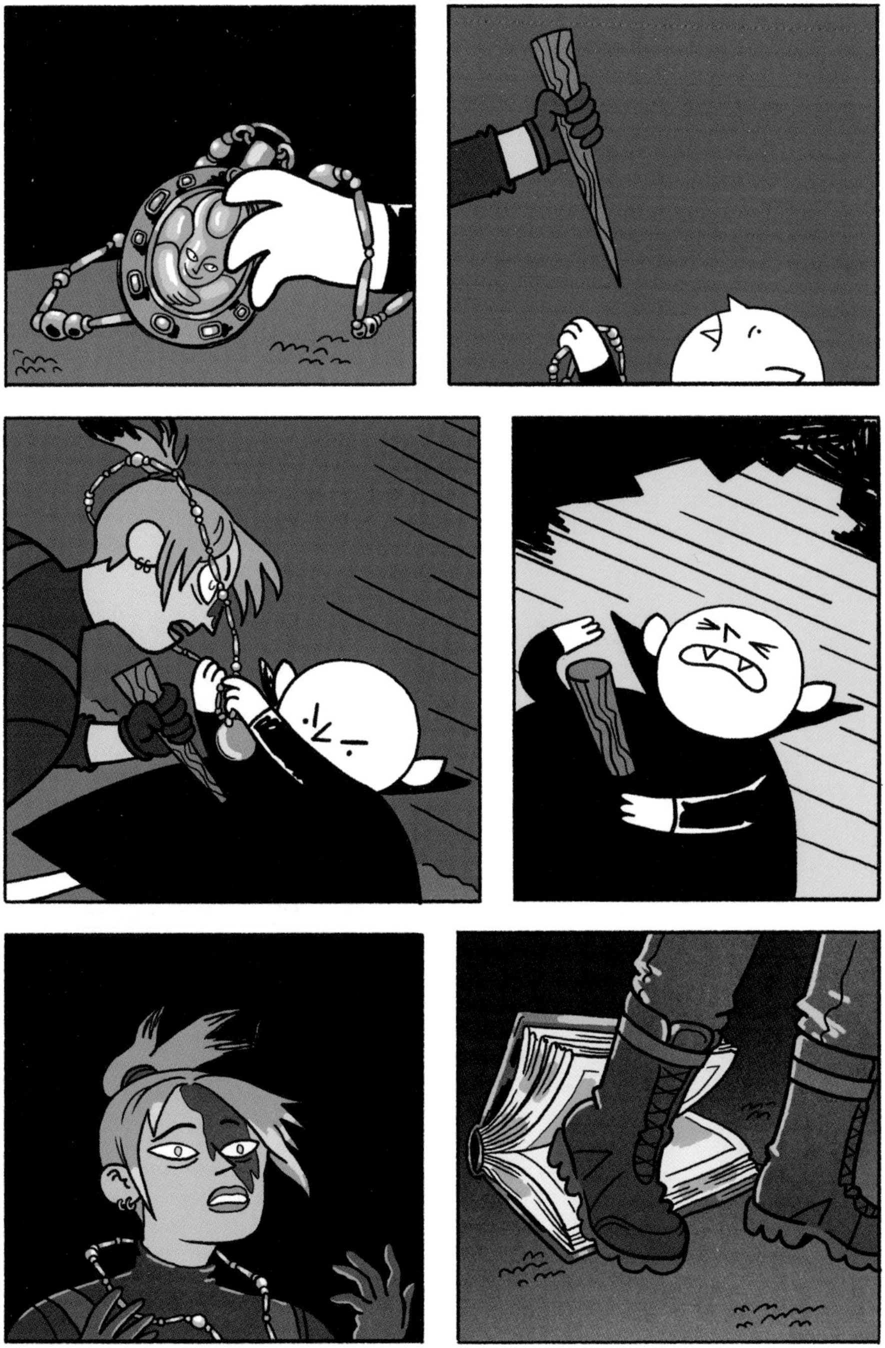

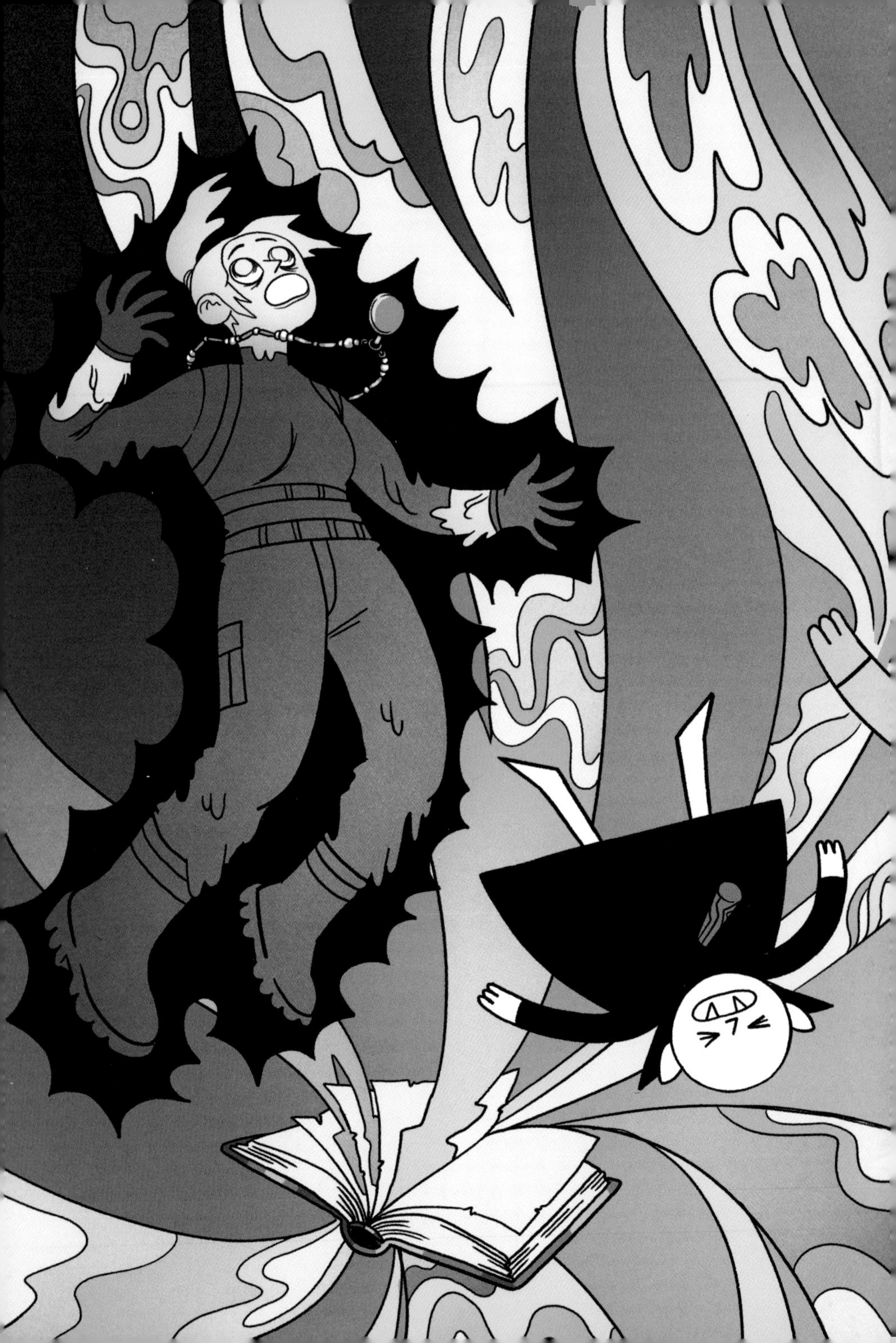

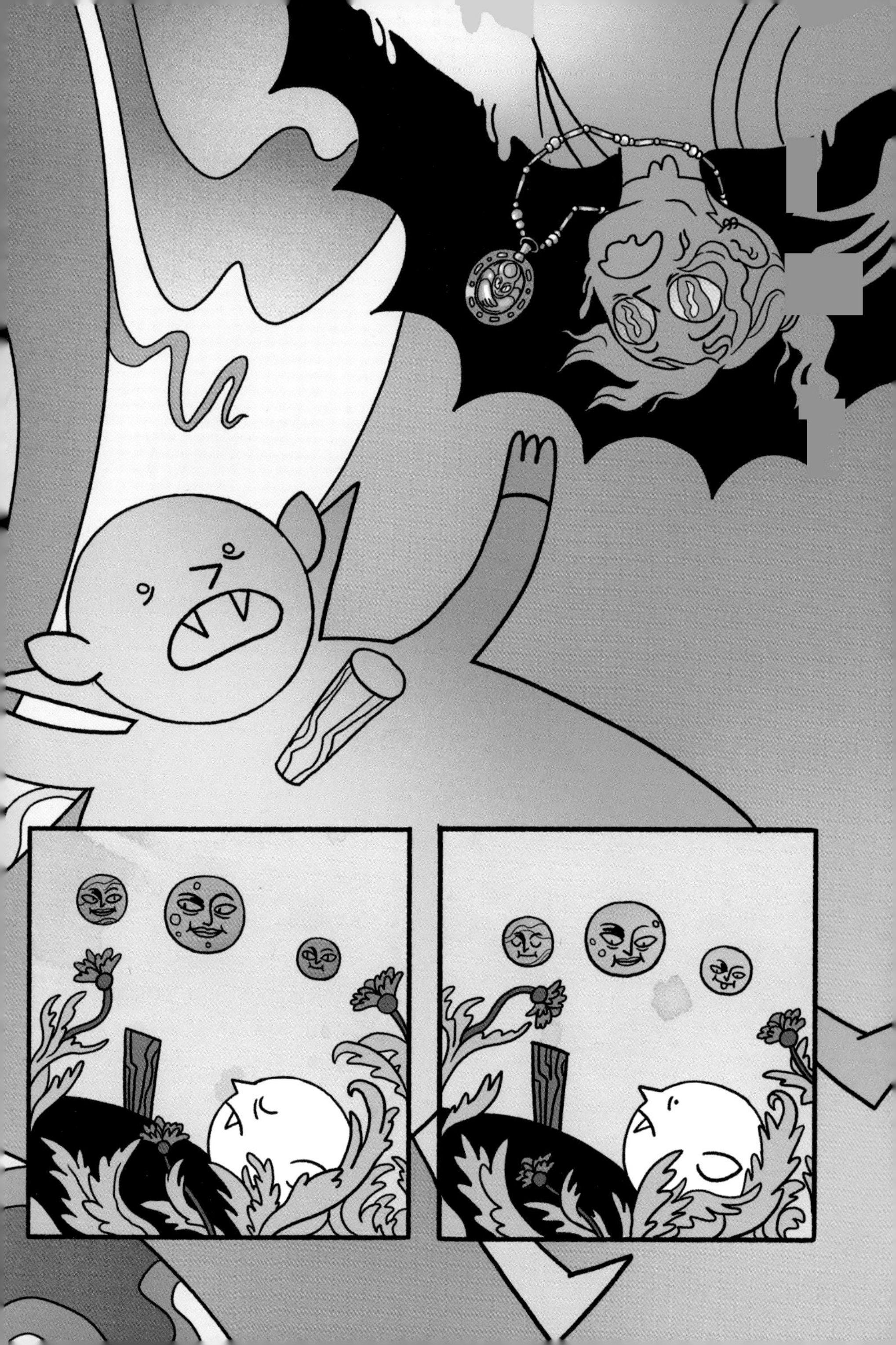

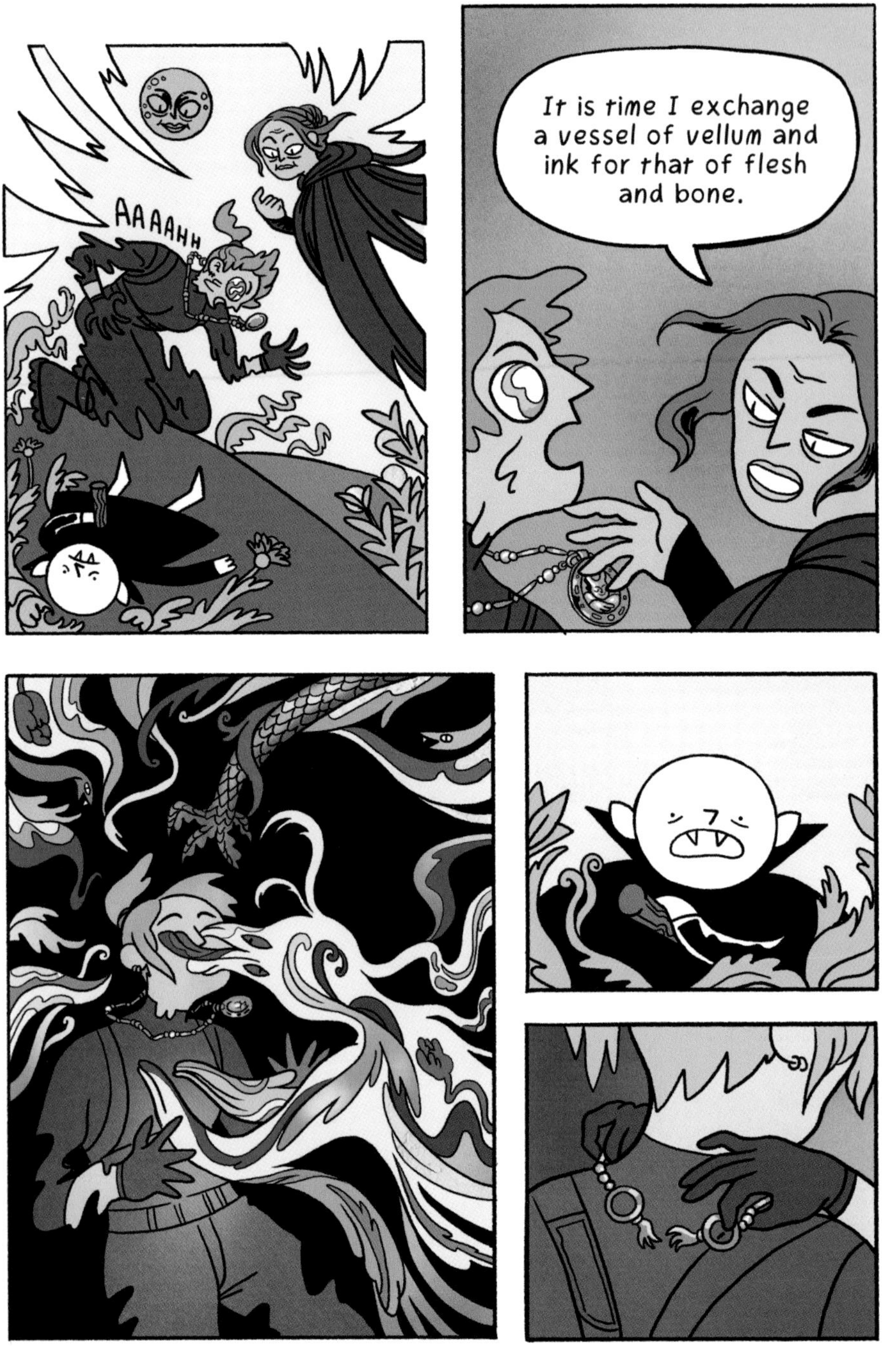
AAAAHH
It is time I exchange a vessel of vellum and ink for that of flesh and bone.

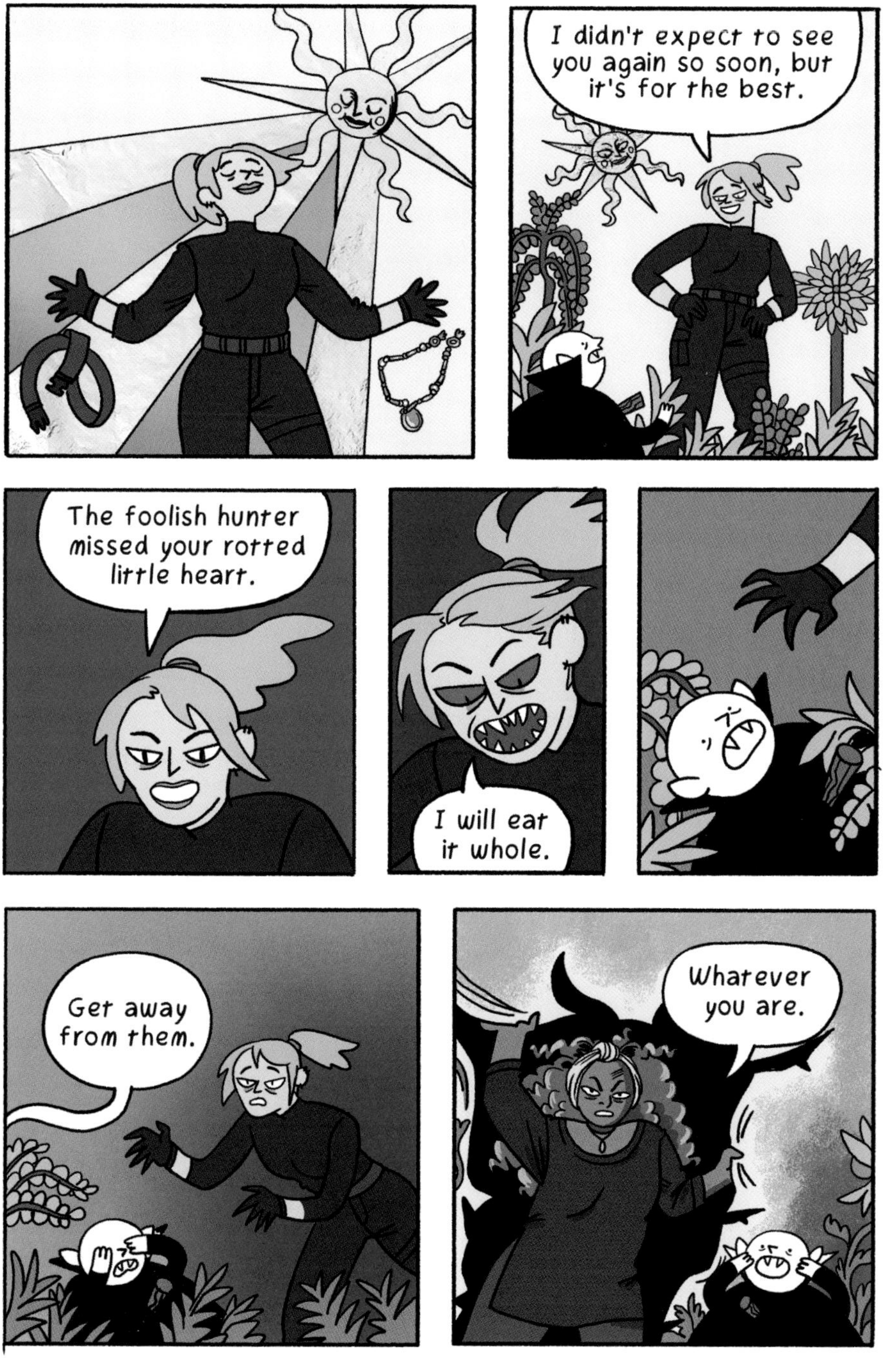
I didn't expect to see you again so soon, but it's for the best.
The foolish hunter missed your rotted little heart.
I will eat it whole.
Get away from them.
Whatever you are.

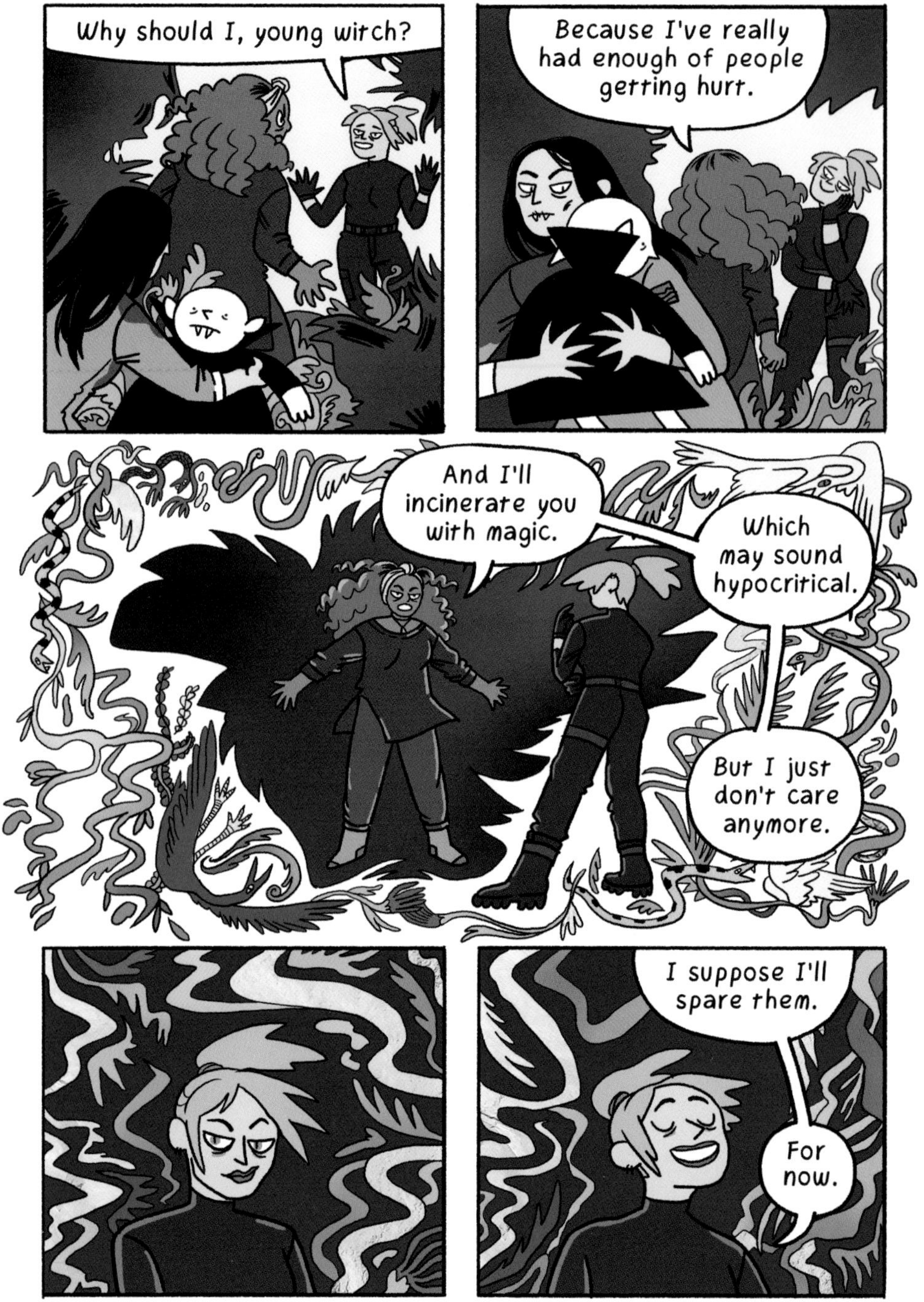

Why should I, young witch?
Because I've really had enough of people getting hurt.
And I'll incinerate you with magic.
Which may sound hypocritical.
But I just don't care anymore.
I suppose I'll spare them.
For now.

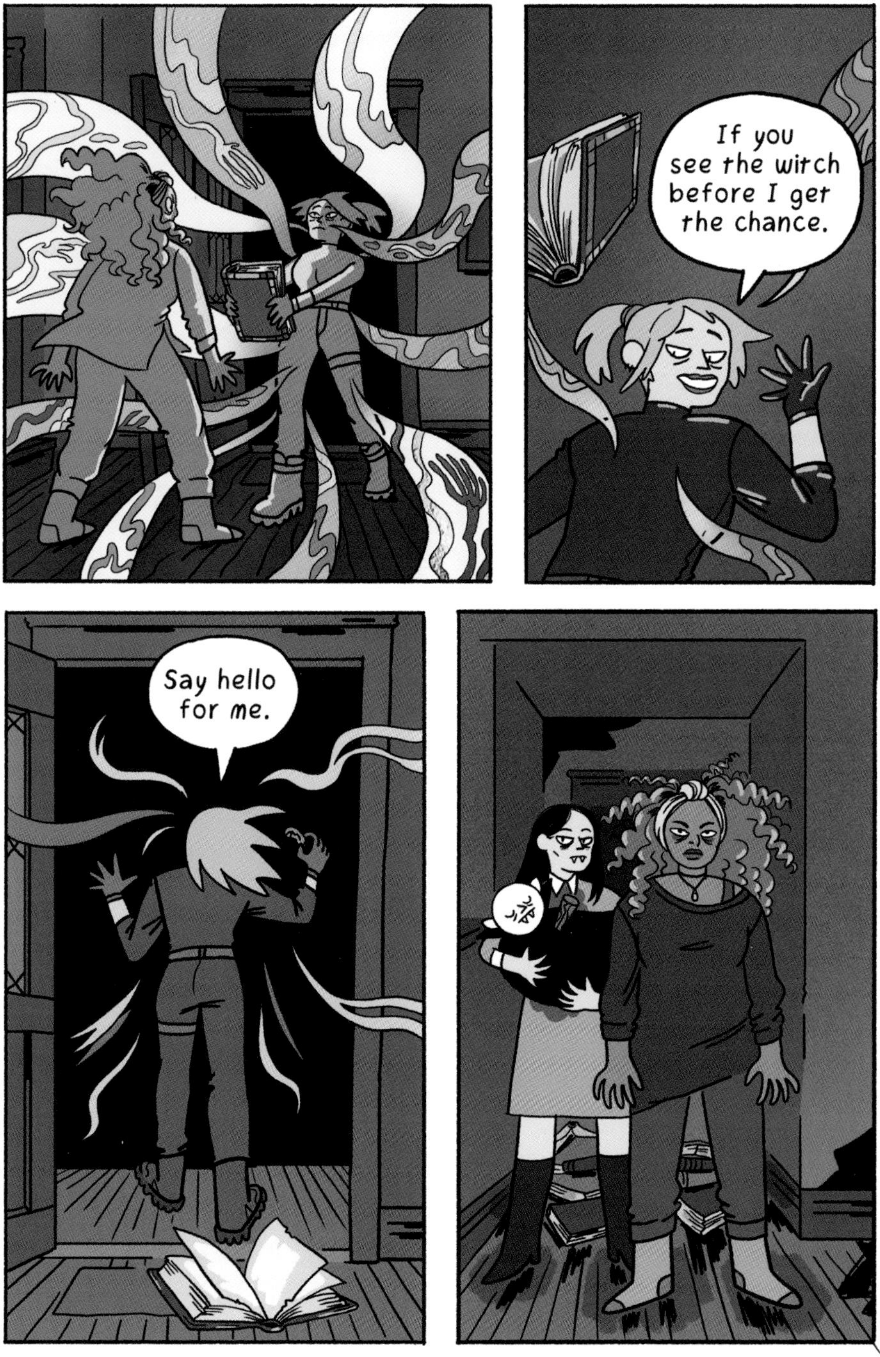
If you see the witch before I get the chance.
Say hello for me.

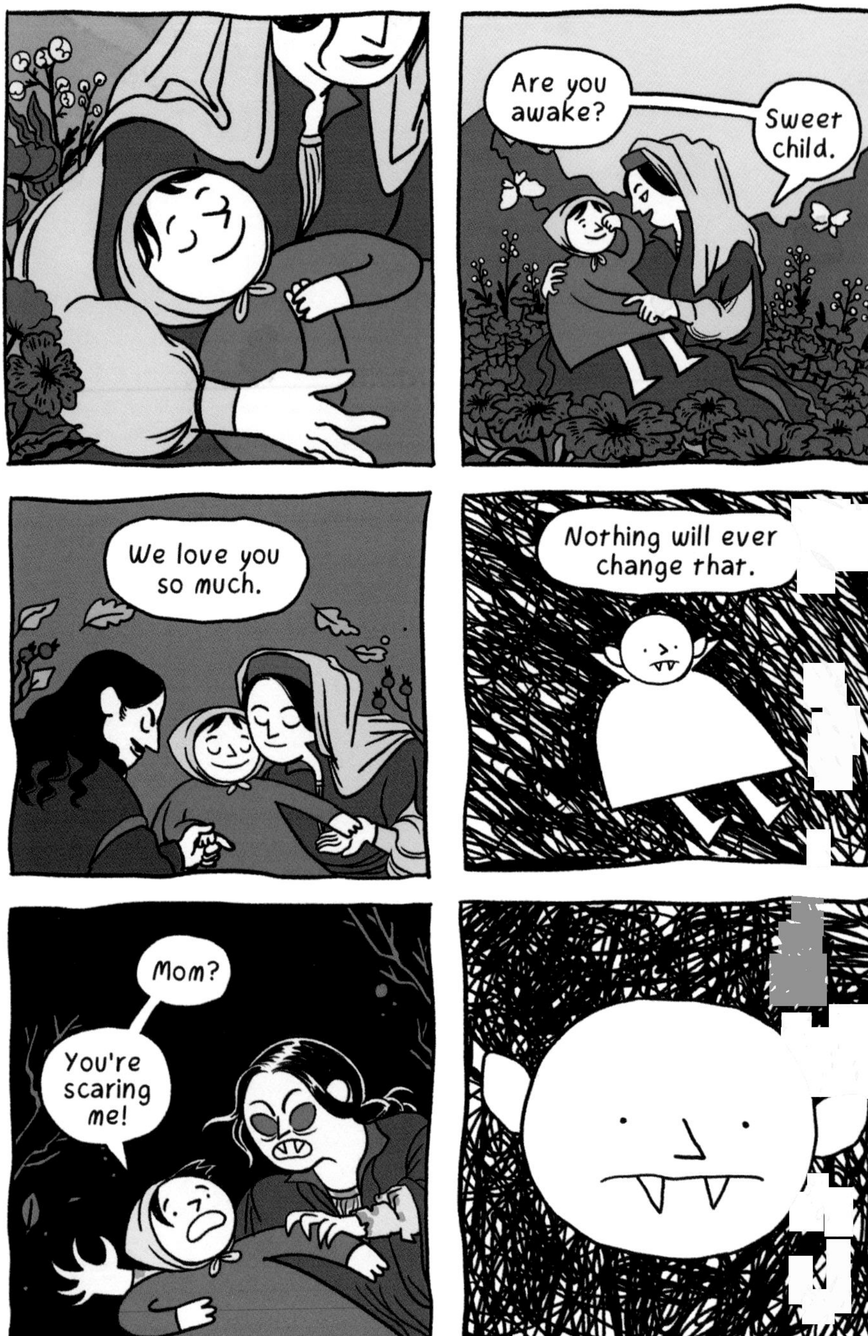
Are you awake?
Sweet child.
We love you so much.
Nothing will ever change that.
Mom?
You're scaring me!

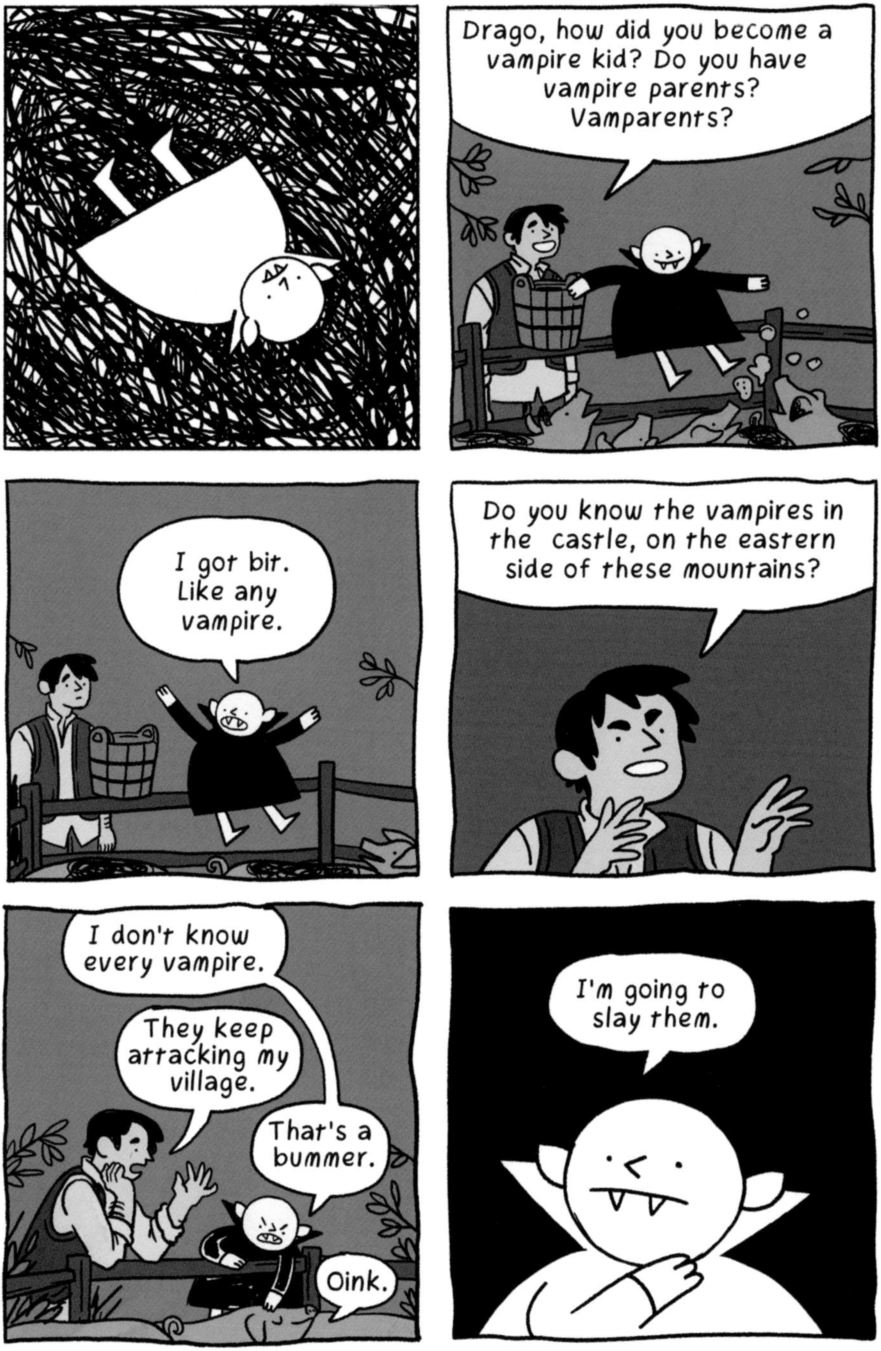
Drago, how did you become a vampire kid? Do you have vampire parents? Vamparents?
I got bit. Like any vampire.
Do you know the vampires in the castle, on the eastern side of these mountains?
I don't know every vampire.
They keep attacking my village.
That's a bummer.
Oink.
I'm going to slay them.

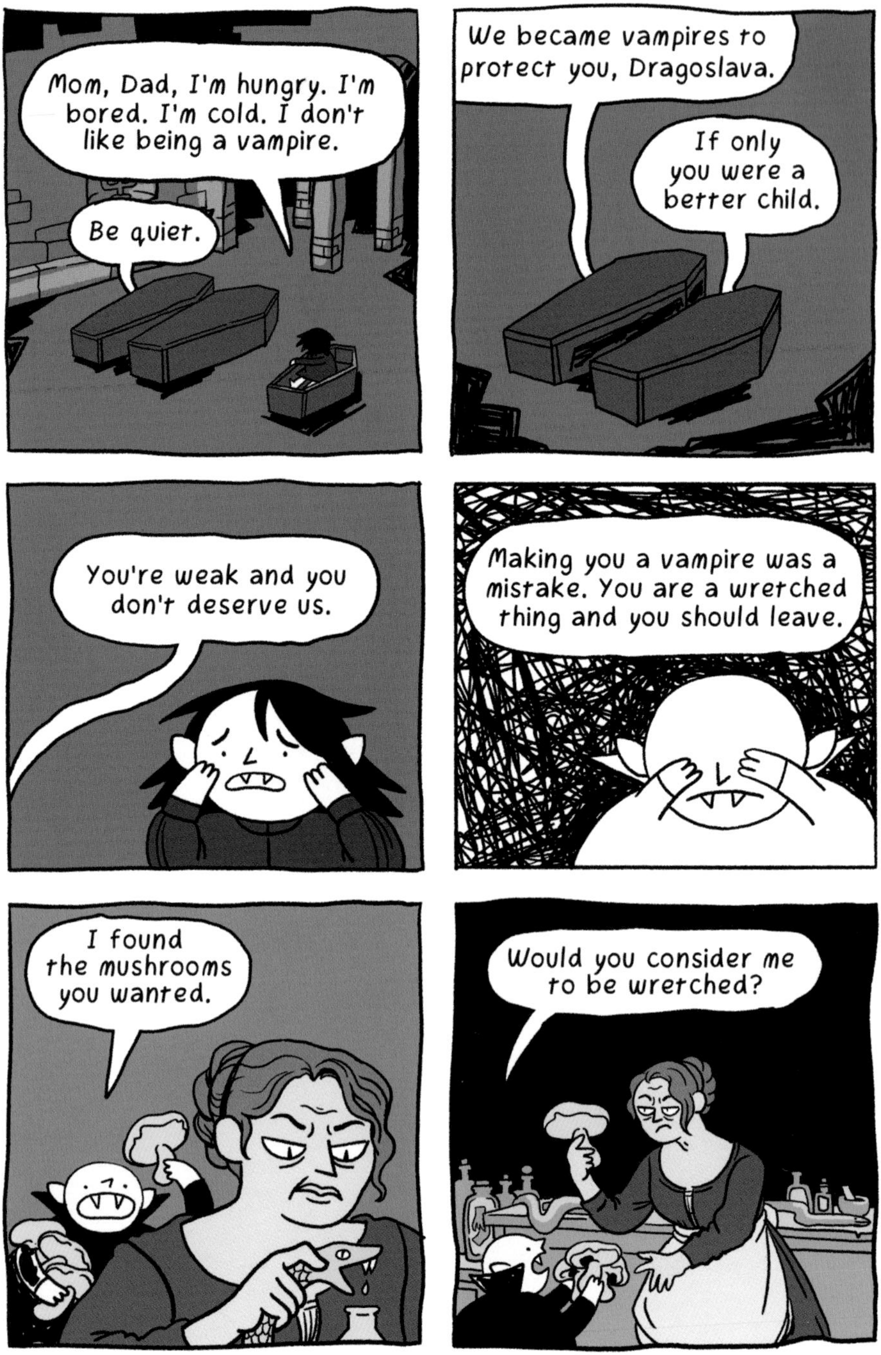
Mom, Dad, I'm hungry. I'm bored. I'm cold. I don't like being a vampire.
Be quiet.
We became vampires to protect you, Dragoslava.
If only you were a better child.
You're weak and you don't deserve us.
Making you a vampire was a mistake. You are a wretched thing and you should leave.
I found the mushrooms you wanted.
Would you consider me to be wretched?

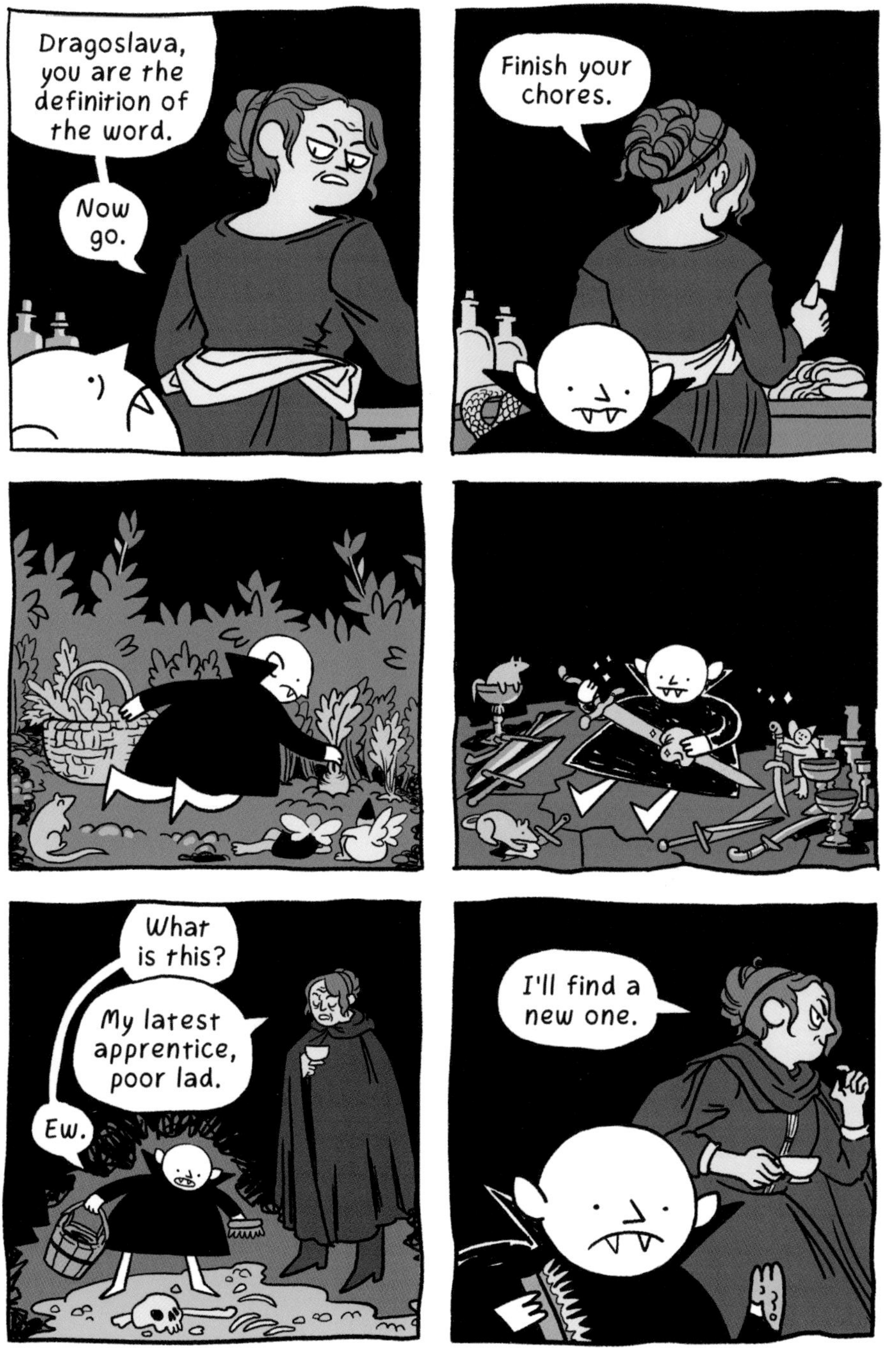
Dragoslava, you are the definition of the word.
Now go.
Finish your chores.
What is this?
My latest apprentice, poor lad.
Ew.
I'll find a new one.

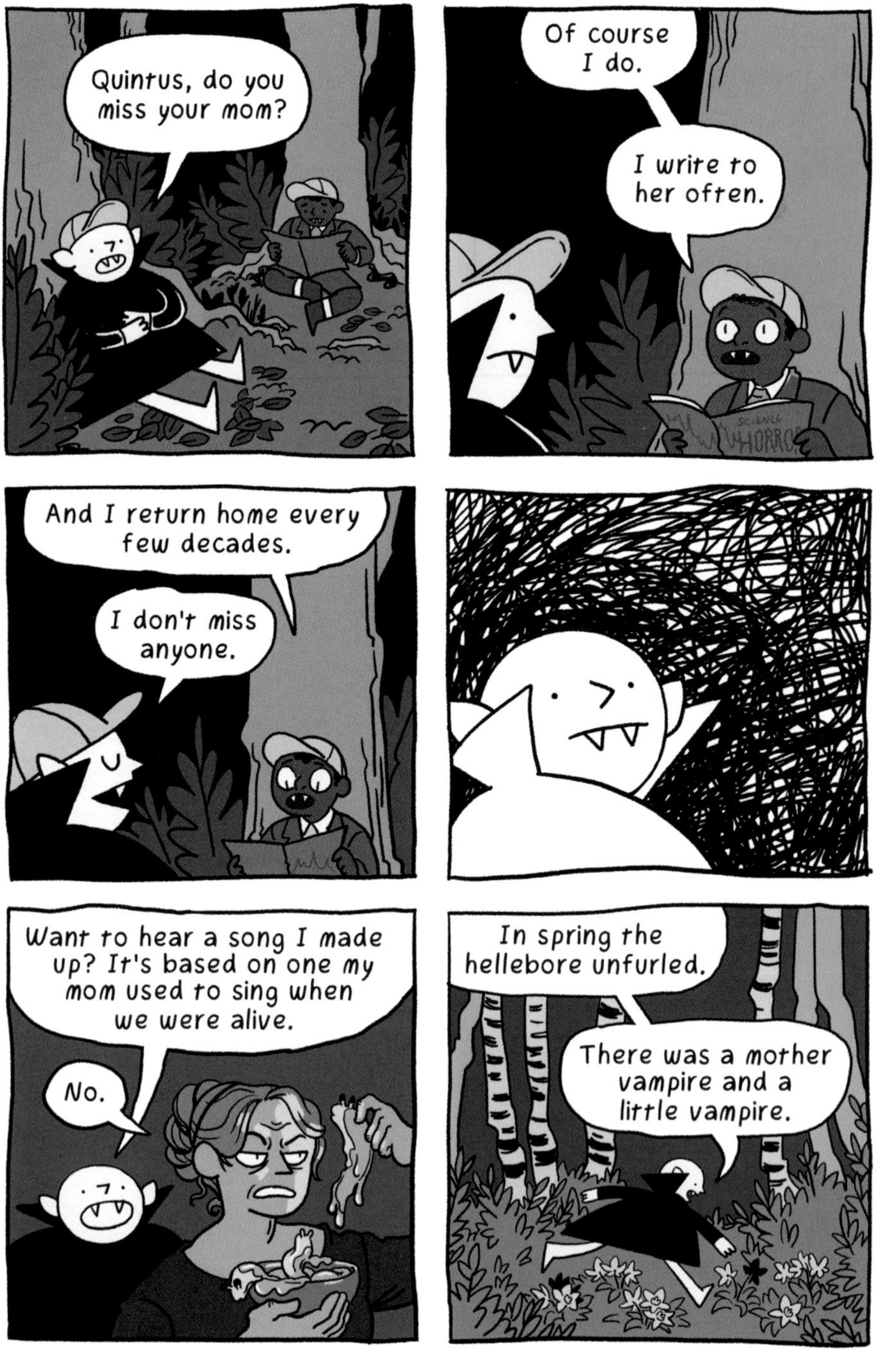
Quintus, do you miss your mom?
Of course I do.
I write to her often.
And I return home every few decades.
I don't miss anyone.
Want to hear a song I made up? It's based on one my mom used to sing when we were alive.
No.
In spring the hellebore unfurled.
There was a mother vampire and a little vampire.

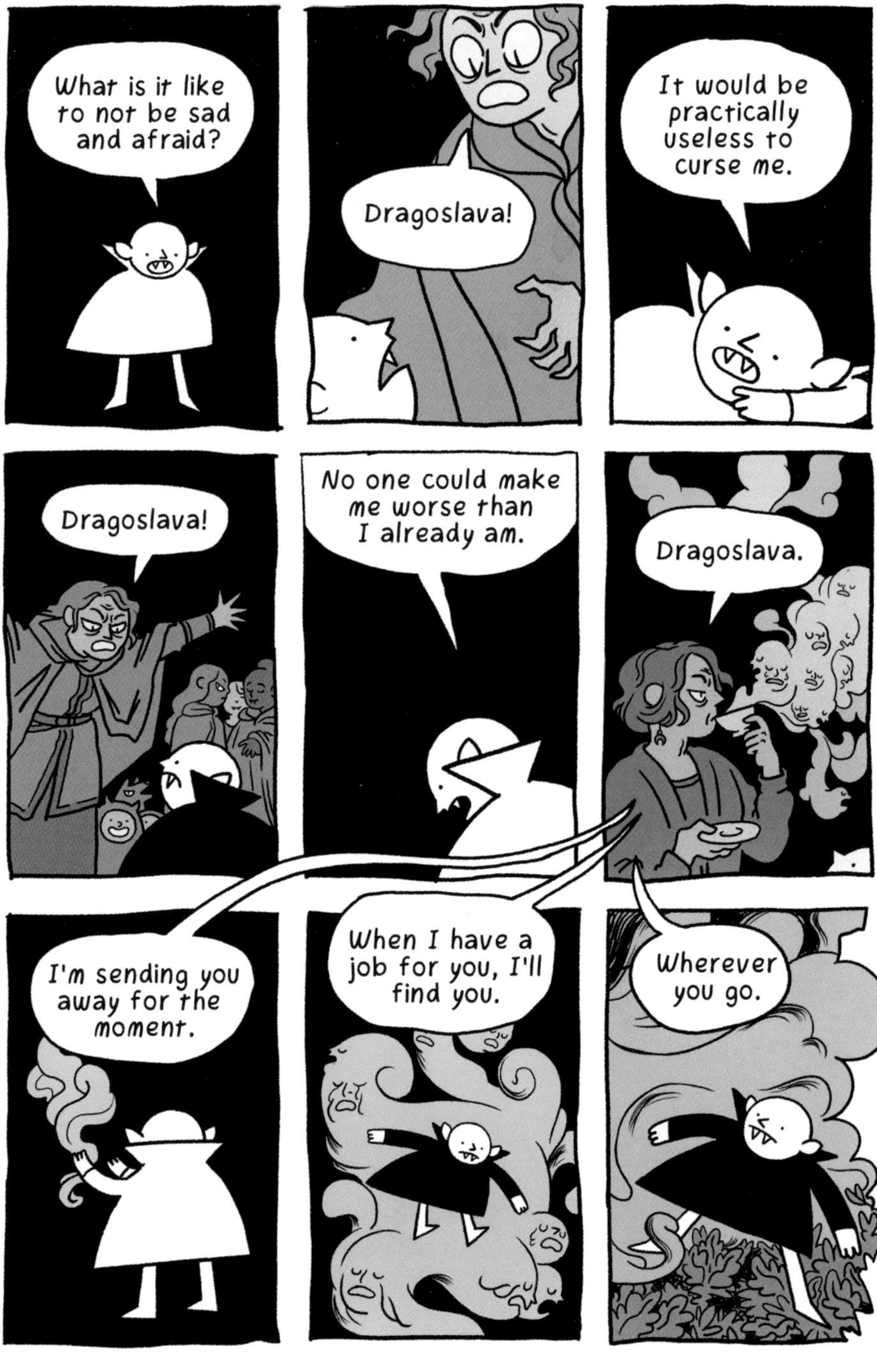
What is it like to not be sad and afraid?
Dragoslava!
It would be practically useless to curse me.
Dragoslava!
No one could make me worse than I already am.
Dragoslava.
I'm sending you away for the moment.
When I have a job for you, I'll find you.
Wherever you go.

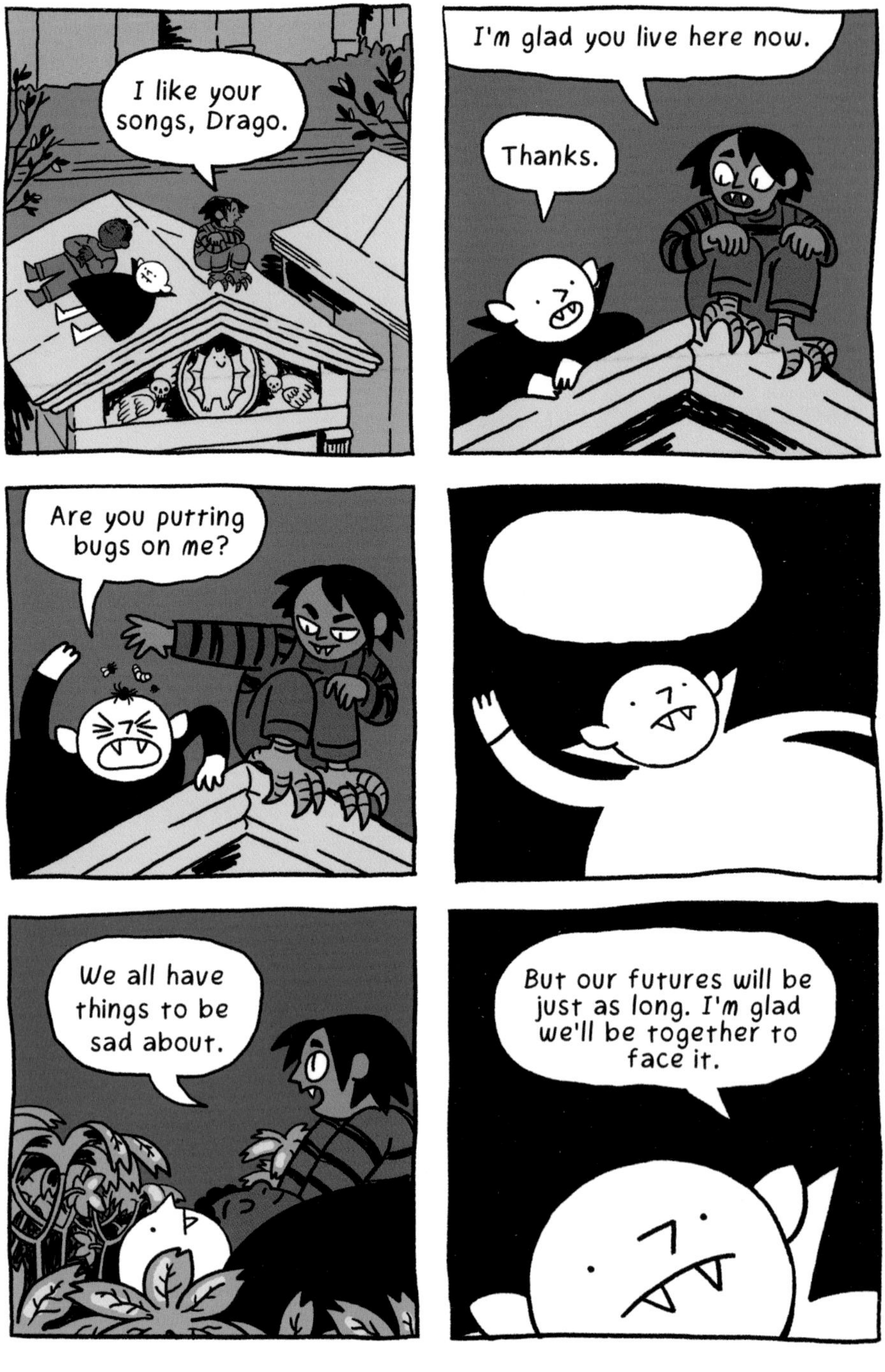
I like your songs, Drago.
I'm glad you live here now.
Thanks.
Are you putting bugs on me?
We all have things to be sad about.
But our futures will be just as long. I'm glad we'll be together to face it.

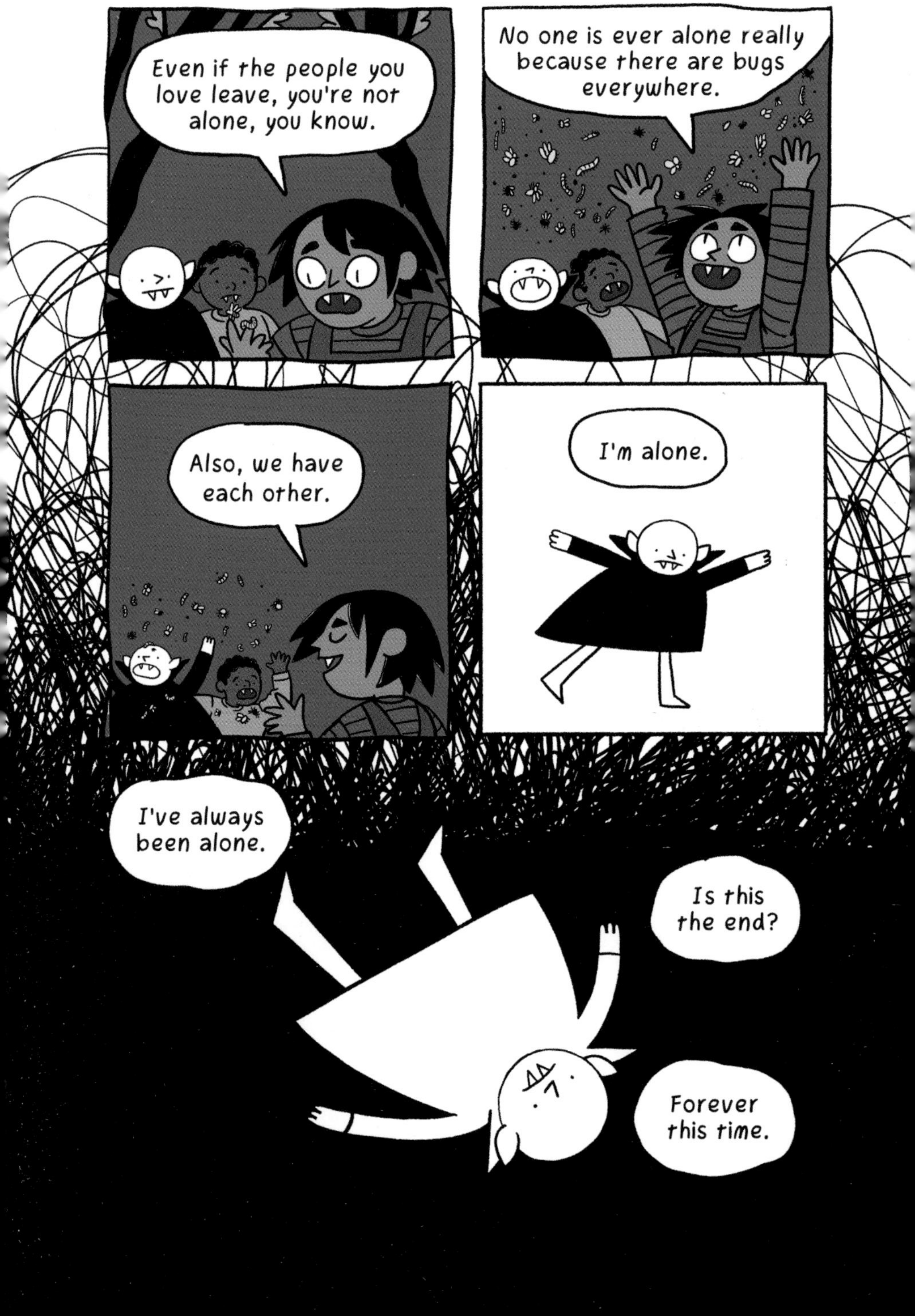
Even if the people you love leave, you're not alone, you know.
No one is ever alone really because there are bugs everywhere.
Also, we have each other.
I'm alone.
I've always been alone.
Is this the end?
Forever this time.

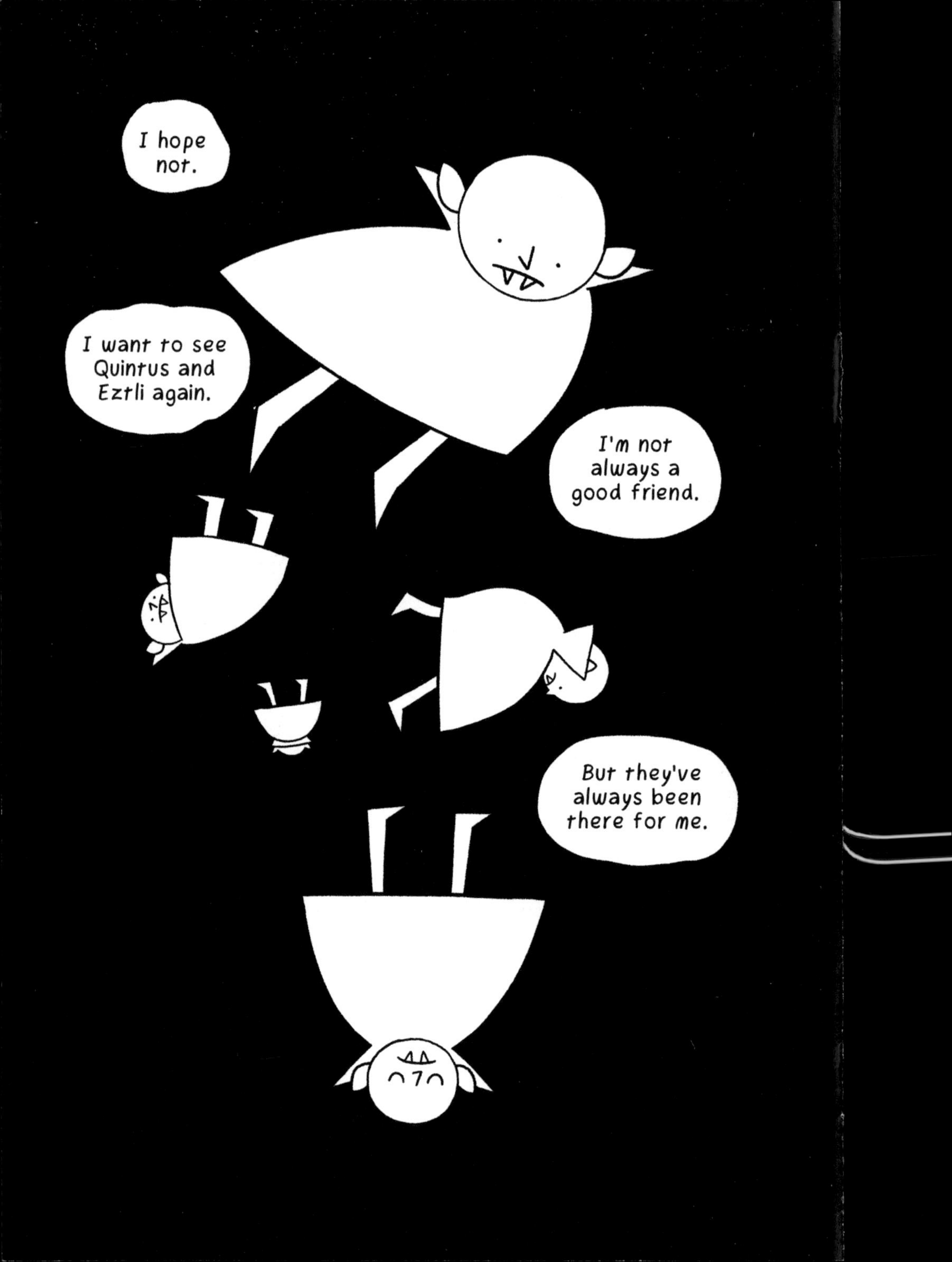
I hope not.
I want to see Quintus and Eztli again.
I'm not always a good friend.
But they've always been there for me.

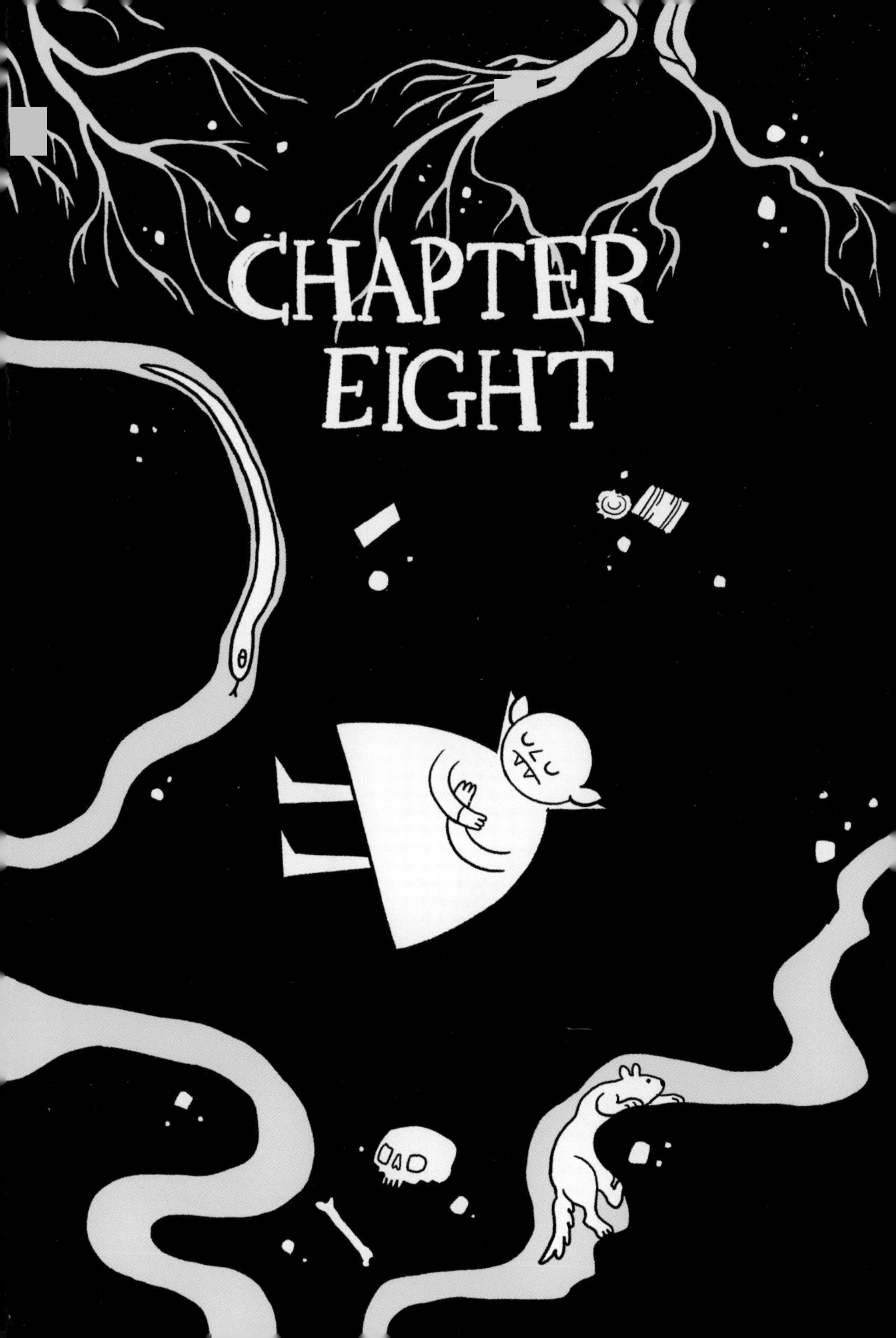
CHAPTER
EIGHT

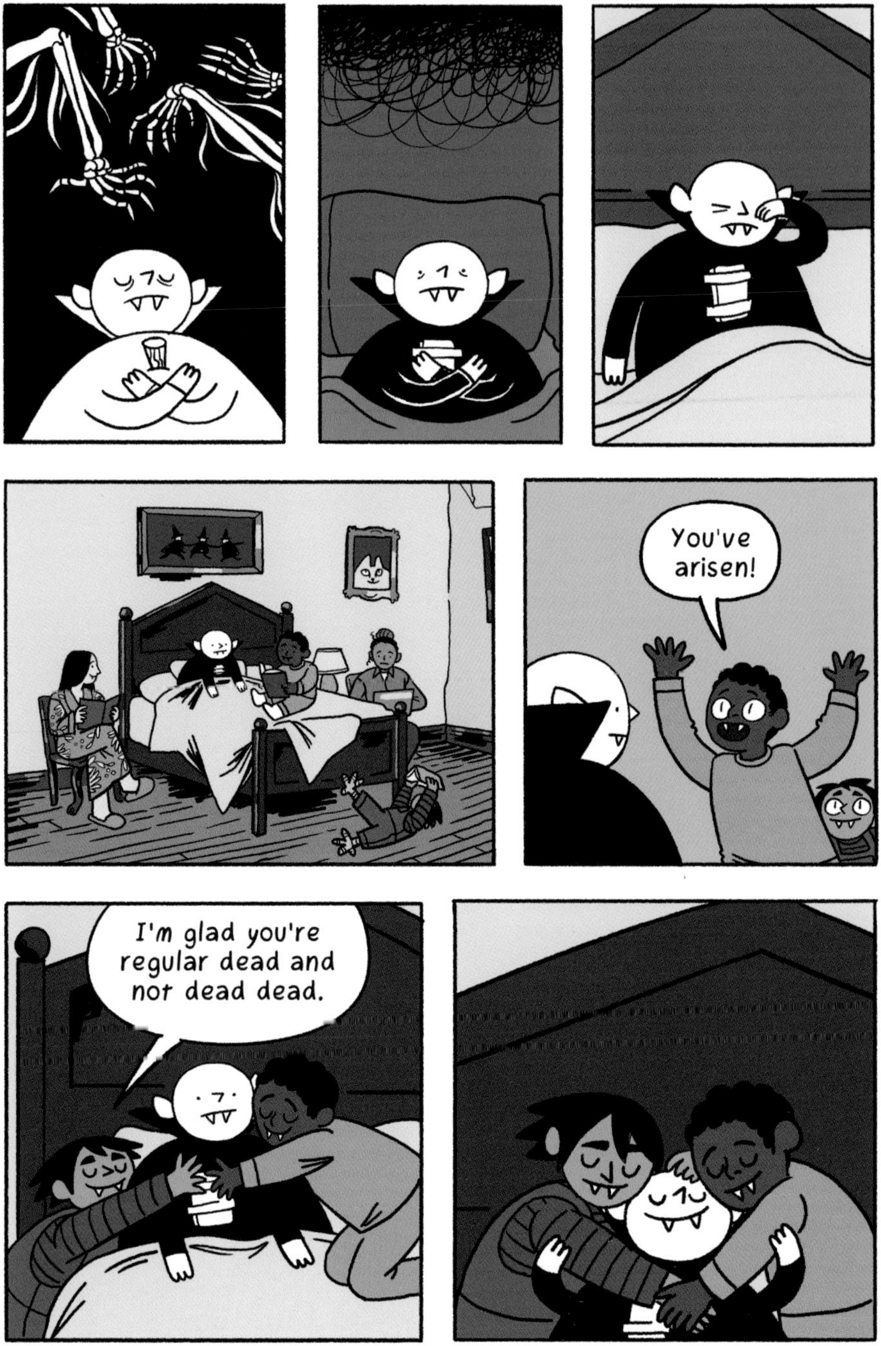
You've arisen!
I'm glad you're regular dead and not dead dead.

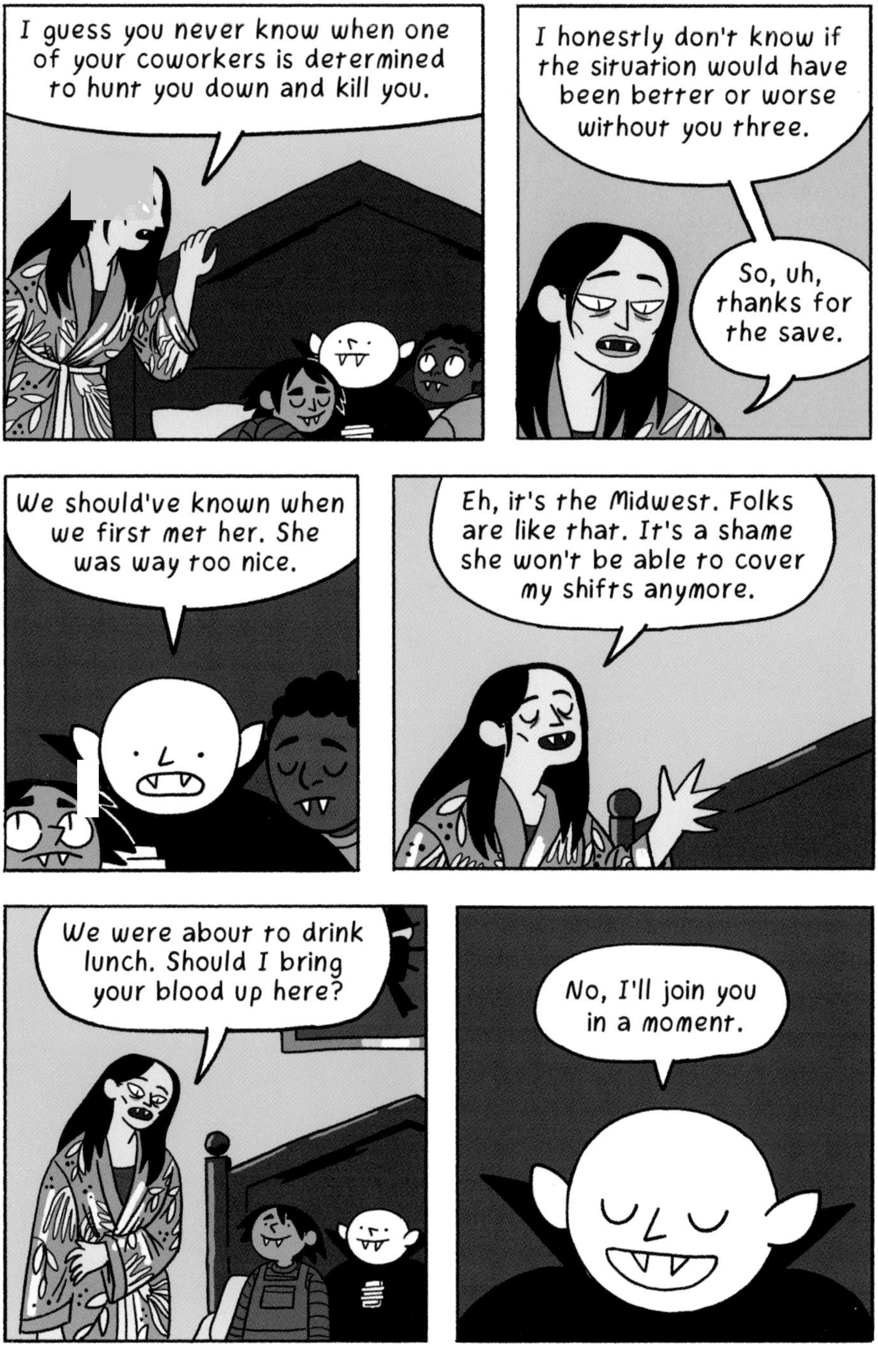
I guess you never know when one of your coworkers is determined to hunt you down and kill you.
I honestly don't know if the situation would have been better or worse without you three.
So, uh, thanks for the save.
We should've known when we first met her. She was way too nice.
Eh, it's the Midwest. Folks are like that. It's a shame she won't be able to cover my shifts anymore.
We were about to drink lunch. Should I bring your blood up here?
No, I'll join you in a moment.

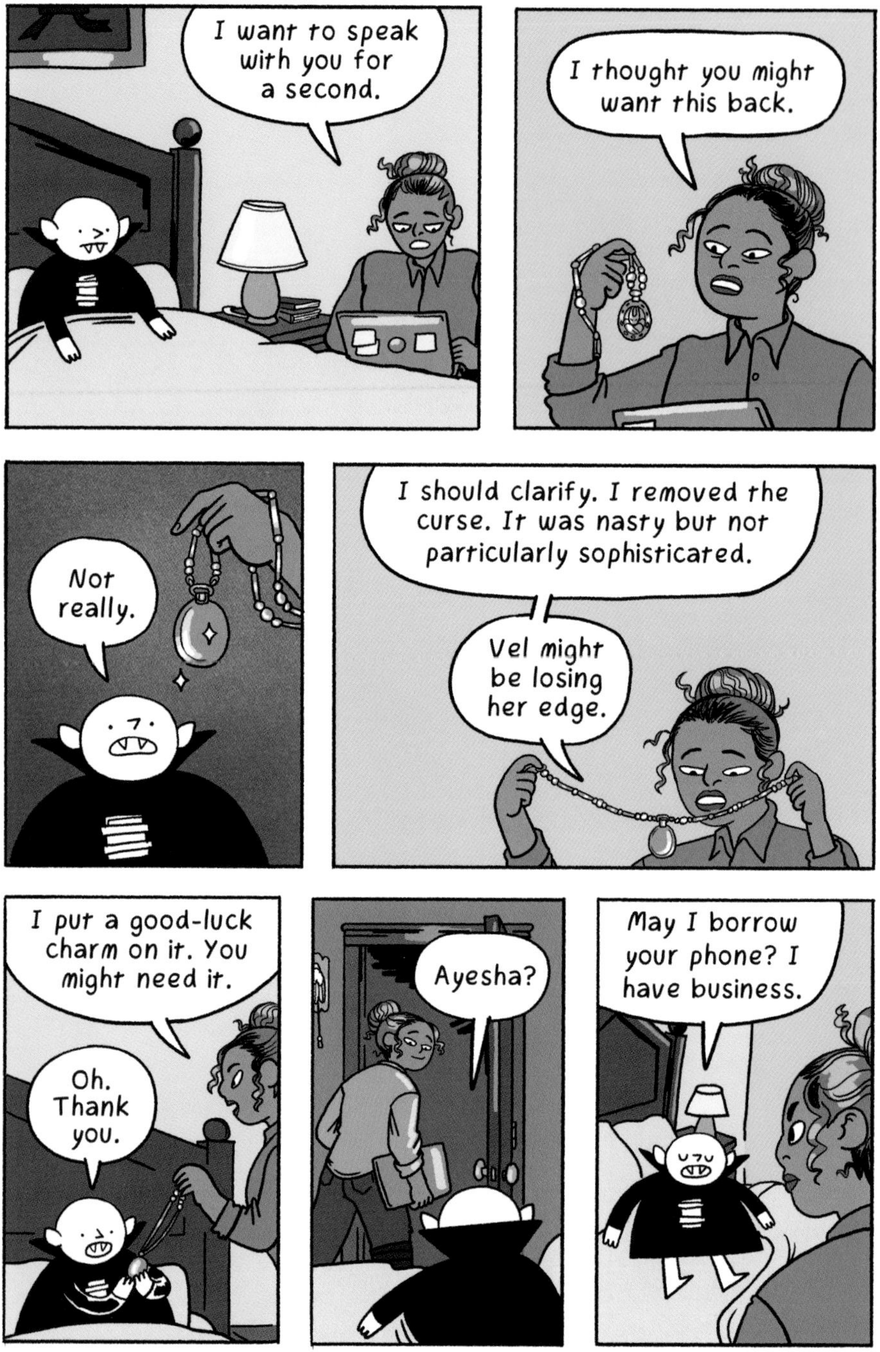

I want to speak with you for a second.
I thought you might want this back.
Not really.
I should clarify. I removed the curse. It was nasty but not particularly sophisticated.
Vel might be losing her edge.
I put a good-luck charm on it. You might need it.
Oh. Thank you.
Ayesha?
May I borrow your phone? I have business.

Sure.

Good luck.

If you need to talk after, I'll be around.

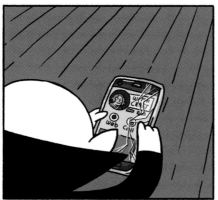

Ayesha?

No. It's me. I'm calling to quit.

Quit? Quit what?

Quit whatever it is I do for you.

Find another errand vampire.

Find another chump to threaten into doing your dirty work.

163

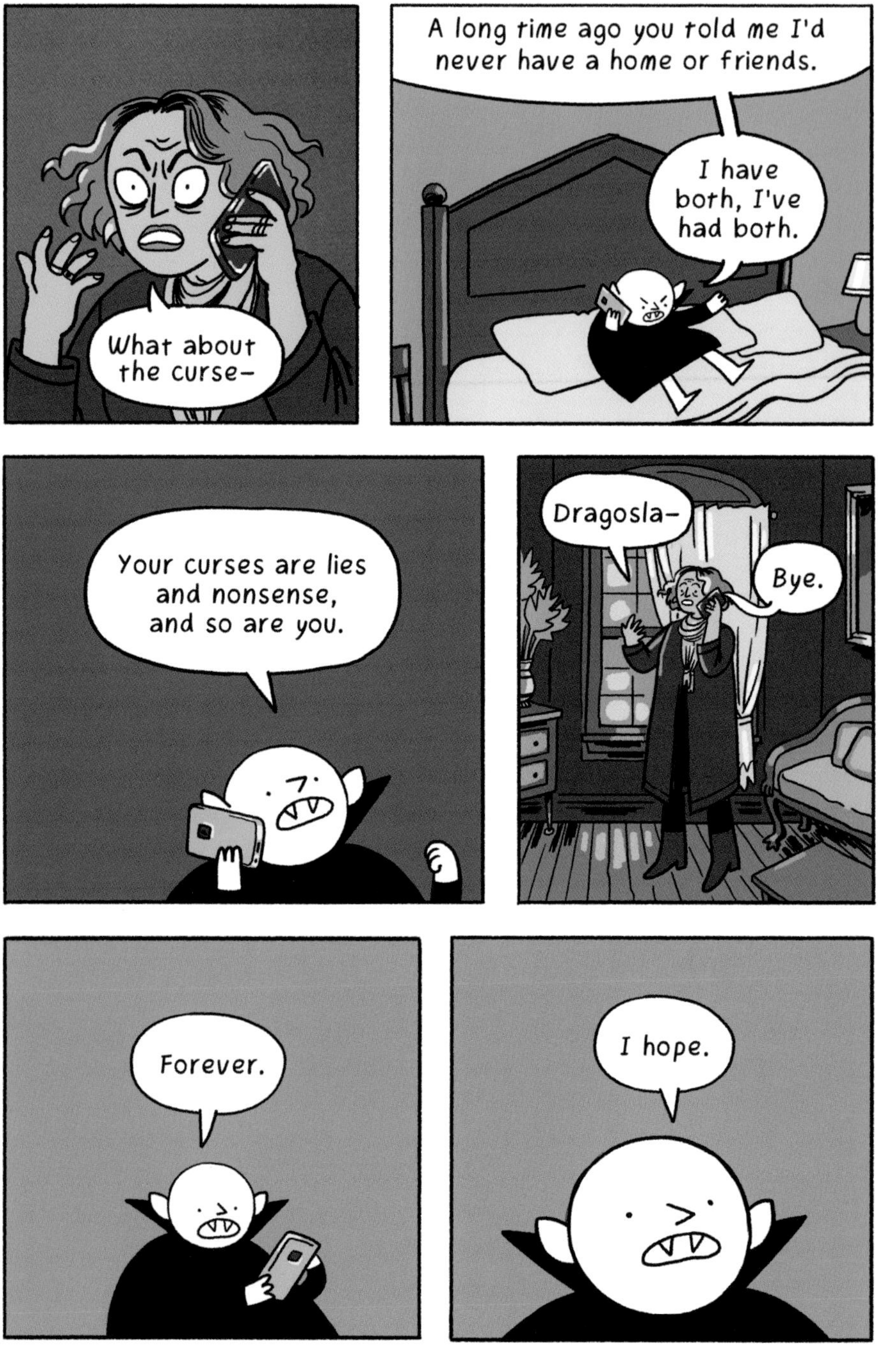
What about the curse-
A long time ago you told me I'd never have a home or friends.
I have both, I've had both.
Your curses are lies and nonsense, and so are you.
Dragosla-
Bye.
Forever.
I hope.

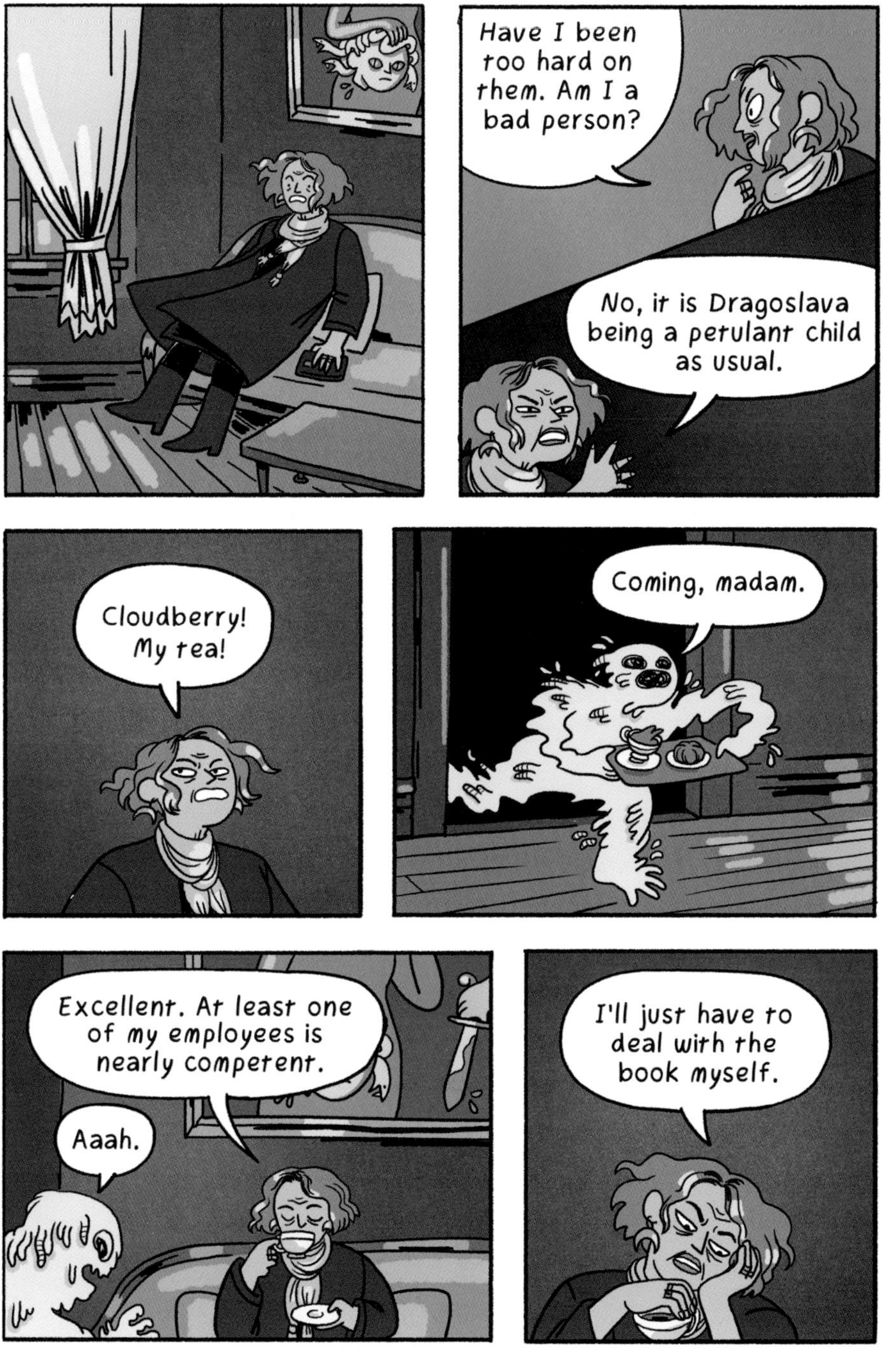

Have I been too hard on them. Am I a bad person?
No, it is Dragoslava being a petulant child as usual.
Cloudberry! My tea!
Coming, madam.
Excellent. At least one of my employees is nearly competent.
Aaah.
I'll just have to deal with the book myself.

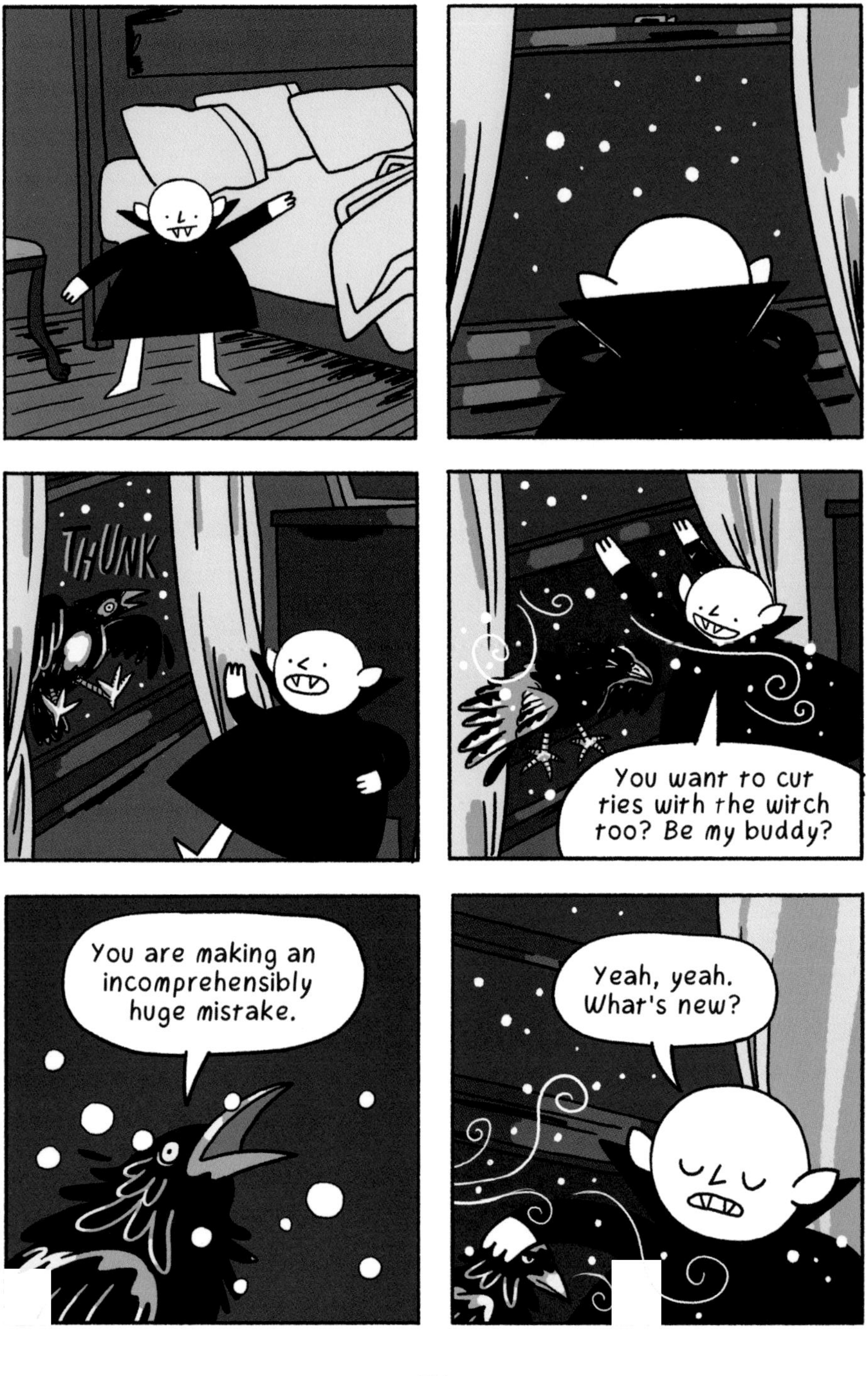
THUNK
You want to cut ties with the witch too? Be my buddy?
You are making an incomprehensibly huge mistake.
Yeah, yeah. What's new?

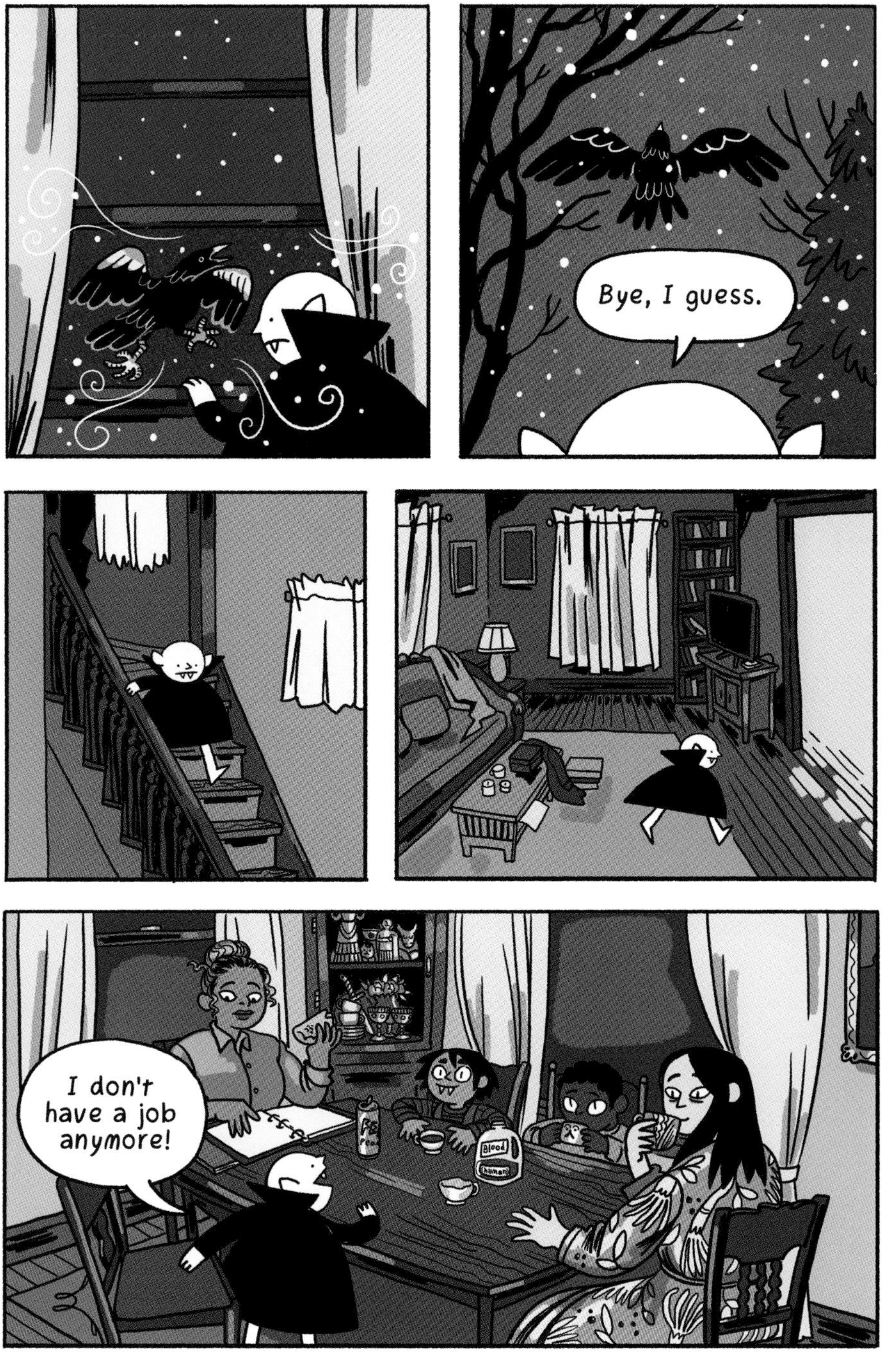
Bye, I guess.
I don't have a job anymore!

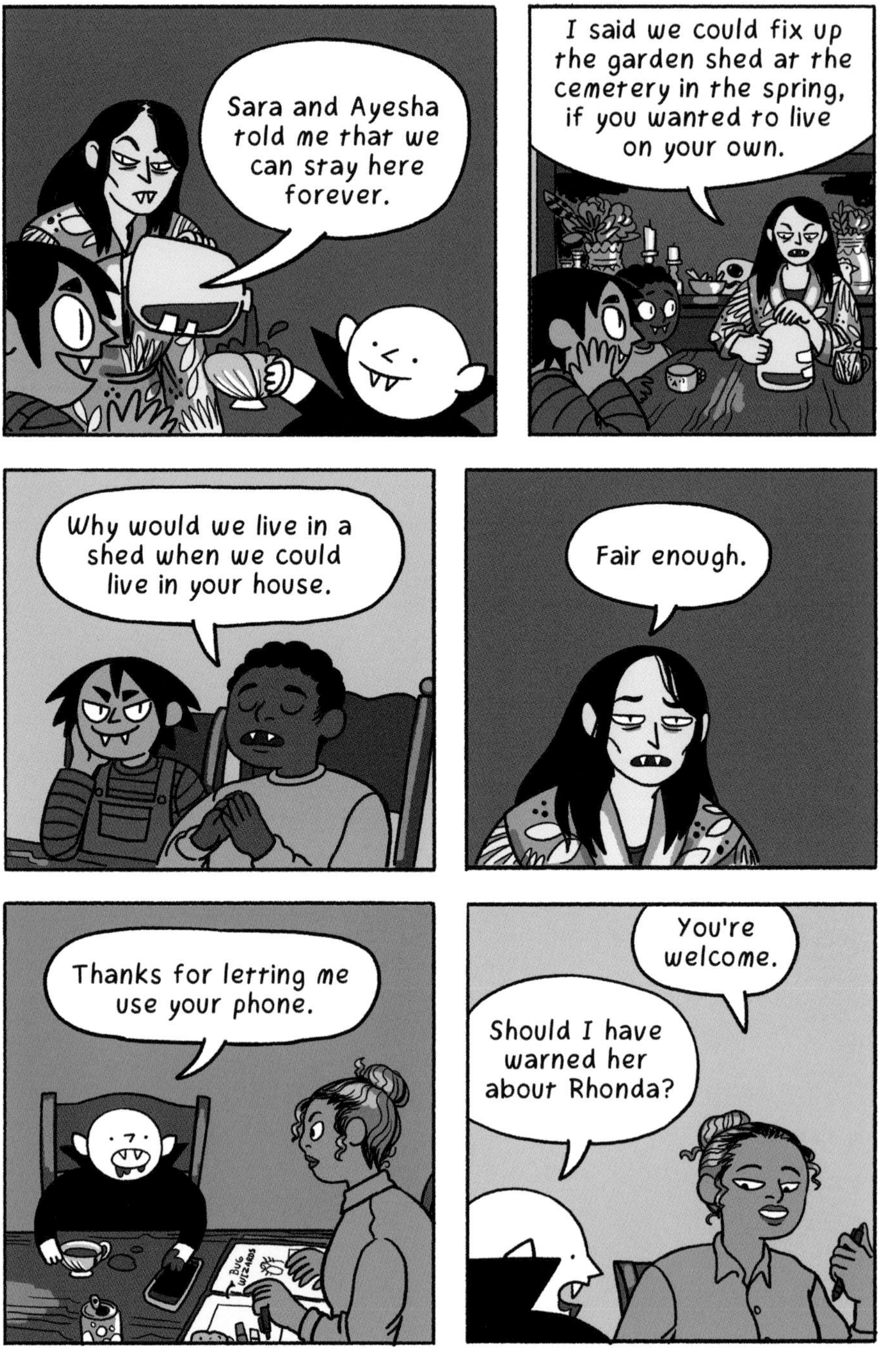
Sara and Ayesha told me that we can stay here forever.
I said we could fix up the garden shed at the cemetery in the spring, if you wanted to live on your own.
Why would we live in a shed when we could live in your house.
Fair enough.
Thanks for letting me use your phone.
BUG WIZARDS
You're welcome.
Should I have warned her about Rhonda?

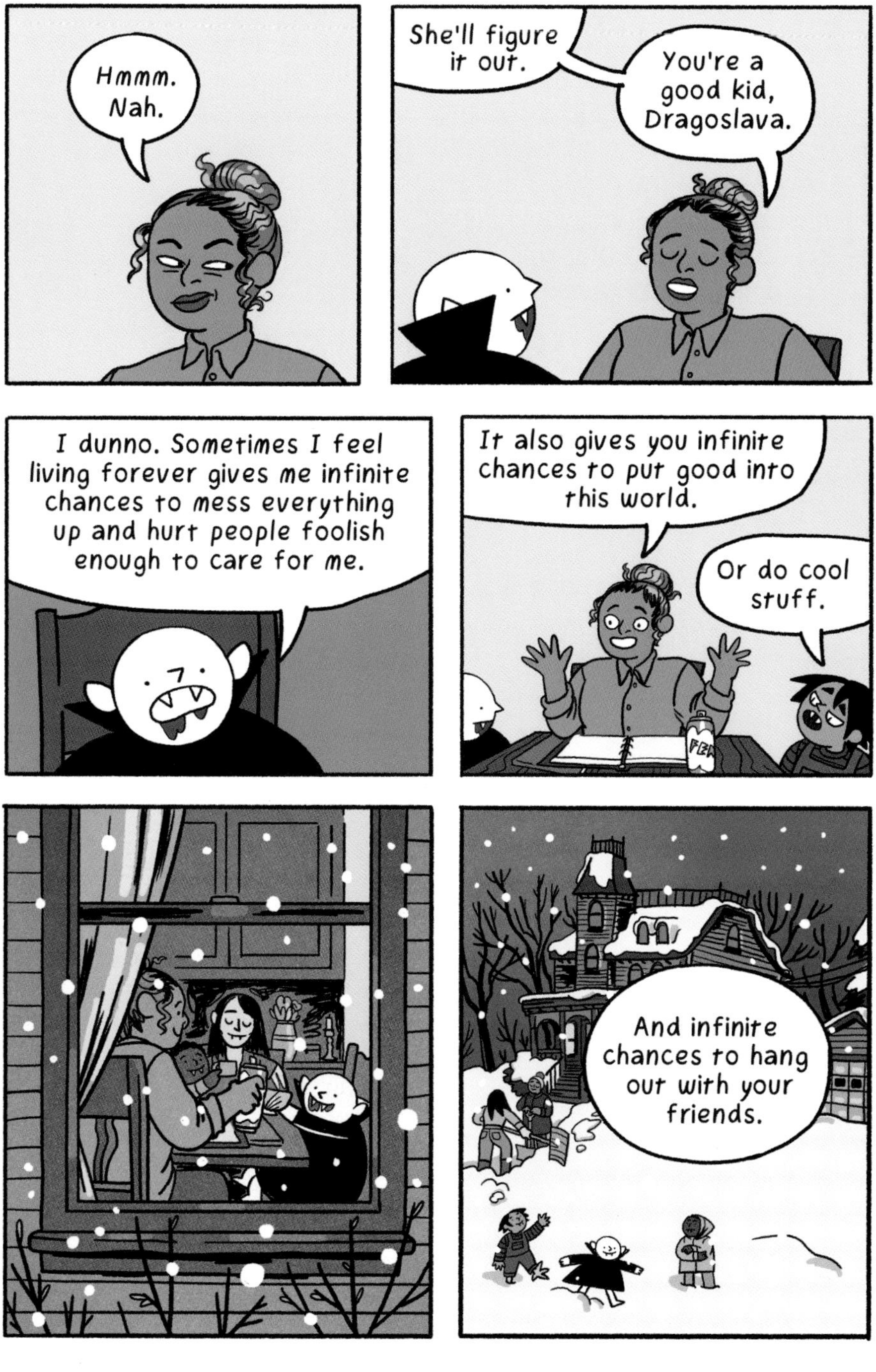
Hmmm. Nah.
She'll figure it out.
You're a good kid, Dragoslava.
I dunno. Sometimes I feel living forever gives me infinite chances to mess everything up and hurt people foolish enough to care for me.
It also gives you infinite chances to put good into this world.
Or do cool stuff.
And infinite chances to hang out with your friends.

ACKNOWLEDGMENTS

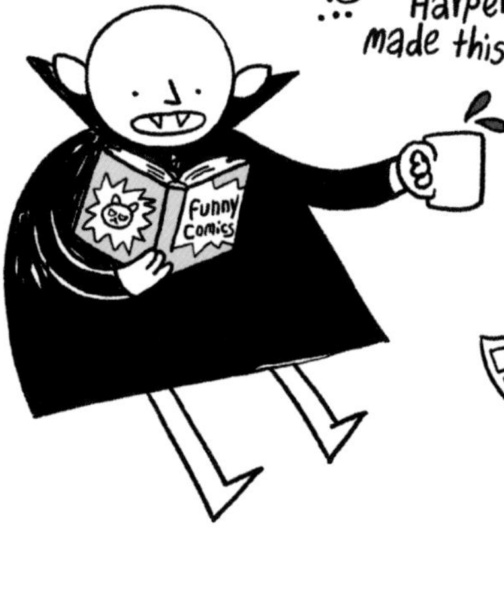

Now that we've got that out of the way, I can get back to doing what vampires do best—
drinking blood and reading comics.
Funny Comics

Color Flatting by **Andrew George** Thank you!

Infinite thanks to my editor, **Andrew Eliopulos,** and to **Catherine San Juan, Erin Fitzsimmons,** and everyone else at HarperCollins who made this book happen.

Thanks to my literary agent, **Linda**.

Thanks to my family, to my teachers and mentors.

Thanks to my wonderful friends for the love, support, critiques, and reassurances. There are too many of you to name.

The biggest and most humble of thanks to my roommates (and friends!) **Ry** and **Kaz**, who had to listen to me whine about this book for the first half of 2020.

DEVELOPMENTAL SKETCHES

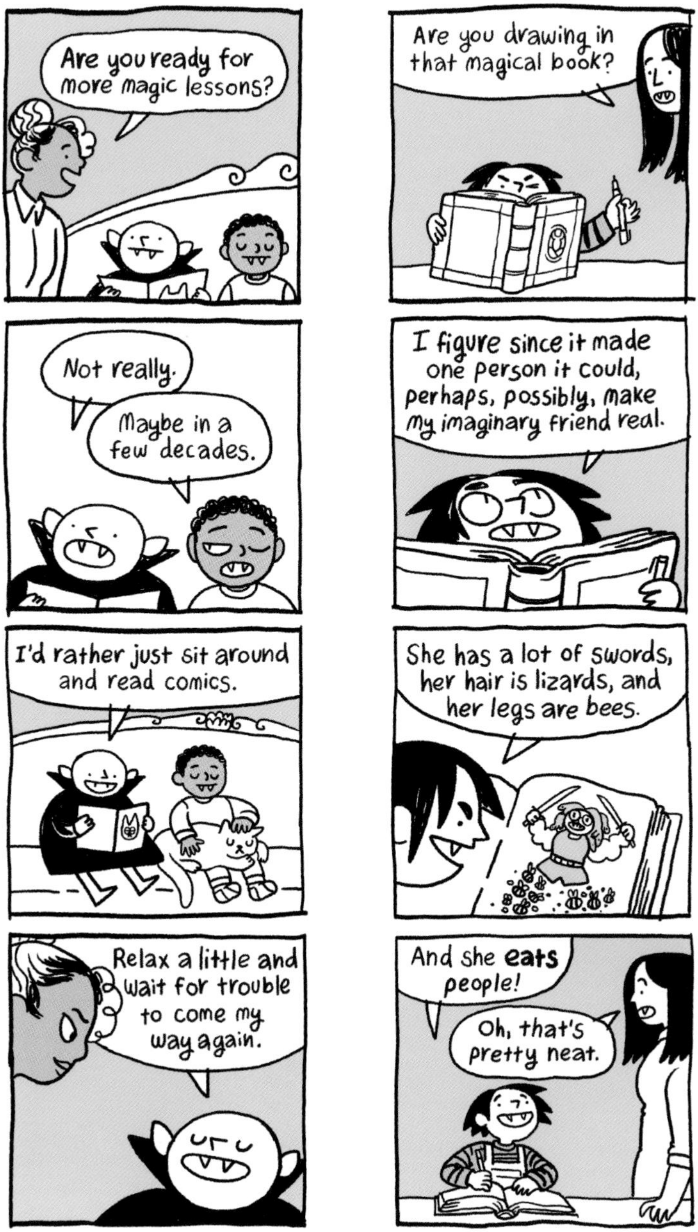
Are you ready for more magic lessons?
Not really.
Maybe in a few decades.
I'd rather just sit around and read comics.
Relax a little and wait for trouble to come my way again.
Are you drawing in that magical book?
I figure since it made one person it could, perhaps, possibly, make my imaginary friend real.
She has a lot of swords, her hair is lizards, and her legs are bees.
And she **eats** people!
Oh, that's pretty neat.

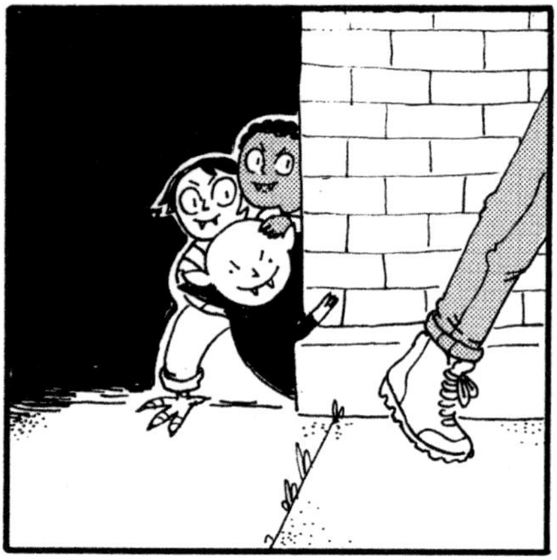

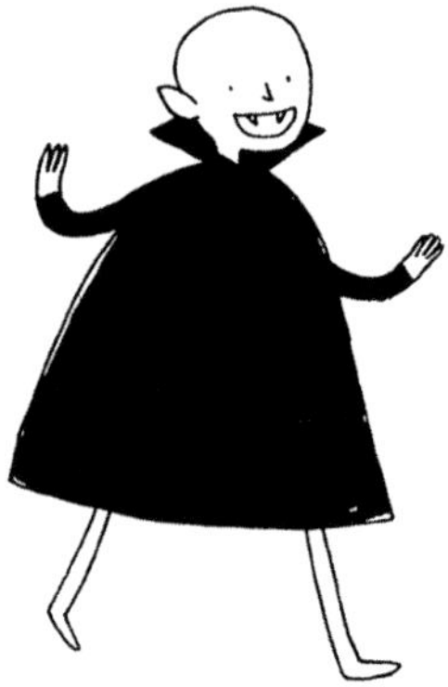

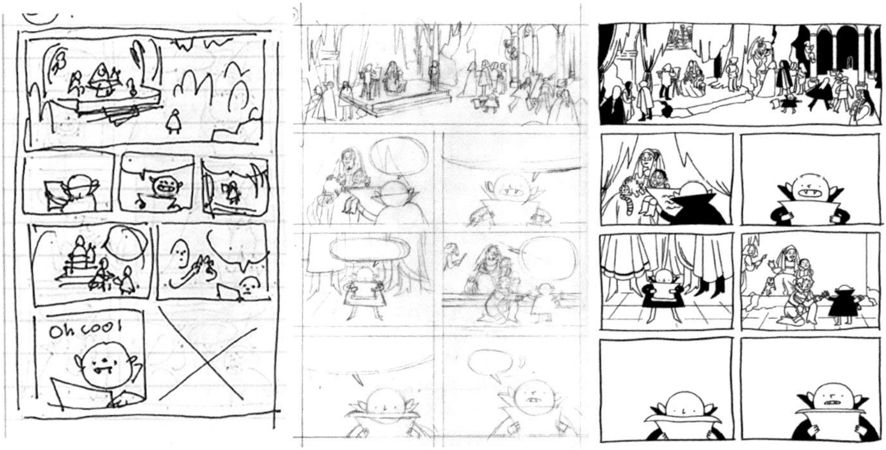
Oh cool

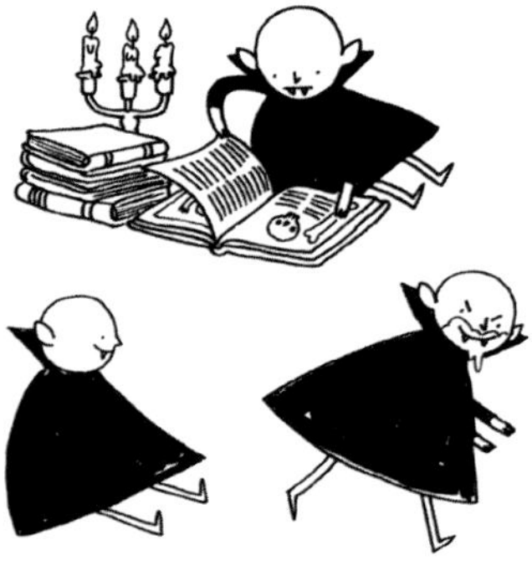

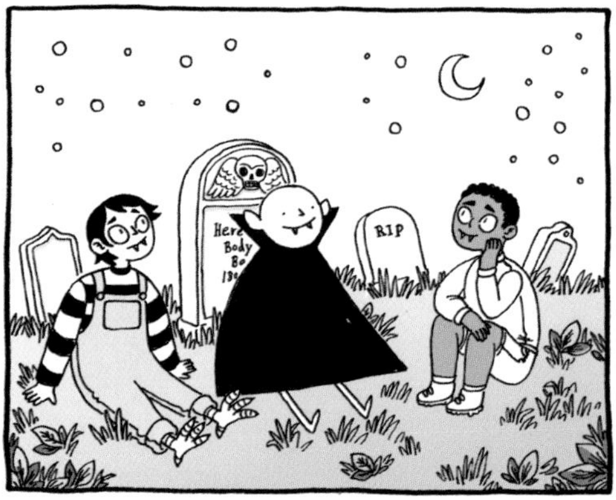
Here
Body
RIP